CHECKLIST: A, B, C

A Checklist Series Box Set

L. DuBois

Published by:
Farm Boy Press,
Sacramento, California, United States of America.

First electronic edition: August, 2013
This edition: April 2021

Proofread by Sharon Muha, Fedora Chen
Cover design by Lila Dubois
Book formatted by Farm Boy Press

ISBN: 978-1-941641-21-7 (ebook)

ISBN: 978-1-941641-62-0 (print)

Publisher's note:
This book is a work of fiction. The names, characters, places, and incidents are products of the writer's imagination or have been used fictitiously and are not to be construed as real. Any resemblance to persons, living or dead, actual events, locale or organizations is entirely coincidental.

CONTENTS

Primal Passion

Scorching Desire

After Burn (free short story)

Forbidden Legacy

Hidden Devotion

Elegant Seduction

Secret Scandal

Delicate Ties

Beloved Sacrifice

Masterful Truth

Fiery Surrender

The Trinity Masters: Volumes 1-4

Warrior Scholars - Trinity Masters Novellas

Hollywood Lies

Joyful Engagement

BDSM Checklist, BDSM Erotic Romance

Writing as L DuBois

A is for…

B is for…

C is for…

D is for…

E is for…

F is for…

G is for…

H is for…

I is for…

J is for…

K is for…

L is for…

M is for…

N is for…

Undone Lovers, *BDSM Erotic Romance*

Undone Rebel

Undone Dom

Undone Diva

Undone Toy

Standalone BDSM Erotic Romance

Betrayed by Love

Dangerous Lust

Red Ribbon

The Glenncailty Ghosts, *Modern Gothic Romance*

Redemption

Lovers

Ghosts

Bones

The Wraith Accords

Carnal Magic

City of Angels, Supernatural

Writing as E.M. Nally

Faith of Beasts

Monsters in Hollywood, *Paranormal Romance*

Dial M for Monster

Thank you to all of the readers who took a chance on this series.

A IS FOR...

CHAPTER 1

Pain or pleasure. In the end it didn't matter. She craved both.

Anna kept her breaths slow and even, trying to make as little noise as possible. Drawing attention to herself right now would be like a mouse squeaking in a room full of hungry jungle cats.

The submissive kneeling beside her shifted, wincing a little. Anna's legs hurt too—they'd been waiting here for over half an hour, and the concrete was hard against her knees and toes. She wanted to raise her head and look around, but she didn't dare.

Slaves and submissives knelt in various states of undress in the center of the large open space. Some sat back on their heels, others were kneeling up, their bodies straight from head to knee. Still others sat cross-legged with their hands laced together behind their backs.

The Masters and Doms lounged on couches or in chairs along two of the walls. More were in the seating area in the converted hay loft, leaning forward to look down at the bounty of flesh on the ground floor. Some prowled the edges of kneeling men and women like predators circling a heard of prey.

They were assembled in the barn, the only space in Las

Palmas large enough to house everyone. To outsiders it might seem like nothing more than an upscale adobe-style barn, built to match the massive, sprawling mansion a hundred yards away. Las Palmas was a beautiful property north of Los Angeles, named for the twin rows of palm trees that lined the drive and circled the mansion. The barn was only one of the many outbuildings and, despite its name, was nicer than most people's homes, with brushed concrete floors, air conditioning and teak doors on the ten large stalls. It had been built to house finicky purebred horses, but both the barn and the mansion served a darker purpose.

Wood groaned as the heavy double doors opened. Anna caught her breath and dropped her chin to her chest. She stared at the top of her own breasts, exposed to just above the nipple by the black corset she wore. Matching stockings, panties and a garter belt completed her ensemble. Outside Las Palmas the lingerie would have been exciting and racy. Here it was the equivalent of a t-shirt and jeans.

Footsteps clicked on the concrete—two pairs of boots and a pair of high heels. She'd been a serious submissive for several years now, and after spending that much time with her head down, she'd become very good at identifying the sound of footsteps.

"Masters, Mistresses, thank you for joining us. Subs, focus on us."

Anna raised her head. Around her the other subs and slaves shifted to obey, rearranging themselves and focusing their attention on the three people standing in the center of the assembly.

Master Leo, Mistress Faith and Master Mikel drew the eye and commanded attention. Each was tall and slim. Master Leo and Mistress Faith wore half masks. Master Mikel did not. He had a narrow, strong face and dark eyes, which regarded the submissives with a sort of lazy pleasure.

They were the owners of Las Palmas, and overseers of *Las*

Palmas Oscuras—The Dark Palms—the name they'd given to the exclusive and secretive BDSM club housed on the estate. Referred to simply as Las Palmas, anyone who overheard a member talking about it and went snooping would find a website detailing the architectural and cultural history of the property.

"We've called you here for a very serious reason," Mistress Faith said, her voice cool and clear. She was in her early fifties and favored trim, tailored dresses instead of leather pants or latex gloves. She radiated power like a fire gave off heat.

"We've become complacent," Master Leo added. "Each of us has found pleasure and pain, often both, within these walls."

"And yet," Master Mikel continued, "we do not push ourselves. Comfort and safety is for the mortals out there." He threw out one long arm, his dress shirt pulling back to expose his strong brown wrist. For a moment Anna thought she could see bruises, like those left by a cuff, but that couldn't be. "We are gods, gods who are growing lazy and stupid in our complacency."

Anna's heartbeat raced. Though the subs and slaves remained still, she saw the Masters and Doms straightening, some who were seated rising to their feet.

"If you want to play the same games, if you want the safety of the known, then we invite you to leave. The contract you signed when you joined will remain in effect. Any discussion of who we are or what we do will be met with swift, harsh retribution."

There were several long minutes of silence. No one moved. Membership at Las Palmas was limited to a very select few— wealth, beauty and depravity were all required to even be considered. Anna suspected that many of the people in the room were like her—they didn't just enjoy this place, they needed it. It soaked up and exercised a darkness within them that otherwise might have run rampant.

"I warn you," Mistress Faith said, "the offer will not be made again. By remaining here you consent to the...activity." The syllables of the word "activity" rolled from the Mistress's mouth, as if she'd been savoring them before speaking.

There were a few chuckles, some muttering from the Doms and Masters, but again, no one left.

"Very well," Master Leo said. "Let's explain the rules."

Master Mikel went to the door of the tack room. He wheeled out a large board draped in black cloth, and positioned it against the wall.

"My friends and companions in debauchery." There was a hint of amusement in Master Mikel's voice. "Prepare yourselves." He pulled off the cloth.

Four neat rows of silver letters were revealed—the alphabet, A to Z. Anna looked from the board to the overseers and back. She didn't understand.

"When you joined us you completed a sex, kink and fetish checklist. Some of you have updated it as your tastes evolved, others have only one on file." Master Mikel dropped the drape to the floor.

"Of all the hundreds of delicious sexual things on that list, many of you have only tried a few," Mistress Faith scolded. "We will no longer allow that."

Anna swallowed. What did that mean?

"Each of you has been assigned to a letter, and with it, every kink and fetish in that part of the alphabet."

Now even the subs were shifting nervously. Anna couldn't remember much about the checklist except that reading it had made her crave a Dom's touch.

"You have one month to try your letter's items."

"Wait a minute, you can't expect us—" A Dom in the hayloft started to protest, but it was cut short when Master Leo held up a hand.

"We've also become complacent in our playmates. Those

subs who are bound to a Master will be assigned to their Master's letter. Those of you who aren't formally bound or whose file says that you are willing to share or be shared, may be partnered with someone new. Possibly more than one someone."

Anna's stomach twisted. She was tempted to look around and find the tall, strong form of Master Jensen, but she obediently kept her gaze on the overseers.

"Not every pair or group will be able to complete all items under their letter." Master Mikel started wandering between the subs, touching heads and shoulders as he passed. "Masters will be limited by the sub's checklist. The game does not give anyone the right to override a sub's limits. You may not do anything the sub has not indicated a desire or willingness to try."

He picked up a lock of Anna's hair and let it slither between his fingers as he passed. She shivered as he walked away. His footsteps stopped and he let out a little laugh. "Don't worry, most of these pretty little things were quite liberal with their limits."

"Masters! Come pick up your envelopes." Master Leo motioned and Gabriela, a pretty Hispanic sub, rose and disappeared into the tack room. She returned holding a box, the tops of the envelopes within scraping against the bottoms of her naked breasts. "Each of you will receive your letter, the names of your assigned partner or partners, the list of associated activities, kinks and tools, and your partner's checklist. Those of you who have reserved space in the mansion for this weekend are expected to begin your checklist activities tonight. The rest of you should begin planning and make reservations."

The subs were dismissed as the Doms formed a line in front of the overseers. Anna followed the others out the double doors and along the path that led from the barn to the mansion. When the walkway split, Anna and the other subs took a smaller pathway that led not to the front doors, but to a side entrance. The mansion was designed around a series of gardens and court-yards. There were over ten different playrooms, and at least that many bedrooms. Occasions like this, where attendance was mandatory for all members, were rare. She wondered if everyone was staying the night, or if members who hadn't reserved play and sleeping rooms would be leaving.

Anna and the others went to the Subs' Garden—a small courtyard circled by two large living rooms, three dressing rooms and two bathrooms. It was the submissives' safe haven, acting as both a lounge and waiting room. Anna sank down onto a chair in the smaller living room and checked the knees of her stockings for rips.

"What do you think?" Sarah, a lean, athletic blonde wearing only a pair of high-waisted leather panties asked as she took the chair opposite Anna.

"I don't know." Anna wasn't sure what to think—mostly because she was both aroused and terrified.

"Are you and Master Jensen bonded?"

Anna took a shaky breath. "No. Not yet."

Sarah winced. "You think he'll be okay with someone else playing with you?"

Anna let out a choked laugh. "No. Not in the least."

"Then you better prepare to have your butt beat black and blue when he gets you back."

Anna licked her lips at the thought. That would almost be worth it. She pictured Master Jensen's face and her heart clenched.

"What do you think, should we have a girls' night?" Mae slid onto the arm of Anna's chair. She was in her early thirties, about five years older than Sarah and Anna, and had beautiful red, curly hair and full breasts. She wore a short zebra print robe belted loosely with a pink sash. One shoulder slid down her arm, revealing a breast and lots of creamy skin.

"Girls night?" Sarah raised one brow. "A bit risky."

"Hardly. If they didn't want me to have champagne they wouldn't stock the good stuff."

Anna tried to relax. "A girls night would be fun." Not all the submissives would be called, and in the past when things like this happened those left in the Subs' Garden made use of their free time and the amenities of the mansion. "I guess it depends on what letter we each get assigned." And more importantly to *whom* they were assigned.

Mae brought over champagne flutes, bottles of sparkling mineral water and a four hundred dollar bottle of champagne. A few other subs wandered over to sit near them, the mood quickly turning festive. Those subs that had standing rules about things like drinking opted for sparkling water. Anna thought it was a bit risky for anyone to choose champagne— what if they were called and the Dom who they were paired with objected to them drinking before hand?

She took a sip of icy mineral water as Mae finished playing hostess and resumed her seat.

"Do you remember?" Mae leaned forward, smiling and wiggling her eyebrows.

"Remember what?" Sarah took a small sip of Champagne and hummed appreciatively.

"What's on the list?" A blonde Anna didn't know was toying with the fuchsia lacing along the edge of her black and silver animal print bra. "I've been wondering, too. I don't remember."

"Some of the letters will be easy." Sarah crossed her arms, her bare breasts squeezed together by the movement. "Think about 'Q.'"

"What about 'B'?" Mae tugged her robe up. "That one will have bondage, branding, beating, breast play, boot worship, breath control—"

They were joined by another sub Anna hadn't met, but whom Mae seemed to know well. While the others tried to guess every item on the checklist, Anna sat quietly, wondering what was going to happen to her. Wondering where Master Jensen was. Her mind drifted back to the last time she'd been with him.

"You're mine, Anna." Master Jensen twirled the crop he held.

Anna could only murmur, "Yes, Master." She was dancing on the razor's edge of an orgasm. Master Jensen had bound her hands to the foot-board of the bed and forced her to bend at the waist while he worked her over with the crop. Arching her back she lifted her ass, hoping to tempt him into fucking her.

The crop ran over her rump. "Are you trying to tempt me?"

Anna tossed her head and looked at him. "Maybe. Is it working, Master?"

Master Jensen grinned. He was bare chested, his heavily muscled body gold in the warm light of the bedroom play space they were using. He wore faded jeans that dipped low on his hips. She could see the bulge of his cock behind the denim.

He brought the crop up from below, striking her dangling breast. Anna gasped as the sweet sting of pain sent little ripples of pleasure down her belly to her pussy. Reaching under her, he tugged at her nipple, toying with it while he swatted her ass with the crop.

She was wet and aching for him. He'd been playing with her for what seemed like hours.

Grabbing something off the bed he dropped to one knee beside her. Anna moaned as he pinched her nipples, then yelped as clamps bit down on her nipples.

"You like that, don't you?"

"Yes, Master."

"I want to hear you jingle while I fuck you."

The crop landed on the bed and in the next moment his cock was sliding into her aching pussy. Anna grabbed the footboard, bracing herself as he fucked her hard and deep. With each thrust the bells dangling from her clamped nipples tinkled.

"You're mine, Anna. Mine."

"Yes, Master. I'm yours."

"I still think 'S' is the scariest."

The comment brought Anna's attention back to the present. It came from a black sub, whose name Anna couldn't remember, was sitting cross-legged on the floor, a glass of water in one hand. She wore a thick collar and leather bra and panty set. "Spanking, speculums, strap-ons."

"Stop," Anna begged, holding up a hand to stop the litany. "I need to keep calm." Thinking about Master Jensen was enough to have her wet and needy.

"Are you scheduled to be here this weekend?" Sarah asked.

"Yes. I'm supposed to be here with Master Jensen." Anna had spent the last few days of her work week fantasizing about his hands on her body, his breath on her neck, his cock thrusting into her, pounding her until she couldn't think.

"Oh, that means that—"

The speaker mounted in the ceiling hummed for a second before a robotic voice said, "Sub Anna. Orion Room."

"—you might get called soon." Mae finished.

Anna froze and time seemed to stand still. She'd been called, not to meet with Master Jensen, but with a Dom or Doms unknown. Anxiety was a heavy knot in her belly and yet she rose, moving on auto pilot, obeying the command to go to one of the play rooms. With a nod to the other submissives, Anna rose to her feet and left the safety of the Subs' Garden, heading for the Orion Room and the unknown pleasures and pain that waited for her there.

———

IT WAS EMPTY. ANNA CLOSED THE DOOR AND exhaled, shutting herself in the dark opulence of the Orion room. There were six rooms around the Constellation Courtyard and Anna had played in several of them, but never this one, which seemed larger than the others. Like all the rooms in this section of the mansion, the Orion room was a study of dark and light. The walls and ceiling were midnight blue and set with tiny lights meant to represent stars. She'd heard from the other subs that the constellations the rooms were named for were outlined in the lights. Anna had never been positioned on her back long enough to learn if that were true. Columns of light shot up from the floor, and spotlights in the ceiling shone down onto several play areas. In a place of honor in the center was a St. Andrew's cross, the straps dangling loose, the metal buckles gleaming silver.

Anna adjusted her corset and stockings, and then padded over to an empty pool of light. She knelt there, assuming the waiting position Master Jensen preferred. If she'd been paired with a different Dom for this insane "game," she might already be in trouble—every Dom had different preferences for how a sub should enter the room, how they should wait, and what they should, or shouldn't, be wearing. Normally the sub would know all this going in, because the play time would have been negotiated, but she was trusting Las Palmas, and had to believe that whoever walked through the door would be skilled and experienced enough to dominate her. Her heart was fluttering in her chest and a shiver ran over her. She'd never imagined that anyone but Master Jensen would touch her again. She hadn't felt this kind of anxiety in years. The feeling was similar to pre-first date jitters, but more powerful. A first date was nerve-wracking, but usually involved nothing more threatening than a kiss. The first time with a new Dom meant giving control of body and mind to someone.

The floor was glossy wood, and much nicer on her knees than the concrete in the barn. She focused on her breathing, taking each breath gently and carefully, noting the way the air felt as it passed over her lips and tongue. Normally this would be enough to take her in to sub-space, but she was too nervous.

She'd become lazy and comfortable after so many months with Master Jensen. If the overseers had decided to do this a few months from now she would have been safely bonded and no one else would have been able to use her—but now she was alone, and risked not only her body and mind at the hands of an unknown player, but the ire of her Master.

The door opened and the fading sunlight that filled the courtyard streamed in, adding golden tones to the blues and whites of the room. Footsteps tapped across the wood, and the door swung shut, sealing her in here with a Dom she couldn't yet see. She risked one glance at the wall then dropped her eyes. When the overseers turned what had once been bedrooms into play rooms, they eliminated the closets, using the space they gained to create viewing rooms sandwiched between the larger play spaces. Though it was difficult to see anything in the darkness beyond the spotlight, she knew there would be a large one-way mirror on the wall, which allowed people seated in the viewing room to watch what was happening, either for their own enjoyment or to protect those inside.

The tips of a pair of glossy black dress shoes appeared at the edge of the ring of light. Anna caught her breath, holding very still. Not Master Jensen—he wasn't the dress-shoes type. Anna blinked to dispel the tears that gathered in her eyes. Up until that moment she'd secretly been expecting her Master, Master Jensen, to walk in to the room.

Should she refuse to submit? Should she use her safe word, get up and walk out? Anna tensed, unsure what to do.

The Dom didn't say anything. Turning to the right, he circled her, staying in the shadows so that all she saw were his expensive shoes and the cuffs of his black dress slacks.

She could protest, say that she wouldn't submit for anyone but Master Jensen.

He stopped in front of her and took one step forward, bringing everything up to his chest into the light. He wore a perfect black one-button suit with a crisp white shirt and thin black tie. His left hand was tucked into his pocket, pulling the side of his jacket back. His right hand was encased in a black leather glove. He pointed to her with the first two fingers on his right hand then tipped them up. Anna stared at him, not sure what she should do. It was the first time she'd failed to instantly obey an order in years.

After a moment of silence the Dom walked away. He stepped into the light, this time holding a riding crop and a pair of cuffs.

They were symbols, items so quintessentially linked to BDSM that when she saw them Anna remembered why she chose to submit, and what that submission meant. The overseers were right—her relationship with Master Jensen had made her complacent. Surrendering body and mind to gain sexual and emotional fulfillment had kept her sane. It was dangerous to forget that she didn't just enjoy being mastered—she needed it.

She wouldn't flee, wouldn't protest being dominated by someone new, because though her emotions were involved with Master Jensen, she was a true submissive. She'd given Las Palmas power over her body and choices, and she would obey.

Anna took deep slow breaths letting go of her questions and worries. Her heart clenched, and there was still part of her that was crying out for her Master, but she was well trained, and would obey as she should. After a few minutes of practiced breathing she was calm, her body warm and ready for a Master's touch.

"I'm sorry, Master. I'm yours to use as you see fit." Her words hung in the air. Though his shoulders and head were still in shadow Anna could just make out the movement as he nodded.

Anna bowed her head, waiting for his first command.

CHAPTER 2

The tip of the crop tapped the underside of her chin. Anna looked up. The Master dropped the cuffs to the floor and again gestured using two fingers.

Sub sign language.

When Anna had first been introduced to the world of BDSM she'd set out to learn everything she could about it, including taking an online class on "sub sign language" designed to be used to maintain secrecy in the vanilla world or when the Dom preferred silence. She'd never been with a Master who used it, but she had a bad feeling she might have indicated that she knew it on her BDSM Checklist.

Anna slowly rose to her feet, guessing as to what the gesture meant. The tip of the crop slid down her breasts. The Dom motioned again, this time raising pinky and thumb. Anna bit her lip, then clasped her hands together at the small of her back.

Crack. The crop struck the bare skin of her thigh above the top of her stocking. Anna sucked in a little breath as he repeated the gesture. This time she raised her arms, lacing her fingers together behind her neck. The crop rose and Anna winced, hating that she'd made such a terrible first impression on this

Dom. First she'd been hesitant to obey an order, now she wasn't obeying correctly.

He touched the tip of the crop to the center of her forehead. Anna blinked, then closed her eyes. The folded leather slid down her cheek, over her chest to her right breast. She breathed a sigh of relief that she'd gotten it right. Her whole body was on alert. She'd forgotten how stimulating the fear of the unknown could be, and this Master was a dangerous mystery.

He took two steps and then the crop was gone, replaced by hands. He cupped and kneaded her breasts through the thin fabric of her corset and Anna couldn't help but moan. The Dom slid his fingers beneath the material, lifting her right breast and then folding her corset down, creating a shelf for her now exposed breast, presenting it to him.

At the touch of the cool air her nipple beaded, and Anna wished she could squeeze her legs together to address the aching in her pussy. The danger this Dom presented and the unknown pleasures and pain that lay before her had her nearly at the point of climax.

The Dom walked away. Anna kept her eyes closed and focused on her breathing. She tried to stay in the moment, to be the good submissive she'd been trained to be, but she couldn't stop her thoughts from shifting to Master Jensen. Would he be angry that another man was using her? He would. He'd be furious that anyone else had touched her, but he knew, as she did, that being a part of this lifestyle meant that until they made their relationship formal there were no guarantees.

If she'd been a different kind of woman—a woman who thought pain had no place in sex and that bruises from a lover's hands were a sign of danger—she would have run screaming from Las Palmas rather than let another man touch her. But she was a submissive, and when she gave herself over to this life she did it wholly, and without reservation. She'd forgotten that for a moment, but wouldn't make that mistake again. Her checklist would indicate that she was willing to play with any Dom, because she'd completed the list and set her personal limits before Master Jensen entered her life, and before they'd developed the relationship they now had.

Jensen was the Master. If he didn't want her to be used by someone else, it was up to him to stop it.

That thought brought a little smile to her lips. Her job was to submit and obey—she shouldn't have to worry or plan. She got to leave those things behind when she drove up the palm lined driveway.

The Dom returned, standing so close to her that she could feel the heat of his body. He stroked her right breast, the leather of his gloves buttery soft. He pinched her nipple, twisting and then lifting it until she gasped and rose onto her toes. He released her, leaving her right nipple throbbing and her left aching for want of the same treatment. Something cool touched the inner swell of her breast, tracing a path up to her collar bone and then down the other side. Anna wanted to open her eyes, but she obediently kept them closed. What had he applied to her breast?

He moved away and she heard the door open. Anna froze. Had he left, or someone else entered?

"Open your eyes to see your letter," a female voice said.

Anna opened her eyes and looked around. She could see the shadowed outline of a woman kneeling five feet in front of her. The Dom was nowhere in sight.

Anna looked down at her bare right breast. It took her a minute to understand what the red lines painted there represented. Her lips twitched.

"A scarlet letter." The painted 'A' glistened against her pale skin.

"Please position yourself on the St. Andrews cross," the woman said.

Anna kept her hands behind her head, turned, and with a

slow, graceful walk went over to the leather covered "X." The bottoms of the leg portions ended in padded platforms. Anna positioned her back against the cross and then stepped up onto the platforms. It spread her legs wide, enough that there was no way to pretend she was anything other than on display. She unlinked her fingers and raised her arms, laying them along the upper pieces.

The woman had followed her, and when she stepped into the light Anna could see she too was a sub and naked except for a body chain that started in a choker around her neck, and draped and swaged its way down to her pussy. Clamps on her nipples and pussy lips helped hold the jewelry in place.

The dark haired sub attached straps around Anna's ankles, thighs, waist, ribs, upper arms and wrists. When she was done, the sub turned and walked to the door, slipping out.

Anna was left alone to contemplate her situation. The St. Andrew's cross leaned back slightly, and the center supported her back. On either side of her were large rectangular boxes, which she knew contained the mechanisms that allowed the cross to rotate from upright to flat and then to upside down, depending on how the Dom wanted to use the sub.

A minute passed, then five. Anna struggled to keep from screaming. If Master Jensen were here, he'd take one look at her and know what she needed—a good, hard fuck. She closed her eyes and imagined he was there, his rugged, scarred body naked from the waist up, his stubbled cheek scraping hers as he leaned in to demand that she beg to be fucked. When she did, he'd rip open his jeans and thrust his long, hard cock into her.

She was so lost in the fantasy that she didn't register the sound of returning footsteps until they were close.

The Dom stepped into the circle of light. His face was shadowed by a fedora. All she could see was the edge of a smooth jaw. In his trim, elegant suit with the hat shading his face he looked like a celebrity hiding from photographers.

The brim of his hat dipped a bit as he looked her over. Anna could only hope what he saw pleased him. She was lightly muscled and toned—she worked hard for this body—but that didn't mean he'd like it. Maybe he preferred larger breasts, or more curves. Maybe he liked girls with darker skin who wouldn't bruise as easily.

He circled around behind her and took a fist full of her hair, pulling her head back so she was looking at the ceiling and the pattern of stars represented there.

"What's our letter?" he whispered.

"A," she replied. His hold on her hair tightened. "A, Sir," she repeated, louder this time.

"What do you think is on our list?" He hissed the question.

Anna licked her lips. She had the first letter of the alphabet —lucky her.

"I don't remember what's on the list, Sir."

He released her and walked away. From somewhere in the dark a whip cracked against the floor.

Anna whimpered at the implied threat. "I don't remember, but I can guess, Sir."

Silence.

"Anal," she said. "Anal would be on there." She shivered. Anna wasn't an anal virgin by any means, but she didn't have the same level of experience as many other subs did. She considered it foreplay. Anna never really felt satisfied unless a session ended with a good, hard pussy-fucking, but she knew there were Doms and subs who would do nothing but anal.

He returned, holding a dark blue velvet bag in one gloved hand, the crop in the other. Setting the bag down, he got out a pair of scissors. Anna knew what was coming. She spent more on lingerie in a month than some people did on their mortgage payments.

The Dom stroked her naked right breast, then pinched her left nipple through the material of her corset.

He undid the strap over her ribs, and started popping open the front closures of her corset. Anna was surprised—she'd been sure he would cut it off, but instead he opened it down the front and pulled the fabric free from behind her back, tossing it to the side. He ran the tip of the scissors lightly down the center line of her body, then flipped it in his hand and rubbed the curved handle against the mound of her sex.

Anna jerked forward, gasping at the sudden spike of pleasure. She hadn't been expecting the touch, didn't have time to think—only react.

He chuckled lightly and she glanced up. The warm chuckle was exactly the kind of response Master Jensen would have had and for a moment her gaze narrowed, examining the Dom, but it wasn't Master Jensen. He was shorter and broader than this Dom. His legs brushed hers as he refastened the strap across her ribs.

Pulling the leg of her panties away from her hip, he snipped through the fabric with the scissors, then repeated the action on the other side before tucking the scissors back into the velvet bag. Her panties clung to her, stuck to the wet flesh of her pussy. He pressed the fabric into the crevice of her sex with his fingers, then lightly stroked her clit.

"Sir, I'm going to come," she gasped after only a few moments. She was too wet, too ready—she couldn't control herself, couldn't delay the pleasure.

"No."

He pulled the fabric away, lifting it to his face and inhaling before casting it aside. She was now naked except for her garter and stockings. Lifting the crop, he used the tip to flick each of her nipples, then tap the mound of her sex—both of which were things she loved.

Tingles of pleasure and anticipation rippled through her as he stepped back. She wanted him to do it again, to strike her most sensitive and vulnerable places with the crop. The Dom stripped off his jacket, throwing it aside with none of the care the fine garment deserved. Next went the tie.

He rolled his shoulders and opened the neck of his shirt. "Ready, love?"

The Dom removed the hat, and with a flick of his wrist, sent it spiraling off into the darkness of the Orion room.

Master Jensen grinned at her.

"Master!" Anna gasped.

Master Jensen prowled forward, planting his hands on either side of her and leaning his face towards hers.

"Who did you think it was?"

"You're wearing a suit." He never wore suits.

He wrapped a fist in her hair and growled. "Do you want to rephrase that?"

Anna licked her lips. "I mean, I was surprised that you were wearing a suit, Master."

"I wanted to surprise you. Did you really think I'd let anyone but me touch you?"

Anna's lips twitched. "I knew you'd be upset, Master."

"And did you want another man doing this?" He reached between her legs and tugged on the lips of her sex.

"I'm happy to serve any Dom." Anna blinked innocently.

"How noble and obedient," Master Jensen growled.

"The greatest pleasure is to serve."

"And it doesn't matter who you serve?"

"Of course not, Master. I serve all equally." It was the right thing to say, but the words felt off.

Master Jensen's lips twitched. "Liar." He slid two fingers deep into her pussy. "You know no one will ever fuck you the way I do."

It was true, she was a liar. While the possibility of the unknown had aroused her in a way she wasn't used to, seeing Master Jensen had taken it to a whole new level—he knew her, body and mind, in a way no one else on earth did. Another

Dom offered the possibility of pleasure. Master Jensen guaranteed it.

He didn't look like himself—he was a worn-jeans and bare-skin man. The suit and clean shave, as well as the cologne that masked his natural scent, had been an effective disguise. His dirty blond hair was parted and combed, something she'd never seen before. Now that she knew it was him, she realized the cut of the suit made his broad shoulders look narrower.

"The overseers knew I wouldn't be happy if anyone but me was partnered with you."

"That's very possessive, Master."

He continued to lazily fuck her with two fingers as they talked. "You're going to be mine, permanently."

"I look forward to that."

"So do I." He kissed her hard and deep, invading her mouth with his tongue even as he pressed a third finger into her pussy.

They were both panting when he pulled back. Slipping his fingers from her sex, he lifted them to her lips. Anna licked her juices from his hand.

"Do you like your scarlet letter?" He tweaked her right nipple.

"Very literary, Master."

"You never told me what you think is on our list, besides anal."

"That's the only one I can think of."

"Do you want to know?"

"Are you going to tell me, Master?"

"Damn right I am. I can't wait to see your face."

He crouched next to the velvet bag, reached in, and pulled out a folded sheet of paper. As he leaned forward, the shirt stretched across his shoulders. The material was thin and she thought she could almost make out the patches of scar tissue on his back. He'd never said it, but Anna was sure that one of the reasons he went shirtless so much was that he was daring someone to say something about his injuries.

"Can you guess the first one?" He waved the paper back and forth.

"Anal?"

"No."

"Anal…something?"

"You seem anxious to have me play with your tight little ass. It'll happen. But not yet."

He reached back into the bag and pulled out a hair brush. It was wide, with a wooden back and board bristles. Anna bit her lip. She couldn't wait to feel the back of that brush smacking her ass.

"Does this give you a hint?" He asked.

"Spanking."

"That doesn't start with 'A.'" Master Jensen pressed a button on the electronic base beside her and the cross started to rotate. Anna's head went down as her feet came up. He switched off the spotlight that was directly overhead and activated two others that were offset to the sides, allowing her to look up at the field of indoor stars above her. He reached under her and pulled the neck piece into position, giving her something to rest her head against.

He laid the brush, bristle side down, on her stomach between the straps and stroked her cheek with the back of his hand. "This list means I'm going to push us, both of us. They weren't wrong when they said we were complacent. I never want you to be bored."

"I never will be, Master."

One corner of his mouth kicked up in a grin. "Then we'd better get started. After we've played their game, I think we might have to do our own version and go through the complete alphabet."

He unfolded the sheet of paper. "Here's the list: abrasion,

age play, anal sex, anal plugs small, anal plugs large, anal plugs in public under clothes, animal roles, arm binders, aromas, asphyxiation and auctioned for charity."

His words hung in the room, exciting and terrifying.

"Of those, you didn't check animal roles and anal plug under clothes. I don't like age play or auctioned for charity. That leaves six things, most of which involve your tight ass."

"Asphyxiation?" she asked. That one scared her. Technically any kind of breath play was illegal in California. She couldn't believe that she'd opted for that one.

Jensen held up her list so she could see where she'd initial the box "willing to try" next to that item.

"Don't you trust me, Anna?"

"Of course, Master."

"Then trust me."

CHAPTER 3

J ensen picked up the brush and looked at the beautiful woman bound and waiting before him. Anna was his. He wanted and needed her on a base level. Out there, in the vanilla world, he did his best to act normal, but he wasn't. Life had stripped him bare, leaving him feeling more animal than human sometimes. BDSM gave him a way to express his base needs without hurting himself or his partner.

In another few months he'd be bonded to Anna, the formal ties between Master and sub cemented in the eyes of their BDSM community. After that neither of them would touch another person sexually without the consent of the other. In a world where monogamy was considered passé, they would be the exception. Maybe someday he wouldn't feel so raw, and he'd be able to include others in their sexual exploration, but for now it was all he could do to keep from tearing away the expensive suit pants another Dom had loaned him as a disguise and fucking her until neither of them could think.

Picking up the brush, he stroked the fronts of her thighs with the smooth wooden back. He'd gotten a quick and dirty lesson on abrasion play in the Masters' lounge, and there were

Doms on the other side of the glass who could help if he needed it, but for now he'd make do with what he knew, and let Anna's reactions guide him the rest of the way.

Flipping the brush over, he stroked her thigh with the stiff bristles. She jerked a little.

"Does that hurt?"

"No, Master, it surprised me."

"The purpose of abrasion is to make your skin sensitive, so that even the lightest touch is both pleasure and pain."

He carefully undid her garters and pushed her stockings to her knees. He stroked the front of each thigh ten times. Her skin grew pink, and faint lines appeared where some of the stiffer bristles had passed.

He did the same to the insides of her forearms, just below the wrist strap, but when he moved down to the softer skin on the inside of her upper arms she hissed and flinched away.

"Did that hurt?"

"N-no, Master."

He knew his sub. She was lying, thinking that saying yes would displease him. Jensen went to the bag of toys and slipped the brush in, returning with a strange pink mitt, which he'd been told was a loofa. He fitted it over his hand, feeling the abrasive material against his palm. He started with her upper arms, stroking until the skin was pink. This time she frowned a little, but it was an expression of confusion rather than pain.

Moving down, he rubbed his hand in a circle over her belly, then along the crease at the top of each thigh where it met her torso. She wiggled a little when he did that. Finally he went to her breasts, cupping the upper swell with his free hand to hold the firm mounds in place as he stroked the underside.

When he was done, her eyes were half closed, and she was breathing softly. There were faint pink patches on her pale skin, and he had a moment of remorse. She was so beautiful it should be a crime to mark her. The only thing that had him going to the bag and pulling out the next item was the fact that he could see her sinking into the place she could only reach when he used and abused her far beyond the bounds of what society found acceptable.

She found peace in that place, and that peace passed through her to him.

Jensen took the piece of tweed fabric and wrapped it around his fingers.

———

ANNA GASPED AS THE ROUGH CLOTH TOUCHED HER thigh—it felt like burlap or cheap wool. Master Jensen raised his hand, showing her the fabric he held. It wasn't burlap, but simple tweed—rough, but not nearly as rough as it felt.

"It feels…" She shook her head, feeling silly.

"Tell me," he demanded.

"It feels like something much rougher."

He switched to the other thigh. The muscles in her leg twitched in response.

"Do you like it?"

"I don't know. It's not arousing, I don't think." Anna laid her head back. It wasn't a sexual touch, and yet it was sexual. After a moment of contemplation she realized why. "I like that you're doing this to me. I like that you can make me feel things that don't even make sense."

He stroked her stomach and she tightened her core muscles in response. He worked his way around her, finishing with her breasts. The undersides were sensitive to begin with, and after only a few passes of the cloth she cried out.

"It's too much, Master."

Master Jensen dipped his fingers into her sex. Anna moaned in relief. This was a touch she knew and understood.

"You're wet."

"Yes, Master."

He wiped his fingers on the fabric square and went to the bag. When he came back he was holding a simple white cotton ball. Anna signed in relief. Jensen traced a swirling pattern down her thigh.

"Master!" Anna felt it in every fiber of her body, her nerves lighting up as if he'd struck her with the crop.

He smiled, hazel eyes sparkling. "That good?"

"Yes, Master."

Jensen worked over every inch of exposed skin. The difference in sensation when he moved between un-abraded and abraded skin made her gasp and shiver. The anticipation of the pleasure-pain and the inability to control or stop it had her dancing on the edge of a dark, delicious precipice.

When he reached her breasts, he bent and took a nipple into his mouth. Sucking hard, he lifted her breast, while tracing his fingers over the extra sensitive skin. Anna pulled against her restraints, leather creaking.

"You're beautiful like this," he whispered. "Fighting but enjoying."

"Fuck me, Master. Fuck me, please."

"Another night I might have, but we have work to do."

Stepping back, he brought the cross upright, then undid her straps. He caught her as she stepped off and let her rest against his chest as she regained control of her arms and legs. He cupped her sex, lifting until his palm dug into her soft, wet flesh. She ground herself against him even as she kept her head burrowed against his shoulder.

He pushed her head up with a thumb under her chin. "Strip."

Anna undid the garter belt, then rolled the stockings down and off, twisting her body as she did so to show off her ass and breasts. Hooking her thumbs in the garter belt, she worked it down her hips.

"Face down this time," he demanded.

Anna bit her lip, then turned and obeyed, climbing back up onto St. Andrew's cross.

Master Jensen strapped her upper body and arms in place, then tilted the table so she was flat with her belly and arms supported while her head and breasts dangled in the open space between the upper pieces. He adjusted the lower pieces of the table, bringing them together to form a "Y" rather than "X" shape.

"Pull your knees up. I want your ass in the air."

When he was satisfied, he attached a strap over her calves and another over her ankles. The tops of her feet were pressed flat against the leather. He put a square bolster under her belly, which helped support her. The bolster rubbed against the sensitive patch of skin and she shivered.

"Tell me if your neck gets tired."

"Yes, Master."

"I want to be thorough, so I'm going to do some abrasion on your back, but since I have you like this, I think I should also start in on that pretty ass."

"If it pleases you, Master."

"It does, Anna." He slid one finger into her pussy. "And it's going to please you too."

He applied the boar bristle brush in long strokes from her shoulders, down her back, over her ass and along the backs of her thighs. Now that she knew what the result was, she enjoyed the process much more, arching into the increasingly intense feelings of the strokes. He moved on to the loofa mitt, going over the skin he'd already abused.

When he reached her ass, he pulled the cheeks apart and stroked her anus with the loofa. Anna yelped.

"Does that hurt?" he asked, still rubbing her.

"Yes."

"I won't give you the full treatment here, but I want you to be fully aware and feeling when I put the plug in you."

Rather than a scrap of tweed, this time he went over her with his discarded tie, the silk seemingly as rough as denim.

"How do you feel?"

"My skin is sore."

"How is your neck?"

"Fine."

He grumbled then came around and crouched to look in her face. "I know when you're lying."

"I'm not lying."

"Even when you don't know you're lying, I know you're lying."

Jensen fiddled with the underside of one of the cross pieces, then pulled a head rest into place. It was like the ones attached to massage tables. Anna rested her face in it, and the strain on her neck disappeared.

"Thank you, Master."

He reached out and pinched a nipple. "I need you to tell me if something feels wrong, Anna." He dug into his pocket and pulled out some wooden clothespins.

"No! Master, I promise I will. I didn't realize my neck was hurting."

"Then this will remind you to check in with your body."

"Master, please."

"Open your mouth, Anna."

Anna lifted her head just enough to open her mouth. Master Jensen pinched her tongue in two fingers and pulled it down, snapping two clothespins onto it. Anna cried out.

She hated clothespins on her tongue. For another sub it might have been odd or even stimulating, but for Anna it was a true corrective action. It had been an accidental discovery, and ever since then her Master had used it as punishment—real punishment, not the kind that was actually a sex act in itself.

Anna didn't like the way it pinched her tongue, didn't like that it made her drool and kept her from talking.

"You'll keep them on for five minutes."

Master Jensen left her there, her body offered up and ready for him, but untouched and unused until her punishment was complete. When he returned, he ducked to look up at her face.

"Anna, for the rest of this weekend you will make sure to pay attention to your body. You will let me know if something hurts, or feels strange. I may not stop, but I want to know."

He pulled the clothespins off and Anna blinked back tears, hiding her throbbing tongue in her mouth.

"Yes, Master," she whispered meekly. "Thank you, Master."

He rubbed her lower lip with his thumb. "Good girl."

Anna focused on breathing, trying to get back the level of arousal she'd reached before. She shouldn't have worried, because the next thing her Master did was to slide his tongue over the abused skin at her shoulder blade. He kissed, nipped and licked his way along her back to her ass. Every touch was a shock on the hyper-sensitive skin.

"Usually you hold so still." Jensen ran his fingertips down her back and she shivered. "It's fun to see you twitching."

Anna clenched her teeth, reveling in the need that pulsed and pounded within her. She wanted him to climb up behind her and slide his cock into her pussy, fuck her until the desperate need inside her was satisfied.

Two fingers sank into her sex. "Yes, yes," she moaned. Her body clenched around the small invasion, wishing it was more.

"Not yet." He pulled out and patted her ass.

Anna heard him walk away, heard the sound of drawers opening and closing. If she strained, she could lift and turn her head, but she didn't.

"You've never been fond of anal, have you?" His voice grew louder as he returned.

"I enjoy it, Master."

"But not as much as when I fuck your sweet pussy."

"No, Master."

"It's partially my fault. You're very fuckable." He ran his hand possessively over her ass. "It's hard to wait."

Anna would have smiled, but she was too wound up, too aware of how close he was to her exposed sex and ass, too aware of her naked breasts and hyper-sensitive skin.

There was a click and then something cold trickled down the crack of her ass.

Jensen rubbed the lube over her puckered anus. He stroked and massaged her, paying much more attention to her rear entrance than he ever had before. Anna was by no means a prude, but she'd never considered having her ass played with pleasurable in and of itself. It had always been a part of her submission—Doms and Masters used her there, taking her because they could, because they controlled her body and her pleasure. The feeling of being dominated and used had been the source of her enjoyment, but the longer Master Jensen rubbed her, his fingers sliding smoothly over the soft ring of flesh, the more she enjoyed the feeling.

The sensitive skin of her anus started to throb the way her nipples did when he played with them. Her aching pussy clenched with each pass of his fingers.

"You're enjoying this."

"Yes, Master. I am. I didn't realize."

"Didn't realize what?"

"That it would feel this good."

"And this?" He pushed one lubed finger into her.

Anna's ass clenched around him, his finger feeling thicker and wider than it ever had before.

"Anna, how does it feel having my finger in your ass?"

"Good, Master. It feels good."

"I don't want good." He pushed his finger deep, until his knuckles dug into her butt cheek.

Anna leaned forward, trying to get away from the pressure. "I'm sorry, Master."

"Don't be sorry." He pulled his finger out. "It just means you need something more back there."

Jensen came around to her head and crouched, holding up something for her to see. "This is the first plug. The small plug."

It was clear and nearly six inches long, but not very thick, with a gentle taper from tip to widest part, then another easy slope from that to the neck. The base was long and flat, made to fit between the butt cheeks.

Anna breathed a little sigh of relief. She'd had plugs like this used on her before, and though it was by no means insignificant, it wouldn't be too much. He pressed the tip against her lips and Anna licked it.

Jensen rose and circled to her ass. He stroked her from the small of her back over her bottom to her thighs. Kneading her ass cheeks with his hands, he pulled them apart, exposing her.

"Relax," he ordered as he released her. The top of the lube bottle clicked and Anna imagined him coating the plug. The hard tip pressed against her anus. His other hand spread her ass apart once more.

"Anna, relax," he barked.

Taking a shuddering breath she released the tension in her leg and ass muscles. The tip of the plug slid in.

"Good girl." He applied pressure and the thick acrylic entered her, pressing deep into her body, each millimeter opening her more.

The widest part entered. Anna felt the plug narrowing. The base pressed against her and she breathed a sigh of relief. Master Jensen thumbed her pussy, rubbing her clit.

Anna moaned in pleasure, perilously close to orgasm. Jensen chuckled. "Not yet, love."

He undid the straps holding her down and helped her off the

cross. Anna clung to his shoulders as she stood, the plug shifting within her.

"Master," she whimpered.

"The sun has barely set. I'm not nearly done with you."

Master Jensen left her there, disappearing into the dark. A minute later the lights came up—spotlights dimming while recessed lights turned on, filling the room with a blue glow. It was twilight, with the starry pinprick lights still visible in the ceiling, but she could now see the rest of the room, beyond what had been illuminated by the spotlights. Master Jensen stepped up to a pommel horse near the large mirror. He patted it and then crooked his finger at her.

"Come here, Anna."

CHAPTER 4

Anna walked carefully towards her Master, aware of the plug shifting with each step. She paused beside the waist-high padded bar. Like the equipment used in gymnastics, it had two legs and a thick upper cross piece. Unlike in sports, it was covered in black vinyl, and straps and chains dangled from the underside.

Anna stopped two feet back and licked her lips. She'd never been used on the horse before, though she'd seen it used in a variety of ways. She hoped he was going to have her sit on it and spread her legs so he could fuck her. The presence of the plug in her ass made it impossible to calm the need inside her. To be a good sub was to live in conflict, relishing in near-constant arousal while simultaneously being serene and accepting.

Right now she didn't feel serene. She felt like she was barely controlling the urge to jump on Master Jensen and ravage him.

"Come here, lean against the horse."

Anna brushed Master Jensen as she passed him, enjoying the small contact. She leaned her hips against the horse.

"Hands behind your back."

Anna rested her wrists on the small of her back, palms facing out. She felt him bend, felt his lips brush the centers of her palms before he took her wrists and separated them.

"Don't just cross your wrists, fold your arms." Jensen walked away.

Anna stared at the mirror, wondering who was on the other side, who was watching them. She folded her arms as much as she could, cupping the opposite forearms with each hand to better maintain the position.

Her Master returned, stroking her forearms with the tips of his fingers. She heard a zipper, then felt fabric brushing her arms.

"Master?"

"Did you already forget what was on our list?"

He tugged her arms away from her body, slipping something between them and her back. The zipper *snicked* softly and the fabric pressed against her forearms.

"Arm binders," she whispered. A shiver raced down her back.

Master Jensen tugged, the fabric binder tightening. It completely encased her hands, forearms and elbows. Anna had to lean into the horse to hold her balance.

"This is a simple version. You get to keep your arms in a relatively comfortable position and it's made of canvas. I can adjust the fit with laces." His voice was soft. "If I enjoy this, then next time I'll get a more extreme one. I'll force your arms down straight and lace your arms in leather or vinyl. Uncomfortable for you, but it will present your breasts."

Grabbing her hip, he spun her around. She fell back against the horse. Jensen eyed her—starting with her head and moving down her naked torso. His lips twitched. "You're helpless like this, aren't you?"

Anna shivered. "Yes, Master."

He grabbed the tip of her breast and pulled. Anna took a half step forward. He released her nipple then slapped her breast, making the flesh jiggle.

"It's different than cuffs isn't it?" He asked.

Anna nodded—he'd said exactly what she was thinking. He'd restrained her more times and more ways than she could count, yet this felt different. She was far more vulnerable strapped to the St. Andrew's cross or hogtied, but the total immobility of her arms while the rest of her was free and able to move around was disconcerting.

"Yes, Master. It feels strange and frightening."

Jensen grabbed her upper arms and jerked her against his bare chest. He stared into her eyes. "Do you trust me, Anna?"

She met his gaze, understood that this wasn't a casual question. She rose up on tip toe and kissed his cheek. "With my life," she whispered.

They held each other's gaze for a moment. Then, without speaking, Jensen spun her to face the mirror and shoved her down over the horse. Anna exhaled as her belly hit the padded top.

He slapped her ass and Anna wiggled until she was firmly planted on the wide top piece, her toes braced on the floor. It felt odd and a little uncomfortable to have her arms behind her back in this position.

Jensen touched her shoulder. "Relax your arms, the binder will hold them in place. Good girl. Now spread your legs."

Anna inched her toes out to the side, the plug shifting as she moved.

"Good girl," he said again, and her pussy clenched at the words. She loved it when he called her that. Raising her head, she watched him in the mirror. The sight of him—all raw power and strength towering over her as she lay helpless and bound before him was thrilling.

"How does that pretty little ass feel?" He tugged on the plug.

"Good, Master."

"Are you ready to take the next size?"

"Next size?" Anna squeaked.

"This one isn't even as thick as a cock. Did you think this was it? Before we're done this weekend, you'll be taking a large plug up that pretty ass—a very large plug."

Anna gasped and licked her lips. She let her head hang for a moment, her hair falling around her. The idea of being forced to take something larger than his cock—which was, until now, the largest thing that had even been up her ass—was darkly thrilling.

His thumb stroked the outer lips of her sex. She was wet with need and his finger slid smoothly over her skin. Pinching and tugging the lips of her pussy was enough to have her rocking against the horse, but not enough to give her the direct pleasure she was craving.

"Master, please." The words burst from her lips.

"Please what?"

"Please, fuck me."

"No." As he spoke, he grabbed the plug and pulled. It took her by surprise and without thinking, she clenched down, trying to hold it in. The plug came free, forcing the tightened muscles of her ass to expand. Anna hissed and gasped at the pleasure-pain.

She heard the acrylic toy hit the floor the second before he started spanking her in earnest. His hand landed hard enough to have her screeching. "Master."

He was silent as he continued to spank her. Anna's toes left the floor as she thrashed under the painful swats. Each one spread fire over her ass, down to her pussy. The ultra-sensitive skin he'd abraded stung, throbbing like a bruise. Her nipples were rock hard, her pussy flooded with fresh moisture. The pain of the spanking made her clench her teeth even as she longed for him to escalate it, to move from his hand to a paddle, from a paddle to a whip.

As suddenly as it had begun, the spanking stopped. Over the sound of her own gasps, Anna was vaguely aware of Jensen's labored breathing.

She slumped over the horse as he walked away. Her ass hurt, the stinging turned to throbbing. She raised her head, watching him return. The angle meant she couldn't see his hands, and whatever it was he might be carrying. Planting a hand on the small of her back, he pressed something into her pussy.

Anna screamed in pleasure. It was as thick as his cock, but unlike his flesh, was cold. It didn't go very deep, but that first moment of penetration was so intense that pleasure shot through her like lightening.

"Naughty girl, did you come?" Master Jensen twisted the thing inside her.

"No, Master. That just felt very, very good." Anna sometimes wondered if these shocks of pleasure weren't what other women called orgasms. She suspected that those who weren't privileged to be used and played with by a Master didn't know the soul-shattering pleasure that she called orgasm. Really it was a matter of semantics, and she certainly wasn't going to admit that she sometimes had little mini-orgasms.

Maybe she wasn't the *most* obedient submissive.

"Do you know what this is?" he asked, pulling the toy out only to thrust it back in.

"A dildo, Master?"

"No, my pretty Anna." He held it up so she could see it.

A silver plug gleamed in the light. It was short and very thick, more closely resembling a mushroom than the long, slender plug he'd pulled out only moments before. He twisted it and she could see that the flared base was set with a large glittering hunk of quartz. The neck of this plug was almost as wide as the largest part of the last one.

"This is your medium plug," he said. His smile was devilish —his lips curled at one corner, his eyes sparkling.

"Medium?" she asked, looking between him and the plug.

"Well, it's larger than the last one, but smaller than the next one I intend to shove into your ass." His fingers dipped to her pussy, tracing a path up to her ass. He slid one finger into her. Anna shoved back against it.

"That...sounds like medium," she said, barely paying attention to what she was saying. Master Jensen added a second finger, tunneling them into her ass. His thumb pressed against her abused butt cheek.

"It's very heavy, so it will be hard for you to hold it in. As your ass muscle stretches and gets tired, you're going to have to concentrate and focus on keeping it in."

"How long do I have to keep it in, Master?"

"As long as it pleases me." He withdrew his fingers, then pulled her ass cheek to the side.

The tip of the plug centered on her anus and Anna clenched. She couldn't help it. The plug was too big, too heavy, too scary.

"Relax or I will force it in."

"I—I can't," she whimpered.

"You have until the count of five. This can be very painful, or simply uncomfortable. The choice is yours, but this plug is going up your ass. One."

Anna took a shuttered breath. The churning mixture of arousal, fear and submission made it hard to think.

"Two."

The part of her that enjoyed masochism wanted to stay clenched, to feel the force and power of him as he bowed her to his will.

"Three."

Her submissive part wanted to relax and let the plug slide in, stretching and filling her.

"Four."

Anna took a deep breath, released it, and relaxed. She was, above all, a good—if not always completely obedient—submissive. If her Master wanted the plug inside her, she would submit; she would do what she could to give him what he wanted, to accept his dominance with grace—and she would trust that he knew her well enough that he would give her that pain she craved when it pleased him to do so.

"Good girl."

The plug pressed in. There was barely any tapering. It almost felt as if he were trying to shove something flat into her. Anna took deep, slow breaths, struggling to relax. Jensen pulled the plug back, then pressed it against her again. This time her body gave, yielding to the heavy, hard thing. Her anus stretched, past the point of comfort. Anna cried out.

"Almost there," he soothed. "Take this for me, my Anna. Yes, that's a good girl."

"It's so big."

"I know. I want you stretched."

It slid in deeper, opening her further and Anna dropped her head, tears stinging her eyes. Jensen's other hand was firm on her back, holding her down as he focused on her exposed and abused ass.

"A little more," he soothed, his thumb rubbing the stretched ring of muscle. He shoved and Anna screamed.

"That's it," he whispered. "This is the widest part. I'm going to hold it here. I want you to accept it. Feel how stretched you are."

"Y-yes, M-master."

Anna's anus tightened around the plug, clenching the massive thing. She cried out at the pain, at the invasion...and cream flooded her sex.

"Do you like it when I hurt you like this?"

Anna raised her head, met Master Jensen's gaze in the mirror. They both knew the answer, but she said it anyway. "Yes."

"Don't look away." With their eyes locked, Jensen pushed, the plug sliding all the way in, her body clenching around the neck. Compared to a moment ago, the neck was much smaller, but by no means small. There was no way for her to ignore how she was being stretched.

Jensen's fingers slipped into her pussy. "You're tight."

"Your fingers feel big. Really big."

He stroked her spine. "Finger. That's only one finger."

"One finger?"

He laughed at her shock. "I was going to fuck you, just enough to take the edge off." He leaned against her, letting her feel the long, hard length of his cock. "But I don't think I'll fit."

"You'll fit." Anna had no idea if that was true, but she wanted his cock in her, no matter the cost.

"I'll fit somewhere," he said darkly.

He circled the horse, showing her the crop he'd picked up off the floor. Laying it across her back, he undid his pants. Anna could have cheered. He was, unsurprisingly, underwear-less. His cock was long and thick. The tip was glistening, the foreskin pulled back to show the delicate mushroom head. She knew his cock almost as well as she knew her own body.

Anna wiggled off the horse, groaning as the plug pressed against her. She couldn't wait to drop to her knees and take him into her mouth.

Crack.

The crop struck her left breast, beside the nipple. Anna jumped, nearly falling due to her arms being behind her back.

"Back over the horse. I didn't give you permission to move."

Anna scrambled to obey, the harsh, angry tone one she rarely heard from him.

"I'm sorry, Master. I'm sorry."

He grabbed a fistful of her hair, jerking her head up. His cock was there, the tip brushing her cheek. "Open."

Anna opened her mouth, neck straining. He pushed his cock in, the head rubbing over her tongue and the roof of her mouth. She wasn't used to sucking him in this position and she gagged and sputtered, spit leaking from the corner of her lips.

He pulled out then thrust in again. There was nothing elegant or skilled about this oral sex. He was using her, fucking her mouth. She drew in a breath as he pulled back, exhaling just as he thrust in.

"Good girl." His tone was still rough. "I expect you to take my cock, even if the position is uncomfortable."

There was nothing she could do but to accept the long, thick column of his dick as it pressed into her mouth.

"Lift your feet off the floor."

Anna struggled to understand. That was all she had to balance.

"Lift them." The crop lashed against her already-spanked ass.

Her submissive nature took over and she lifted her toes, bending her legs until her heels touched her butt. Now she was balanced on her stomach. The horse was plenty wide enough to support her, but she didn't feel steady or secure. It felt like she was balanced on a wire, the only thing holding her up his grip on her hair and his cock in her mouth.

He bent his knees, adjusting the angle. Anna closed her eyes and gave herself over to her master, trusting him, submitting to him. She was his, he was hers. He continued to fuck her mouth, and as soon as she stopped worrying, her arousal returned with a vengeance. This was what she wanted—for him to use and fuck her. To have all control stripped away, to have every part of her touched, whether it be by pain or by pleasure.

The crop struck her ass, a much gentler swat than before. It was a quick sting followed by pleasant heat.

Tap, tap, tap. The crop worked the cheeks of her ass as he held her hair and fucked her. She knew he was about to come—could feel it in the way his cock twitched, hear it in his rapid breathing. The knowledge that she was going to make him come made her pussy and ass clench, the plug stretching that sensitive entrance to her body.

"Anna." He breathed her name. It sounded like a prayer when he said it.

She worked her tongue along the underside of his cock. Swallowed the head when he thrust in deep. In the next moment, he was coming against her tongue. Anna cradled the head of his cock with her lips as he groaned.

Releasing her hair, he cupped her shoulders. She held his cock in her mouth, knowing he was too sensitive just after orgasm to enjoy stimulation. Her thighs were trembling from holding her legs bent up, her shoulders ached from the pressure of the arm binder, her belly hurt from lying over the horse, and her ass ached from the beating and the heavy plug that was still inside her.

Jensen pulled back, his semi-erect cock slipping from her mouth. She swallowed.

"You may put your feet down."

She lowered them gratefully, adjusting her position on the horse and rolling her stiff neck. She could taste him on her tongue and she throbbed with the need to have him inside her.

He touched the plug and she jumped. Next, his fingers dipped into her pussy, stroking the swollen, aching lips of her sex.

"How close are you?" he asked.

"Very close, Master."

"I think it's time my pretty sub came."

"Oh thank you, Jesus."

Jensen barked out a laugh. He cupped her hips and in the next moment she felt his breath on her wet pussy.

"I don't think I've ever seen you this wet." He pinched her labia and pulled them open, exposing her aching core.

"I can't remember the last time I was this aroused, Master."

"You're enjoying trying new things—abrasion, arm binding, anal."

"Oh yes, Master."

"Good, because we've got more to do. Come when you're ready."

His lips closed over her clit. Anna screamed. The direct contact with the throbbing bundle of nerves was so intense that her toes curled. Jensen held her upper thighs as he lapped at her clit. Broad strokes of his tongue fanned the already wild fire of her desire. He pulled back and blew on her wet flesh, then circled her clit with the tip of his tongue.

"Master!"

Knowing she had his permission—and she was so aroused that even if she hadn't she would have come—Anna gave in to the orgasm building in her belly. She sobbed as the pleasure washed over her in heavy, thick waves. Her nipples were diamond hard, her ass throbbing, her channel clenching.

He pulled her deeper under the waves of pleasure, using the flat of his tongue to gently massage her throbbing clit. Anything more direct would have been uncomfortable in her pleasure-sensitive body, but he knew her, knew that he could prolong her orgasm.

Anna sucked in great sobbing breaths as her legs trembled and her pussy throbbed. The last wave crashed over her and she went limp, her head hanging down, her hair nearly brushing the floor.

"Come on, love," he whispered, lifting her limp body off the horse. With quick movements he undid the arm binding, then massaged her upper arms and shoulders. Anna leaned against him, panting. He cupped her face, rubbing her cheeks with his thumbs. He kissed her, murmuring sweet nonsense as she slowly came down to earth.

Finally, Anna blinked, focusing on him.

The corner of his mouth kicked up. "Enjoy that?"

"Yes, thank you." She tried to tell him with her eyes that she was thanking him for more than just this session, more than this one wild orgasm.

They kissed again, this time Anna a much more active participant.

"Thank you, Master," she said as he pulled back. She shifted her weight and gasped as the plug moved.

Jensen raised an eyebrow. "Forgot about that, did you?"

"Yes, Master."

"How about we go get some food? I'm hungry."

Jensen pulled on the suit pants. Picking up the gray bag and another larger black one, he shoved the toys inside. Anna bent to help him, then stopped. The plug was heavy, and for a moment she thought it might slip out. Now that she was standing, she could feel the hard, cold edges of the quartz set into the base.

"Problem, Anna?"

"No, Master."

"Liar."

"Sadist," she countered, knowing he enjoyed the banter.

He laughed. Another Dom might have beaten her black and blue for talking back, but Anna hated being limited to "no, Master," and "yes, Master." Lucky for her, Jensen felt the same.

Slinging the bags into a corner, he offered her his arm. "My lady."

Anna started a mock curtsey, but froze as the plug pushed against her.

Jensen wrapped an arm around her. His hand slid over her ass, then touched the base of the plug. "Is your pretty little ass having a hard time keeping it in?"

"Yes, Master."

"You *will* keep it in."

"I don't know how much—"

"You will keep that plug in your ass." His gaze searched her face, his expression hard and relentless. "I want it in you."

Anna shivered. "Yes, Master."

He laced her arm through his, and then led her to the door and out into the hall.

CHAPTER 5

J ensen felt her hesitation as they left the Orion room. Though he'd come less than 30 minutes ago, his cock twitched. Anna was the perfect woman and three hours ago he would have sworn that their BDSM play couldn't get any better. She was submissive but feisty, wickedly smart yet soft and yielding. What he hadn't realized until now was how much he'd enjoy pushing her, how much her uncertainty and fear would bring out both his need to protect her and his desire to dominate her.

The way she trembled against him as they walked along the open hallway that ringed the Constellation Court made him want to throw her over his shoulder and take her back to the Orion room. The plug was big, and if not for the prompting of the checklist game, he wouldn't have used it on her. He imagined it was hard for her to walk with it in.

Anna stopped, clutching his arm. "Master…"

"What is it?"

"The plug. I think it's going to slip out." Her eyes were wide.

Jensen's nostril's flared. "I told you to keep it in."

"It's so heavy…I'm trying."

Another couple—an older Dom with salt and pepper hair leading a twenty-something sub in a school girl uniform, passed by. Anna turned into Jensen, hiding her nakedness. Jensen growled and grabbed her wrists. Forcing them behind her back he turned her face out, exposing her naked body.

The Dom stopped, looked Anna over from head to toe. "You have the first letter?" He pointed to Anna's breast.

The large "A" he'd applied with body paint was smudged, but readable. "Yes," Jensen answered.

The other Dom nodded to him, then walked away.

Anna sucked in a breath. Jensen was just as surprised by what he'd done as she had to be. He didn't like to share. He wanted Anna all to himself. He didn't mind people watching from behind glass, but Anna's naked body was his, and his alone. Normally when they were out in the public areas she wore lingerie.

Jensen took a minute to examine his feelings, his motivation. He knew Anna had gone naked in Las Palmas, and even been used in the large public play rooms, but that was before he'd joined the club with the express purpose of dominating her.

"Master?"

"I've never had you naked in the hall before, have I?"

"No, Master."

He took both wrists in one hand, then gripped her hair, tipping her head to the side. "Right now I enjoy showing you off, showing everyone your pink ass, the plug, your pussy still shiny with your juices."

The words were true, and it was a new feeling for him. Anna's breath caught, and she shifted restlessly. He released her and she turned to face him.

"You will keep the plug in through dinner."

Her eyes widened in alarm.

"If you think you can't do it, you may crawl." The words were harsh, the impetus even harsher. He wanted her used, filled, stretched, and if that meant she had to crawl like a slave, naked for all to see, then he would make her do that.

She bowed her head, then sank to her hands and knees. Jensen's cock hardened in the tight slacks. The chunk of quartz in the base of the plug glittered in the dim light. It drew the eye, demanded that anyone who passed by look at her ass, which was red from the abrasion, spanking and crop. They would know that her ass was owned and filled.

"Come," Jensen said. Anna crawled after him as he made his way towards the dining room.

ANNA'S KNEES THROBBED BY THE TIME THEY REACHED their destination, but that paled compared to the throbbing in her pussy. Exhibitionism wasn't one of her kinks, and yet she couldn't help but find Jensen's newfound desire to display her arousing. It wasn't like him, but this weekend was about trying new things, and it seemed her Master had taken that to heart.

She'd lost track of the people who'd passed them—she was moving slowly, since the tile and wood floors were not the easiest thing to crawl on. Murmurs of "lovely" and "well done" had washed over her, embarrassing yet thrilling.

The plug shifted inside her with each movement, but at least it wasn't in danger of slipping out. Part of her doubted it would have happened even if she'd remained standing considering how thick it had felt going in.

Finally they entered the dining room. Set with a variety of tables and lounge areas, the dining room served brunch and dinner Friday to Sunday night, which was when most people came to Las Palmas. The food was catered by a five star restaurant in Malibu and the wines were all award winning vintages.

Jensen led her to a sunken seating area. Stepping down, he sat on the padded bench that lined the square. A low table in the center had discrete rings set into the sides so it could be used to restrain and display subs. Jensen stretched out his long legs.

Anna still knelt on the floor. Their heads were nearly level. Jensen smiled, but his eyes were serious, his desire like a cloak around him.

"Steak and veggies," he told her.

Anna licked her lips. "Yes, Master. I will have to stand."

"I expected so. Keep the plug in."

She nodded once then rose to her feet.

Anna felt the eyes of the other diners on her as she crossed the room. The "A" on her breast seemed to burn, declaring to all that she was the first to play, the first to be subjected to this wicked game.

She was by no means the only naked woman, and yet it was the first time in a very long time that she'd been naked in one of the public spaces. Though there were over one hundred members of Las Palmas, it was an intimate group, and everyone came to know one another by sight and reputation if not by name. Anna had no doubt that others would be discussing her nakedness, wondering why Master Jensen, who was so deliciously possessive of her, would show her off.

She also had no doubt that they were looking at the "A," then at the plug in her ass, and wondering what else she was going to be forced to submit to.

She selected a plump filet from the warming dish and then added veggies to the plate. Next she poured a glass of Master Jensen's preferred red wine and carried both the plate and the glass back to him, taking the steps down into the seating area and placing his dinner on the low table.

Anna paused beside Jensen, unsure what to do. Normally she'd sit next to him and cuddle against his heat, feeding him bits of dinner as they chatted quietly. Tonight wasn't normal. She couldn't make any assumptions.

"Kneel on the side," he commanded, cutting his first bite of steak.

Anna climbed out of the seating area and knelt on the floor, her movements hesitant.

"Ass facing me," he said casually.

She turned so her bottom faced the seating area. She was grateful—it meant she was looking out towards the center of the dining room, with only a few people at the table along the wall looking at her ass and pussy.

Silverware clinked, and she could hear Master Jensen chewing. Anna took advantage of the position and looked around. It was a risky move, since many Doms expected a sub to keep their eyes lowered at all times. Though Jensen wasn't one of them, it wasn't unheard of for Doms who'd caught a sub looking up and making eye contact to request that the sub be punished by their own Dom.

Master Carter, an older, super-strict Dom, had once asked Jensen to punish her. She'd accidentally made eye contact with Master Carter while she'd been watching him drip candle wax onto his sub's pussy lips, sealing them closed with black wax.

Master Carter had marched over to Master Jensen, lit candle still in his hand, and demanded that Jensen punish Anna. Jensen had stood up, stepped in front of Anna and told the other Dom that he didn't take orders from anyone, and that Anna would be punished when and if he saw fit. Then he'd returned to his seat and pulled Anna onto his lap.

If Master Carter were to come back right now and demand that she be punished, Anna didn't know how Jensen would react. He was newly unpredictable, and she didn't know if she liked it.

The door opened and a younger man entered, holding a leash in each hand. Two subs in puppy gear crawled in behind him. Both wore full leather masks that covered their heads. Dog ears and snouts, also made out of black leather, were mounted on thick straps and worn over the masks. The female of the pair had a short curly tail, like that of a pug. Fastened to a plug, it curled up over her ass. The male had a longer, hard-plastic tail that stuck straight out from his ass. They each wore a leather-strap harness that circled and crossed their upper bodies. The male's made an "X" across the chest and back, while the female's had bands above and below her breasts. As they came farther into the room, Anna got a better look at them. Tags dangled from their collars, their hands were encased in mitts, and they wore pads similar to those a baseball catcher wore on their lower legs, protecting their knees, shins and feet as they crawled. Thin cords crisscrossed between the cheeks of their asses, probably holding the plugs in place.

Anna turned to say something to Master Jensen about the cords that held the plugs in place, or the pads they wore on their knees. She wanted to make a joke or say something clever about how she didn't have either of those things.

Jensen held his wine glass in one hand, but he wasn't eating dinner. He too was watching the puppy play subs. Their eyes met and Anna's breath caught. She faced forward and lowered her gaze. Her heart was racing, but she didn't know why.

Master Jensen stroked her thigh, and then pushed two fingers into her pussy. The sudden invasion startled a cry out of her. Pleasure rippled along her back and she bit her lip to hold back the moan. She hadn't realized how close to the edge she was.

"Do you see the puppies?"

"Yes, Master."

"You're wet. You got wet watching them."

"I... I..."

He set his wine glass down and reached under her to fondle her breast. "What's our letter, Anna?"

"'A,' Master."

"I decided there were things I didn't want to do from our

letter. They didn't interest me, or weren't allowed on your list. One of the things you'd said you didn't ever want to do was animal roles."

Anna struggled to breathe normally as his fingers lazily slide in and out of her pussy. The plug in her ass meant he was hitting her G spot with each stroke. Her arms trembled and she locked her elbows to keep herself upright.

"Do you want that, Anna? Do you want to be my little puppy? Or maybe you want to be my little kitty."

He pulled on her nipple, twisting and pinching it. Anna gave in and bowed her head, eyes squeezed shut.

"I'd get you a nice collar, and a tag with your name on it. I'd keep you on your knees, and when I wanted to fuck you, I'd pull your tail out and slide my cock up your ass."

Anna wasn't interested in animal play—it always seemed a bit gimmicky to her. Not that it wasn't sexy or interesting. She certainly liked to watch when the pony play people did their annual races, but it wasn't for her. And yet...and yet right now she would do anything he asked of her. Nothing seemed outside the realm of possibility—whatever limits and reservations she had were gone in the face of overwhelming arousal and complete submission.

"Watch, Anna, watch them."

Anna heard him, but was too distracted to obey. Jensen grabbed her hair and forced her head up. Across the room, the puppies' Master had taken a seat, one sub on each side. He unfastened the panel of leather that covered their mouths, then fed them each a piece of meat. The female puppy whimpered and inched closer, resting her head on her master's lap.

"No," he said, shoving her head off. He picked up a cane from the table and smacked her with it. She dropped her head and shoulders to the floor. Her master used the crop to push on her tail, and Anna imagined how the plug felt shifting in the other sub's ass.

Master Jensen pulled his fingers from her pussy. "No," Anna gasped, but then her Master took a hold of the plug and tugged it, mimicking what she was seeing happen to the other sub.

"Shall I ignore your checklist, Anna? Do you want me to treat you like a little puppy?"

Across the room, the Master had grabbed the male puppy by the collar and dragged him around to where the female was. "Calm her down," he commanded. The female puppy tried to crawl away but the male grabbed her. With the fist mitts on, the only thing he could do was wrap his arms around her hips. The female whimpered as the male dragged her back, pulling her into position under him. As the male puppy mounted the female, sliding his cock into her and then fucking her rapidly, their Master went back to his dinner.

Anna watched the woman, her head covered by the hood and dog mask, her body wrapped in leather and restraints, her ass filled, her pussy being brutally fucked by another sub, also dressed like a puppy. That sub had no control, no input. She'd been reduced to something base, and yet sexual. Anna imagined it was her in that hood, her on her knees being treated like an animal, being fucked.

Anna shook with arousal, her breathing hard and fast.

"Yes," she whispered. "Yes, I want that."

"Do you?" Master Jensen grabbed her by the waist and dragged her down into the seating area. He turned her to face him. Anna grabbed his shoulders, leaning into him. She inhaled, drinking in his scent.

He forced her wrists behind her back, binding them in one hand. He grabbed her neck with the other, holding her still so he could look at her. His gaze searched her face. "You would let me do it. You'd let me make you into my little puppy. You wouldn't use your safe word."

"Yes, Master, yes. I'll be your puppy."

"No, Anna. That won't happen. Look at me."

She met his gaze, her teeth clenched in frustration that he wouldn't give her what she wanted, that he wouldn't accept her submission and use it to do anything, and everything, to her.

"I'm going to push us, but not past our hard limits. You wouldn't want this if you weren't so fucking worked up. Right now I could do anything to you." His hand tightened a fraction on her neck. "But I won't. You need to know that. You need to hear that."

Anna took a deep breath as his words penetrated. He was right—she was totally defenseless right now. Subs were given the illusion of control with safe words and checklists, but the reality was that once they were in subspace, they would agree to almost anything.

His hand dropped from her neck and Anna rested her forehead on his shoulder. She was shaking.

"Deep breaths."

He rubbed her back, then eased her away. Anna expected that he'd call a halt for the night and take her to the bedroom, but instead he forced her to kneel on the table with her legs spread and her bottom facing the dining room. She knew people could see her wet pussy and plugged ass. That knowledge did nothing to dim her arousal, but she was no longer confronted by the visual stimuli of the puppy subs.

Jensen finished his meal, then fed her roasted vegetables and sips of his wine. By the time they were done, Anna was calmer, if no less aroused.

"Come," he said, rising to his feet. "You can walk, but remember, the plug stays in."

She felt eyes on her as they left the dining room, heard other members whispering about the first letter of the game. Half way to their room, she had to drop to her knees and crawl behind her Master. When they reached the door to the bedroom, Jensen helped her to her feet. He swept her up into his arms and carried her across the threshold.

CHAPTER 6

M aster Jensen laid her on the bed.

"Roll over, and get up onto your knees."

Anna obeyed, clenching her fists in the soft cotton duvet cover. He steadied her with a hand on the small of her back as he grasped the base of the plug.

"Relax." He started to draw it out, the thick bulb pulling against her anus from within.

Anna cried out, clenching against the pain.

"I said relax, Anna."

"I can't."

Jensen dipped his head, his lips finding her pussy, tongue stroking her clit. Pleasure flickered along her nerve endings. He continued to pull the plug as he licked her clit. The pressure within her ass morphed from scary and painful to pleasure-pain.

"Master," she moaned. "May I come?"

He lifted his head and slid two fingers into her pussy. "No." He yanked the plug out.

Anna screamed, biting the duvet. Master Jensen continued to work his fingers in her pussy. Sensation rolled through her—she couldn't define it as good or bad. It simply was.

Jensen rolled her onto her back, pushed her legs apart. "Spread for me," he demanded.

Anna spread her legs open, pulling her knees up. "Master, please fuck me."

He came down over her, his big body crowding her, his chest close enough that her nipples brushed him, but he held the weight of his body off her with his arms. His cock slid into her, full and thick, filling her in the way she needed, the way she craved. Anna wrapped her arms around him, clinging to him as if her sanity depended on it.

Often, it did.

His breath was heavy on her neck, his chin rough against hers. They clung to one another. It was the most basic kind of sex —just two people and their desire—and yet at the end of a long evening of play, it was the most important, the most meaningful.

"Master," she whispered, unable to say more.

"Come," he groaned, thrusts hard and fast as his orgasm approached.

Anna gasped as she came, her pussy and lower belly muscles clamping down, making Jensen's cock feel even bigger inside her. He groaned, holding himself deep inside her as he came.

Jensen rolled over, pulling Anna onto his chest. "We're done for now."

Burying her face against him, Anna started to sob.

"It's okay, love." He sat up, back against the headboard, and cradled her on his lap.

Anna gave in to the overwhelming feelings. It was always like this for her after a powerful scene—she wasn't sad, or in pain. Sometimes the physical pleasure of sex and orgasm wasn't enough to release the emotions that had built up in her, so she cried. She'd spent her adult life learning to lock down her feelings. Only here did she allow herself to laugh and cry when she felt like it, without stopping to analyze or consider the ramifications. Master Jensen didn't ask her what was wrong, didn't tell her to stop crying. He knew her, knew she needed this as much as she needed his hands on her body.

As her sobs quieted, he slipped from the bed, carrying her to the bathroom. He turned on the shower, testing the water before getting in and pulling her in after him. He washed her until she was able to take the soap and do it herself. He didn't leave—he stayed with her in the warmth, occasionally touching her, but never in a sexual way. She washed his back as he scrubbed his hands through his hair. Once they were done, they toweled each other dry.

Jensen held a robe for her and she slipped into it.

"I'll give you a few minutes." He motioned to the vanity, where her toiletry bags rested.

"Thank you."

"Anna?"

"Yes?"

"When you come out, we start again."

Anna opened her mouth, then closed it, dropping her gaze.

"I know, normally we'd stop for the night. This time is different."

"Yes," she agreed. It was different.

He took her hand and kissed her palm. "Have fun doing... whatever that is." He motioned vaguely to the vanity.

Anna rolled her eyes and took a seat. Jensen grunted as she started pulling out bottles, then left the bathroom. Anna moisturized, taking her time with her nightly beauty routine, all while being careful not to think about what would happen when she left the bathroom.

When she was done, she shed the robe and walked out.

Jensen was waiting for her. He'd pulled on a pair of silk sleep pants. She knew he'd prefer fleece or plaid flannel, but he'd given in to her looks of disgust and upgraded. With his arms crossed over his muscled chest he looked like a sultan waiting for a harem girl.

When she was close he pulled her in for a long kiss. She slid her fingers into his still-damp hair, loving the feel of it, relishing in the freedom to touch him.

"We need to sleep," he said as they broke apart. "I have plans for tomorrow."

"You said we were starting again."

"We are." He motioned to the bed.

Lying on the white duvet were two long, black pieces of leather. Anna looked from them to Master Jensen.

"Bondage sleeves," he said in answer to her unspoken question. "They're a variety of arm binding. I figured you'd want to try more than one type."

"*I'd* want to try more than one?"

"I'm just thinking of you, love."

Anna raised one brow.

Jensen grinned, totally unrepentant. "Right arm."

He slid the sleeve onto her, then started to tighten it. The leather was smooth on the inside, and covered her from above her biceps to her palm. Her fingers were free, but a wide strap went around her palm, locking the sleeve in place with her thumb pressed against her hand, almost like a fingerless mitten. Laces ran up the side, allowing it to be tightened. Jensen adjusted it until it was snug, but not tight. The leather was thick and stiff, and she could bend her elbow only a little bit. Buckles around her wrist, elbow and upper arm made sure she couldn't slip it off.

Anna's breath caught when he was done with it. If she'd seen another sub wearing this, she would have assumed it was decorative more than functional, but it felt like he'd wrapped her in rope. Though it wasn't restrictive, it was holding her, owning her. Suddenly she wanted nothing more than to bend her arm, the one thing she couldn't do.

"How does it feel?"

"It's strange. I didn't think it would make me feel like this."

"Explain." He started to work the second sleeve onto her free arm.

Anna fought the urge to back away. "It's big, and heavy. I can't bend my elbow. I didn't think it would make me feel so... so owned."

"Owned?" He paused to cup her chin and kissed her hard and fast. "You're damned right, you're owned."

Anna smiled and dipped her head, submitting as Jensen finished lacing her other arm up. Once he was done, he added padded restraints to her ankles and thighs.

"Okay, into bed." He threw back the covers.

"Like this?"

"Yes."

"I can't sleep like this."

"You're going to."

Anna sat, the thick cuffs around her thighs rubbing each other. She lay flat on her back, her heavy arms resting at her sides.

Jensen climbed in beside her.

"I can't move," she said.

"Maybe I'll get some sleep."

"You always sleep."

"Only because I can sleep though a beating. You punched me in the kidney last week."

Anna choked back a laugh. "I did not."

"You're the most restless sleeper I ever met." He looped the straps that dangled from the ends of the sleeves through the "D" rings in the cuffs on her thighs.

"So I have to stay like this all night?"

"No. I'm not fastening the straps. They will pull free if you work at it, so you can change position. However, every time I wake up I'll strap you in again."

Anna had slept in restraints before. It hadn't made her feel much besides stiff and slightly irritated—she did like to move around in her sleep. But that was before Jensen. As he turned out the lights and pulled the covers over them, her body started to tingle. Her nipples were stiff, rubbing against the sheet. Her pussy started to throb. She held still, tried to calm her mind, to relax, but sleep wouldn't come.

"Master?"

He grunted.

"I can't sleep."

"Are your arms okay? Anna you have to tell me if it's too tight." He touched her fingers, checking to make sure they were still warm. If the sleeves were too tight they would restrict circulation to her fingers, which would get cold.

"My arms are okay."

"What is it?"

"I'm...I'm..." Anna was at a loss for words. She wouldn't have had any trouble telling him she was aroused in the heat of a scene, but somehow lying here, helpless, made it seem like a strange thing to say.

After a moment of silence, his hand slid from hers, across her belly to the mound of her sex. Anna parted her legs. He dipped his fingers in.

"You're soaked. I didn't think you liked overnight bondage."

"I don't."

"Really?" He rubbed her clit and Anna arched up off the bed.

Master Jensen cupped her pussy, his palm over her mound, two fingers nestled between the lips of her sex, the others alongside the outer lips. He dragged his pillow next to hers, and lay down on his side. "Go to sleep, Anna."

"Like this?"

"Yes."

Within minutes Jensen was asleep, his hand cupping her sex. It was a long time before Anna joined him.

Anna jerked awake. She'd tried to roll over, but her legs wouldn't straighten out. After a minute of maneuvering, she realized that at some point she'd curled up, and Jensen had attached the straps from the sleeves to the ankle restraints, essentially hogtying her.

He was sleeping beside her, lying on his back with his head turned away. She tugged until the straps slipped free and she was able to straighten her legs. Lying on her back she stared at the ceiling.

Quiet mornings were hard for her—they allowed for too much thinking. Anna usually fell into bed exhausted at night, so mornings were when her mind raced. It didn't help that she'd been in the middle of a bad dream, the same one she'd had for years.

In the dream, she was sitting in a stiff plastic chair in a waiting room. That was the whole dream—waiting. Waiting for news, waiting for her heart to break.

Anna closed her eyes, willing away the memory, and the accompanying feelings. She was here now, getting what she needed. Jensen was right beside her.

But she could still remember the smell of that waiting room —coffee and old paper. She'd sat in a plastic chair until her legs went numb. She'd lied to get in there, saying she was the soldier's fiancée, instead of his ex-girlfriend. She'd been in her final year of law school at the time and she couldn't help but run through the ramifications if she were caught lying to the US Army. Eighteen hours after she'd gotten the terrifying phone call, and fifteen since she'd arrived at the base, a trim woman in a frumpy suit had stopped in to tell her that the boy she loved was alive. She'd pressed her hands over her face and sobbed, finally pulling herself together enough to ask when she'd be able to see him.

They were college sweethearts who'd carried their relationship over as he went off to the army, fulfilling his ROTC obligation. She'd worked at a non-profit for a year after graduation before starting law school. He'd come back from his first tour tired and bitter, mumbling about shitty equipment and even shittier maintenance plans. She'd listened, but hadn't really heard, too wrapped up in the drama of her first year of law school. Over the course of the next year, they'd grown apart. Anna had slipped into the polished, wealthy world of law, while the boy she loved struggled and slogged through war zones, piloting helicopters.

The last time she'd seen him she'd dragged him to a cocktail party, despite the fact that he was due back at the base early the next morning. The firm she wanted to work for was hosting the party, and she needed to make an impression if she was going to land the all-important summer internship. She'd wanted to show off her handsome US Army Lieutenant. In the world of trim lawyers he was a gladiator, his height and imposing physique making him seem like a god among mortals.

He'd been quiet and standoffish, finally telling someone point blank that the thing they were talking about was stupid. The night had ended with them screaming at each other, all the differences that now separated them mounting up like a wall neither one was willing to scale. He'd packed his things and left. Anna cried herself to sleep, and by the time she woke up the next morning it was too late—he was already in transit to the Middle East.

Eighteen months later she'd received a call from the Army. He hadn't updated his emergency contact information, and when the phone call woke her, some instinct had kept her from revealing that they hadn't spoken in eighteen months. He'd been in a helicopter crash and was being brought home for medical treatment. She'd jumped in her car and raced down to Camp Pendleton, tears streaming down her face.

That was three years ago.

Anna turned her head, looked at Jensen's scarred back. As if he felt her looking, he rolled over, rubbing a hand over his face. He blinked, then frowned.

"Anna? You okay, love? You hurting?"

"I'm okay."

"You're crying."

"I am? I didn't realize."

"What's going on?" He undid the buckles on her left arm.

"I was having a bad dream."

His fingers stilled. "The waiting room dream?"

"Yes."

He pulled the sleeves off her. "Come here."

Anna cuddled against his side, breathing in his scent. He let her rest there for a while, but then his hand stroked her from collar bone to hip, fingers bumping over her nipple. "Anna, you haven't been addressing me properly."

From one breath to the next, Anna's mood went from melancholy to excited. "I'm sorry, Master."

He rolled her onto her belly, stroking her back and ass. "I can still see the marks from the abrasion. I like it."

"I liked it too, Master."

"And this?" His hand slipped between the cheeks of her ass, rubbing her anus. Anna sucked in a breath.

"I'm sore, Master."

"But did you like it?"

"Yes, Master."

He bent and kissed her ass. "I'm sorry you're sore. I'm afraid I'm still going to use you here. I want to see a large plug in you."

"Yesterday's was large."

"Not large enough." He dipped his fingers into her pussy, wetting them, then slipped one finger into her ass. Anna winced, then moaned and lifted herself, inviting more of the sweet torment.

"It's really your fault." He pulled his finger free and slid from the bed to sit in a large plush chair.

Anna watched his hard cock bob as he walked. "What's my fault?"

"Your ass is far too fine to be ignored."

"The fact that I suffer through squats three times a week to have this ass means it's my fault that you're obsessed with it?"

"Yes. Come here, Anna."

She slid from the bed, stretching her stiff muscles as she did.

"Over my knee."

Biting her lip, she obeyed, draping herself over his knee, with her elbows and legs resting on the seat of the wide chair. He rubbed her legs, massaging his way up to her butt. He kneaded the globes, pulled them apart to examine her rear entrance.

"We have a long day ahead of us." *Smack.* He spanked her left ass cheek.

"One. Thank you, Master."

"After I'm done spanking you, I'm going to lock you in a chastity belt, so no one can get at that pretty pussy." *Smack.*

"Two. Thank you, Master."

"Then I'm going to send you to hang out with the other subs while I get ready."

"Get ready for what, Master?"

"What fun would it be if I told you?"

"I don't think that would be fun."

Smack, smack, smack. "I think it's more fun to surprise you."

Anna groaned. She'd lost count, but she didn't think it mattered. He continued to lazily spank her as they talked, alternating between hard swats and soft taps.

"And before you leave I'm going to write a big 'A' on your breast."

"Yes, Master."

"You never know, maybe I'll change my mind about auctioning you off for charity. This pretty ass would bring big bucks at auction."

"You'd...sell me, Master?" A strange mix of horror and arousal slid through her.

Jensen lifted and turned her so she straddled him. He leaned back into the chair. Anna sank down onto his cock, sighing in pleasure as it filled her. His eyes closed, jaw clenching. Bracing her hands on the back of the chair she rode him, pleasuring him.

"Sell you?" he said, after a few minutes. "No, you're not my slave, and I don't want you to be. But I'd auction you off. I'd put you on display, let everyone look at you. Then I'd buy you for myself."

"What if someone outbid you?"

Jensen grabbed her by the hair, pulling her forward and capturing a nipple in his mouth. He bit her. Anna yelped.

"I'd fucking kill them. Then I'd spank you for making me spend so much damned money."

"You'd punish me...because you put me up for auction."

"Exactly. Get off. On your knees."

Anna grabbed his shoulders, hating the order. She wanted his cock in her.

"Anna. On your knees." His tone was pure steel.

"Yes, Master." She climbed off him, her pussy clinging to his cock. He scooted forward and she took him into her mouth. Her sex throbbed. Wrapping one hand around the base, she licked the tip, then nibbled her way down the shaft before sliding her lips over him. She knew what he liked, knew how to bring him release. Within minutes he was groaning, hands tight in her hair as he came in her mouth. When it was done, he went to his bag, coming back with the chastity belt.

"Master, I don't get to come?"

He grinned. "No, you don't."

"I'll go insane."

"You have ten minutes in the bathroom. Don't touch your clit."

Anna used the restroom, brushed her teeth and then put on her makeup. Her pussy throbbed, her body still hoping for the orgasm she craved.

"I was fast," she said as she emerged.

"You always are when you think you might get an orgasm."

"And do I, Master?" She stopped in front of him.

Master Jensen forced her legs apart. "No. I want you riled up and thinking of me while you wait."

The chastity belt was made of a curved, flat piece of hard plastic, shaped like a teardrop and covered in leather. It was positioned over her sex and held in place by metal-studded straps. The narrow end of the hard piece was positioned between her legs, covering the entrance to her sex. He fastened it, making sure the rear strap was wedged firmly between the cheeks of her ass.

"Bring me something I can write on you with."

Walking carefully, Anna went to the bathroom. The chastity belt actually provided some stimulus. It was pressed against her in a way that made her intensely aware of her pussy lips rubbing over her clit, but she knew it wouldn't be enough to make her orgasm.

She brought him waterproof liquid eyeliner. He looked at it the way he would a grenade. Anna hid her smile and opened it for him. He drew a large black "A" on her breast, then turned her and wrote something on her ass.

"Master?" she twisted, trying to see what was there.

"I added my initials, just in case."

"Yes, Master."

"I have one more thing. You're not going to like it." Master Jensen picked up a posture collar off the table.

Anna fell back a step. "M-master?"

"I know you. After an hour you'll start thinking about your life outside of here. I don't want that. I want you to feel and know that the waiting is part of the game."

"But the belt—"

"The chastity belt is for me, so I know no one can touch you. The collar is for you."

Anna curled her hands into fists, fighting the urge to refuse him.

"Come here, Anna."

"Master, please. I won't—"

"I gave you an order. I will have you caged and collared if you're having trouble remembering who is in charge here."

"No. Master."

"Lift your hair."

With trembling fingers, Anna lifted her hair away from her neck. The posture collar was prettier than most, with bands of metal connected to plates at the front and back. The plate at the back had a hinge, while the front had a series of metal closures. He slid it around her neck and closed it with a small click. It was wider in front, dipping down to touch the top of her breastbone.

"You will be careful while you wear this."

"Yes, Master."

He pulled a small Allen-wrench-like key from his pocket and used it to screw the fastenings together. There were no buckles, no safety latches. He'd fastened her in and only the key he held could get her out. Anna trembled, her eyes on the far wall. The posture collar kept her chin raised a fraction higher than was comfortable. She could still talk, and turn her head a limited amount.

"Look at me."

Anna met her Master's gaze. He stroked her cheek. "I know you hate it, but you're beautifully submissive when you wear it."

It was true. Though her arms and legs were free, she felt as bound as if she were hanging from the ceiling in rope.

"I'm happy to please you, Master."

He squeezed her breast.

"I need to prepare for the rest of our day. Go to the Subs' Garden. You aren't allowed to view any other play sessions, or to leave the garden. Understand?"

"Yes, Master."

He kissed her hard and deep. "Good. Go."

Arousal still humming through her, Anna left their room. She hoped he didn't make her wait too long.

CHAPTER 7

By the time he called for her, Anna was so lost in her own head that she almost didn't hear the announcement. It wasn't until another one of the subs touched her shoulder that she realized what was happening.

"Sub Anna. Orion Room," the metallic voice droned.

She rose, leaving behind the half eaten plate of food someone had brought her. Head held high—because she didn't have any other choice—she made her way through Las Palmas. She had no way of ignoring the Masters and Doms who examined her as she passed. The "A" on her breast let them know what was going to happen to her, while the chastity belt made sure everyone knew that her pussy was owned. They may not have been formally bonded yet, but Master Jensen had left no doubt as to whom she belonged to.

Above all there was the posture collar, forcing her to face her choices, and her submission.

Anna had no desire to wear a permanent collar once they were bonded. A piece of jewelry wouldn't make Jensen any more or less her Master. She understood the appeal of the collar, and certainly enjoyed them—except, perhaps, for the one she wore now. But Anna could not, as much as she might want it, give herself over to her submission. The person she was outside these walls would no more wear the same necklace every day—especially a choker style one, which hadn't been in fashion since the 90's—than she would go to work in mismatched shoes.

The only jewelry she wore with any regularity was her engagement ring. She'd taken it off as soon as she'd arrived at Las Palmas. It had no place here, the same as a collar had no place in the outside world.

She stopped outside the Orion Room and took a deep breath.

"Wait."

She jumped. A dark haired sub decked in body jewelry and chains appeared beside her. It was the same woman who'd been there yesterday.

"Your Master has commanded me to take you to the bathroom."

"Oh. Thank you."

"It's over here."

Together they slipped into a bathroom located a few doors down.

"Inspection," the dark-haired sub said.

Anna stiffened, but then spread her legs and raised her arms, lacing her fingers behind her neck. She touched the warm metal of the collar and wondered if the sub had the key.

The other woman undid the chastity belt, then slipped out, allowing Anna to relieve herself. She washed her hands and fixed her hair, then examined herself in the mirror.

There were still faint patches of pink on her fair skin from the abrasion, and she could see one or two spots of darker pink from the various spankings. She'd cleaned herself up after she'd used the toilet, but she could already feel her sex growing wet once more. Her eyes seemed larger and darker than normal.

The collar made her neck seem slim and pale, held delicately within the hard ribs of metal. She touched her pulse point and swallowed. She knew what was coming. It was all she'd been able to think about.

Slipping out, she found the other sub waiting for her. Together they returned to the Orion Room.

"What's your name?" Anna asked the other woman.

"Pet."

"Your name is Pet?"

"I am my Master's pet."

Anna took a deep breath. "You're a slave, not a sub."

"Yes."

It made sense that Master Jensen would have asked one of the Owners to loan out his slave to be used as a helper. Most slaves lived the lifestyle 24/7, and had no expectation of pleasure the way a sub did.

Anna opened the door.

As before, the room was dark, and it took her eyes a minute to adjust. The pinpricks of light sparkled in the ceiling overhead. A single spotlight highlighted a large steel structure. There were two upright metal pieces supporting a long horizontal bar ten feet off the floor. Add stacks of weights, pulleys and hand grips and it would be gym equipment.

Instead of rubber grips and stacks of weights, this piece was outfitted with rings, straps and chain.

Master Jensen stepped into the light.

Her breath caught and a flood of desire poured over her. Just the sight of him was enough to have her teetering on the brink of orgasm. He looked more himself than he had yesterday, wearing nothing but jeans. His arms were folded, showing off his imposing muscles. His hair hung over his forehead and his stare was intense.

"To me, Anna."

Naked save for the collar, Anna walked over to him. She dropped to her knees. She could look neither up nor down. He circled her, touching her head, her shoulder, her breast.

"Hands."

She held up her arms, wrists together. She heard footsteps, then Pet appeared and handed him something. He held it down for her to see.

"Do you know what these are, Anna?"

"Cuffs, Master."

The black restraints were thick, with a single large buckle on each. They were lined with a softer material that looked like suede. Instead of an "O" or "D" ring, there were straps attached perpendicularly to the cuffs so that when they were on, the straps would drape over the back of the hand.

"Not, just cuffs. Suspension cuffs."

Anna started to look up but her head hit the back of the collar and she winced. That explained the straps, which would distribute the weight, allowing the sub to hang by the wrists without damaging the fragile joint.

Master Jensen fastened the cuffs around her wrists, tugging to check the fit. Then he drew her to her feet. Taking the key from his pocket, he undid the posture collar. Anna blinked back tears as it was taken away.

"Thank you, Master," she whispered.

"Was it so hard to be reminded you're mine?" He touched her cheek.

"No, Master." She wanted to kiss him. "I like knowing I'm yours."

"Good."

Master Jensen positioned her under the bar, and then raised her hands, attaching her to the frame with chain. Her arms went straight up from her shoulders, and were pulled tight enough that standing flat footed wasn't comfortable. She rose onto the balls of her feet, swaying a little. She wouldn't be able to stand like this for long, but there was enough play that she could drop down onto her heels to rest her calves.

"Comfortable?" he asked.

"Not exactly."

He grinned. "Good." Jensen circled her, touching and rubbing her, making sure every inch of her belly, breasts, back and ass got attention.

He stopped in front of her, and the grin was gone.

"Do you remember what's left on our list?"

"Yes, Master."

Jensen fondled her left breast, then slid his hand up to her neck. "Are you scared?"

"I don't know."

"Bring me the first mask."

Anna heard Pet's footsteps. Her heart was pounding in her chest. What mask had Pet gone to get? A gas mask? A hood?

"Trust me, Anna."

"I do, Master."

Pet returned and Jensen released her to turn to the other woman. When he turned back, Anna saw panels of black leather and straps.

"Smell." He lifted the thing he held.

Anna took a deep breath. "Sandalwood."

"Figures that you'd know the proper name for it. Remember the items left on our "A" list?"

She took another breath, inhaling the warm, woody smell that was distinctly male. "Aromas," she exclaimed.

"Exactly. Did you know that the sense of smell is most closely tied to memory?" He circled behind her, pulling her against his chest. His cock pressed against her ass and she danced on her toes to keep her balance. "I'm going to make sure that when you smell this, you have very, very good memories."

He lifted the leather mask and pressed it over her face. It wasn't just a mask, it was a muzzle. The heavy leather covered her from just below her eyes to her chin. A strap ran up from the bridge of her nose, over her head to meet the straps that crossed her cheeks. It wasn't tight to her face and that, coupled with the vents, meant she could breathe normally—but each breath she took was rich with the scent of sandalwood. He must have coated the inside of the muzzle in scented oil.

"Can you breathe?"

She nodded.

"Okay, baby, are you ready for some fun?"

Pet appeared again, this time she holding a Hitachi Magic Wand. She dropped to her knees and opened a small panel in the floor, plugging the heavy-duty vibrator in. Behind her, Anna heard a zipper, then felt the hard length of Jensen's naked cock against her ass.

His hands cupped her breasts, lifting and squeezing them. His thumbs flicked her nipples, then he pinched them, tugging gently.

"Use the vibe on her pussy. Not her clit yet."

Without hesitating, Pet reached for Anna's pussy, rubbing it before flipping the vibrator on. The rounded head of the wand pressed against her, just above the start of her slit. Anna moaned as the vibrations trembled through her.

Master Jensen pulled harder on her nipples and Anna arched into his hands. She was dancing on her toes, spreading her legs to give the vibrator better access. Jensen grabbed her left leg at the knee and lifted, folding it up along her side. For a moment she was off balance, hanging by her wrists, but then she adjusted her weight to her right leg. Pet pulled the vibrator back, the hum of its motor and Anna's breath echoing in the muzzle the only sounds.

Her Master's cock rubbed against her pussy. The head bumped her clit and Anna gasped. She sucked in a breath, the air perfumed with the scent he'd selected. Holding her leg in one hand, the other arm wrapped around her torso, hand on her breast, Master Jensen adjusted his hips and then his cock was at the entrance to her body.

He slid up into her in one long, smooth stroke. Anna

dropped her head back onto his shoulder. His cock retreated, then slid in again.

"I can feel you around my cock. You're hot and wet. You like being chained up and fucked."

Anna mumbled into the muzzle as the rhythm of his fucking picked up.

"Pet, put the vibe on her pussy."

The vibrator rubbed over the lips of her sex, making circles along her sensitive flesh yet never touching her clit. Jensen adjusted his grip and then slammed his cock into her. The force of his thrusts lifted her off the ground. Anna gasped into the mask as pleasure ripped through her.

Master Jensen pulled his cock from her aching pussy and lowered her leg. Anna swayed before finding her balance. Pet still held the vibrator against her, and Anna's leg muscles twitched from the pleasure.

"Stop."

Anna's head jerked up. He couldn't stop now, her body was warm and tingling with pleasure. A few more minutes of the vibe and his cock in her and she'd be orgasming so hard the whole mansion would hear her.

Jensen reached back and undid the mask. "Where there's pleasure, there's pain."

Both her Master and Pet disappeared into the darkness outside the circle of light. Anna sighed in frustration, but knew that a spanking—which is what she guessed was coming— would only make it all the better when she finally did orgasm.

Master Jensen carried a simple wood horse, the kind they sold at home improvement stores, over. He positioned it in front of her, then reached up and undid the chain.

"Put your chest on the horse, breasts on either side."

Eager to get the scene started again, Anna obeyed. Pet returned, carrying the same gray bag Jensen had used yesterday. She passed Jensen another mask.

"Lift your head and open your mouth."

Anna obeyed. This mask didn't smell like sandalwood, but sage. It was a gag, with a small black piece that fit into her mouth. Two straps ran alongside her nose to meet on her forehead. It had the same cheek straps that connected to the one on the top of her head. Jensen fitted a hose into the front and squeezed the pump he held. The piece in her mouth started to inflate.

Anna grunted as it pushed her tongue back and pressed against her cheeks. Jensen kept pumping. She looked at him, shook her head. Jensen grabbed her by the hair and forced her cheek against the wood. A shiver ran through her. Her mouth was stuffed full, painfully so. Her nose wasn't covered, but the scent of sage was still strong.

"You notice this one has a different aroma. This scent will remind you of pain."

There was no teasing in his voice. He sounded grim and determined. She didn't want pain—she wanted the wonderful pleasure of a few moments ago.

He locked the suspension cuffs together behind her back, then took a short belt from the bag. He strapped her elbows together, forcing her shoulders back.

"This is punishment, Anna. Not play punishment, not pain as a path to pleasure, but true punishment."

Anna wanted to beg him not to do it, to plead with him not to hurt her when she'd done nothing wrong.

But he was her Master. It was his right to use and train her.

Her arms were lifted away from her back, increasing the pressure on her shoulders, and attached to the frame high above her. More straps secured her legs to the legs of the horse. Her ass and pussy were extended out over the end of the bench, leaving them completely vulnerable.

"The paddle."

Pet passed Master Jensen a long wood paddle with holes

drilled into it. Anna's eyes widened and she thrashed, trying and failing to scream.

"Take deep breaths and calm down. I'm going to paddle you, and it is going to hurt."

Anna sucked in air laced with the scent of sage. Master Jensen rubbed the cheeks of her ass.

Crack.

The first blow stung, the pain lasting far longer than that from a blow with a hand or crop did. Anna's scream was only a muffled squeak.

Crack.

She pressed her face against the wood, tears filling her eyes.

Crack.

The paddle made a whistling noise as it descended to strike her vulnerable and waiting ass.

Crack.

"Pet, deflate the gag."

Anna's relief as the thing invading her mouth grew smaller was short lived.

"This is the last one for now."

Crack.

The blow was harder than the others. Anna sobbed as the pain radiated up from her ass. She barely noticed her legs and arms being released, or Master Jensen helping her to stand before he pulled the gag off. She cuddled against his chest, taking great shuddering breaths.

He eased her away and held up the muzzle. Anna jumped back.

"What are you doing?" she asked.

"I'm putting this back on you."

"Wait, wait." She held up both hands. "You're going to do it again?"

"Yes."

"All of it?" she whispered in horror.

His face was hard, merciless. "Yes."

"No, Master, please."

"No? You have a safe word. Use if it you want."

"Safe word?" She didn't want to walk away, she just wanted him to be gentler. She didn't want him to push her, didn't want to be taken to her limits.

Anna bowed her head. She was a liar—she called herself a good submissive, and yet when faced with a true test, she was failing.

"Anna. Safe word or raise your arms."

Anna met his gaze, hoping he would see in her eyes that she wanted to obey, but was terrified.

"We've become lazy, love. Six months ago you would have obeyed me, even after a paddling. Now you want to run away."

"I'm scared."

"But do you trust me?"

"Yes."

"You trust me, but you want me to be predictable. You don't want to be challenged."

"Master, I want anything and everything you'll give me. I just...I didn't expect this."

"And I've let you become complacent. It's my fault."

Anna looked at the dangling chains above her.

"Safe word or raise your arms," he repeated.

Anna raised her arms.

Master Jensen reattached the suspension cuffs, then put the muzzle on her. The warm scent of sandalwood filled her nose. He stroked and petted her, licked and kissed her nipples while his fingers danced over her clit. Faster than she would have believed possible, the fear and pain of a moment ago was forgotten.

He lifted her by the hips and impaled her on his cock. Anna wrapped her fingers around the straps of the suspension cuffs and locked her legs behind his back as he fucked her. Master

Jensen ordered Pet to stand beside them. She maneuvered the vibrator between their bodies so that with each thrust, Jensen was pushing the head of the wand against her clit.

When she was on the verge of climax, Master Jensen pulled out. He switched the muzzle for the gag while she was still suspended. As she took her first breath of sage-scented air, fear settled over her, but this time it was different. The fear was laced with acceptance and need. She was a submissive. Her Master wanted to beat her, hurt her...and so she wanted it, too.

Bound and helpless over the horse, she cried and screamed as Master Jensen delivered another five punishing blows, but this time when he lifted her up, she merely waited for the next order.

"Your ass is red, love."

"Thank you, Master."

"You found your subspace this time, didn't you?"

"Yes, Master, I did."

"You know I'm going to keep going, don't you?"

"Yes."

"Arms up."

He pushed them through three more rounds of pleasure and pain. By the end, she'd had twenty five strikes from the paddle and the pain in her ass was constant. He'd incorporated other toys—clamps on her nipples for pleasure, weights on her nipples for pain. His finger in her ass for pleasure, a drop chili oil on her anus for pain. He didn't speak as he lifted her up the last time. She raised her arms even as she swayed. He strapped her in.

"No more pain, just pleasure."

It was the first time he'd spoken in what seemed like hours. Pet put the muzzle on her and Master Jensen dropped to his knees and pressed his tongue to her pussy. He licked and sucked her until she was moaning, then he went around behind her, his hips against her burning bottom. His cock slid into her pussy, filling her aching core. At his command Pet applied the vibrator to her clit.

The cock filling her, the pain in her ass, the fingers on her nipples and vibrator on her clit all combined into a dense ball of feeling low in her belly. Her breathing labored through the mask, her mind was blank. She needed and wanted nothing more or less than whatever he would give her.

"Come for me, Anna."

Her world exploded in a sea of colored lights and crashing waves of pleasure. It was as if every nerve ending had lit up at once. Her toes curled, her fingers clenched. Jensen groaned against her shoulder as he too came.

He hadn't ordered Pet to stop using the vibrator. As her pussy clenched on his cock, the incessant buzz against her clit threw her into another orgasm.

When she came down from this one, Jensen waved the slave away. "Enough, Pet. Thank you. You may go."

With gentle hands he freed her, stripping away the cuffs and muzzle. He then lifted her, carrying her into a corner and laying her down on a chaise. He lay beside her. Anna rested her head on the chest of the man she would have sworn couldn't surprise her.

"Master," she whispered.

CHAPTER 8

S he didn't sleep. She drifted in the twilight world of post-pleasure. When Jensen got up she clung to him, not wanting to lose his warmth, but he soothed her with soft kisses, then drew a blanket over her.

Anna's ass ached dully, as did her shoulders. She felt calmer, and more humble, than she had in a long time. She, who prided herself on being a good sub, had balked when her Master had demanded true surrender, the surrender that came with giving up both control and expectations.

It had been a long time since a scene had given her such utter peace. She hadn't felt like this since Master Jensen had first dominated her.

"Anna, baby, wake up."

"I'm not asleep." She rolled onto her back to look up at him and hissed as her ass pressed against the chaise.

"Let me see."

She rolled off and stood, presenting her back to her Master. He'd raised the lights, giving the room a twilight glow. He stroked her spine, fingers dipping to the top of her ass, but not touching her abused skin.

"I hurt you."

"Yes, Master."

He turned her with a hand on her shoulder. "I've never pushed you that hard. I need to know how you're feeling."

"Ashamed."

"Ashamed? I didn't mean to make you feel ashamed."

"No, I'm ashamed of myself. Ashamed of the way I reacted. You're my Master. I trust you, and I want—" she shook her head. "I *need* you to push me, with pleasure and pain. I love the way you treat me, love that you're possessive and protective, and I got too wrapped up in that."

He threaded his hand through her hair. "It's too easy to fuck you."

"And that's a bad thing?" She tried and failed to stop the smile that curved her lips.

"It is when I'm fucking you instead of doing other stuff to you."

"Yes, Master."

"Anna, you're really okay?"

"Yes." She touched his cheek.

"Good, because we're not done."

The smile faded from her face. "Yes, Master." She curled her hands into fists. If he spanked her in the condition she was in now, she didn't think she'd be able to take it, yet she knew that she had to find a way.

"Trust me."

"I do."

"On your knees and crawl over to the ottoman."

Across the room, near the St. Andrew's cross, was a large ottoman. It was covered in easy to clean black vinyl. A spotlight shone on it, but the difference in lighting wasn't as apparent when the rest of the room wasn't drenched in darkness.

Anna stopped beside the ottoman and waited for his next order. Instead of trying to figure out what he had planned, or what was left on the list, she was happy to simply sit and wait. It was the patience and calm acceptance of subspace.

"It's been a while since you were this deep," he said from behind her. She knew he meant this deep in subspace, and she was both surprised and glad he could tell.

"Yes, Master."

"On the ottoman, head down, ass up."

She climbed up, and despite the pain in her bottom, she dropped her shoulders and head to the vinyl.

"Spread your knees. More. Perfect." Master Jensen circled the ottoman, inspecting her. "I'm not going to restrain you. You will hold still."

"Yes, Master."

He left, only to return a moment later. There was a click and then something cool and slippery dripped between the cheeks of her bottom. Anna shivered as the cold lube touched her.

"I thought about giving up on this. Your ass has been through enough. But I want to do it. I want to see you accept it. I want to push you again, to see what you can take, to make it pleasure even when there's pain."

Anna's pussy clenched at his words.

"Relax your ass," he ordered. Two fingers slid through the lube, then the tip of one finger invaded her rear entrance.

Anna blew out a slow breath, relaxing into the invasion. His finger pumped in and out and her pussy fluttered in response.

"Good girl," he whispered.

His finger withdrew and then a second joined it. Anna winced against the initial stretching, but when he started thrusting, she was again swamped by pleasure. His other hand dipped into her pussy, testing the wetness there.

"You're enjoying having your ass used, aren't you?"

"I am, Master, I am."

"Good. You're going to take more now." He added a third

finger and Anna's nails pressed into the vinyl. "Relax," he demanded. "You will take three fingers in your ass."

"Y-yes."

He rocked his fingers, barely moving them. Slowly her body relaxed, opening to him. He pushed his fingers deeper and she felt the hard ridge of his knuckles. She cried out as he stretched her.

"Good girl. Good girl."

Anna's breathing was shallow, her nipples hard points under her, her clit throbbing. He pulled his fingers free. Anna drew in a deep breath, then let out a whimper as he pulled the beaten cheeks of her ass farther apart. More lube poured over her anus.

There was pressure against her puckered hole, something smooth and firm. Her master applied force and it sank into her ass, opening her a little more with each centimeter. The smooth surface of the plug was easier to accept than his fingers. Her body stretched and stretched. The first twinges of true pain made her twitch her hips.

"Hold still. We're half way."

"Half way?" she whispered.

"Yes. And what do you say?"

Anna sighed. "Thank you, Master."

"Good girl."

Deeper and deeper it went, stretching her anus until it burned.

"You look so sexy like this." She could hear his arousal in the growl in his voice. "You're marked from the beating, and your tight little ass is stretched open so wide."

Anna drank in his words, reveling in the darkness he'd pushed them to. The plug slid in another inch.

"This is the widest part. I've never opened your ass this wide."

Anna couldn't reply, she could barely breathe. Dark pleasure filled her. Her sex was throbbing, her skin tingling. Jensen pressed his palm against her ass cheek. Anna shrieked in pain. Her anus clenched around the massive plug, but it was so big that her muscles could only tremble against the invader.

Jensen pushed and the plug slid in. Her body closed around the neck, which, while narrower, was still wider than anything she was used to.

"Beautiful. You took that beautifully. Hands and knees."

Anna pushed herself up, bracing her trembling arms. Jensen dropped down beside the ottoman. He reached under her and rubbed his palm against her nipples with one hand, while the other slid into her pussy. His wrist pressed against her ass and the pings of pain only increased the throbbing in her belly. One finger slid into her pussy and his pinky rubbed her clit.

An orgasm ripped through her. It was unexpected and violent. Anna screamed, her muscles clenching which only made her more aware of the plug. Her arms trembled, and if not for the fact that her Master quickly braced his forearm under her ribs, she would have dropped down.

"It's okay, baby. It's okay. Just let it come."

Anna shivered, little lightning strikes of pleasure zipping through her still.

"I'm sorry, Master."

"For what?"

"I didn't have permission to come."

"Did you know you were going to come?"

"No, Master."

"Then don't apologize. That was one of the sexiest things I've ever seen."

He slid onto the ottoman, then pulled her on top of him. She straddled his thighs, resting her chest and head against him. He stroked her sides and back.

"Thank you, Master."

He kissed her temple. "You're welcome, but we're not done yet."

ANNA CLUNG TO HER MASTER'S ARM. THE PLUG IN HER bottom made walking feel strange.

"Lovely ass. Well done, Jensen."

Master Jensen acknowledged the other Dom's comment with a nod. Anna blushed, but she kept walking. He'd decided that it was time to go back to their room. As before, he'd given her the chance to walk there, but if the plug started to come out, she'd have to ask to crawl. She doubted the massive plug currently filling her would come out, but it was turning out to be a slow walk.

She was completely naked, her abused ass on display, the black "A" still marking her breast. Master Jensen had allowed her to hold his arm, since she felt unsteady on her feet, but he didn't let her turn into him, wouldn't let her hide from the people who walked past. She knew he did that for her.

While yesterday he'd seemed to enjoy putting her on display, now he had returned to his normal attitude, which involved wanting no one but himself to see her stripped bare both emotionally and physically. He tensed every time someone came near them, and his right hand fisted when someone commented on her body or the plug. He forced her to parade through Las Palmas in order to remind her of her submission, and to allow her to display her marks and bruises.

When they reached their room, Jensen swept her up into his arms, carrying her in and laying her gently on the bed.

"Are you alright, Master?"

"I didn't beat the crap out of anyone."

"Very grown up of you."

He grunted. "Roll over."

Anna rolled onto her belly. He touched her hip and she drew her knees up under her, presenting her ass.

"Turn and put your knees on the side of the bed."

She adjusted her position, grabbing fistfuls of the duvet to hold herself in place.

Two fingers entered her pussy and Anna arched her neck, moaning. The plug was so large, her pussy so tight, that his fingers felt as thick as his cock.

He grunted. "I don't think I can fuck you with that thing in."

Despite the wild orgasm of half an hour ago, Anna was aroused again. "Please, Master." She didn't care how full she was, she wanted his cock inside her.

He tried to fit a third finger into her and Anna hissed as sharp pain shot through her.

"I have a better idea." Jensen's fingers disappeared, to be replaced by his tongue on her clit. He licked and sucked the bundle of nerves, drawing her closer and closer to orgasm.

She moaned, thrusting her pussy back against his face. "Master, please, please," she begged.

He grasped the base of the plug, tugging it in time to his tongue's movements over her clit. The added stimulation had her gasping and withering. One knee slid off the bed and Master Jensen paused long enough to help her reposition so she lay with her belly flat on the mattress, her toes braced on the floor.

"How does that feel?" His fingers danced over her clit, sliding easily through the wet folds of her pussy.

"Good, so good."

"Concentrate on my fingers on your clit."

The plug moved inside her. She felt the tips of his fingers against her anus as he grasped the base. He pulled, nearly lifting her off the bed.

"Master..."

"Concentrate on your clit."

Around and around his fingers went, occasionally slipping deep into her pussy. The pressure on her ass increased as he continued to tug, timing the pulls to the spasms of her sex. Anna's hips rose and fell. She couldn't, wouldn't stop the instinctive movement, the helpless thrusts that showed him exactly how much she wanted him, how much she wanted to be fucked.

Pain shot through her as the widest part of the plug pulled free. Anna slid forward, straining to escape the plug entirely, but he didn't let her. Her master held it in place, keeping her ass stretched and open.

"Master, master!"

"This ass is mine."

She shuddered. "Yes, Master."

A stroke to her clit sent a fresh wave of pleasure through her, all the stronger because of the pain. Anna raked the bed with her nails, sobbing with arousal. Jensen pulled the anal plug all the way out in one fell swoop. Her anus clenched tight. Her ass felt empty, but not for long.

Master Jensen's cock slid into her. Anna's breath hissed as he pressed deep into her, his hips rubbing her abused butt cheeks.

"You're going to come for me, Anna. You're going to come for me while I fuck your ass."

She wanted to tell him that she couldn't. Wanted to tell him that the pain and discomfort she felt were stronger than the pleasure. She needed clit or pussy stimulation to orgasm.

Those would have been lies. As he fucked her ass, his hips mercilessly slapping the butt he'd paddled only hours ago, the orgasm built in her belly. This time Anna recognized it, and could identify the pleasure from the anal fucking, so different and yet similar to what she was used to.

"Master, please…"

"Come, Anna."

She screamed, arching her neck. He leaned down and bit her shoulder as she came, his cock planted firmly in her ass.

Anna's head dropped down onto the bed, her arms and legs trembling. Jensen pulled out and Anna crawled up onto the bed, curling up into a satisfied ball. She heard him moving around and then the mattress dipped.

"Come here, Anna."

He was sitting at the head of the bed, back propped up by pillows. His cock rose proudly, the veins standing out sharply. He hadn't come, which meant that he wasn't done with her. She crawled toward him, licking her lips in anticipation of taking him in her mouth.

"On my lap."

She looked up in surprise, but obeyed. Straddling his thighs, she held herself up, her dripping pussy barely an inch above the swollen head of his cock. He plumped her breasts, then flicked her nipples until they were erect pink buds. He showed her the nipple clamps he'd hidden next to his leg. They were simple screw clamps. Licking her lips, she cupped and lifted her breasts, moaning in pleasure as he closed the clamps over her nipples, tightening them just a bit.

"Beautiful."

"Mmm, thank you, Master."

"You're ready for another orgasm, aren't you?" He fingered her pussy.

"Yes, Master."

"Good." He took two pairs of cuffs from under the pillow behind him.

Anna narrowed her eyes, wondering what else he was hiding. He locked one side of a set around each wrist, leaving the other cuffs dangling.

"Lock the cuffs to the headboard behind me."

Anna leaned forward, her captured nipples rubbing his shoulders. He kissed her neck and chest as she locked the cuffs around the vertical slats of the headboard. The cuffs had a longer than normal connecting chain, and she was able to lean back enough to look into his eyes. She expected a grin, but his face was serious.

"We have one more item on our list."

Anna realized what was about to happen the instant before he looped a thin white scarf around her neck. The ends dangled against her back.

"Master, I'm scared."

"Don't be." He touched her face. "I'm going to apply just enough pressure to restrict, but not truly cut off, your breath." He adjusted the loop of fabric that circled her neck. "This is about pleasure, not pain."

She dropped her forehead to his. Her safe word hovered on her lips. He held completely still, letting her come to terms with this. A too-hard paddling would result in bruises and maybe a blood blister. Asphyxiation was something much different, and much more serious.

He'd protected her, used her, pushed her to her limits. She'd trusted him with everything else, and she'd trust him now.

Anna leaned back, then nodded once.

"Fuck yourself on my cock."

Anna sank down onto his thick length. After a few strokes, she forgot everything but the delicious fullness of his cock in her pussy. She loved looking at him as she rode him, it made her feel like a harem girl, who lived to pleasure her sultan. She rocked her hips, then lifted herself until he almost slipped out, only to sink down again. Her eyes closed, her head fell back. The clamps on her nipples added delicious pressure to the sensitive buds.

The scarf tightened around her throat. Her breath hitched in her chest and her blood pounded. As soon as she realized the pressure was there, it was gone again. She faltered for a moment, but Master Jensen squeezed her ass, eliciting a yelp.

"Focus, Anna," he admonished her.

"Yes, Master."

She went back to fucking herself on him, using the slow, grinding rhythm she knew would drive him wild.

Again the scarf tightened, restricting her breath for just a moment longer than the first time. She looked at her master, her lips parted to take the breath he held captive. Their gazes locked as he tightened the pressure for the third time, this time holding it long enough that her chest heaved.

A spike of pleasure shot through her. Anna's eyes widened in surprise.

"What?" he asked, seeing her reaction.

"That felt...that felt good."

He nodded once. "It's restricting the oxygen flow to your brain. Carbon dioxide is accumulating and that's what's making it feel good'. It's like being at a high altitude."

She listened vaguely, glad he knew the physiology, but not wanting to think about it too much, in case it distracted her from the pleasure.

She could feel his fists on her back, knew he held the ends of the scarf there. It both thrilled and terrified her that he controlled her so completely.

"Faster," he growled, and Anna increased the speed of her hips.

He stole another breath from her, holding it long enough that her body spasmed, reacting to the denial with an illogical pleasure. Giddiness swept through her.

"Faster," he demanded again.

Anna braced her forearms on his shoulders, threw her head back and fucked him hard and fast. Her ass slapped his thighs and the resulting pain was sweet pleasure.

He pulled the scarf tight around her throat.

"Come, Anna," he demanded.

Anna's whole body convulsed in pleasure. The split second of oxygen deprivation tricked her body into a heightened state of pleasure. Her chest heaved, she could feel her pulse fluttering in her neck. She was owned, controlled, pleasured and worshiped. She trusted him completely. He mastered her, body and soul, and she owned him in returned. The scarf went slack and his hands grabbed her hips, holding her still as he jackhammered up into her pussy, shouting as he came deep inside her.

Anna collapsed against his chest, the scarf still snug around her neck.

CHAPTER 9

For the second time that day, Anna broke down. She sobbed, releasing the last bits of tension she held in her body. He freed her from the cuffs and clamps, then laid them down and curled around her, holding and protecting her. When she rolled over to face him, she could see the power and impact of what they'd done in the tense lines of his face. She kissed and stroked him, her touches not meant to arouse but to calm. He laid his head on her breast, the tension slowly leaving his body. She rested her hand on his back, feeling the scars there.

"They're not sexy scars," he said quietly.

He'd said it a million times before. She doubted he knew how much it revealed about his internal wounds.

"They mean you survived," she replied simply.

Anna closed her eyes, going back to that waiting room. She remembered the moment they'd come for her, taking her into the hospital, where she'd gotten her first look at the boy she loved. But it hadn't been a boy who lay there, it had been a man, his body wrapped in gauze, forty percent of him burned, the result of a helicopter crash.

In the eighteen months since they'd broken up, she'd landed

the job she wanted. She'd even tried to date—but it hadn't worked. She found the men she met at the firm or at posh cocktail parties weak and insipid. She'd longed for her former boyfriend's strong hands—and she'd hated herself for choosing a career over a future. Though only in her mid-twenties, she'd started to feel like her life was over.

She'd been rescued, given an outlet for those dark feelings by a senior partner in her firm, Ramon Leo. He'd noticed her disdain for the men in their circle of acquaintances. He'd invited her out for drinks, plied her with expensive champagne, and asked her about her love life. Too tired and drunk to care, she'd told him how much she missed a strong man.

The next weekend, he'd brought her to Las Palmas as a guest. Senior partner Ramon Leo turned in to Master Leo. He'd tutored and guided her as she explored her submissive side. When she'd received the call from Camp Pendleton, Ramon Leo had been one of the first people she'd told.

When she returned to work a week later, after making sure her ex-boyfriend was safely set up in a good hospital, she'd unloaded on her boss, admitting that he was the reason she craved such strong men, and that it was killing her to see him so badly hurt. Seeing her beloved again, and seeing him in such pain, had made the outlet Las Palmas gave her all the more important.

For a long painful year, she'd split her time between her job and her beloved's recovery. One weekend a month she gave herself over to Las Palmas, desperately needing to be mastered. It was the only way she'd managed to stay calm and in control the rest of the time.

"What are you thinking about?" Master Jensen asked her.

"You."

"Don't. Don't think about it. It's over."

It was amazing what a difference a few years could make. If someone had told her two years ago that she'd be junior partner at her firm, a full member of Las Palmas, and that she'd be preparing to be bonded to the perfect Dom, she wouldn't have believed them. Two years ago, the future had been a terrifying prospect.

"How's your neck?" he asked, kissing her.

"Fine."

"And your ass?"

"Sore."

He kissed her slow and deep.

"Anna?" he whispered against her cheek.

"Yes, Master?"

"I'm starving. Let's go get dinner."

Anna chuckled. She slid carefully off the bed, then went to the bathroom. When she came out, he was wearing jeans.

"Put something on. I'm done sharing you."

Anna's lips twitched. She went to her overnight bag and pulled out a pink and black bra, panty and garter set. Careful of her ass, she got dressed. Master Jensen kissed the upper swell of her breast, then led her toward the door.

TWENTY-FOUR HOURS LATER, ANNA ZIPPED HER SKIRT and checked her reflection in the mirror. She'd come right from work on Friday, and hadn't brought any casual clothes with her. She'd be going home in the tailored Chanel skirt suit she'd been wearing when she left the office.

Friday felt like a million years ago, instead of only two days. It was even stranger when she considered that she'd spent most of today sitting quietly with her Master and watching the players who'd been assigned to the letter "B." She'd thought "A" was intense until she'd seen what the "B" subs were being subjected to.

She placed her toiletry bag in the locker she'd been assigned in one of the Subs' Garden rooms. Picking up her overnight bag, she pulled out the ring box. Extracting the antique, three-carat sapphire engagement ring, she slid it onto her finger.

She waved to the other subs, both those who were changing into street clothes and those who were lounging in various states of nakedness, their play not yet done. She hadn't exactly gotten the girls' night they'd talked about, but there would be other weekends to play with her fellow subs.

Anna smoothed a lock of hair back towards the chic chignon that was her signature hairstyle.

Her Sergio Rossi heeled sandal—alternating thick and thin straps of hot pink and zebra print with a fuchsia heel—tapped on the concrete as she left the mansion and made her way toward the parking area. A handsome, blond man was leaning against the fender of a sleek, silver Aston Martin DB9. Anna smiled at her fiancé.

"Hello, gorgeous."

"Hello, solider."

The corner of Jensen Couper's mouth kicked up when she used the nickname she'd coined for him back when they were undergrads.

She kissed him, plucking at the ugly polo shirt he wore. "I'm going to throw this thing away."

"There's nothing wrong with this shirt."

Anna rolled her eyes.

"You're the only one who cares what I wear." He took her bag and put it in the trunk.

"At least you dress up for client meetings."

Jensen snorted. "Only because you make me."

"When people are giving you millions of dollars, a tie is appropriate."

He grinned. Looking at him now, with his hair glinting in the fading sunlight, she could see traces of the boy she'd fallen in love with all those years ago. They'd been through more than some people twice their age—he'd gone to war and nearly died. She'd nursed him back to health, while struggling to control her feelings for him and simultaneously dealing with her personal sexual demons.

When he'd been near the end of his recovery and leaned in to kiss her, she'd had to haltingly tell him about what she'd been doing to satisfy her sexual needs, even while she'd emotionally committed to him and his recovery. Jensen hadn't judged her, and they'd agreed to remain friends. Anna hadn't wanted to take advantage of his gratitude by starting another relationship. Jensen hadn't wanted to stand in the way of her exploration of BDSM.

It had been a painful, if productive, period of their relationship, with each of them trying desperately to deny their feelings for one another, and learn to be friends as adults.

Anna had helped him to set up a small engineering firm. Within six months he'd designed a new missile mount for military helicopters. Uneven weight distribution had caused the crash that had nearly killed him, and his design corrected that error. She'd represented him in the patent filing and subsequent multimillion dollar sale of the design. As a result of bringing him on, she was made a junior partner in her law firm, and Jensen was owner and chief designer of an ever-growing mechanical engineering company that specialized in military equipment.

A year ago she'd arrived for one of her monthly visits to Las Palmas where Master Leo had introduced her to their newest member—a handsome, young millionaire who went by the title of Master Jensen.

Anna had thrown herself into his arms and cried. He'd done this for her, she knew that. Later, Leo had told her that Jensen had come to him looking for advice and training. He'd spent six months secretly exploring the world of BDSM before officially joining Las Palmas. That first weekend, she'd been eager to show off for Jensen, and volunteer to sub for a Master who was known for putting on lovely bondage displays.

Jensen had lasted ten minutes before he'd jumped on the stage, demanded that the other Master release her, and then hauled Anna away to fuck her senseless.

They'd spent forty-eight hours locked in a room, exercising years of pent up desire. When they'd left after that first weekend, Anna had told Jensen that outside of Las Palmas she wasn't sub Anna. She wanted to keep that part of her life separate. He'd understood, and that night he'd taken her home and dropped her off at her front door like a proper gentleman.

The night after that, Anna had shown up at his condo in nothing but a trench coat. Much to their delight, they discovered they could still set the bed on fire outside the D/s relationship.

Two weeks later they'd moved in together, and a month after that Jensen had proposed.

"Baby, you okay?" His question shook her from her trip down memory lane.

"Yeah, just thinking. It's been a crazy few years."

He picked up her hand and kissed it. "I would be lost without you. You know that, don't you?"

"I love you. I hate how much time we lost."

"Don't think about it. It all happened for a reason. We might never have found Las Palmas if things had been different."

"Is kinky sex really worth almost dying?"

Jensen snorted. "Uh, yeah."

Anna laughed. She waited at the passenger door for him to open it, then held his arm as she gingerly lowered herself onto the seat.

"I'm sorry, gorgeous." He kissed her temple as she winced.

"No, you're not."

"Yeah, I'm not."

"Jerk."

"Nympho."

Jensen slid behind the wheel. Reaching into his pocket, he pulled out a slip of paper. Rubbing it on the back of his hand, he then cupped her chin and pulled her in for a kiss. The smell of sandalwood flooded the car. Anna gasped as her nipples tightened and her pussy clenched.

"You bastard," she breathed. Taking the slip of paper, she sniffed it. The scent of sandalwood made her head spin.

"Damn that's hot." He rubbed the back of his hand over her breast. "Why didn't we do that before?"

"Drive, damn it."

"Yes, Ma'am." The engine purred to life and Jensen maneuvered the car out of the parking lot and down the long driveway.

"And the joke's on you. We're eating Chinese food for Thanksgiving." Anna rolled down the window to clear out the scent before she went crazy.

"Huh?"

"Sage. The other scent you used was sage. It's one of the main herbs in stuffing. Since I'm never getting near sage again, we will be eating Chinese food, or Thai food, for Thanksgiving."

"Damn it, I love stuffing."

"You really have no one to blame but yourself."

"I guess I'll just have to teach you to love sage again."

"Remember, we only have two more weekends here before the wedding."

Jensen's eyes twitched at the mention of their upcoming wedding. It had been nearly ten months since he'd proposed, assuming they'd get married the next week. Anna was unrepentantly planning a six-figure dream wedding. Theirs was an epic love story—it deserved an epic wedding.

"I will buy you a house in France if you'd just elope with me."

"Nope. But you're going to buy me a vacation house in France anyway."

Jensen shot her a disgruntled look. "Then how about we move up our bonding ceremony?"

Anna pretended to consider it. "Wedding first."

"Damn it, woman. Do you realize what I would have done if they'd tried to give you to someone else this weekend?" The primal violence in his voice made her shiver. After all they'd done this weekend, she should have been too exhausted to even think about sex, but when it came to Jensen, it seemed that she could never get enough.

"I was a little concerned," she admitted. "But I know you enjoyed making me sweat by pretending to be someone else. Besides, if you get lazy with the sex post-marriage, I might have to find a new Dom. Don't worry I'll still have vanilla sex with you."

"It's cute that you think I'll ever let anyone else touch you."

"Maybe I'll marry you but get bonded to a different Dom. A husband and a lover. I'd get double presents on Valentine's day." Anna fluttered her eyelashes.

"Maybe I'll buy an island and keep you there naked and chained up."

Anna laced her fingers with his. "Promises, promises," she said with a smile.

As they sped down into the city, she felt the real world closing in around her. She'd work ten hour days the rest of this week, and meet with her wedding planner and bridesmaids in the evening. Jensen was finalizing the bid for a DOD design contract, so she probably wouldn't see much of him until Thursday. Despite the fact that their day-to-day lives left little time for emotional or physical intimacy, they'd be alright—the closeness from this weekend would linger, holding them together even when they were apart.

"Back to the real world," he said as he parked in their garage. He helped her out, then pressed her back against the car. Jensen kissed her slow and deep.

"You're mine," he whispered. "Always and forever."

Anna touched his cheek. "Always and forever."

MASTER LEO TOOK THE LARGE LETTER "A" OFF THE board. One letter down, twenty-five to go. His submissive, Gabriela, knelt at his feet. She shifted, the tiny bells that dangled from her nipples jingling. Her breasts were marked by thin stripes from the cane he'd used on them earlier. Watching the people he'd assigned to the letter "B" had inspired him to do some "breast whipping" of his own.

"Come," he said. "Let's go see how they're going to handle 'branding.'"

B IS FOR...

CHAPTER 1

S ome people craved the sweet pleasure of submission. Some wanted the heady sting of pain. Some had no choice. For some, the darkness inside could only be eased with the dangerous games played here.

Xavier tossed his bag into one of the elegant mahogany lockers in a small dressing room, anticipation making his movements hard and sharp. He needed this. For months he'd been wanting it, lying awake at night dreaming of having a woman bound at his mercy. A week ago it had gone from "want" to "need" when the darkness inside him reached critical levels. He rubbed his bare face, grimacing, then tucked a handful of leather into the front pocket of his black jeans.

He headed for the well-stocked bar in the next room. The Dom's Lounge, affectionately called the den, was an elegant room with wood paneling, floor to ceiling bookshelves, and robust leather furniture. It had an air of wealth and power, both of which the people who used this room possessed. One wall was all windows, taking in the view of golden hills and palm trees, rather than the verdant English countryside one might expect.

Las Palmas was a sprawling Spanish-style estate north of Los Angeles. Its size and architectural history meant it was mentioned in various guides, but very few people could claim to have ever been inside. Las Palmas was the home of *Las Palmas Oscuras*—a BDSM club for the wealthy, powerful, and kinky denizens of the City of Angels.

"Welcome back, Xavier."

Glass in hand, Xavier half-turned to see an elegant woman in her fifties rising from one of the leather wing-back chairs. Mistress Faith was one of the overseers of Las Palmas, and a woman he was lucky to call a friend.

"Mistress." Xavier used the title both as a sign of respect and affection.

When she offered her hand, he took it and bowed stiffly over it. There were lines around her eyes that Xavier hadn't seen last time he was here, though she looked elegant and powerful in a tailored black skirt suit. Outside the Doms' section of the estate she wore a porcelain half-mask, both to protect her identity and hide her age. That was something Xavier understood, though at thirty-nine it was not his age he was hiding.

"I didn't think you'd make it for our meeting." She patted his arm just above the leather bracers he wore on each wrist.

"Meeting?" Apparently he'd missed something. Not a surprise, given his life outside of here.

Mistress Faith sighed. "I suppose you haven't read your email?"

"I've only been back for—" Xavier started to reach for his phone to check the time, then remembered he didn't carry it while here. It was a way to separate who he was to the outside world from who he was at Las Palmas. "—less than a day."

"Then your timing is simply excellent. We have an hour before everyone is expected in the Conclave."

"You mean the barn?"

"If it has air conditioning, it's not a barn. If it's elegant, it's not a barn." Faith had helped develop Las Palmas, and had overseen the renovations.

Xavier snorted. "It's nicer than 99% of the world's housing, but it has horse stalls. It's a barn."

She sniffed. "You weren't always so obstinate."

Xavier was tired of small talk. "What's going on? Is there something wrong?"

"Not at all. Have a seat; I'll have someone bring us food."

"I'm fine." He tossed back his drink and poured another, though this one was simply mineral water. It was time to go find a submissive, one of the women who would gladly accept and submit to his aggressive desires.

"You need to eat." She motioned to the chairs.

"I need a sub and an empty room. Food can wait."

"Let's feed your body, then we'll feed your soul." Faith slipped her arm through his. For a moment Xavier resisted, but when Faith tapped his arm he gave in and let her guide him to a chair. He chose his seat, mindful of his positioning and how much of his face she could see.

Xavier set down his drink and tugged the heavy leather mask from his pocket, laying it on the side table. It seemed he wouldn't be getting to put it on for another few minutes. If anyone else had tried to detain him, he would have shut him or her down. But Faith was one of the few people he respected enough to put aside his needs—as long as it was a short delay.

"Has anyone ever told you that you're bossy?" Xavier forced himself to relax into the chair, though his blood was humming and he was mentally preparing to enter the Las Palmas general rooms, where members mingled and those who were not bonded or owned found partners and negotiated scenes.

"All the time, darling. All the time."

Mistress Faith used a phone that waited on a desk facing the windows to place an order. When she returned, she picked up a glass of champagne from the side table and raised it in a toast. "To new adventures."

Xavier swirled the liquid in his glass. "I'm not in the mood for an adventure."

"No. I suppose you're not."

There was a wealth of understanding in her words, and Xavier kept his gaze on the windows, not wanting to see the pity in her eyes.

"I'll rephrase. We're going to play a game."

Xavier took a long drink, now wishing it was more than water, before replying. "You and I are?"

Mistress Faith laughed. "No, regrettably. All the members of *Las Palmas Oscuras*."

"What game?"

"You'll find out soon enough."

―――

AN HOUR AND A HALF LATER XAVIER STOOD, shoulder propped against the wall, as the overseers exercised their power.

"When you joined us you completed a sex, kink, and fetish checklist. Some of you have updated it as your tastes evolved; others have only the original on file." Master Mikael pulled a cloth covering off of a large board. Mounted on it were cards— one for each letter of the alphabet.

The Dom standing beside Xavier snorted in apparent amusement. "This almost reminds me of school."

"I don't like naughty pupil scenes," Xavier replied.

"I wouldn't expect so." The words implied a lot of things about Xavier's tastes. Most of which were probably true.

Xavier knew his reputation within the club, and it was deserved but surprising considering how rarely he was able to play.

"You're James?" he asked. He recognized the man.

The other Dom nodded, his gaze focused on the three over-seers, who were still explaining whatever it was they were up to.

Xavier's patience was wearing very thin, so he switched his attention to the subs and slaves who were seated or kneeling on the floor in the center of the large space. He saw a few subs he'd played with before, the kind of women who liked their pain tinged with pleasure and who had been to the darkest parts of their own souls. When he got his hands on one of them…

Mistress Faith's voice snapped his attention back to the overseers.

"Of all the hundreds of delicious sexual things on that list, many of you have only tried a few. We will no longer allow that."

Xavier frowned, his attention now on Faith, who was scanning the Masters, Dominants, and Owners who stood near the walls or were seated in the lounge-like loft overhead. She raised a brow slightly when her gaze met Xavier's. "Each of you has been assigned to a letter, and with it every kink and fetish in that part of the alphabet."

"This… could be interesting." James's tone was tinged with surprise. Others in the room were shifting and muttering.

Xavier had to agree. He remembered completing the BDSM Checklist—a list of activities and implements used in BDSM play. Filling out the checklist was a good way to find partners who had the same interests, and a way to negotiate hard limits up front. He'd actually had to do it twice, each time spending hours thinking about the items before deciding what his response would be. He looked at the letter board—he could think of a few things he hadn't had a chance to try. Hopefully he got a letter that would provide him some novelty, and could snatch up one of the subs he'd noted earlier.

"We've also become complacent in our playmates." Master Leo, the third overseer, raised his voice to be heard over the protests and comments of the Dominant members, who were starting to voice their questions. The subs and slaves were, of course, obediently silent. "Those subs who are bound to a Master will be assigned to their Master's letter. Those of you who indicated that you are willing to share or be shared may be partnered with someone new. Possibly more than one someone."

They were assigning the subs? Now the Doms were grumbling in truth. Xavier shrugged mentally. They'd assign him someone who could handle what he'd do to her. They wouldn't dare do anything else.

Twenty minutes later he found out how horribly wrong he was.

"Master Xavier, you have the letter B." Mistress Faith handed him an envelope containing the name of his assigned partner and copies of both of their checklists.

Stepping to the side, he ripped it open and pulled out an eight-by-ten glossy photo of his sub.

"Fuck."

James looked up from his own envelope. "Problem?"

Xavier held up the picture. James looked from it to Xavier and then started to laugh.

The woman in the picture was gorgeous—soft red curls framed her classically beautiful face and soft, kissable lips. In the photo she was wearing a ruffled white corset, lace panties, and stockings printed with pink hearts, which showed off her lush figure. She was the kind of sub who liked to be cuddled and kissed, and to squirm and giggle while being spanked.

The women Xavier played with made a lot of noises, but they didn't giggle.

"Mae is a lovely sub." James clapped him on the shoulder. "Don't let her looks fool you. She's also very smart and has a quick wit. She's a pleasure to talk to."

"I'm not looking for a fucking therapist." Xavier rubbed his cheek just under the edge of his mask.

James shrugged. "I didn't say she was one."

"Isn't she the one who did that ribbon bondage presentation?" Occasionally members hosted demonstrations. The last time he'd been here there'd been one on "gentle bondage" and he was fairly certain this pretty redhead had been part of it.

What the fuck was the point of gentle bondage?

There was something about her though, a kind of magnetism and confidence that made submission powerful. A weak-willed woman who submitted wasn't interesting. At the demo she'd been bound to an upholstered ottoman with wide red ribbon and then gently spanked. As uninteresting as he'd found the setup, he remembered Mae because he'd stayed to watch her, if only because it was impossible to look away.

"Just…try not to break her." James nodded once and then headed for the door.

Xavier examined the photo one more time. She was the perfect sub…*for someone else*. She was silk ribbon and champagne. He was steel cuffs and whiskey. He needed to find Mistress Faith and get a new assignment. Yet he found himself still standing there, long after the Conclave had cleared out, staring at Mae's photo.

Shaking his head, he shoved the photo back into the envelope, then pulled out the two checklists inside. Looking first at his own, he scanned the list of things that began with the letter B. It was a long list.

Flipping to Mae's checklist he read through, cursed, then scanned the "B" section again, sure he was misreading it. He wasn't.

MAE POURED HERSELF ANOTHER GLASS OF champagne and curled up on a delicate love seat in the lounge of the Subs' Garden, a pretty suite of rooms reserved exclusively for the use of submissive members of *Las Palmas Oscuras*. It was nearly midnight and there were only a few other subs milling about. Members who hadn't reserved play time or space for this weekend had gone home. Others were off meeting with their checklist partners, planning when they'd work through their letter. Some were ensconced in playrooms with their Owners or Masters, since the rules said that they had to complete their checklist items within the month, not that they were restricted from any play that wasn't part of the game.

A few hours after the announcement, Mae had ventured out to see what was happening, and who was playing with whom, in the public spaces. She watched Master Carter drip black wax onto a sub's nipples—a fairly regular occurrence since Master Carter was a wax connoisseur—and tried to not let herself get too worked up by the woman's moans of pleasure. A few of her favorite Doms had approached her while she watched the scene, but she'd gently replied that she wasn't free to play, making sure her smile let them know how much she regretted her reply. It wasn't a lie, but maybe it wasn't the whole truth.

In the six hours since the game had been announced, it seemed that club members all knew who their partners were, what their letter was, or at least when they were expected to be here to play. Mae knew nothing. She hadn't been contacted, either over the loudspeaker system that allowed the Doms to make announcements in the subs-only spaces, or by paper message delivered by a few slaves who'd been tasked to play mail carrier. Envelope after envelope had arrived to the Subs' Garden, announcement after announcement had been made, but none addressed to Mae.

Taking a sip of champagne, Mae tugged the shoulder of her kimono-style robe up over her shoulder, covering her breast, and tried to keep her mood light. Her emotions were a mess of arousal—which was an almost Pavlovian response to being at Las Palmas, frustrated—since it didn't seem like a scene or orgasm was coming her way any time soon, angry—that her partner hadn't contacted her, and worried that somehow, for some reason, she hadn't been included in the game. Mae wasn't used to being alone. When she came to play, she never doubted that there would be Doms delighted to have her submit to them, if only to have her sitting on their laps while they drank and chatted.

Polishing off the champagne, she decided it was time to give up hope of being contacted. She'd chosen to come here, to play and be played with, but it seemed that wasn't going to happen. She could stay the night and see what happened in the morning, using the downtime to get some work done—her phone and tablet were in her locker—but if she was going to work she might as well go home. Plus at home she had a lovely box of toys she could play with.

Letting irritation mask feeling sorry for herself, Mae set her glass down with a snap, glad to have a plan. She was in no shape to drive home immediately, but she could change into her street clothes and get ready to go. Rising to her feet, she left the lounge for the locker room, keying in the code and taking her phone and glasses out of her designer purse. Slipping on the glasses, she started typing an email to her assistant, letting her know that, despite what was on her calendar, she would be available to take meetings and approve designs this weekend.

"Mae?"

Startled by the sound of her name, Mae jumped slightly, knocking the locker door closed. Gabriela, Master Leo's bonded submissive, was standing in the doorway. She was a lovely Hispanic woman and older than Mae, but maybe not as much as anyone would have guessed. She had waves of lush dark hair and wore a long black silk robe, held closed by an under-bust corset.

"Gabriela, you startled me." Mae tapped her chest, just over her heart. "I was just going to change."

"Don't. Come with me."

Mae's stomach muscles tightened and irritation morphed into trepidation. The only people who could send Gabriela to do an errand were the overseers, which meant that they wanted to talk to Mae about something serious. Was she being kicked out? Was that why she hadn't gotten a letter? The idea of being shut out of Las Palmas was enough to make Mae physically sick.

"Let me put my stuff back in my locker." She reached for the keypad but stopped when Gabriela spoke.

"Now, Mae." Gabriela's tone was soft, but firm. In the hierarchy of club submissives you didn't get any higher than Gabriela, and only the unwise ignored an order from her.

Tucking her phone and glasses into the sleeve pockets of her robe, Mae followed Gabriela out of the locker room. The abrupt change from ready-to-go-home to mysterious summons left her feeling off balance. If Gabriela had come even thirty minutes earlier Mae would have been prepared, but mentally she'd already started to check out, leaving her submissive side behind.

They left the Subs' Garden, which did indeed have a native plant garden in the small courtyard around which the submissive-only rooms were arranged. The hallways were mostly empty, with only a few people out and about, most of them wearing the cat-that-ate-the-canary smile that indicated they were in the middle of, or had just finished a scene.

A few minutes later they reached a part of the estate Mae knew existed, but had never been to. The Spanish-style of the buildings meant that everything was arranged around courtyards, and the various playrooms had been named to go along with their gardens. Each court, and each playroom, had different equipment and amenities. The Constellation Court had six rooms, each unsurprisingly named after a constellation, and rooms large enough to accommodate large pieces of bondage equipment. The Sub Rosa Court, where Mae most often found herself, had playrooms modeled after bedrooms or living rooms and were named after famous roses breeds.

For the first time, Mae found herself in the Iron Court, so named because instead of lush plants, the courtyard held a statuary garden, each piece rendered in metal and stone. The figures were those of naked men and women, each shown in some sort of bondage—a stone woman encased in bands of steel, a bronze male figure with chain wrapped not only around, but seemingly through, his arms and legs. Mae folded her hands together, letting the sleeves fall over them to hide how hard she was clenching her fingers. The Iron Court rooms were for people who liked their BDSM physical and dangerous.

Gabriela stopped at one of the doors. There was no label on it, no name to the place she'd been brought.

The other sub reached over and pushed one shoulder of Mae's robe down so it pooled at her waist, exposing her right breast. "You'll be okay." She knocked three times on the door.

With that Gabriela departed, leaving Mae staring at the closed door with no idea who, or what, was on the other side.

CHAPTER 2

"Come in."

The muffled words made Mae's already racing heart beat so hard that she could feel her pulse in her fingertips. Taking a deep breath, she steadied herself, drawing on her submissive persona.

Everything is going to be fine. They're just going to explain your part in the game. This room is probably the only one not in use tonight.

Mae arranged her hair over her shoulder, fixed the bow at the small of her back from her double-wrapped sash, quirked her lips in a sexy little smile, then opened the door.

It was a dungeon.

An elegant dungeon, but a dungeon nonetheless.

The floor was massive terra-cotta tiles, cold even through the soles of her shoes. The walls were rough stucco, painted a classic Spanish cream color, but that didn't make the space seem any less threatening. Metal-studded wood panels, vertical bars, and horizontal boards were mounted around the room, providing plenty of places where someone could be bound. The high ceiling with its exploded wood beams was partially obscured by a grid of pipes, almost like the lighting rigging in a theater. A dark-stained wooden horse and straight backed chair were tucked against the far wall, and there was a stack of padded mats, the kind used for wrestling or in a gym, in the corner by the door.

In the center of the room was a single brown leather armchair. The occupant was hidden by the uneven low lighting. His splayed lower legs were on the edge of a pool of light while his upper body was in shadow. He wore black pants and dark boots.

Mae hesitated on the threshold. Whoever this was, it wasn't one of the overseers.

"Close the door." His voice was a delicious low timber, his tone tinged with either impatience or irritation. There was no denying the command in his voice.

Something in that voice called to her, stirred something inside her. The world seemed to spin, as if she were standing in the eye of a hurricane while the madness of the storm whipped around her. It was strange and thrilling to have such an instant and powerful reaction to someone she couldn't even see. Her self-preservation instinct told her to run, flee this man and this moment before everything changed. Before he changed everything.

But she was a moth to a flame—dangerously curious about something that was undoubtedly hazardous to her sanity.

Mae tugged the door closed, sealing herself in the room with the unknown Dom.

XAVIER'S FINGERS TIGHTENED ON THE ARM OF THE chair until the wood creaked. His palms tingled with the need to touch the beautiful creature who'd just stepped into the playroom.

Mae was even more lovely in person than he remembered,

and than her photos showed. Her skin was pale and creamy, making her red hair gleam, but the photo must have been a few years old. In person she was more mature in her face, placing her in her late rather than early twenties. Or perhaps it was the way she was dressed in the photo that made her seem younger. Tonight she wore a short Asian-style robe. It had fallen on one side, leaving her breast exposed. Her nipple was a lovely shade of rose, the tip hardened into a sweet little bud. A wide pink sash around her waist emphasized the curves of her hips. Her legs were bare and she wore black shoes with white puffy things on the toes.

He wanted to rip the clothes from her and cane her ass and breasts until she begged him to fuck her.

Xavier closed his eyes and reined in his impulses. This was exactly why he couldn't be paired with Mae. Hours of arguing with Mistress Faith and he hadn't gotten anywhere. He'd been tempted to walk away, forfeiting his membership, but Faith had convinced him to at least meet with the sub, and trust that the rules of the game, and the rules of BDSM, would protect both of them.

Xavier took that to mean that once the pretty Mae met with him she would run screaming from the room. Pre-scene it was the submissive who held all the power, because the sub decided whether the Dom merited the trust needed to proceed. Mae would refuse and he would be free to find another sub to play with for the limited amount of time he had here. Though technically if Mae walked away, she'd be in violation of this ridiculous checklist game, Xavier had made Faith agree not to kick the submissive out if she did indeed run from him.

What Xavier didn't understand was why Faith was putting him through this. She knew he needed his time here to fight back the darkness inside him. Forcing him to waste a night like this was cruel...which considering the source shouldn't surprise him.

But whatever lesson Mistress Faith wanted to teach him, Xavier doubted she had any idea how truly torturous this was, because though he and Mae were as different as silk and steel, there was something about her that called to him.

She was smiling slightly when she entered, but the longer she stood there in silence the more the expression faded. Good. He wanted her scared enough to walk away. When she shifted her weight and clasped her hands together, Xavier decided it was probably time to show her exactly what was going on. Placing his hands on the arms of the chair, he rose and stepped into the light.

OH SHIT.

Mae's breath hitched in her throat when the Dom came out of the shadows.

Master Xavier.

There were a handful of truly terrifying Doms at Las Palmas, and this was one of them. Though he was an infrequent player, Mae recognized him. Even if she'd never seen him, she would recognize him from his description.

Master Xavier always wore a black leather hood-mask, and rumor had it no one at Las Palmas had ever seen his face.

The mask covered his whole head and neck except for his mouth, lower cheeks, and chin. A sub Mae knew named Sarah, who had submitted to him several times, said it was like Batman's mask. They'd giggled about that, but quietly, as if Master Xavier might hear them otherwise.

He was muscular, but not bulky, wearing a tight sleeveless top that hugged the muscles of his chest and firm belly. He folded his arms, which were thick with muscle. The unrelenting black of his clothing and mask drew attention to the skin that was bare. Mae focused on his lips, which were fuller than she'd remembered from the few times she'd seen him.

"Mae."

A shiver ran down her back when he said her name.

"Master Xavier." She bowed her head submissively, but looked at him through her lashes.

"You know me."

It wasn't really a question, but she answered anyway. "Yes, Sir. I recognize your mask."

He let out one hard laugh. "Fine. Do you know why you're here?"

"No, Sir."

"We're partners in the game. The checklist game."

Mae wasn't really surprised—there was no other reason for him to have called for her, but hearing him say it made her stomach knot.

She popped her hip to the side, propped her hand on it, and said, "I almost left, it took you so long to contact me."

She hadn't planned to say that, hadn't planned to act like that, but it was an automatic response, a defense mechanism. Mae teased and pouted, sassed and misbehaved. That's who she was. When Doms came looking for her, that's what they wanted.

And it was the wrong thing to do with a Master like Xavier.

Master Xavier started walking toward her. He didn't say anything, didn't run or yell. He just walked.

When he was five feet away Mae took a small step back. Then another. Her shoulders hit the door behind her. In the next breath Master Xavier was there, looming over her.

"Are you criticizing me?" That deliciously rich voice of his had deepened further. Each syllable seemed to glide over her skin.

"I was only teasing, Sir." Mae kept her gaze focused on the neck of his shirt and reminded herself that he wouldn't, couldn't hurt her. They were just talking—they weren't in a scene, hadn't negotiated to play.

But as he loomed over her, she felt that strange stirring again, this time accompanied by the urge to sink to her knees, to spread her legs and bow her head in that simplest of submissive postures.

"You're teasing me?"

The dismissive tone irked her and the urge to kneel disappeared. "Yes. I am. Though it *was* a little rude to make me wait so long." Mae pouted a bit as she said it.

Bad idea.

Maybe if she hadn't had so many glasses of champagne, or been mentally out the door when Gabriela's arrival yanked her back, Mae would have been able to bite her tongue and play the kind of sub Master Xavier was used to. But she wasn't feeling submissive. She felt ready to poke and prod this man until she figured out why she felt this inexplicable attraction to him.

Behind the mask she saw his eyes widen at her response. His eyes were green. Not hazel, but a pretty true green.

He leaned closer. "Little girl, you don't want to play with me. Tell the overseers that you won't sub for me."

Mae's hands curled into fists. "I'm not your little girl." There'd been a time when she'd reveled in being called that by a Dom, but her tastes had changed.

He reached for her hair, fingers stopping just short of contact. "No, you're not." He stepped back.

Mae's mouth opened in surprise. Was that regret in his voice?

"Tell the overseers you can't be partnered with me." He turned his back, apparently done with her.

"Why?"

Master Xavier faced her, clearly surprised she was still in the room. "Is this what you like?" He motioned to the dungeon-like playroom. "This is what I like, and unless you want to be spread open on the floor so I can whip your pussy, I suggest you leave."

Mae dropped her gaze, biting the inside of her cheek as a shiver took her. She didn't want that. She wanted to be kissed and cuddled and spanked. Yet her body was thrumming with arousal, and her pussy was so wet she was afraid to move.

"I meant why don't *you* tell them, Sir?" The words were breathy, but she got them out.

Xavier crossed his arms. "I did. I spent the last few hours arguing to have our pairing reassigned, but Mistress Faith refused. I was given the option of meeting with you or resigning from Las Palmas. Since I do not want to lose my membership, it's up to you to walk away. You will not be punished for doing so; I saw to that."

An unfamiliar feeling settled over Mae. She'd been blessed in life by being smart, pretty, and having the kind of personality that drew people to her. There were very few times she'd ever been rejected, romantically, sexually, or as a friend. It took her a minute, but she realized what this feeling was.

Embarrassment. Embarrassment and shame. He was rejecting her, without even getting to know her. She should get the hell out of here and back to the safety of the Sub Rosa Court and Doms who enjoyed the kind of submission she was willing to offer.

She should, but she wasn't going to.

Mae raised her chin and folded her arms. "No."

XAVIER NARROWED HIS EYES. "WHAT DO YOU MEAN, 'No'?"

"I mean that I'm not going to tell the overseers that I can't be partnered with you. Everyone has to play the checklist game, and I'm not going to get in trouble just because you would rather have a different sub."

Rather have another sub? Xavier shook his head—if only she knew how hard he was fighting his attraction to her. He needed her to get out of here before he lost his internal battle and gave in to his desire to dominate her.

"I told you, you won't be in trouble. You're making a mistake, little girl."

"Don't call me that."

"If you sub for me, I'll call you whatever I want." Her attitude was both irritating and rather engaging.

"Well I'm not subbing for you right now."

"If you're still standing here in five minutes you will be."

"Fine, then I'll stand here for five minutes." Mae stepped out of her shoes and kicked them to the side. He saw her bare toes curl against the cold tile.

Those cold little toes disturbed him. He didn't like seeing her uncomfortable. And damn if that wasn't the dumbest thought considering what he wanted to do to her.

Xavier grabbed a mat from the stack and tossed it on the floor in the center of the room. He pointed, silently commanding her to stand there. Mae's chin notched up in an even more defiant expression. Xavier had to admit he was impressed. She was ballsier than he'd expected.

Their gazes met. Her eyes were the color of storm clouds. Xavier held her gaze, unafraid of the intimacy of such an action.

A little shudder went through her. She lowered her eyelids, her defiant stance softening. She padded over to the mat.

Xavier took a deep breath as the air in the room thickened. He'd felt it when he looked into her eyes—the first hints of the power transfer that was so critical to BDSM play.

"Kneel." The order was a test, as much for him as it was for her.

Mae hesitated and looked at him. He could see the war

inside her—the battle between the desire to submit and the urge to fight back, to remain in control. She pressed her lips together, looked at the floor and then back to him.

Now he read something else in her expression.

Help me. Help me submit.

He'd been with subs who needed that first push, but they hadn't said "help me." They'd said "make me," their defiance carefully orchestrated to give him the opening to grab them by the hair and force them to their knees, giving both of them what they wanted.

Letting instinct guide him, Xavier reached for Mae, giving her the physical contact that would help her submit. Instead of grabbing her by the hair, neck, or arms, Xavier ran his hand along her bare shoulder down to her breast. He caressed the tip with his palm, and when her nipple beaded, he pinched it between his curled index finger and thumb. Still holding her nipple, he repeated the order.

"Kneel, Mae."

She dropped gracefully to her knees, whimpering slightly when the movement pulled the tip of her breast from between his fingers.

She was sitting with her legs pressed together, her hands curled into little fists. Her hair spilled over her bare shoulder, almost long enough to cover her nipple.

Xavier returned to the chair, bracing his elbows on his knees. Nothing was going the way he thought it would. Instead of running away, the lovely woman was far stronger than he'd imagined, and most surprisingly, was now submitting, despite an initial show of defiance.

"I'm going to give you one more chance to leave. But only one. If you stay, you're agreeing to submit to me, to be mine, until we've completed the checklist items. Do you understand?"

"Yes, Sir."

Xavier picked the envelope up from the floor under the chair. "Once you hear the list, you'll realize you're not ready for me."

That brought her chin up, her gaze defiant even as she remained submissively kneeling. "What letter are we?"

"B, as in bondage."

MAE'S WHOLE BODY WAS THROBBING WITH AROUSAL. She hadn't been this turned on this quickly, or with such little physical contact, since she first discovered the delightful worlds of kink. Despite that, one thought was running though her mind on a loop.

What are you doing?

When the big bad wolf tells you you're free to go, a smart person leaves. Apparently Mae was not as smart as she thought she was, because not only hadn't she left, but she'd taunted him. She was setting herself up for a corrective punishment, and coming from this Dom that would probably be far more than she was equipped to handle.

And yet...when he'd looked at her she felt something, something she wanted to feel again.

Master Xavier pulled some papers out of an envelope. "Do you remember what you put on your checklist?"

Mae barely remembered filling out the checklist. "No, Sir."

"Once we begin—if we begin—you will call me Master Xavier."

"Yes, Master Xavier." She liked the way that felt, liked saying it.

"I'll start by reading off the list of items under B." He flipped the page, scanned the text, then looked at her. "Ball gag. Beating, soft. Beating, hard."

Mae was acutely aware that he was studying her reaction to each thing he said. She winced at "beating, hard." The idea should have dampened her arousal, but didn't. If anything it increased it.

"Blindfolding. Being serviced. Biting. Breast bondage. Breast whipping."

Mae's breathing was fast, her fingers clenching rhythmically. She shouldn't want these things. This wasn't who she was.

"Branding."

Mae's gaze jerked to his, that one word enough to knock her out of the arousal-fueled daze. "We only do the things that both of us said yes to on our lists."

Master Xavier nodded and Mae relaxed. There was no way she'd marked branding as an interest.

"There's more. Boot worship. Bondage, light. Bondage, heavy." His voice got deeper, and she realized he was aroused too. "B is a good letter. Bondage, multi-day. And finally, one more bondage, but this one is public under clothing."

Now that he'd listed them off, Mae remembered the checklist. She remembered the desperate arousal she'd felt while reading it.

"If you choose to stay, you will remain with me from now until Monday morning. This is a purely BDSM scene, meaning there will be no sex, except as it relates to 'being serviced.' I have a copy of your hard limits, and know your safe word, but that doesn't mean that you wouldn't find submitting to me very difficult. I would not be easy on you, just because you're..." he motioned vaguely.

He thought she couldn't handle him. Well she could. Maybe. She was stronger than anyone ever gave her credit for, and she wanted Xavier to know it. "I wouldn't want you to be." The words were mostly bravado, and she had a bad feeling that it would take only a matter of minutes for Master Xavier to push her deeper than she'd gone before.

Master Xavier searched her face. "You're not what I expected."

I'm not what I expected right now either.

Mae didn't know how to respond, so she tucked her chin down and stared at her knees. It wasn't exactly a compliment, but it made her feel strong, as if defying his expectations freed her to be complicated.

"Push down your robe, Mae. Show me your other breast."

With a shrug of her shoulder the robe slid off, the fabric now held in place by the sash at her waist. The first hints of arousal curled in her belly and her blood heated in anticipation.

Xavier stood and circled around behind her. He cupped her neck, thumb and middle finger pressing lightly on the soft spots just behind her jawbone. It forced her head up and back, so she was looking at him.

"You understand what I'll do to you?"

"Yes, Master Xavier."

"I want to hear it."

"You'll do everything on the checklist that both of us said yes to."

"That may be only one thing." His thumb moved in a small circular caress over the sensitive skin below her ear. "It may be all of them."

"Yes, Master Xavier."

"I won't fuck you, but that doesn't mean I won't touch you, use you."

"I know."

He held her gaze for another moment and then released her. He made a noise of either anger or disgust. Mae had a moment to wonder what she'd done wrong while he stalked away, but then he turned.

"Last chance, little girl."

"I'm not your little girl."

"Okay, Red, you're right. You're not a little girl." Master Xavier took out a pocket knife and flicked the blade open. "But what you are is mine."

CHAPTER 3

Xavier pressed his thumb against the blade of the small knife, hard enough that he felt it, but not enough to draw blood. He needed the pain to center himself. This wasn't supposed to be happening; she was supposed to be long gone, fled back into the arms of men who would kiss and cuddle her, then "punish" her with orgasms.

Strangely, he wanted to kiss her, something he rarely did. But the cuddles...well.

"Stand."

Mae pushed to her feet, her hands still clasped together in front of her. She had lovely breasts, large enough to make breast play interesting, and her nipples were excitingly pink against her pale skin.

"Hands at your sides."

She hesitated long enough that he was tempted to grab a crop. He wouldn't have tolerated this from anyone else.

Mae unclenched her fingers and let her arms dangle, taking a shuttered breath as she did so.

Rather than punishing her for being slow to obey, he found himself reaching out to caress her left shoulder and breast, rewarding her for her bravery. "Good." She calmed slightly at his touch.

Xavier hooked two fingers in the tie of her robe, slid the blade of his knife under the fabric, and cut it.

The sash dropped and her robe fell open. In the next breath the fabric lost its tenuous hold and slithered to the floor, revealing a pair of hot pink lace boy-cut panties with a large fabric bow on the back.

Xavier circled her, examining her near-naked body. "I haven't had a sub who wore pink panties in...ever."

Mae cleared her throat. "What do your subs normally wear?"

"Black."

"You don't like pink?"

Xavier squeezed her ass. The bow was completely ridiculous, and yet he found himself admiring the way it framed her bottom. He rubbed her back and shoulders, palmed her breasts, and ran his hands up and down her legs, getting her used to his touch.

Mae was breathing hard, enough so that Xavier was concerned. For whatever reason, this lovely, soft woman had decided that she was going to subject herself to him. He knew all about using BDSM to exorcise personal demons, so he wasn't going to judge her, or refuse to play with her. But he was going to protect her, if even from herself—at least until his own needs reared their ugly head.

He'd never felt this protective urge. Usually he was all about pushing, both himself and his subs, to the edge.

Right now he needed to know why she was breathing so hard.

"Mae, look at me."

Her eyes were wide, the irises a lovely shade of gray. There was no distress in her gaze. It wasn't fear that made her tremble.

"Mae, are you wet?"

She nodded jerkily.

"Put two fingers in your pussy. Show me."

Her hand dipped into the pink lace, and her eyes fluttered closed as she touched herself. Xavier grabbed her wrist, squeezing enough that her eyes popped open.

"Show me, Mae."

She held out her hand, two fingers coated in cream. The smell of her arousal was strong in the air. Xavier inhaled, startled and delighted by how wet she was at this early stage.

"Clean your fingers."

She seemed surprised by the order, and for an instant irritation rippled over her features, but then she put her fingers in her mouth, licking them clean. As he watched her, Xavier started to suspect that there was far more to this submissive than anyone knew.

"You're aroused, when everything I know about you, and how you normally play, says that you should be terrified."

"I am scared, Master Xavier."

"Are you? Or have you been lying to everyone here, including yourself?"

MAE OPENED HER MOUTH TO PROTEST. SHE WASN'T lying to anyone. The words caught in her throat, and for the first time she really was afraid. Not by what he'd do to her body, but by what being with Xavier would reveal about her.

"Kneel."

She dropped down, kneeling amid the discarded fabric of her robe, glad that she didn't have to reply to his question. Master Xavier grabbed a duffel bag from the shadows under the wooden horse and dumped it into the chair to rummage through it. When he turned to her he had a handful of black straps and rope.

"Give me your wrists." Xavier draped some of the restraints around his neck, freeing his hands to work the black and silver cuffs he held. They were padded nylon, the outside reinforced with gleaming steel and set with heavy D rings.

With quick, sure movements Master Xavier fastened the cuffs around her wrists. They were heavy, probably a pound each.

"Kneel up and put your toes on the mat, ankles bent."

Mae let her heavy wrists drop to her sides and adjusted her feet. When Xavier dropped to one knee beside her, she was nearly overcome with the urge to lean into his warm, hard body, to cuddle against him.

She bit the tip of her tongue to get herself under control. Cuddling would only reinforce what he thought about her.

Master Xavier fastened cuffs around her ankles. "Stand up and follow me."

Mae took a second to look down at herself—the heavy metal-studded cuffs were unlike anything she was used to.

Xavier was standing beside one of the sections of ladder-like bars on the wall. The horizontal wooden boards were evenly spaced, starting at the floor and going nearly all the way to the ceiling. It was deceptively simple, almost decorative, but with each step she took, Mae knew that whatever was about to happen would be anything but simple.

XAVIER AGAIN CHECKED HIS URGE TO PUSH MAE TO move faster. He could feel her nervousness, just as he could feel her excitement. Or maybe it was his own nervousness and excitement that he was projecting on her. Ridiculous that he should be nervous. He was an experienced player who knew how to plan a scene and read a sub. What was about to happen would not challenge him—it was about challenging her.

Mae stopped in front of the restraint wall, examining it with trepidation. Then she took a tiny step to the side, toward him, as if seeking his protection.

It was time to show her that he was the one she needed protection from.

"Back against the bars, arms up." This time when she didn't move fast enough he hooked a finger in the D ring of her right cuff and forced her hand up. She stumbled, eyes wide, then quickly got into position. Taking a strap from around his neck Xavier quickly secured that hand, repeating the process on the left.

"Is this the light bondage?" Mae spoke softly, her eyes on his face. Her hands were spread up and to the side, wrists just slightly above shoulder height, with enough room so she could bend her elbows.

Xavier pulled another strap from around his neck. "I would barely consider this bondage."

She shivered and dropped her gaze.

"Legs together. Are you right or left-handed?"

"Right, Master Xavier."

"Then lift your right foot off the floor." He gave her a minute to find her balance on her non-dominant foot, then grabbed her right knee, lifting her leg and pressing it to the side. He didn't know how flexible she was, so rather than force her knee up by her ribs he raised it only slightly higher than hip height before wrapping a strap several times around her thigh and the bar behind it, buckling the strap in place. He also secured the ankle cuff to the next bar down, and finally tied the cuff on her left ankle to the lowest rung of the restraint wall.

Mae wavered, upper body tilting to the side as she tried to adjust to the position. She was totally exposed, her breasts and sex both easily accessible. Though she was still wearing the panties, Xavier could clearly see the lips of her sex. She was so wet that the lace was plastered against her pussy.

"This isn't bondage?" Mae squeaked.

Xavier smiled. He couldn't help it. The outburst should have yielded an immediate punishment, but he liked knowing what she thought. "It's light bondage. Very light. Here." He reached up and cupped her hand in his. Her fingers trembled. "Hold on to the strap. That keeps you from straining your shoulders and back."

Xavier reached across her to help her grab the other strap, bringing his chest within inches of her. Her head was tipped back, her pink lips slightly parted and oh-so-kissable. Xavier cupped her cheek, rubbing his thumb over the corner of her mouth and lowered his head.

What are you doing?

Before he did something stupid, Xavier jerked back. Mae looked both disappointed and confused, the expressions flashing across her face.

He went to his bag of equipment, using the action to gain control of himself.

"I apologize, Mae."

"You're apologizing, for *not* kissing me?"

"We're here for BDSM play. Not sex or sexual contact."

"Wait...you were serious about the no sex thing?"

Xavier pulled his single-tail whip out of his bag and looped it over his chest. "You thought I wasn't?"

Mae didn't respond. Her eyes were fixed on the whip. Xavier grabbed an eye mask and held it up so she could see it. "I'm going to blindfold you. I'd prefer something more substantial, but this will have to do for now."

Mae was still looking at the whip. "Are you...are you going to use that?"

"What?"

"T-that."

"Ask me properly."

She took a breath then met his gaze. "Are you going to whip me, Master Xavier?"

In response he slipped the eye mask over her head.

"Master Xavier?" She turned her head side to side, a hint of panic in her voice. He touched her cheek and she calmed.

Xavier uncurled the whip, took two steps back and snapped his wrist. The *crack* of the whip's tip was a sonic boom. Mae screamed, turning her head into her arm.

In the ensuing silence Mae's ragged breathing was the only sound. She lifted her head from her arm.

"You *jerk.*"

Xavier narrowed his eyes. "Excuse me?"

"You scared me."

Xavier pushed the mask off her face. "What did you just say to me?" He spoke softly, putting a hint of menace in his voice.

"You scared me." This time her words trembled.

Xavier flipped the handle of the whip and pressed the butt of it up under her chin, forcing her face up.

"Tell me, Red, when you submit, who's really in control?"

"The Dominant, Master Xavier." The words were awkward because of the placement of the whip handle, but she got them out.

"You're lying again. You're in control, aren't you? You get exactly what you want, how you want it. But you make them think it was their idea."

"No, no. I don't."

Xavier trailed the thick handle of the whip down the center of her body, then pressed it against her sex. Mae shuddered and dropped her head forward.

"Have you ever done a scene where you didn't get fucked or fingered, didn't come?"

"No, Master Xavier."

He moved the handle slightly, giving her just enough stimulation to distract her, keep her from being able to lie. "In the past who's been in control? You or the Dom?"

Mae's lips trembled and there were tears in her eyes. "I don't...I don't know."

Xavier retreated and snapped the whip again. She flinched at the sound and let out a little cry, though she could see that it was nowhere near her.

"Please, Master," she begged.

"Please, what?"

She dropped her head. "I don't know. I don't know what I want."

Xavier grabbed her by the hair, forcing her to look at him. What he saw in her eyes was both familiar—the raw expression that submissives wore when they began to truly give in, and strange—a kind of delicate beauty that urged him to protect and cherish. Tightening his hold on her hair, Xavier pressed his body to hers and whispered in her ear. "I do."

MAE WANTED TO CRY WHEN MASTER XAVIER LEFT HER, returning to that sinister duffel bag. The loss of his body heat made her shiver, even as her scalp ached from his hold.

She couldn't stop thinking about what he'd said. Had she been topping from the bottom?

This time when Xavier returned he had a flogger. Mae tightened her hold on the straps attached to her cuffs. She wanted him to flog her. She wanted to wear the marks from his beating.

This isn't you.

"There's something we haven't talked about." Master Xavier rubbed his cheek just under the edge of his mask. She wondered what he looked like without it. What color was his hair? How old was he? He was fit, but had the kind of presence that made her think he might be older.

"Mae?"

"Yes, Master Xavier?"

"Did you hear what I said?"

"No, I'm sorry."

"What were you thinking about?"

"You, Master Xavier."

He rocked back on his heels and crossed his arms. "And what were you thinking?"

"I was wondering how old you were and what you looked like under the mask. Why do you wear it?"

"It's not your place to question me."

Mae dropped her gaze to the floor. "I'm sorry, Master Xavier."

He was silent, and she thought he was angry, until he said, "Why do you think I wear it?"

"Because it makes you look like Batman."

Xavier blinked twice, then started to laugh. He laughed so hard that he braced his hand on the wall near her. His laugh was a wonderful, rich sound. Mae found herself smiling, and wishing she could hold him, feel that joy and mirth against her body.

"Batman?"

"One of the submissives called it a Batman mask. Though no one would dare say it to your face."

He shifted closer, bracing one forearm above her head so they were separated by mere inches. "Except you?"

"I'm not thinking straight."

"Really? Or do you like teasing and sassing your Doms?"

Mae couldn't deny that. "Is it really such a bad thing?"

"Before meeting you I would have said so, but now...I think it isn't. But you have to be willing to pay the price."

"And what's the price?" she whispered.

His lips brushed her ear. "Whatever I want it to be." Smooth leather strands trailed over Mae's upraised leg and she whimpered.

"Are you scared, Mae?"

"Yes."

"Scared of me, or of the flogger?"

"You."

"Why?"

"I've played with a flogger before, but I don't think... I think it will be very different if you're the one using it."

"Smart girl. It will be. And that brings me back to what we need to talk about."

Xavier pulled some folded papers from his back pocket and flicked her nipple with them. "This is your checklist."

"Yes, Master Xavier." She was so wet, so ready, that if he just flicked her nipple a few more times she might be able to come. Bracing her hips, she thrust her chest forward, begging him without words to touch her.

Xavier stepped back. Mae nearly growled.

"What do you remember about filling out your checklist?"

Mae blew out a frustrated breath. "It was years ago."

"Years? How long have you been a member?"

"Six years."

That seemed to surprise him. "How old are you?"

"Don't you know you shouldn't ask a lady her age?"

"Don't you know that you should answer when a Master asks you a question?" His voice was cold with warning.

"I'm thirty-one, Master Xavier."

He grunted in surprise. When he didn't say anything, Mae had to wonder if her age changed the way he thought of her.

"You didn't answer my question."

Shit. "I'm sorry, Master Xavier, could you repeat it?"

"What do you remember about filling out your checklist?"

"I remember reading it was arousing."

He flipped to the last page, held it up so she could see. "You signed this list, and it's part of your membership contract with Las Palmas."

Mae frowned. Why was he pushing this issue? "Yes, Master Xavier." That was definitely her signature—she'd used glittery purple ink.

"For the purposes of the game, and therefore this scene, you're bound by what you put on this list. Anything you marked "yes" or "maybe" to is a valid option."

"I understand, Master Xavier."

He turned a few pages, then again held it up for her to see. She recognized her own handwriting—the checkmarks and initials she'd used to indicate her level of interest in each item. Mae narrowed her eyes, wishing for her glasses. Xavier held the paper close to her face.

It was the page with all the "B" items, everything he'd read out loud.

And she'd said yes to every single one.

Mae's mouth fell open in dawning horror. Suddenly Xavier's actions made much more sense. She'd been paired with one of the most dangerous Doms, insisted on playing with him even when he'd warned her away, all without realizing that her checklist gave him carte blanche.

"Oh..."

"I was more than a little surprised when I saw your checklist." There was a hint of amusement in his voice—but not the funny "ha ha" kind.

"I don't...I don't remember doing that." Surely she wouldn't have said yes to beatings and branding.

"Are you accusing me of something?"

"No."

The flogger struck the wall with a heavy *thunk*. "No, what?"

She flinched. "No, Master Xavier."

"I gave you the chance to leave, Mae. That opportunity is gone. You still have your safe word. What is it?"

"Banana."

"Say it again."

"Banana."

"Good. Using your safe word will pause the scene."

"Pause it?"

"Yes. Everything I'm about to do to you, you said you were interested in. If I were to end the scene when you used your safe word, you would be in control. But for the next forty-eight hours I'm your master. Everything you have, everything you are, is mine. Use your safe word if you need to, but understand that I will decide if we need to stop, or if you simply need a different approach."

"Master Xavier, the things on that list. I didn't understand. I don't want—"

He pressed the flogger up under her chin, snapping her teeth together and stopping her mid-sentence.

"Don't insult either of us by pretending you didn't know what these things were. If you were that ignorant you would never have been allowed in to Las Palmas."

He moved the flogger, giving her the chance to continue her protest, but she didn't. She couldn't. He was right. She'd known what each of those things were, what they meant…she'd just never assumed they would happen to *her*.

After all, she was the cute, sassy sub who got over-the-knee spankings and punishment by multiple orgasms.

"You want this Mae. You wouldn't have insisted on staying if you didn't want it."

She lowered her head, unable to deny it.

"I won't go easy on you." He seemed to want her to acknowledge what he'd said.

Taking a deep breath, Mae mustered all her courage. "I don't want you to, Master Xavier."

CHAPTER 4

Xavier watched Mae shift nervously as she stood beside the wooden horse, which he'd moved into the middle of the room. The top was a two-by-six piece of cherrywood that was turned on its side so the upper surface was the narrower two-inch face. There were rings set into the underside of the crosspiece and along the edges of the slanted legs. Xavier left the cuffs on her wrists and ankles, but decided against binding her to the convenient tie points on the horse. It was time to see exactly what Mae could handle, and how obedient she could be.

"Do you know the difference between a hard and soft beating?" he asked.

Mae opened her mouth, but closed it.

"No?" he prompted.

"I can only think of sassy things to say."

"Why don't you say them?"

Mae eyed the flogger in his right hand. "Maybe later."

Xavier chuckled. She was fun. It had been a long time since he'd had fun with a sub.

"All right, Red. I want you to face the horse, bend at the

waist, and rest your arms on the top. You can fold your arms if that's more comfortable."

He helped position her, having her step back until her body made a ninety degree angle and her cheek rested on her folded arms atop the wood.

"Very good. Legs together."

The metal on the ankle restraints clanked as she brought her feet side by side. Once he was satisfied, he swung the flogger against his own leg, letting her get used to the sound.

"Do you want to know the difference between a hard beating and a soft beating?"

"Yes, Master Xavier."

Thwack, thwack, thwack.

The flogger's steady rhythm was like a metronome as he spoke. "The difference is in how long the sub wears the marks. A flogging is a light beating, because your skin will be red for a few days. Paddles, canes, a tawse, and whips are hard beatings."

"What's a spanking?" Her words were slightly muffled because of the way her face rested on her arms, but he understood.

"A spanking is foreplay. A spanking is what little girls get when they want to pretend they're being punished."

That wasn't exactly true—spanking was an art form in itself and a well-administered one could have longer-lasting effects than a caning, but he was guessing that those weren't the kinds of spankings Mae got.

"Are you punishing me? Is that why you're beating me?" Her question was soft, and when he looked, her eyes were wide and dark, fixed on his face.

"No, Mae. I'm going to beat you because I want to. Because I need to. And because you need to be beaten."

He'd kept up his steady movement of the flogger. Without breaking rhythm he raised his arm, this time striking Mae's ass.

She yelped, jerking upright with her hands braced on the horse.

"Back in position." He struck her ass again, this time with more force.

She cried out in either shock or pain, looking back at him with wide eyes. Her hair fell in soft waves around her face. Her lower lip was wet and pink, trembling slightly. Her eyes pleaded for mercy, pleaded for him to stop and kiss her, hold her.

Xavier understood how she'd managed to go so long without being properly mastered. He understood, but he wasn't so blind to her real wants as others had been. She was going to accept her beating, and nothing she did or said would change it.

Holding her gaze, he struck her ass again, even harder than last time. This one had to hurt, and there was a flash of anger in her eyes.

That's right, Red, you're mine, and you're about to find out exactly what that means.

"Back in position, Mae. I won't tell you again." Master Xavier pulled the flogger back.

Mae was frozen, the tension in her arms, back, and legs seemingly turning her to stone. The first blow had taken her by surprise, the second stung enough that she'd jumped, and the third one *hurt*.

Thwack.

Pain set fire to the back of her thighs and ass as the hardest blow yet landed. Jolted from her paralysis, Mae yelped and took two steps forward, turning so that Master Xavier's flogger couldn't reach her ass.

"Mae, you're making me angry."

"Master Xavier, that hurts."

He tilted his head. "Of course it hurts, Mae. It's meant to hurt."

"But I don't want it to hurt." He swung the flogger towards her and Mae pressed herself harder against the horse, staying just outside its reach.

"I understand that you don't want it to hurt. But that doesn't matter."

Unexpectedly, tears of frustration filled her eyes. "It should matter."

"It doesn't."

"Why?"

"Because it's not up to you. I decide if you get pleasure or pain. I decide how much pain. I'm your Master."

His words flipped a switch inside her and Mae shuddered. Her outrage and anger faded, replaced by a dark need. The need for pain, the need to give up all control.

She couldn't stop herself from trembling, but Mae turned around, presenting her back.

"Back in position, bend at the waist."

Mae resumed her position, hiding her face against her forearms. Part of her was amazed that she was doing this, that she hadn't walked out. A larger part of her desperately wanted to know how far he would take it, how much he would do to her.

Master Xavier tugged her panties down until they pooled at her ankles, leaving her totally naked for the first time.

Thwack. This time the blow landed on the back of her thighs, avoiding her ass. The reprieve was short-lived, as the tails of the flogger once more landed on her sensitive ass.

She was tensing before each blow, whole body drawn tight in anticipation. For what felt like an hour but could have been no more than five minutes, he kept up a steady rhythm, the strength and placement of them alternating. At first she tried to keep quiet, but was soon gasping and whimpering.

"Relax, Mae. You can't control this. Can't stop this."

The words freed something inside her. Mae let out a little sob, and the tension faded from her body. When the next blow came she accepted it, her soft flesh taking in the pain more readily.

The fiery ache in her ass and thighs grew until she was moaning steadily.

"Open your legs."

She didn't question, didn't hesitate. She stepped out of her panties and spread her legs, wide as she could while keeping her balance. She wanted him to have access to her sex, wanted him to use her in whatever way he wanted.

The tails of the flogger came up between her legs, smacking her pussy. The gentle blow had only the barest hint of sting, hidden under a jolt of pleasure. Or maybe it was that she was so aroused it didn't matter what kind of attention her aching pussy got.

Master Xavier alternated gentle swats to her inner thighs and pussy with harder floggings of her ass. Her whole body was trembling, and Mae didn't know if it was pleasure or pain that made her shake.

"Can you come from pain alone?"

Master Xavier's words barely penetrated the twilight-like space where she seemed to float.

"No, Master Xavier."

"Are you sure?"

The tip of the flogger tails landed on the inner curves of her ass, near her anus, and the sting of pain sent a jolt of pleasure through her pussy.

"No, Master. I'm not." She wasn't sure of anything anymore.

A warm palm came to rest on her back. "These last few will be the hardest."

That was the only warning she got before pain exploded across her ass. Mae screamed, tears leaking from her eyes.

"You'll take another one." Master Xavier's voice was deep, his breathing a bit ragged too.

Mae couldn't speak, but she arched her back, presenting her ass more fully.

"Good girl."

Crack. Crack. Crack.

The final three blows came in quick succession. Mae didn't have time to scream, she barely managed to breathe. Her legs started to give out and she reached back with one hand, grabbing Xavier's forearm, holding on to him as if he were a life raft in the middle of a stormy ocean.

He grabbed her by the upper arm and neck, raising her to a standing position and turning her to face him. Within the shadows of his mask his eyes glowed like emeralds. He was breathing hard, his jaw muscles tensed.

Mae realized that he was as lost in the storm as she was. This is what had always been missing from her scenes before. Never before had doing something to her, playing with her, had the kind of impact on a Dom that she could see in Xavier's eyes.

The ground shifted under her feet, the earth seeming to tip sideways only to right itself, the world slightly different than it had been a moment ago.

"Master, please."

He searched her face. "What do you want? To come? To get fucked?"

With the last of her courage she reached up, laying her palm on his cheek, feeling both skin and leather under her hand. "Kiss me."

Xavier's eyes closed and he bent his head, resting his forehead on hers. Mae's heart clenched, and she knew, though she couldn't say why, that though he was the Master of pain and pleasure, power and control, he didn't know gentleness.

She took the flogger from his fingers, dropping it to the floor, then guided his hands to her waist, resting them there. Rising onto tiptoe, Mae kissed him.

Xavier tasted like mint, and his lips were firm and wet against hers. For a moment he didn't react, and Mae felt a pang of fear—she'd overstepped, she'd read the moment wrong.

Xavier shuddered, then his arms were tight around her back, crushing her against him as he ravaged her mouth.

Mae's nails scraped against the smooth surface of the mask. She wished she could bury her fingers in his hair, wished she could see his face.

Xavier deepened the kiss, his tongue dipping into her mouth. Mae sucked on his tongue, and when he shifted, one leg sliding between hers, she eagerly ground against his thigh. She couldn't wait to have him inside her, his cock filling her.

When he wrenched away, taking three quick steps back, Mae was left gasping, her body thrumming with need.

"Our play time does not include sexual contact, except for what's on the checklist." His face unreadable, hidden from her.

Mae wanted to curse. There'd been something between them. Maybe he hadn't felt it the way she did. That thought made her stomach knot, but it didn't feel like the truth.

"What if I want sex? What if I want to add that to our session?"

Xavier didn't answer her questions. "It's nearly four a.m. You'll sleep in the Subs' Garden."

"What if—"

Xavier grabbed her by the back of the neck, his will washing over her. "You will sleep in the Subs' Garden."

"Yes, Master Xavier." She didn't bother to hide her frustration—both sexual and emotional, and it showed, her words sarcastic and biting.

Master Xavier's hold tightened just a fraction, but his jaw clenched, lips a thin line. She'd pushed him too far.

Xavier took her by the upper arms and forced her to bend over the horse. His movements were sharp but controlled.

"Grab your ankles."

"Master Xavier, I'm sorry, I just—"

"Now, Mae." He pressed his hand against her abused ass.

The flare of pain sent a shudder through her. Disappointment and frustration from the truncated kiss were suppressed by a resurgence of the sweet submissiveness that had filled her while he beat her.

Mae hooked her fingers in the D-ring cuffs around her ankles.

"You're going to sleep in one of the bunks in the Subs' Garden. You will meet me back here at noon. Eat before you arrive. You will not orgasm, either by touching yourself or by asking another submissive to touch you. Do you understand, Mae?"

"Yes, Master Xavier."

"It seems you have a hard time remembering your place unless you're actively being dominated." He pinched her abused ass.

Mae was having trouble thinking; all the blood was rushing to her head. "I'm sorry, Master."

"It is who you are." The words were matter of fact, and it gave Mae some hope that he didn't sound disgusted. "It means that I cannot let you go without reminders, as I have no desire to start over again. Have you been trained for anal?"

"Yes, Master Xavier."

"What have you taken up your ass?"

"Plugs and cocks." She forced the words out, terribly aroused.

"Can you sleep in a plug?"

"I never have before, Master."

"Then you will tonight. Stand up."

Mae straightened and braced her hands on the horse. Xavier

reached around her and casually pinched her nipples. "I'm going to get a few things. I will be gone no more than five minutes."

"Yes, Master Xavier."

He grabbed her jaw, turning her to face him. "I don't want to leave you unbound. Have you ridden a wooden horse before?"

Mae shivered. "No, Master. I promise I won't—"

"You won't worry about it. You're mine, and you will trust me to give you what you need, and what I want you to have."

Mae bit her lip to stop from screaming that what she wanted was for him to kiss her again, for him to put his hands, mouth, and cock between her legs.

"Straddle the horse."

With a moan of dread, Mae obeyed. The wooden horse was a diabolical device, consisting simply of a wooden beam that the sub was made to straddle. Then either the sub's legs were tied up or the horse was raised so that she couldn't touch the floor, forcing her to rest her body weight on their sex.

She was tall enough that she had only to raise her heels an inch off the floor to keep her body weight off her pussy.

"Arms folded behind your back." Xavier attached a strap to the D ring of her right cuff, brought the strap around her front, then attached it to her left wrist so she couldn't straighten her arms. In this position she was slightly off balance, which was going to make it harder to keep her weight on her toes.

Xavier cupped her left breast, thumbing the nipple. It felt so good that Mae's concentration broke. She tipped off balance, sitting hard on her already abused pussy. Yelping she jumped back onto her toes, her sex throbbing.

"Mae?"

"Yes, Master Xavier."

"You're not allowed to come." He pinched her nipple for emphasis, then left, boots ringing on the tile.

Mae practiced her yoga breathing and tried not to think about how desperately she wanted Master Xavier, or how much she'd enjoyed this time with him. She hadn't come, and yet she'd felt more satisfaction than she had in her last play session, which had included more orgasms than she could count. Neither of those things made any sense.

XAVIER LEANED BACK AGAINST THE DOOR. WHAT THE hell had just happened? It was a simple flogging, followed by a bratty sub stealing a kiss. Neither should have affected him the way they did.

Mindful of Mae's situation—though he knew the room was being monitored, as all playrooms were—he headed for the Den and the stash of toys the Dominants, Owners, and Masters kept there.

A few other Doms were winding down their evening with drinks, among them James. Xavier grabbed what he wanted from the cabinets, then on impulse stopped to talk to the other man. After a minute of conversation, and raised eyebrows from James, Xavier was on his way back to Mae.

He had more arrangements to make for the weekend, but they would wait until the pretty sub was safely in bed.

When he opened the door he was greeted by the site of Mae's pink and red ass. Parts of it were dark enough to match her hair. She was swaying slightly, her delicate calf muscles tense. He watched her lower herself onto the horse for a second, just enough to press her feet flat to the ground, before popping back onto her toes. He'd been very gentle when flogging her pussy, but still the combination of that plus a few minutes on the horse must have made her sore.

He was glad. He wanted her sore, wanted her thinking about him, feeling his touch on her body, even as she slept.

Without a word, he helped her swing a leg over the wooden horse and dismount. Dropping to one knee, he pushed her knees open, examining her pussy. The labia were bright pink and slightly swelled. He pinched them, testing how sensitive she was. Rather than a yelp of pain she moaned, pressing her crotch toward him.

Xavier fought the urge to bury his face in her pussy and his finger in her ass.

Satisfied that she'd be able to handle what he planned for her tomorrow, Xavier stood. Mae's arms were still bound behind her back, which made it easy to guide her to the armchair and bend her over the back. He tapped her legs open with a foot between her ankles. Taking a small packet of lube from his pocket, he ripped it open and squeezed it onto her anus.

"I'm going to place a plug in your ass. You're to sleep with it in. If you wake up and are uncomfortable you may take it out for an hour. Set an alarm and when the hour is up, you must reinsert it. You're to keep track of how many times you take it out. You may remove and wash it in the morning, but then immediately reinsert it. Do you understand?"

"Yes, oh yes, Master Xavier."

"You're looking forward to this?"

"I'm going to go crazy if I don't get something."

"You mean have something penetrate you?"

"Yes, Master Xavier."

He coated a simple plastic training plug with the last of the lube, then placed the tip against her rear entrance and used the toy to move the lube around. He was careful not to use his fingers, which like the kiss, were things he considered too personal and intimate for a scene that was only designed for BDSM play. "You are not allowed to come."

"I remember, Master Xavier."

"Good." He positioned the plug and pushed it all the way in with one hard thrust. Mae screamed and wiggled. He hadn't given her any warning, and the sudden invasion would have hurt, which is what he wanted.

He was surprised when Mae moaned and shuddered. He could see the shivers that trembled through her. It almost looked as if...

"Mae," he barked. "You are not allowed to come."

"I'm trying not to, Master."

He pinched her reddened ass.

Mae moaned again. "No, Master, I'll come!"

He took his hands off her and watched for her trembling to subside before crouching by the seat of the chair where he could see her face. "Were you really going to come just from that?"

She nodded jerkily. She looked baffled and scared, as if she didn't know what her body was doing. Her eyes were luminous with tears, her lips flushed pink from arousal.

"Mae, did you know that you're masochistic?" he asked softly.

"I'm not a pain slut." She seemed shocked by the very idea.

Xavier decided to leave the issue. He suspected she'd been through about all she could handle today. Tomorrow he'd help her explore this aspect of her submission.

Raising her to a standing position, he held her when she swayed and when she sagged back against him, turned her face so she could rest her cheek against his shoulder. He didn't have the heart to push her away. He knew it was a mistake, but it felt too good to have her body curled against his like this.

When she'd stopped trembling, he stepped back. "Mae, look at me. You're going to keep the cuffs on overnight, and wear this."

He picked up a small drawstring bag he'd brought with him, taking out a simple leather dog collar.

"This is just a training tool, something to help you." A collar was a significant symbol in BDSM, used to signal that a submissive had been permanently bound to, or was owned by, a Dom or Master.

Her lip curled.

"If you'd rather not wear a collar I can respect that." There were some who considered using collars for training unwise because it could confuse the submissive.

"It's not that I object to wearing a collar. I just don't like *that* collar. It's ugly."

Xavier looked from Mae to the collar and back. Shaking his head he slid the collar around her neck and buckled it loosely.

She pursed her lips. "It doesn't match the cuffs."

Xavier let out an exasperated grunt. "That's what you're focused on?"

"I take accessories very seriously."

"I don't even know what to do with that statement."

She giggled.

Xavier tensed, expecting that their banter and her sass would have knocked her out of subspace, but she didn't try to take control as she had when she kissed him. She stood obediently, pretty face turned up, waiting to see what he'd do next. But she'd giggled. His subs didn't giggle.

The final items in the bag were a set of belled clamps. He poured them into his palm to show her. "There are four clamps. One for each nipple, and two for the lips of your sex. You'll put them on as soon as you wake up. You may take them off to use the restroom, but then, as with the plug, you must put them back on immediately. Do you understand?"

"Yes, Master Xavier."

"Do you know why I want you to wear these?"

"No, Master."

"You will in the morning. Also, there's been a change in plan. Go to the Griff's Red room at 11:30."

"In the Sub Rosa Court?"

"Yes."

Though she was clearly curious, she didn't ask any questions. Xavier unstrapped her arms, rubbed the circulation back into them, and then picked up her robe, draping it over her shoulders, and handed her the bag of clamps. "Tomorrow you'll wear nothing except what I've given you tonight."

She frowned.

"Is there a problem, Mae?"

"Nothing matches." Her lips twitched before she got her expression back under control. She looked up at him through her lashes and he realized she was teasing him.

Xavier caught her chin, forcing her to look up. "You don't know when to quit, do you?" He meant it to be harsh, a warning, but his heart wasn't in it. He liked the sass. God help him, he even liked the giggle.

Her eyes fluttered closed as she shivered. "No, Master."

Desire roared through Xavier.

"I will see you tomorrow, Mae." He helped her put her arms through the robe, then felt something in the sleeve. Curious, he reached in and pulled out a phone and a pair of dark-framed glasses.

"Oh uh, those are mine." She tried to take them, but Xavier held them out of reach.

Unfolding the glasses, he slipped them onto her face. Mae blinked up at him from behind the lenses. She looked different with them on, older and more confident. He had several extremely vivid naughty librarian fantasies. Taking them off her face, he handed them to her.

She tucked them away. "Goodnight, Master Xavier."

"Goodnight, Mae."

He walked her to the door of the play room, and watched her leave, the hem of her robe flapping around her upper thighs. He realized she was barefoot. Ducking back into the room he grabbed her shoes but when he stuck his head out into the courtyard she was already gone, leaving him standing there with a pair of black kitten heels, and the strangest feeling that he'd just let Cinderella slip through his fingers.

CHAPTER 5

The next morning Mae carefully brushed her hair, hyper aware that each movement caused the bells that dangled from her nipples to jingle. She'd wanted to shower, but Master Xavier hadn't said she could take off the cuffs, and she wasn't sure if she should get them wet. Luckily her hair still looked good despite yesterday's dramatic events, and after washing her face and taking a sponge bath, she'd felt more herself.

There were faint circles under her eyes, which she covered up with concealer before putting on subtle makeup, just enough to make her feel prepared to face the day. She hadn't slept well, her dreams a chaotic mix of nightmares and erotic fantasies. After waking from a nightmare in a cold sweat, she'd crept out of the comfortable bed in the dorm-like room where subs slept when not ensconced in a play or sleeping room. She'd taken out the plug, hoping the relief from the stimulation of that would allow her to calm down. After an hour of dozing in an armchair, her phone alarm had gone off and she'd had to reinsert the plug, which only brought her arousal roaring back to life.

"Mae, your bottom!"

Mae looked over to see Alice, one of the subs she was friends with, staring at her ass.

Alice had only recently made the transition from the sweet, if kinky, role of being a "little" with no pain play to being a BDSM submissive. She was still shocked by some of the less obviously-sexy aspects of the BDSM world.

"Hi, Alice."

"What *happened* to you?"

Mae frowned. Alice's reaction wasn't totally unexpected, but she found herself irritated that the other sub couldn't see how pretty her ass, red from the flogger and bearing a few darker splotches that might be bruises, was. Though it hurt to sit, Mae had been admiring it all morning.

"I got a beating."

"Oh *no*. I'm so sorry."

"Don't be. I enjoyed it."

"You did? But I didn't think you liked stuff like that."

Neither did I.

Mae shrugged and finished applying her makeup. "I liked trying something different." The clock on the wall read eleven-fifteen. Time to go.

"Wait...you said a beating. Does that mean you got the letter B?"

Mae smiled. "Yes, I did. Did you get a letter?"

"No, just a note to show up next weekend."

"Sounds fun. Be good, Alice."

"Mae, you didn't tell me who your partner is."

Mae tucked her makeup bag into a cubby in the dressing room and checked her reflection—the belled clamps dangled from her breasts and sex, the heavy cuffs made her wrists and ankles look tiny and delicate, and the plain leather collar around her neck made it abundantly clear that she was dressed this way by command. Not that anyone who knew her would think she'd have chosen to present herself like this.

She looked at Alice and smiled. "Master Xavier."

Alice's eyes went round as saucers. "The one with the mask?"

Mae laughed and nodded.

A delicious mix of trepidation and anticipation filled her as she exited the Subs' Garden and headed for the Sub Rosa Court. She'd never had anything but fun in those rooms, and wondered what Master Xavier had in store for them there. It was brunch time and there were plenty of people out, most like her having just woken up. Heads turned as she moved, the bells drawing everyone's attention.

She knew now why Xavier had wanted her to wear them. The surprised stares and raised brows were a repeat of Alice's reaction, emphasizing that Xavier had done something to her that wasn't usual. He'd mastered her in a way no one else ever had. Mae was not particularly modest, especially here, but she rarely was nude in the public spaces, and that added to the sense of otherness she felt.

His possession of her body and control of her submission was like a cloak around her, both highlighting her nakedness and protecting her from the opinion of others.

When she reached the Griff's Red room she found the door already open slightly. This time Mae didn't bother to arrange her hair or think about her expression. She slipped into the play-space, nervous excitement causing butterflies in her belly.

The elegant chamber was dominated by a four poster bed. There was a large armchair, the seat wide enough for two, an ottoman perfectly sized to have someone kneeling on it, and an *en suite* bathroom with a claw footed tub. An antique screen in the corner created a dressing area, an armoire full of toys and linen beside it.

A set of French doors in the exterior wall revealed a wide expanse of lawn, and off to the left, the double row of palm trees that lined the drive and gave the estate its name.

"Mae, it's a pleasure to see you." Master James rose from a replica turn-of-the-century armchair, closing the book he'd been reading.

"Master James." Mae jumped when she saw him, then dipped her head. "My apologies. I must have misheard my instructions for the morning. Please excuse me." She backed toward the entrance.

"No, Mae. You're in the right place. Close the door and come here."

Mae's heart leapt into her throat. "Master James?"

He took a seat on the extra-wide chair and patted his knee. "Come to me." It seemed like he expected her. That he'd been waiting for her.

Was this some kind of test? Where was Xavier? Her excitement was morphing to dread.

"Master James, I was supposed to meet Master Xavier."

"Is that what he told you, or did he tell you to come to this room at 11:30?"

A ball of icy disappointment and shame solidified in her belly. Mae closed her eyes, fighting back tears. "He told me to come here, Sir."

"You obeyed him, and now you'll obey me, won't you?"

"Master James, I..."

"You can use your safe word, if you feel the need. Otherwise you're still under Master Xavier's control, and must obey his orders."

Mae didn't move. She couldn't.

Last night both she and Xavier had acknowledged that they weren't exactly a good fit, but once they'd started, their chemistry had been amazing, leading to one of the most intense sexual experiences of Mae's life. But clearly Xavier hadn't felt the same.

"Do you need to use your safe word? I'll tell Master Xavier and the overseers, so you don't have to."

Mae cleared her throat. "No, Master James. It's my pleasure to submit." The words rolled off her tongue with ease—a formulaic response.

She wanted to demand answers, but she bit the inside of her cheek, making her way to Master James, now hating the stupid bells that jingled with each step.

"On my lap."

It was an order she'd heard plenty of times before, from James and others. She slid onto his lap, straddling his thighs with her legs on the seat. James spread his own legs a bit, forcing hers open further. Mae pressed her nails into her palms.

James flicked the bells dangling from her pussy lips. "You don't seem happy to see me, Mae."

"My apologies, Sir." She tried and failed to smile, to pretend everything was all right when inside she was so very angry and upset.

"You're also being uncommonly obedient."

The casual comment, said with a smile, cut deep. Mae took a shuddering breath. "Was I... Am I a bad submissive?"

James stroked her arms with his palms. "No, Mae. You're a lovely sub to play with."

Her throat was too tight for words, so Mae only nodded in acknowledgement.

James carefully took the clamps off her pussy lips, massaging them gently. Mae's sex clenched when he brushed her clit, but it was a purely physical reaction.

"What's wrong, Mae? I thought you'd be happy to be here with me."

This time she forced a smile and tossed her hair, struggling to put aside what she was feeling and present herself the way she normally did. "Of course I am, Sir."

Master James raised one brow, clearly not believing her.

She toyed with the top button of Master James's shirt. "Did you miss me?"

Master James frowned.

Desperation curled in Mae's belly. She'd disappointed Master Xavier and now it looked like she was disappointing Master James.

"I want to be a good sub." That much was true. She ran her hands down Master James's chest, then brushed her palm against his crotch. "May I, Sir, please?" If she could pleasure him in this most basic way, he might not notice the pain she was sure was hiding in her eyes.

"Don't you want me to play with you first?" Master James ran two fingers over the lips of her sex. "I heard that your scene with Master Xavier was pure BDSM. No sex, no pleasure."

"Did Master Xavier tell you that?" Mae tried to keep her tone light, to pretend she didn't care what Xavier had said about her, or thought about her.

But Master James didn't answer her question. "I saw the marks. Did you like your beating?"

She didn't have to answer. Her body did it for her, a small moan escaping her before she clamped her lips closed.

"Do you wish he'd fucked you?"

Mae closed her eyes.

"Answer me."

"Yes, Sir."

"If you agreed to add sex as part of your session, you'd be completely at his mercy. There would be no restrictions on how he could touch you."

The idea of being at the mercy of Master Xavier sent arousal shooting through her. James's fingers dipped into the entrance of her pussy, finding the fresh wetness there.

"You're wetter now, Mae. Is that because I talked about Master Xavier?"

A tear slid down her cheek. "Please, Sir. Let me suck your cock. I don't want to talk about Master Xavier."

"Because you're scared of him?"

"No, because...because I'm not scared. I should be and I'm not and I hate it that he didn't want me." Mae couldn't hold in her feelings anymore. She covered her face with her hands.

James pulled her against his chest, rubbing her back until she calmed a bit. "You've been lying to all of us, haven't you?"

"What?" Mae sat back, shocked at his words. She shook her head. "I haven't lied."

"You have, but you lied to yourself more than anyone. Mae, you need more than this." Master James gestured around the pretty room.

"No, I love this." She did. This is who she was.

"You've grown as a submissive." He lowered his voice. "I know who you are outside of these walls, and you can still be that person. Wanting something darker and harder doesn't have to change that."

Mae bowed her head. "I'm not what Master Xavier wants. I can't be what he wants."

"You shouldn't want to be anything but true to yourself. I think you've been hiding for far too long. Maybe it's time to move on from being the naughty girl or sassy princess." Those were only a few of the pet names she'd been called over the years.

"It's who I am."

"It's who you were."

"Please, Master James. I can't talk about this." Mae jumped off his lap, suddenly frantic to get rid of the collar and cuffs. To free herself of any reminder of Xavier and return to the kind of BDSM that she was comfortable with. Master James stood and reached for her but she stumbled back. She ripped the clamps from her nipples and threw them aside, then jerked at the buckle of the collar.

"Mae, enough." The deep voice cut through the buzzing in her ears. Like a tolled bell it focused her thoughts and calmed her mind. Mae looked slowly to Master James, who indicated with a jerk of his head that she should turn around.

Master Xavier stepped out from behind the dressing screen. He was again wearing all black clothing and the severe mask. He was a menacing, raw presence, out of place in the elegant room, but no less powerful or in command here than he had been in the Iron Court.

She looked from James to Xavier, the pieces clicking together.

"You—" Her voice broke. Mae took a breath that was meant to be calming, but instead all it did was fuel the fire of her rage. "You *son of a bitch.*"

Mae leaped at Xavier, wanting him to feel some of the pain he'd caused her. She had the satisfaction of seeing his eyes widen before James caught ahold of her, pulling her back toward the bed.

"You complete ass." Mae struggled against Master James. "Let me go."

"No, Mae. I won't. Calm down and think."

"I am thinking." Her hair whipped over her face, obscuring her vision. "He tricked me. You tricked me." Mae tossed her head to the side, managing to knock Master James's chin. With an *oomph* he let go of her.

Mae brushed her hair out of her eyes with her hands, ready to let Master Xavier have it.

But he was already there. Mae squeaked in surprise to see him looming over her, but before she could do or say anything he grabbed her arms, forcing her back three steps and then raising her hands above her head, clicking the D-rings on her cuffs onto a chain that dangled from the bedpost. In a matter of seconds he took command of her body, his control precise and absolute.

He pushed her back against the post and he curled one hand

around her neck, digging his fingers into the pressure points at the back of her jawbone. "Enough."

Mae closed her eyes, competing feelings of relief and anger warring within her. Relief from having him in control and anger for this heartless charade he'd put her through.

"Look at me."

Mae met his gaze, and there was something in his eyes that seemed to echo what she was feeling. He tipped her head back a fraction, gaze hardening until his eyes were as unreadable as his masked face.

"You will submit. You will behave."

"Yes, Master Xavier," she murmured.

"Good." Xavier released her.

James was rubbing his jaw and looking at her in a decidedly unfriendly way. "Mae was always a bit bratty, but this is new." He looked from Xavier to her. "You two need to talk. I have this room reserved for the weekend. You're welcome to it until this evening."

The other Dom clapped Xavier on the shoulder before leaving and closing the door behind him.

Now that she was alone with Master Xavier, Mae didn't know what to say, what to feel.

Their gazes met once more, and she had this strange feeling that Xavier was just as much at a loss as she was. She'd never even spoken to him until twelve hours ago, and yet the idea that he'd dismissed her by passing her off to another Master had shredded her heart. That he had the power to impact her so heavily was beyond worrying. It was terrifying.

"I didn't mean to upset you."

His words were both unexpected and infuriating. "You gave me to another Dom." Mae tried to keep the emotion out of her voice, to match his level tone. "How did you think that would make me feel?" She wasn't succeeding—pain leaked into her words.

He shook his head. "I don't own you. I couldn't give you away, even if I wanted to. And I don't."

"I thought…" Mae blinked to keep tears from falling.

"James is the kind of Dom you like. I thought you'd be comfortable with him."

"I didn't walk away last night when you told me to, so now you're trying to get rid of me this way? Then you could have a sub who won't ever talk back or be scared." Mae spat each word, losing the battle with her feelings. Pain and a sense of betrayal made her long to lash out again.

Xavier grabbed her hips, jerking them against his. For the first time she felt the hard length of his erection. The evidence of his desire took her breath away.

"I thought you'd be comfortable telling him the truth." Xavier's face was only inches from hers, his voice a growl.

"Truth about what?" she breathed.

"Whether you really wanted to include sex in our session."

Chain rattled as Mae reached for him only to be brought up short. "How could you doubt it?"

"A Dom can't change the terms of a scene while it's happening. Submissives will agree to things they shouldn't when they're in subspace." Xavier's hand moved up her side until his thumb was poised at the bottom swell of her breast. "They'll do things like say yes to everything on the checklist because they're turned on while they're filling out the form." His lips twitched and the corners of his eyes—just barely visible behind the mask —crinkled. Mae blushed.

"I needed to know if you really wanted more than straight BDSM play." His eyes were new-leaf green, the daylight making them appear lighter than they had last night. "What James said was true—you'll be completely at my mercy. I told you that I'd push you. I did, and I will, because there's something inside you begging to be let out. And because it's what I want, what I need to do to you."

Mae closed her eyes. The answer to the question of sex was a resounding "yes," but the rest of it was a bit more complicated. They'd spent only a few hours together and yet he'd had more impact on her than any other Dom in years. If they kept going there was no telling who she'd be when they reached the other side.

"I want you." It was the simple truth, and Mae hoped it was enough. "I want you to touch me, dominate me. In every way."

Xavier's hand closed over her breast as his lips captured hers in a savage kiss. Mae arched into him, wanting every bit of contact he would give her. She moved her hips side to side, rubbing his cock with her lower belly. His free hand closed over her abused ass and she bit his lip in reaction to the sudden stab of pain.

Xavier growled and jerked her head back. "Did you just bite me, Red?"

"It was an accident, Master." She was half distracted by the nickname, but the intensity of his stare warned her to concentrate, to watch him and obey his commands.

"I'm going to bite you, and it's not going to be an accident." He smiled darkly. "Good of you to remind me that we have checklist items yet to complete. I think we should take care of 'biting' right now."

Master Xavier dropped to one knee, his mouth level with her bellybutton.

"Spread your legs, Mae."

She inched her feet apart, exposing her wet core. Her heart was pounding so loud she thought he'd be able to hear it. It wasn't fear of him biting her sensitive pussy that had her blood racing, but anticipation of him finally touching her.

Xavier lowered his head, Mae sucked in a breath, and he bit the inside of her right thigh.

The pressure-pain of the bite was so close to her aching pussy that it only made her body throb harder.

"Master Xavier, please. I can't wait any more." Couldn't he see how wet she was? How much she needed him?

"You *will* wait." His words brushed her pussy. "I like you this way. Wet. Needy."

Mae let out a frustrated little scream, banging the cuffs back against the bedpost. In response Xavier placed a second bite next to the first, this one a bit harder, lasting a bit longer. Mae trembled, but didn't protest or move her leg away. The sweet sting of pain wasn't the orgasm she craved, but it was satisfying in a way she didn't fully understand.

"You'll have a bruise there." Xavier traced the marks he'd left on her thigh.

"Thank you, Master." And she was thankful. She wanted him to mark her.

"I have something of yours." He went to the screen and came back carrying her shoes. Dropping to one knee he carefully helped her slip them on.

Mae looked down at her naked body and her lips twitched. "Master?"

"Yes, Mae."

"They don't match the collar either."

CHAPTER 6

Xavier laughed so hard he had to sit on the bed. Mae shifted around to look at him, her arms still chained above her head, pulling her body into a pretty, taut line.

He grinned at her, genuinely amused. "Next time I'll do my best to use bondage equipment that matches your shoes. If it exists."

"Oh, it exists." Her tone was wry, as if she knew something he didn't.

When it came to coordinating accessories and bondage equipment it wasn't hard for him to believe.

"If you say so." He pushed off the bed and retrieved his bag from behind the screen where he'd waited to hear her responses to James's questions.

What he'd heard was more than he could have hoped for, and far more than he had a right to ask. Mae hadn't just been willing to deepen their play, but she'd obeyed Master James in his stead and most surprising, she'd become upset when she thought he would no longer be the one Dominating her.

He'd given her another chance to escape him, and again

she'd refused. Every time he pushed her away, she only pressed closer. It was disconcerting.

Today would not be easy, for either of them. He doubted that she'd look at him with that alluring mixture of trust and desire by the time he was done.

He dumped the duffle bag on the bed then looked around the room, eyeing the possibilities before undoing the carbine clip that attached the cuffs to the chain.

Mae folded her arms across her waist and leaned toward him, brushing his arm with hers. It was a small moment of contact, one that he could pretend was accidental, but knew wasn't. Mae needed, wanted, to touch him.

"On your knees on that ottoman."

She obeyed without question or comment, positioning herself perfectly with her knees on the edge, head down, and arms stretched out and grabbing the opposite side of the padded top.

He took a minute to examine her ass. There were a few spots that would bruise, but the rest of it would have faded by tomorrow. Her pussy lips were full and pink, but he doubted that was left over from last night. She was so wet even the insides of her thighs were damp, her body's moisture coating the bite marks he'd left there.

The plug was firmly ensconced in her pretty bottom. Taking hold of the base, he started to tug it out. Mae moaned as her anus was stretched.

"How many times did you take it out last night?"

"One, Master."

"And did you put the plug back in?"

"After one hour."

"Did you touch your pussy?"

"No, Master."

"Did you want to?"

"Yes, Master...but not as much as I wanted you to."

"But I'm not going to." He removed the plug, watched as her ass clenched closed.

"Master? I thought…"

"We've agreed that sex can be included in our activities." He grabbed her under the arms and hauled her up so that she was standing beside the ottoman with her back against his chest. "That doesn't mean I'm going to fuck you. That doesn't mean you get to come."

Mae's whole body stiffened and he could feel her need to protest, to pout and beg until she got what she wanted.

Xavier reached for the collar. Slipping the tail out of the buckle, he pulled, tightening it just enough so she felt the pressure around her throat. With his other hand he cupped her breast, squeezing hard.

Mae relaxed against him, her head dropping forward. "Yes, Master."

Xavier inhaled slowly, savoring the moment. She'd gotten used to topping from the bottom, but she was submissive in her core. He was so accustomed to hyper-obedient subs that he'd forgotten the thrill of winning these small battles for control.

He took the collar off her, then removed the cuffs from her ankles and wrists. Despite the fact that he'd just put them on her, Xavier had her slip out of the froufrou shoes. He tucked everything into the bag, leaving her wholly naked, her creamy skin now marked by his touch.

He laid out the things he'd brought with him. There were two wide black leather belts, a heavy molded blindfold and a ball gag.

Mae took a half step back when she saw the tools. He put a hand on her back, both stopping any further retreat and reassuring her.

"What are you thinking, Mae?"

"I don't like gags, Master Xavier."

"Of course you don't. It's hard to top from the bottom if you can't say anything."

She stiffened. "I wasn't doing it on purpose."

"I understand that. And I even understand the allure of giving in and letting a sub like you be sassy."

"You do?"

"I do. But, when you're mine," he lowered his voice so she'd know how serious his next words were, "you submit, and you behave." Xavier picked up the wider and longer of the two belts. "Raise your arms, wrists on top of your head."

He placed the belt around her upper back, then buckled it in place over her breasts. It compressed her tits, binding them so that they swelled prettily above and below the leather.

"Take a deep breath. How does that feel?"

"Tight."

"Are you having trouble breathing?"

"No, Master."

"Good." He paused, waiting to see if she'd say whatever comment or question was clearly on the tip of her tongue.

She met his gaze, then pressed her lips together. He smiled.

"This is a form of breast binding." He put two fingers between the belt and her ribs, double checking the tightness. "I've chosen to bind you this way because I have other plans for your breasts later."

The second belt was only a few inches wide, and twenty inches long. This one he wrapped around her neck, creating a thick collar. It wasn't a posture collar, designed to keep her chin up, but its size meant that it would be uncomfortable if she lowered her chin too much.

Picking up the blindfold and ball gag, he decided to wait on those and give her the chance to see what was about to happen.

"Come with me, Mae."

MAE KEPT HER GAZE ON MASTER XAVIER'S SHOULDERS as they passed through the halls and courtyards of Las Palmas. The surprised glances she'd endured this morning when the other members saw her marked ass and unusual attire—or lack thereof—was nothing compared to the looks they were getting now.

People actually stopped and stared when they saw Xavier coming with Mae one step behind him, naked except for the thick collar and breast binding.

The library was one of the public rooms of Las Palmas. It was always open, and anyone was welcome to spend time there. Dominants, Masters, and Owners could book the small circular stage for demonstrations or to use when putting their sub on display. There were bookcases along one wall, but instead of books, the lighted shelves displayed various BDSM equipment, some new, some antique. There was an L-shaped bar in one corner, with usually a submissive or two behind it playing bartender. Cocktail tables clustered near it were made of massive wine barrels supporting round glass tops. On the far side of the stage from the bar was a Spanish-style tiled fireplace. Plush rugs and floor cushions were folded and stacked in baskets on either side of the hearth, while several comfortable couches formed a half circle facing the empty fireplace. The tufted dark-leather couches with rounded backs and arms were all the perfect height to have someone bent over them.

The dining room was next door, and when they entered the library there were a few people at the pub tables with plates of food catered by a local restaurant. The occupants were an eclectic mix of people—ranging both in age and how they liked their BDSM. An African American Domme had her feet propped on the back of her submissive, who was on her hands and knees. Beside her an older Master sat with his sub cuddled against his side.

Before now Mae would no more have knelt to be used as a

foot rest than she would have jumped off the roof. She didn't judge people who chose that kind of submission, but she didn't want it for herself. But now she found herself looking at the kneeling woman with greater understanding. She didn't want to do it, but she understood it.

Xavier put a hand on her back and guided her over to the bar area. One of the tables had been taken apart, the wine barrel turned on its side and placed on braces. With the stabilizing pieces under it, the top of the barrel was at waist height.

Mae was experiencing a strange foreboding. Xavier stopped beside the barrel and patted the top. Mae laced her fingers together, looking nervously between him and the people at the nearby table, who were watching with obvious interest.

"No, Red. Look at me."

She jerked her attention back to Xavier.

"Sit up on the barrel."

She kept her gaze down, though she couldn't lower her chin very much, as she backed up against the barrel and with a little jump sat on the curved top. Nerves were making her breathe hard, which made her more aware of the binding around her breasts, which in turn made her wet.

"Spread your legs, Mae."

She whimpered, scared and frustrated. She wanted to be back in a private room with him. Though she had no problem being naked and played with in public, and had been up on the library stage several times as part of demonstrations, she doubted he'd brought her here to fuck her until they both passed out from pleasure, which is what she'd been hoping for.

Xavier fisted his hand in her hair. The instant he touched her she calmed, even as his tight hold made her scalp tingle. Mae spread her legs, tucking her heels along the edges of the barrel. Her desire to be fucked melted away in the heat of a different desire—the desire to submit, to be dominated.

"You should enjoy this, Mae. It's time for 'being serviced.'"

Xavier released her hair. "I'm going to bind you to this barrel. Your pussy will be exposed and available for anyone who chooses to service you. You will be both blindfolded and gagged."

Mae couldn't stop the shudder of combined arousal and horror that shook her. "Anyone can touch me?"

"Yes, Mae. Nothing in your hard limits or checklist prevents that. You have your safe word, if you need it." Xavier laid his hand on her thigh, fingers inches from her sex. "However, you have permission to come. That should please you."

"It does, Master, but I—" *I want to come because you're touching me. I want you to be the one to release me from the prison of need you put me in.* Mae wasn't brave enough to say what she was thinking. She'd already made a fool of herself once this morning. He'd told her that he expected her to be good, be obedient, and she would be both. "Thank you, Master Xavier."

He nodded once. "Lie back."

Xavier positioned her so that she was on her back draped over the barrel. She grabbed each wrist with the opposite hand, letting her arms dangle.

"Bend your knees, spread your legs. I want everyone to have easy access to your pussy."

With her legs bent, Xavier positioned her feet so they were on the very edges of the barrel. After a few other adjustments he crouched beside her. Mae lifted her head slightly so she wasn't looking at him upside down.

"Now I'm going to bind you in place. I am not going to use safety restraints. I want you to experience true bondage."

"Heavy bondage?" she asked, remembering that from the checklist.

Xavier's lips kicked up into a devastating smile. "No. I wouldn't call it heavy bondage. This one can count for light bondage. We'll get to the heavy stuff, but you're not ready yet."

"Yes, Master."

Xavier held up a handful of pale blue, flat rope. "This is nylon strapping. It's the same weight and density of what's used in shipping tie downs." He took a small section and wrapped it around her already linked hands and wrists, leaving the tips of her fingers exposed. "I'm going to wrap it around each of your calves and thighs, just like this, then nail the strapping directly into the wood barrel. Do you understand?"

What she understood was that once he was done with her Mae wouldn't be moving, wouldn't be able to get away. She whimpered.

"Are you afraid or aroused?"

"Both, Master."

"Good."

A crowd gathered to watch as Xavier started weaving the strapping in a figure eight pattern around her thighs and ankles, starting at her thigh, then looping between her upper and lower leg to circle her calf, and crossing back to again wind around her thigh. When her legs were encased from mid-thigh to hip, and mid-calf to ankle, Xavier tied off the strapping with a simple knot, then nailed the trailing ends into the barrel. Mae jumped at the first ringing sound of hammer striking nail, and the barrel vibrated under her with each blow. She raised her head when he was done, looking at the elaborate bindings, which were expertly done, creating almost a woven pattern. With her legs spread the whole width of the barrel, her pussy was on complete display.

Master Xavier was examining her—bound and vulnerable, body exposed and accessible. He traced the outer lips of her sex, his eyes seeming to gleam behind the mask. The sight of him calmed her even as it heightened her arousal.

"How do you feel, Mae?"

"Scared, Master."

He pinched the lips of her sex together and rubbed them over her clit. "Is that all?"

"No, Master," she gasped. It was as if every nerve end in her pussy were extra sensitive. For one wild moment she thought she'd come from that simple touch alone.

"Are you ready to be serviced?"

"No, Master." She didn't think, just answered.

"No?" Xavier released her pussy lips and Mae whimpered. "Explain."

She bit her lip. It would be easy to say that she hadn't meant "no," that she'd been confused or not really paying attention. If she did that the scene would continue. It was a white lie, meant to make life easy. If it had been any other Dom, any other situation, she would have done it without thinking. Instead she took a deep breath. "I don't want them to touch me."

"Are you refusing to complete the checklist item?"

Tears of frustration stung Mae's eyes. She wanted to explain what she was feeling, wanted to express the conflicting desires that roared through her, but she didn't know how.

"Master Xavier, if I may offer my assistance?" Master Anderson rose in one elegant motion, his slightly accented voice not nearly as compelling as Xavier's, but containing the same easy confidence. He was a man who knew that when he spoke others would listen. The submissive kneeling beside his chair watched him with hungry, haunted eyes. He wore a stark black suit, with a white shirt open at the throat. His pale skin, dark hair and eyes so blue they seemed black completed the picture of a stark, debonair man.

"I do not need assistance." Xavier's voice was deeper than normal. He watched the other Master.

"Of course not, but I think perhaps I might know what your sub is trying to say."

Master Anderson had a reputation, but unlike Xavier he was not known for hard physical play. Anyone who subbed for him had to be willing to let him in, not only to their body, but to their mind. Mae had seen subs break down sobbing from the emotional intensity of spending time with him. The Dom slipped his hand under her head, lifting it slightly. When he touched her, Xavier took a half step toward the other man, as if he were going to shove him back.

"Your name is Mae?"

Mae looked at Master Xavier. He didn't intervene, so she answered, "Yes, Sir."

"You're desperate to come, aren't you?"

"Yes, Sir."

"But you don't just want to come. You want your Master, and only him, to be the one to make you orgasm."

Mae looked at Master Anderson, shocked that he'd so precisely put words to her feelings. "How did you—"

He laid one finger over her lips. "I did not invite comment. You will answer my question. Is your reluctance due to your desire to have your Master be the one to experience the gift of your pleasure?"

The way the other Dom phrased it kept it from sounding like her desire was another instance of her trying to top from the bottom. Mae looked at Master Xavier. "Yes, Sir. That's it exactly."

"Your Master wants you to be serviced by anyone who walks into the room. And what does that mean?"

Now Mae looked away from Xavier, staring at the ceiling. "I am Master Xavier's to do with as he pleases."

The other Dom lowered her head, his gold signet-style ring, embossed with a triangular Celtic symbol, catching the light. Mae blew out a long breath. She was relieved that she'd had a chance to express what she was feeling, and glad Master Anderson had reminded her of her place.

Some romantic part of her hoped that Xavier would be so moved that he'd undo the bindings, sweep her into his arms and carry her away to fuck her in privacy. He didn't, and she hadn't really thought he would. If he were the kind of Dom who'd do that, she wouldn't care so much, wouldn't feel the things she was feeling.

The heavy blindfold slid into place over her eyes. Her tension ratcheted up a notch, and without being able to see she had the strangest sense that she was falling off the barrel. Xavier pressed something soft between the tips of her fingers and her forearm. "I'm going to gag you. This takes the place of your safe word. Release the cloth and I'll remove the gag so we can speak. Do you understand?"

"Yes, Master." Something brushed her cheek and Mae could smell the rubber of the ball gag. She twisted her head to the side, sudden panic taking hold of her. "Please, no."

"I want you to open your mouth, Red."

Mae's lips trembled as she fought to push aside her fear and let her submissiveness rise up.

Xavier kissed her.

He cradled her head as his lips pressed over hers. The kiss felt odd, because she was upside down, but then he nipped her lower lip before pressing his tongue into her mouth. Her mind went quiet even as her body flushed with desire. When he pulled back, Mae parted her lips, ready for the gag.

"I could order that you don't come." He traced her lower lip with his thumb. "They would still touch you, play with you, but your orgasm would still be mine."

His. There'd be no relief for this intense ache that consumed her, but he would own another little piece of her.

"If it would please you, Master."

She heard him take a deep breath. "You are so much more than you seem. A man could spend a lifetime exploring your submission."

Mae's heart thumped.

"And I regret that I cannot be that man." The words were so low she could barely hear them, and before she had time to process what he'd said, Xavier pinched her chin, forced her mouth open, and pressed the ball gag into place.

She wanted to ask him what he meant by that. Wanted to push back against the implied idea that it was his choice alone whether he became a permanent part of her life, and remind him that he was only her Dom for the game—even if inside she was starting to feel like the parts of her Xavier owned she might never get back.

She struggled against the gag, trying to spit it out. Xavier cupped her jaw, forcing her to bite down on it. Mae's struggle was short lived. When she stilled, Xavier buckled the straps behind her head, then tugged lightly on the safe word cloth, reminding her it was there.

CHAPTER 7

Xavier examined his handiwork. It was one of his better setups, and yet he felt slightly ill at the thought of actually stepping back and letting everyone touch her.

Mine. Mine. Mine.

The word was a mantra in his mind. In less than a day Mae had invaded his mind and soul, making him want things he couldn't have. The more submission she gave, the more drawn to her he was.

He needed to see others touching her, needed the emotional distance it would provide. She could use her safe word—if she did he'd end the scene, rather than just halting it—but he had a sinking feeling that she wouldn't. Mae had yet to back down from a challenge.

Her pussy was lovely—wet and pink, begging to be pleasured. For someone like Mae, who wasn't used to scenes that didn't include sexual fulfillment, the past twenty hours must have been torture. He had no doubt that she was more than ready to come, no matter who it was who touched her.

Still her admission that she would rather continue to be

denied pleasure and wait for his touch was like gasoline thrown on the fire of his desire for her.

Xavier laid his hand on her stomach. She tensed, then relaxed, almost as if she'd realized who was touching her.

That was the last straw. Xavier stepped away, leaving her alone and exposed in her bindings. He looked at the crowd of fifteen or so people who had gathered.

"Mae is available for you to enjoy. Fingers and mouths only. No fucking." Mae made a strangled sound behind the gag. Xavier raised his voice, making sure everyone heard him. "She is not allowed to come."

Several people chuckled. "What happens if she does come?" someone called out.

"If she orgasms then the breast whipping she has coming will be much more severe." He put menace in the words, wanting to scare Mae, giving her the fear as a tool to help control her body's reaction to what was about to happen.

She moaned, her hips lifting slightly.

Then again, if she was, as he suspected, deeply masochistic, the idea of a severe breast whipping might only arouse her further.

Several people stepped forward. When the Dom who'd helped Mae admit her desires pulled up a chair, positioning it so he could sit while playing with her pussy, Xavier tapped him on the shoulder. He smiled knowingly and silently gave up his seat.

A pretty female slave was kneeling by Mae's head, kissing her neck just above the collar, while her owner fished an ice cube from his drink and ran it over Mae's belly. Xavier had known that every inch of flesh he left exposed would be considered fair game, which is why he'd been sure to cover her breasts, saving those for himself.

Planting his hands on the barrel, he leaned forward and blew across her wet pussy lips, letting her know someone was there.

Mae was breathing heavily through her nose, and he watched

her pussy clench. Xavier used two fingers to further part her outer labia. Her vagina was lovely, the soft folds swollen with arousal, begging to be touched and fucked.

Xavier doubted she'd be able to keep from coming. The mind could not always control the body, but he knew she'd fight the orgasm in an effort to obey. She'd fail, but he wanted to be the one to cause that failure. He wanted to feel her struggle for obedience.

Smiling, Xavier lowered his mouth to her clit.

———

No. No. No.

Mae whimpered into the hated gag as fingers opened her pussy. She was doing her best to ignore the person kissing the sensitive skin of her neck and the cold brush of ice over her stomach, but she wouldn't be able to ignore direct stimulation of her sex.

Something soft brushed her clit, the barest touch. She jumped, a spike of pleasure lancing through her. Clenching her belly muscles, she braced herself to try to stop from coming.

Another soft flick of her clit, and now a finger was stroking her inner labia in a smooth rhythm. Maybe if it continued like this she'd be able to fight it.

Lips pressed over her, a tongue stroked her clit, and Mae almost came.

Jerking her hips up, she sucked air in through her nose, gasping at the sudden, sharp pleasure. She'd moved enough to dislodge the person's mouth, giving her a chance to regain control.

The reprieve from stimulation was brief. As soon as her ass hit the barrel the tongue was back on her clit. Again she tried to lift her hips and break contact, but didn't have the leverage to hold the position for long. The hand running ice over her stomach applied pressure, keeping her in place.

Fingers toyed with her pussy lips, pinching and tugging them, then a finger circled the entrance to her body, pressing in just enough to remind her how achingly empty she was.

Something thick—it had to be at least two fingers—pressed against her entrance and Mae stiffened. She wanted to be filled, to be possessed in this primal way, but she wanted it to be Master Xavier who did it.

The tongue stroked her clit again, this time paired with a sudden thrust that filled her aching pussy.

Mae couldn't hold back the orgasm. She screamed, her legs pulling against the straps, her hips arching up. She started to move her arms but the person kissing her neck held them down. Mae bit down on the ball as the orgasm continued to ripple through her.

The mouth and hands between her legs didn't stop. They went to work on her clit in earnest, alternating flicks with long licks. The fingers inside her twisted, now rubbing her g-spot with each thrust. There were more hands and mouths on her—stroking the exposed lower curves of her breasts, nipping the soft skin of her hip and massaging her upper arms.

Mae sobbed into the gag, her skull thumping against the wood as she sobbed in a combination of exquisite pleasure and disappointment that she hadn't been able to obey Xavier's order. Not only had she failed to keep from orgasming, it had taken less than five minutes for her to lose the battle.

And as much as she regretted that, defeat felt very good.

The mouth and fingers on her pussy stopped their sweet torment, only to return a moment later. It took only a second for her to realize that there was someone new enjoying her pussy—the touch was different, not as precise. The realization that she really was helpless—that she couldn't control who or how many people touched her—made her shudder in submissive delight.

Though she'd come when she shouldn't have, she wasn't draped over this barrel, exposed for use, because she wanted to be.

She was here because her Master wanted her like this.

There was a rush of cold air on her saliva-damp neck as the person there left. She could tell someone else had taken their place, and she knew, though she couldn't see, that it was Xavier. She turned her face to him, straining her head to reach him.

Fingers brushed her cheek, then her hair. "Did you come, Red?"

His dark voice washed over her. She nodded, wishing she could tell him she was sorry, tell him that she'd tried.

"I'm going to punish you for that."

Mae nodded, hoping he couldn't tell that right now the threat sounded more like foreplay. The person between her legs was quickly bringing her close to a second orgasm.

Xavier leaned close, his cheek brushing hers. "You're lovely when you come…and you have a delicious pussy." There was a smile in his voice.

That had been him? Delighted that he'd been the first to touch her, the first to make her orgasm, was quickly followed by irritation that he'd given an order and then made sure she'd fail.

"You jerk. I should have known it was you." Her words were totally unintelligible.

Xavier laughed, as if he'd understood her despite the gag. The hands and mouths pleasuring Mae all stopped. She had the strangest feeling that everyone was looking at Xavier, as if they couldn't believe what they'd just heard.

He brushed his lips over hers, the kiss awkward because of the gag, apparently not aware or not caring that he'd shocked everyone.

"You'd better not come again. If you do I might have to spank that pretty pussy."

Mae came. It took her by surprise, the orgasm caused by the delicious threat, the undeniably erotic situation he'd put her in, and the sound of his voice in her ear. She couldn't stop the moans, or her hips from lifting. Anyone watching would know exactly what was happening deep inside her, despite the fact that at that moment no one was touching her.

With a whimper at failing yet again she hid her face against her arm. Xavier tugged at her collar, then kissed her neck before rising.

Distantly she heard some ask, "Did he just make her orgasm with his voice alone?"

"Never mind that, did Master Xavier just laugh?"

AN HOUR LATER MAE WAS SURE SHE HAD NOTHING left inside her. She was like a wrung-out cloth, tangled and empty. But then someone pushed another ice cube into her ass before rubbing her clit. Mae arched her back, her shoulders and head pressing against the submissive who was supporting her. Ten minutes ago Master Xavier had helped her to half sit up. She was still bound to the barrel, still blindfolded and gagged, but now her upper body was resting against someone, her bound hands looped over her supporter's neck.

"Did you just come again?" Master Xavier was walking toward her. She could tell when he reached her side. It was as if there was a compass inside her, and he was true north.

She shook her head. She hadn't come. At least she didn't think so. Never before had she been exposed to such prolonged pleasure. This made a few "forced" orgasms from a vibrator seem like vanilla sex. If she hadn't been gagged she would have long ago tried to get out of this, either by begging to be fucked or by pleading about how tired and sensitive she was.

With the gag in her mouth that wasn't an option. She still held the safe word cloth, and every so often someone would tug on it, reminding her she had it. If her Master wanted her here, if he thought she could take more, then she would.

Two fingers circled her clit. Mae recognized the touch—Master Xavier had taken more turns than she could count, tormenting her, each time bringing her to a blistering orgasm.

Though she would have sworn she was too worn out to come again, after only a minute he had her sobbing through another orgasm.

When it was through, her stomach and thigh muscles continued to tremble—not with pleasure, but with exhaustion.

"You've been serviced enough."

Mae's arms were unbound and the person at her back gently lowered her to lie over the barrel once more. There was the screech of nails being pulled from wood, then the pressure of her leg bindings loosened. When they were gone she tried to straighten her legs, but they were too stiff. Multiple pairs of hands helped rub the circulation back into her limbs. Finally she was lifted off the barrel. She swayed on her feet, curling her fingers into Xavier's shirt. He guided her a few steps to the left, turned her so that her back was to his chest, and unbuckled the blindfold. Mae blinked, her vision taking a long time to focus.

A naked woman was standing in front of her, a black collar labeling her a submissive. Her pale skin was marked by pink splotches and her face was free of makeup, though there was a streak of mascara along one temple. She was the vision of a well-used submissive, the kind of woman who obeyed without question, who gave everything she was over to a Master.

Mae let out a small sob, touching the red ball gag still in her mouth, watching the unfamiliar reflection mirror the motion. The black band still bound her breasts, her legs were criss-crossed with red stripes from the bindings, the bites on her inner thigh had darkened to semicircular bruises, and her pussy lips were swollen and deep pink, an obvious result of being well-used.

She'd never seen herself look like this, and she wasn't sure what it meant.

Her knees started to buckle and Xavier grabbed her upper arms. She looked at him—a dark presence looming over her shoulder. He looked implacable and hard. He looked like the kind of man who left a sub marked and wrung out.

She touched the gag again, begging without words for him to take it out. He shook his head, heartlessly denying her request. Tears filled her eyes. Mae couldn't bear to look in the mirror anymore.

Turning, she clung to Xavier's chest, sobbing. He held her, hands rubbing her back, dipping down to touch her ass, which only reminded her of the flogging last night. When her knees gave out he lowered her to the floor.

"Hands and knees, Mae." His voice was gentle, though the command was not. He gathered her hair, twirling it into a rope. Using it as a leash he walked over to a couch, Mae crawling beside him.

When he sat she collapsed at his feet, resting her head on his knee.

He stroked her hair, then lifted her onto the couch beside him. Mae blinked back fresh tears of relief. He unbuckled the gag, but when Mae quickly spat it out, he frowned at her.

"No, Mae. Not until I remove it or give you permission."

He held the gag up to her lips. She met his gaze, sure that he wouldn't make her keep wearing it. There was no quarter, no pity, in his gaze. His will washed over her, and she submitted. Opening her mouth she sat obediently when he pushed the hated thing between her teeth.

Mae felt like a plucked string, taut and vibrating so hard that she might snap. Tentatively she crawled onto his lap, nestling her ass between his splayed thighs and resting her head on his shoulder. She waited for him to shove her onto the floor, reprimand her in some way.

But Xavier curled his arms around her and kissed her forehead. Mae closed her eyes in relief. He'd pushed her, demanded more of her than anyone ever had before, but now, in his arms, she knew that he would also protect her.

Mae gave in to the exhaustion that weighed on her, falling asleep in his arms.

XAVIER TUGGED THE GAG FROM HER MOUTH. MAE'S only response was to snuggle tighter against him. He was trying to figure out how to move her so he could undo the breast binding when James dropped down onto the couch beside him.

"Need help?"

"If I shift her can you undo the strap?"

James nodded. Still cradling her in his arms, Xavier twisted Mae's upper body so James could undo the buckle. There were hard red lines along her breasts where the edges of the binding had cut in. Xavier repositioned Mae, then rubbed the marks. Even in her sleep her nipples pebbled at his touch.

"Xavier, you need to be careful." The other man looked troubled.

"Thank you for your opinion." He made sure his tone conveyed that he in fact did not give a shit what the other man thought.

James's jaw clenched. "You're playing a dangerous game with her."

"Exactly, I'm playing the game."

"No, you're opening her up, and I'm worried about her. About what will happen when you leave. She may have been a player in the lifestyle for years, but no one has ever gotten to the core of her, not the way you have."

"And that's on you." Though Xavier liked James, he was

battling a sense of contempt that James and others had dominated Mae without seeing what she really was.

"You're not understanding what's really happening here. I heard about the beginning of the scene."

"What about it?"

"She admitted she would rather be tortured with orgasm denial than to have anyone but you make her come. Don't you get it? That's something a sub does for their Master. *Their* Master. I didn't figure out that Mae needed harder play, because I couldn't. She would never have done that—" James motioned to the far side of the room and the barrel "—for me."

"A good Dom—"

"Don't insult me by finishing that sentence. You know that the chemistry between two people can completely change a dynamic. You two have something."

Xavier stared at the empty fireplace. There was some truth in James's words. His connection with Mae, the way she responded to him and the way she made him respond to her, was unlike anything he'd ever felt before.

"I'll make sure she understands."

"Understands what?" James sounded exasperated.

"Understands that she doesn't want someone like me. Yes, she needs someone who's into more than just spankings. She needs pain play, and more extreme domination. But she doesn't want what I am, what I'd do to her."

"Are you sure about that?"

"No, but I am sure that if she's going to explore this she needs a regular play partner—a commitment."

James shook his head. "It's a shame; the two of you have something."

Xavier wouldn't insult what he felt for Mae, or what she'd gone through, by denying it. "Mae deserves to be collared and bound. I can't do that."

James looked at Xavier's masked face. "I know, and I'm sorry that's the case. For you as much as for her."

When James left, Xavier pulled Mae closer. Giving in to impulse, he kissed each eyelid, her cheeks, and the corners of her mouth. He'd never seen anything as beautiful as Mae writhing in pleasure, never felt anything as powerful as knowing that though there were more hands on her than his, each bit of pleasure she felt was by his will.

It was time to change the plan, to skip ahead a few steps. The sooner he started to put emotional distance between them the better.

But that could wait a few hours. Right now he needed to hold her.

THE KISS WOKE HER. MAE KEPT HER EYES CLOSED AS awareness returned slowly. Her body was still heavy with exhaustion, but she was vaguely aware that she was lying on something soft.

Warm lips slid along her jaw to her neck.

"Mae." Her name was a plea.

"Master." She reached into the darkness, found his strong shoulders. "Xavier."

The heavy weight of a male body settled over her. Mae, eyes still closed, moaned as her nipples brushed against his bare chest. She trailed her palms down his naked sides to his hips.

"Touch me."

Her questing fingers found the hard length of his cock. He was long and thick, his balls already drawn up tight to his body. She should open her eyes, look at what she held, but she was too tired, and this was only a dream anyway.

Mae toyed with the tip of his cock, rubbing the wetness she found there down the shaft.

Then he was pushing her thighs open. She winced slightly as her sore muscles protested, but then his cock was at the entrance to her body. Mae whimpered when he entered her.

"Are you too sore?" Kisses rained down along her cheek and temple.

"Go slow," she replied.

Inch by inch he pressed into her, opening her wide and filling her—not just her body, but filling the well of need deep inside.

When he was fully seated, Mae wrapped her arms and legs around him, clinging to him as he thrust into her. She shivered in pleasure that wasn't quite an orgasm, but was enough to have her moaning.

"Mae, yes." His face pressed against hers, and she was sad to realize that even in her dreams he wore the mask. Then he was slamming into her, groaning as he came.

When he was done and pulled out of her, Mae curled up on her side.

"Go back to sleep." A final kiss to her brow was the last thing Mae remembered of the strange, sweet dream.

CHAPTER 8

Mae stepped out of the shower and wrapped a towel around her head. It felt glorious to be clean and well rested. The last thing she remembered was falling asleep on Master Xavier's lap after that ridiculously intense scene in the Library. She'd slept for close to ten hours, waking at midnight in the same bed she'd used last night. But unlike before she'd slept well, without the restlessness and nightmares that had plagued her the first night. She'd had one vivid sex dream about Xavier, so real she'd still been able to taste his kiss when she woke. Mae might have slept through until morning if someone hadn't set the bedside alarm clock to go off at twelve a.m.

She'd found a note under a water bottle waiting beside the chiming alarm.

1:30 a.m.
Iron Court
Your choice of attire
X

Mae didn't have time to dry her hair, so she braided it before putting on the only other outfit she'd brought with her for the weekend. The steampunk-style under-bust corset and leather panties were a bit less girly than her normal clothes. They were both prototypes, and Mae was glad she'd chosen to test them out this weekend.

She put on an off-the-shoulder sheer lace shirt under the corset, the lace spaced widely enough that it was not hard to spot the pink of her nipples.

Next she put on the panties which were modeled after vintage lingerie cuts—high in the waist and nearly straight across the top of the thigh. These were made of thick brown spandex with panels of faux leather to give it a steampunk look, and there were decorative bits of chain at one hip. The embellishments matched the clasp closures down the front of the corset. She finished the look with sheer white thigh-highs and gold pumps with lacings up the heel that mimicked rope bondage.

Examining herself in the mirror, Mae decided that she did like the outfit. When she got home on Monday she'd make the call on the new line. Though it was different from her original brand—a brand Mae was mother-bear protective of—she could imagine the girl who would buy this and wear it, which was what mattered.

Wishing that she had time to dry and curl her hair, which would help soften the look, Mae instead applied her makeup, and then, with twenty minutes to spare, left the Subs' Garden.

This time no one looked twice at her. With the most obvious of her marks covered, Mae no longer wore the evidence of her submission for all to see. She regretted that—not that she was going to go back and strip—but she'd liked showing off Master Xavier's domination of her.

At this hour of night the club was alive with activity. Subtle lighting made it easy to see where she was going in the myriad of indoor-outdoor spaces, but didn't detract from the darkness of the night. Voices spilled from the library and dining room, but Mae wasn't tempted to stop. Quick steps carried her toward Master Xavier.

When she rounded the corner and saw the Iron Court, her feet slowed. The statuary garden was lit not only with strategic landscape lighting, but by dozens of torches, clustered around a small stage that had been erected in the center. A few Doms were milling around, and when she appeared, their attention snapped to her. Mae snuck a quick glance at the stage, which was three feet off the ground and roughly five feet by five feet, then knocked on the door of the room where she'd first met Xavier.

"Come in."

A sense of *deja vu* washed over Mae as she opened the door. Had it only been twenty-four hours ago that she'd stood here, with no idea who, or what, waited for her on the other side?

Master Xavier wore a gray dress shirt instead of the tight, sleeveless black top he'd had on earlier. It was open mid-way down the chest, exposing golden. The sight of him made her fingertips tingle.

He was standing beside the armchair he'd used the first night. A plain wooden chair held the place of honor in the center of the room.

"Master Xavier." Mae closed the door behind her.

He crooked his finger.

Mae's whole body responded to the casual command—her nipples hardened under the lace, wetness flooded her pussy, and her mouth went dry.

She stopped a few feet in front of him, skin tingling in anticipation of his touch. He looked her up and down, the corner of his mouth kicking up in just the hint of a smile. Reaching out, he tugged her braid, then ran his hands down to her breasts—pinching her nipples and rubbing the lace against the sensitive buds. Mae arched her back, offering him more, offering him everything.

Xavier released her and pointed to the plain chair.

Mae took a seat, knees together, hands braced on either side of her thighs.

Xavier circled her, occasionally dipping one hand into her top to fondle her breasts. When she leaned forward slightly, brushing her cheek against his arm as he passed, Xavier thumbed her lower lip, then stroked her neck. The quiet room made it easy to forget everything but these strange wonderful feelings he elicited in her. He tugged her shirt down enough to expose her right nipple, flicking it with his thumb until she arched her back and gasped.

Mae was perilously close to coming, aroused to the point of orgasm by nothing more than his presence and a few touches. He stopped, which was both a relief and a disappointment, and took a seat.

Half in shadow, he seemed lazily dangerous, like a jaguar napping in the sun. "Blindfold, ball gag, soft beating, biting, breast bondage, being serviced, and light bondage." Xavier tapped his fist against the arm of the chair. "Those are the checklist items we've done."

"Yes, Master Xavier."

"Those are also the lightest items on the list."

Mae shivered, remembering what was still to come.

"I've taken you to your limits, pushed you further than you ever have been before. Am I correct?"

"Yes, Master Xavier."

"And you've enjoyed it?"

Mae nodded quickly.

"I have too." Xavier sat forward, bracing his arms on his knees. "But I need more. I do not play on the darker side of the spectrum because I like it. I do it because I need it. Do you understand, Mae?"

She dropped her gaze. "I bore you."

"You are anything but boring. Being with you has challenged

me as a Dominant. Helping you discover the depth of your submission is rewarding." His tone deepened, hinting at the darkness within him. "But I do not come here for that. I come here because I need things."

"What things, Master? I'll do them." For him, with him, she wanted it all.

He rubbed one hand over the smooth crown of his mask. When he spoke he kept his head down. "You will, at least until the game is done. But understand now I have to satisfy my own needs. I will do things to you that may hurt you or scare you. You trust me, and I am trusting you to use your safe word when needed."

"I'm not afraid." But her voice shook.

"You should be." He stood and cupped her chin, forcing her to look up at him. "You should be, because I've never tasted anything as sweet as your submission, and it makes me want to push you harder."

"I'm willing, Master."

He hesitated and Mae wondered what he was waiting for— all she needed was the chance to show him that she was willing, that she could submit in a way that would fulfill them both.

Xavier walked away, plucking some things off a table along the wall.

"For the rest of the night you will not speak unless spoken to. You will keep your gaze down unless I give you permission to look at me." With each word his tone hardened until it was almost as if he were a stranger—a cold, menacing stranger. "At no time will you attempt to cover yourself, or otherwise interfere with what I'm doing.

"Do you understand?"

"Yes, Master Xavier." Mae curled her fingers around the edges of the chair, keeping her gaze down.

"Spread your knees. You are not to close your legs unless I give you permission. Understand?"

"Yes, Master."

He grabbed her hair, jerking her head back. Mae yelped at the unexpected pain, but she opened her thighs, spreading her legs until her knees were on either side of the seat.

"Do you, Red? You keep your legs spread because this is mine now." His free hand patted her pussy, just hard enough to make her glad for the slight protection the panties offered. "Hold out your arms."

Rough rope wrapped her wrists, the binding quick and rough, nothing like the elegant bondage from this afternoon. With a jerk, Master Xavier lifted and folded her arms, pushing her bound wrists down until her hands were behind her neck. He tied the trailing ends of the rope to one of the rungs of the chair back, the tension on the rope strong enough that she had to arch her upper body to relieve the tension.

The position lifted her breasts, and Mae suddenly knew what was about to happen.

Xavier picked up her braid. "I like this." He pulled the strands apart, then threaded some rope through the braid itself. Mae started to protest, but the words didn't come. He'd ordered her to remain silent, and so she didn't speak as he tied the rope now woven and knotted through her hair to the upper rung of the chair, further reinforcing the arch of her back.

Another rope went around her waist, ensuring she couldn't scoot forward, and finally he bound her legs open, looping rope around first her left knee, then around the back of the chair, before tying it off at her right knee.

Though the bondage was far less elaborate than what he'd put her through earlier, Mae felt it more acutely. The scratchy rope and rough handling made it clear that this time the bindings were not about her pleasure...but about his.

That realization, that what Master Xavier was doing was about his pleasure, his need, brought a flush of arousal to Mae's skin and calmed her racing heart. She wanted him to use her this way.

There was a loud *crack* and Mae flinched. With her head pulled back, she couldn't see much except the ceiling. Xavier appeared in her field of vision. Unsure how to keep her gaze downcast when she was in this position, Mae closed her eyes.

Something traced a figure eight pattern on her chest above the edge of her lace top. Mae licked her lips and fought back nervous shivers.

"Open your eyes, Red."

Xavier was standing beside the chair, close enough that she could easily see him. He held up his hand, showing her the whip he held. It was at least three feet long, with a soft flexible tail at the end that he'd folded back and was holding in place at the handle. Despite her resolve to be strong, she let out a frightened little gasp.

"This is one of my whips." He released the tail and flicked his wrist. The stiff body of the whip trembled, while the flexible end snapped out, cracking in the air. "The shaft is composite and the lash is braided nylon, designed to create that whip sound."

He cracked it again. This time Mae was ready and she managed to stay perfectly still.

"This is not a BDSM toy. This was not designed for play. It's not even something they keep on hand here. I purchased this from an equestrian store, and do you know why?"

"No, Master Xavier," she whispered.

"Because when I whip a submissive, I want a carefully crafted tool. I want maximum impact."

He folded the lash back against the shaft, then used the tip of the stiff part to trace patterns along her upraised arms, tugging at her lace sleeves. The whip teased her nipples, which despite her fear were stiff, the left still semi-hidden beneath her shirt. He caught her right nipple on the edge of the whip, flicking it hard enough that she whimpered.

Xavier reversed his hold on the whip and pressed the butt handle of it against her sex. Mae's hips jerked, the legs of the chair scraping against the tile from the force of her movement. Though she was afraid, her body betrayed her enjoyment of this rough, masterful handling. She was wet and aching, wishing she had come to him naked, so that now there would be nothing separating her vulnerable body from his brutal touch.

"If you want it, beg me, Red. Beg me to whip your breasts."

"Please, Master, please."

"Please what?"

"Please whip me." She stuttered over the words, but still she said them. "Please whip my breasts."

Xavier stepped back, where she could no longer see him. Mae closed her eyes. Dread and anticipation—an uneasy mix of emotion—were making her stomach churn. She braced herself, ready for the first blow, but nothing happened. The silence pressed down on her closed eyes, made each breath heavy. Time passed and all she could do was wait.

Crack.

Mae screamed in surprise and fear. She felt a slight thump on her belly. She waited, but there was no pain. Again the whip cracked, and again the lash struck her well-protected midsection. He whipped her again and again, each terrifying whistle-crack blow making her twitch and flinch, but she felt nothing more than a small thump under the thick leather of her corset.

It wasn't enough.

Frustration flared to life in her belly. She wanted to feel the sting of the whip, wanted him to mark her and hurt her. When she couldn't take it anymore, she broke his command for silence and begged.

"Please, Master. Please whip me."

He growled and then his hands were on her breasts, jerking

the lace shirt down and tucking it roughly into the top of the corset.

She heard the click of his heels on the tile as he moved closer.

"Open your mouth."

The whip pressed between her teeth and she had to bite down to hold it in place. He was standing behind the chair, close enough that her fingers brushed against the rigid line of his cock.

Mae opened her eyes. Xavier was looking down at her, his chest heaving, his eyes seeming to burn with emerald fire. He grabbed her roughly by the back of the neck.

"Eyes closed," he growled.

XAVIER WATCHED AS MAE OBEDIENTLY CLOSED HER eyes. He was fighting his urges—the urge to whip her until she came from nothing more than the pain he inflicted on her breasts. The urge to cut the ropes, drag her to the floor, and fuck her.

He would do neither. At least not yet. He'd promised himself time with her lovely breasts, and he would not let his base urges deny him this opportunity. Her body was bowed and stretched, her breasts lifted like sweet offerings.

Taking the pink tips in his fingers he pinched them, lifting her breasts. Mae moaned around the shaft of the whip, the sound an intoxicating mix of pleasure and pain.

He slapped her right breast, just hard enough to sting, then repeated the blow on the left. Pausing, he lifted the whip from her mouth, laying it over her thighs within easy reach. He wanted her to be able to use her safe word if she had to.

Xavier slapped her breasts again, this time making sure he got her nipples. She gasped and whimpered. Her fingers brushed his cock as she twitched and Xavier's knees trembled. He would not be able to make the scene last much longer—his need for her was too fierce.

He spanked her breasts until they were flushed pink, until Mae no longer jumped with each blow, but lifted her chest higher. He rewarded her with a final strike to each nipple.

Taking the lunge whip off her lap, he carefully detached the lash from the shaft, replacing it with a six-inch popper, designed to make that delightful *crack* noise that evoked visions of a bullwhip. He would never risk hitting a submissive with a tailed whip—though he'd had some who begged for the bullwhip, even after he explained that it would leave them scarred. Instead he used the long lash of this whip, like his bullwhip, to open the mind to the darkness. Xavier tested it against his thigh, making sure the popper wouldn't fly off. Mae stiffened slightly, probably trying to figure out why the sound was different.

Stepping up beside her, Xavier laid the shaft on her breasts, pressing it against her hard enough that there could be no doubt what it was. Mae's sweet, kissable lips parted and she let out a long slow, breath.

She was ready.

With a quick flick of his wrist, Xavier struck her breasts. The *thwack* of the shaft was chased by the cracking sound of the popper snapping the air. Mae gasped, the sharp breath making her abused breasts bounce. Xavier rubbed the whip over her breasts, catching her nipples as he did so. He gave her time, gave her the chance to change her mind.

But the lovely Mae didn't use her safe word, didn't retreat into herself or do anything else that would tell him he had to stop.

Xavier struck her again, this time hard enough that a faint pink line appeared. Then again.

He alternated strikes above and below the nipple. After six he switched sides, making sure her breasts got an even amount of attention. Each bounce of her breasts, each gasp and sigh, made Xavier's cock throb.

Her skin was now nicely marked, her nipples turgid little points. Knowing the end was near, he laid a hard blow on the undersides of her breasts, just below the nipples. Mae screamed, jerking so hard that the chair slid a few inches. She tried to curl up, her upper body twisting awkwardly. Xavier slid the whip between her back and the chair, applying pressure. It was a reminder, and invitation for her to return to her previous position. For a long moment he thought she wouldn't react and he prepared himself for the next step, but then, with a shuddering sob, Mae arched her back, offering her breasts up for the next blow.

The courage that took, the bravery and faith she had in letting him take her to this dark place, was the most beautiful thing he'd ever seen. Xavier longed to kiss her, but the time for that was over.

Thwack.

A thin red line, darker than the pink marks that had come before it, blossomed on her pale flesh. Mae screamed, but then she moaned, her head twisting side to side.

Tossing the whip down, Xavier put one knee on the seat of the chair between her spread legs and leaned over her. Taking a breast in each hand, he squeezed hard.

"Open your eyes. Look at me."

There was a storm in her eyes—as if a hurricane was swirling inside her. She was giving him everything she had, everything she was. And in return she demanded all of him, all the darkness and rage that he bottled up every day.

Wanting, needing, to taste that sweet pain, he took her nipples in his mouth. He wasn't gentle. He bit and sucked, pinched and pulled, drawing on her breasts with hungry hands and mouth. Mae's gasps turned into cries. Rope creaked as she strained against her bonds. Xavier released her, then jerked his belt from the loops. Doubling it in his hand, he choked up until he held a fold that was no more than four inches long.

The leather belt struck the center of her breast, slapping the aching nipple.

"P-please, Master." Her teeth were nearly chattering she was shaking so hard, but it wasn't with pain.

Xavier slid two fingers into her mouth. She bit down, then began to frantically suck on them. He spanked her other nipple.

Mae came. Her already tightly bound body went tense. He could see the muscles in her upper arms, neck, and thighs straining even as her teeth clamped down on his fingers so hard he wondered if she'd broken the skin.

Tossing the belt to the side he squeezed her breasts, holding her as the last of the orgasm rippled through her. Her jaw relaxed and he pulled his hand away.

"It's not enough." The words were faintly baffled, and he wasn't sure if she was talking to him or herself.

Xavier rose and stared down at her. "You came."

Mae's storm-filled eyes met his. "It's not enough."

Grabbing her head, he kissed her savagely. The need he'd held in check slammed against his control, causing cracks in the armor he wore to survive. "No, it's not."

He flicked open his pocket knife and cut through the ropes that bound her to the chair. With her hands still tied together he jerked her up, then dragged her a few feet and forced her to kneel on the seat of the armchair facing the back. Standing behind it, he pulled her upper body down so her midsection was on the padded back and her abused breasts hung exposed and vulnerable below her.

Xavier jerked on the fastenings of his pants, shoving them down just enough to free his cock. He was wet with pre-come, so hard it was almost painful.

He wrapped her braid around one of his hands. "Open your mouth."

The head of his cock slid past her pink lips and into her warm mouth. Xavier thrust, pushing deeper until he felt her throat close around him. He held there then withdrew just enough for her to take a deep breath through her nose, then thrust back in. Mae adjusted her position, bracing her elbows on the chair so her head was higher and at a better angle to accept his cock. Another submissive wouldn't have dared move, but not his Mae. He realized for her the rules weren't as important as the pleasure...and the pain.

He started fucking her mouth in truth, using the hold on her hair to guide and control her. Mae swallowed as his thick length pushed deeper into her, past the point of comfort, to the place where there was no doubt that this was about control and domination.

Xavier reached under her with his free hand and pinched one of her nipples. Mae gasped around his cock, and he took advantage of the moment to pick up the speed of his thrusts. The wet sound of his cock sliding into her mouth was punctuated by her muffled moans as he abused her nipples.

Xavier looked down at her—her lovely body submissively bent before him, her red hair coming loose from the braid to spill around her shoulders. Along the edges of her panties he could see a few marks from the flogging. She was lovely in her submission—not helpless, because even now he sensed that in her core she was still in control. Not of her body, because that belonged to him, but of her mind. He'd opened the door, showed her the darkness on the other side, but it had been her choice to step through. Very few Doms were ever privileged enough to feel this—the humbling power of mastering a submissive who only grew stronger the more he or she gave.

Xavier came, one hand tangled in her hair, the other grabbing the waist of her panties and jerking them up so the fabric ground against her pussy. Mae shuddered through her own orgasm as she sucked the last of his come from his body.

Xavier's legs were trembling when he stepped back. A blessed peace filled him. It was like silence after a lifetime of throbbing noise, or dawn heralding the end of a ceaseless night. He dropped to his knees and rested his forehead against the chair. Mae's cheek dropped to rest on his head, her still bound arms dropping around his shoulders.

She held him as he shuddered and shivered through the emotional release that he'd come here looking for, and that had been building inside him since he first touched her.

For the first time he didn't think about her—what she needed or was feeling. He took rather than gave. Took the release, took the comfort of her touch. He didn't know how long he knelt there, but when he finally sat back he could not pretend that this had been just another session with a sub.

A rush of fear made him get to his feet and turn away from Mae. He'd meant this to be a simple breast whipping, a primer to what he'd planned to do to her in the courtyard. It should not have affected him like this. He should not have felt as if he'd been turned inside out.

He looked back at Mae. She was still kneeling on the chair, elbows propped on the back. She opened her mouth, but when their gazes met she dropped her eyes and closed her mouth. She slowly lowered her upper body until her midsection rested on the back of the chair, resuming the position he'd first put her in.

She'd given him everything he'd asked, more than he could have hoped for, and now she was willing to give him more.

Xavier bowed his head. He was a coward, something he'd sworn never to be. It was time to stop pretending that what he had with Mae was simple, or that he'd be willing and able to give her up when this was done.

He helped her off the chair, taking a seat and pulling her into his lap. She cuddled her head against his neck and rested her still bound hands on his chest.

Xavier kissed her forehead. If it hadn't been for the game, he might have ended the scene here, taking her to a bed where he could fuck her at his leisure. The overseers had said that this checklist game was about pushing themselves. There was almost nothing on the checklist he wasn't willing to try or do, so he'd assumed that Mae was his challenge. Mistress Faith must have seen that she was more than sweetly submissive, and in need of a guide to the darker end of the spectrum. Once he'd seen her masochistic tendencies Xavier had understood why, though they seemingly had nothing in common, he and Mae had been paired.

He knew now that she wouldn't use her safe word, wouldn't back out. She'd take all he'd give her, and she'd be a better submissive for it. But being pushed that far, that deep, could take its toll, and Xavier feared that though Mae would submit to what he had planned, she'd hate him for it.

CHAPTER 9

M ae practiced breathing—in, out, in, out. She'd have thought that by this point in her life she'd have something that fundamental mastered, but it was as if Xavier had drained her of everything… only to fill her back up again. What she'd just been through should have been less intense than this afternoon's session bent over the barrel in the library, but it had been far more so. And the most intense part had been at the end, when Xavier had dropped to his knees. He'd been shaking as if he would break apart into a million pieces, and she'd been gripped by the need to hold and protect him from whatever was raging within.

In that moment, with her body still aching from his touch, she'd had to acknowledge that she had feelings for him. Feelings that went far beyond what a sub should feel for a Dom. Falling in love with a Dom was an amateur mistake, and one she'd never been in danger of making until now.

Once she got away from him, once the game was over, these crazy feelings for him would surely fade. This sense that fate had brought them together was simply a byproduct of their intense play and her own conflict over this new direction her sexuality was taking.

When Master Xavier urged her off his lap, Mae sank gracefully to her knees. Her breast brushed his leg and she winced. Looking down, she was both shocked and pleased by the state of her breasts. They were pink all over from his hands with thin red lines from the whip. Her nipples were plump and still erect. With each breath she was aware of the way the air danced over her skin.

Though she'd come twice—the first time from nothing more than rough breast play, which she'd never have imagined was possible—Mae was still aroused. Her panties now felt like a chastity belt, designed to torment and keep her from her pleasure.

"Stand up; take off your clothes."

Hiding a smile of delight, Mae gingerly pushed to her feet. Xavier cut the bindings on her wrists, freeing her to obey his command.

First she undid the latches on the front of the corset. Peeling it back, she took a few deep breaths, reveling in the freedom. Next she stripped the steampunk undies down and off. The crotch was soaked and the smell of her arousal flooded the room.

She tugged the sleeves of the lace shirt until her arms were free, intending to push it down over her hips.

"No, take it off the other way. Slowly."

Mae shivered, glad that he wouldn't let her get away with anything, glad that he wanted her to feel everything he did to her. Crossing her arms she started to pull the shirt off. The lace felt like sandpaper against her sensitive nipples. She was trembling by the time it was off. She went to remove her shoes and stockings, but he shook his head and she left them on.

"Hands together behind your neck."

Mae did as she was ordered, her beaten breasts now proudly

on display. He examined her, his gaze almost a physical weight on her body. Two fingers dipped into her pussy, massaging her clit. Mae's knees went weak, but his touch was gone far too soon. She watched, mesmerized, as he raised his hand and tasted her. She remembered the way she'd felt when he'd pushed his fingers into her mouth, the way she'd bitten him, too lost in the mad combination of pain and pleasure to consider exactly what she was doing.

"Put the corset back on."

Questions and comments were right there on the tip of her tongue, but she swallowed them, choosing instead to give him the silent obedience that would free him to do whatever wonderful, painful things he had planned.

She'd adjusted the lacing at the back of the corset before even coming to Las Palmas, so it was easy enough to quickly slip it around her belly and fastened the closures down the front. Above and below it she was naked, her breasts and pussy on total display. The constriction of the corset felt odd contrasted with the nakedness of her most intimate places.

Master Xavier grabbed her wrist, tugging until she fell against him, her breasts brushing his chest. "We're not done, Mae. It would be easier if we were, if I could ignore everything and fuck you the way I want to."

Mae's eyes widened at the grim tone of his voice.

"You're masochistic—you enjoy pain, you feel it the way other people feel pleasure. I don't know how you went this long without being tested, but now that you know, you won't be able to go back."

Her stomach churned.

"You'll have to learn your new limits. And you'll have to learn to protect yourself. Masochistic submissives are the most vulnerable in our community."

"Why are you telling me this, Master?" It was the kind of lecture you gave someone before you left them.

"I'm telling you because you need to hear it. And you need to face what it means." Xavier handed her a pair of simple leather cuffs. "Put these on, count to one hundred, then come outside."

THE TORCHLIGHT LENT A PRIMITIVE AIR TO THE already imposing Iron Court. There were more people there now than there had been an hour ago. Some were seated on benches placed on the paths between the statues, others were kneeling and still more were standing around the outer rim of the torchlight. In the middle of it all was the stage. A few short metal buckets sat on one corner, and a large T-shaped wood structure was mounted to the edge closest to her. Master Xavier stood in the center of it all. He'd stripped off his shirt and his bare chest seemed to glisten in the light. With the dark pants and hood he looked like an executioner waiting for the condemned.

When she emerged all eyes turned toward her. Mae dropped her gaze and swallowed.

Run.

She clenched her fists, fighting back the impulse. She trusted Master Xavier, and as scared as she was, she wanted this—whatever dark thing was about to befall her. If he wanted to do it to her, then she wanted to experience it.

The click of her heels was loud on the tile until she stepped onto the crushed sandstone path that led to the center of the court. She could feel the gazes of the crowd—they were looking at her red and beaten breasts, at her marked ass and exposed sex.

She mounted the steps up to the stage. When she reached the top Master Xavier's hand was there, guiding her forward. He took her hips in his hands and turned her to face the corner, where the metal containers were. One was a bucket—filled nearly to the top with water.

The other was a brazier, full of glowing red coals. The handles of three branding irons protruded from the fire.

"No!"

Mae jumped back, smacking against Master Xavier. She shouldn't be shocked—this elaborate set-up and the way he'd spoken to her just moments ago were all clues that this was coming. She'd hadn't seen, hadn't wanted to see.

Xavier steadied her, then took a deliberate step back so he wasn't touching her.

"Branding is one of our checklist items, Mae."

"No, no." Panic was clawing at her throat.

"Are you using your safe word?" Someone in the crowd called out the question, clearly concerned for her.

Mae opened her mouth. *Banana.* All she had to do was say it.

Instead she looked at Xavier. "This is on your checklist?"

He nodded. "I can see the beauty in marking a submissive in this way, if she chooses to bear her submission like this."

"Is this...like collaring?" It would make sense if this were about permanently showing ownership.

"No, Mae. We are not bound. This branding would mean that you submitted fully to me in this moment. Nothing more. Nothing less."

Her heart was breaking and she couldn't breathe. Mae folded her arms against her chest, only to cry out when her breasts throbbed.

"On your checklist, did you say you wanted to be branded?" His tone was firm.

"Yes, Master."

"And now you are presented with that opportunity."

She whimpered and dropped her head.

Xavier touched her cheek. "This is what safe words were made for."

Though she heard him, all she could think about was his touch. It was nothing more than his knuckles stroking her face, but it made all the difference. Mae exhaled, a trance-like calm settling over her. He'd warned her both about himself and about her own desires.

This was the turning point. She could walk away, or she could embrace this.

And then, when her time with him was over, Mae would have his mark. She'd have a way to remember what it had felt like to dance in the dark. Even if no one else ever touched her the way he had, she'd remember these feelings—the pride and desire of walking through the club wearing the marks of a flogger, the delicious helplessness of being mastered by a man who found release by marking her flesh, and above all the way he'd looked at her.

"No, Master."

"You have to say your word, Mae."

"I mean no, I'm not using my safe word." She raised her voice and heard the crowd mutter. "I'm ready."

He took a deliberate step back. Doubt bit at her once his touch was gone, but she clenched her fists and firmed her resolve.

"Mae, this is not a challenge. No one here doubts your submission. Least of all me."

"Thank you, Master."

He snarled, chest muscles flexing. "Use your safe word, damn it."

Mae shook her head. "No, Master."

"Xavier, if you've changed your mind, you too have the right to safeword out of this item." Though Mae couldn't see the speaker, she recognized Mistress Faith's voice.

Their gazes met, and in his eyes Mae saw a terrible dark need.

"I want to brand her. I want to mark her." Master Xavier's

deep voice made the words poetry. "I want to taste her pain and submission and the pleasure it brings."

There were murmurs from the crowd, but she didn't care. Her whole world had narrowed, until all that mattered was his green eyes, staring at her from behind the mask that hid nothing of his soul.

Xavier pointed at the T-shaped wood structure. "If you want this, attach your cuffs to the chains. I will not bind you. You will do it yourself."

Mae looked at the simple cuffs she'd put on. They were one thin piece of leather, held closed by a buckle. A D ring near the closure was the only hardware that distinguished them from a cuff bracelet. It seemed odd that these simple things would be what bound her.

The crosspiece of the T came to just below her breasts. A short chain with a carabiner clip dangled from each end. Using two hands she got her left wrist clip in with no problem. The right took her longer, and she had to stretch and wedge the clip against the wood in order to press the latch and push the D ring in. Her fingers were shaking by the time she was secured, and doubt clawed at her.

She wrapped her fingers around the chains, holding tight.

Footsteps thumped on the wooden stage. "Look at me, Mae.

Turning her head, she watched as Xavier held up a branding iron, the tip glowing red. He pushed it down on the stage and the wood hissed and sizzled. When he lifted the brand, an "X" was burned into the boards.

Mae felt nauseous. The idea of that heat searing against her skin was too much. She shook her head, raising her gaze to Master Xavier's. There was fire in his gaze, a fierce desire to master her body in this way. The desire to submit warred with fear and she dropped her gaze, struggling to sort out her feelings.

She didn't want this because it would hurt, she wanted it

because he wanted to do it to her. Wanted what would come after—the permanent record of what they'd meant to each other.

She was vaguely aware of the sound of water hissing as he dunked the brand into the bucket, though she couldn't see it happening. When he touched her ass Mae screamed, then shuddered when she realized it was just his hands.

"Spread your legs, Mae."

She was shaking too much to obey. He forced them open, then pressed two fingers into her pussy. The penetration sent spikes of pleasure through her. She focused on that—the feel of his fingers inside her.

"I want you to come for me. I want to feel you shaking with pleasure." He brushed her hair aside and kissed her neck. "Can you come for me, Red?"

His fingers scissored around her clit and Mae screamed, her whole body bowed back. Knowing that there was a crowd looking on only spurred her arousal. She shamelessly pumped her hips on his hand, grateful to have this to focus on—the kinky pleasure that she understood so much better than the dark needs he raised in her.

Her orgasm was still shuddering through her when he pulled back. Mae had a moment to focus, to remember where she was, and what was about to happen.

She felt the heat a second before something hard pressed against her right butt cheek near her hip.

Mae screamed. She screamed in terror and in satisfaction. She screamed as the heat penetrated her. It was hot, painfully hot.

...But it didn't burn.

She sobbed, falling forward against the wood support as her trembling knees gave way.

It didn't burn.

That one thought rattled through her. The pressure of the

brand was gone from her skin, having stayed there not more than a second or two.

Xavier wrapped his arms around her, one at her waist, the other at her shoulders, just below her neck. He pulled her back against his body, holding her as she shook. "I've got you. I've got you."

The tears came, great sobs wracking through her body. "You... you didn't?" She couldn't complete the question.

"The brand was hot, but not enough to scald you. I wouldn't do that to you, Mae."

He cupped her jaw, forced her to turn her head and meet his gaze. "It was my choice, and I chose not to mark you permanently. Do you understand?"

She could feel a dull ache on her butt where the brand had touched. Though it hadn't burned her, she was sure she'd have a mark. His grip shifted, pulling her tighter back against him. The hard line of his cock dug into her, leaving her no doubt as to what effect she had on him.

Xavier released her to undo the cuffs from the chain. The instant she lost full body contact with him she started to shake. Holding on to the T-support, she faced him. Feelings she couldn't even begin to name rocketed through her, one after another, coming so fast she couldn't process them.

Xavier reached for her, but Mae held up a hand. He stopped, eyes hot with need as he examined her.

She slapped him. Mae had no idea where it came from, but she hauled her hand back and slapped him hard across the cheek. His head whipped to the side, then slowly swiveled back to her.

Mae straightened, facing him down with every ounce of courage she had left in her body. Her breasts were heaving with her shaky breaths, her whole body ached both from what he'd done to her and the release of tension. His gaze pierced her, his mouth a hard line of anger.

Their eyes met, and Xavier's expression softened, leaving her to wonder what he could see in her face, if he knew how hard she was trying to rebuild the defenses he'd ripped down.

"Come here, Red." He opened his arms.

That was the last straw. Mae couldn't take it anymore.

Whirling, she ran from him. Stumbling down the steps, she lost a shoe, and would have fallen if someone hadn't reached out to catch her. Pushing away from the helper she kicked off her other heel and ran, tears streaming down her face.

XAVIER STOOD ALONE IN THE FIRELIGHT, WATCHING her go. The crowd was muttering, and Mistress Faith came up to say something. He didn't hear her.

He crouched on the steps and picked up her discarded heels. Cradling the silly gold things in his hand, he straightened. Without a word, Master Xavier clenched his fist around Mae's shoes and took off after her.

CHAPTER 10

Mae stumbled into the Conclave. The elegant barn was deserted, the board bearing the alphabet letters the overseers had used to explain this horrible game still in the middle of the open space.

She didn't know how to turn on the lights, so she left the door open. There was enough moonlight from that and the windows to guide her as she pushed open the heavy doors of what had been horse stalls and were now either elegant "cells" for naughty subs, or pens for horse and pony play. She found one that had a twin bed in it. With a sob she threw herself down on the mattress, grateful for whatever person had left soft cotton sheets in place.

She jerked her ruined stockings off, then removed the corset, dropping both carelessly onto the floor. Rolling onto her side she laid her palm over the hot place on her ass. The skin was sensitive to the touch, the residual pain equal to the deepest marks on her breast.

"Mae."

She rolled, looking at the open stall door where a man stood silhouetted in the faint moonlight. She wasn't surprised, but she wasn't happy either. "Go away."

He disappeared, and Mae blinked back tears. It was totally unfair of her to be disappointed that he'd left when she told him to, but right now she couldn't manage fair. Her feelings were too jumbled.

Xavier returned, toting two heavy floor candelabras. The massive iron things went with the elegant Spanish style of the mansion, but when he placed them on either side of the room and flicked a lighter, all she cared about was that he'd made it light when she wanted dark.

"Leave me alone, Xavier." She didn't call him Master, using it to push him away.

"I won't."

"What more could you want from me?"

He dropped to sit on the floor, back against the wall. "I have no right to ask for anything more."

"That's right, you don't."

"But I want to know why you ran."

"You almost branded me. Me." Mae spread her arms. "I don't even have a tattoo, because I couldn't commit to a design. I was going to let you brand me, burn me, with whatever you wanted."

"Is that why you're upset?"

Mae clenched her fists, longing to lash out at him, to break that calm until he felt what she did. "Yes. And no." She ground out the last word.

"Then why?" His eyes bored into her, and despite the walls of anger she'd erected, she felt herself responding to the command in his gaze.

"I ran because…because I was disappointed that you didn't do it." Mae leapt to her feet. "I don't even know you. I've never seen your face. But I wanted you to do it. I wanted to have you brand me so that it would always be there. I'd always feel you touching me."

Xavier rose slowly to his feet. She held out her hands. "No. Don't touch me. I can't stand it. Can't stand that you're so calm when I feel like I'm breaking apart inside."

She knelt on the bed, inching back until she hit the wall, now as far away from him as she could be. "You make me feel things that I can't even understand, and it didn't mean anything to you."

"You think that I don't feel." Xavier's voice was thick with pain. "There are days the rage inside me is enough to make me want to rip my own skin off. I hate myself for wanting this." He cast his hand out, seeming to include all of Las Palmas in the gesture. "But it's the only thing that gives me any fucking peace. You think I don't feel what you do? When I touched you for a minute everything was quiet. Everything was okay. No one's given me that before."

Mae let out a breath, her shaking subsiding as she listened to him.

"You have no idea how much I wanted to brand you. To mark you. But I can't have you."

"Why not?" Mae whispered. Couldn't he see that she wanted him, needed him, for more than just the game?

"Is that really what you'd want, Mae? You're ready to always be the obedient submissive, to spend your time bound and gagged instead of petted and fucked?"

She opened her mouth to say yes, but then looked away.

"I didn't think so." There was defeat in his voice.

That irritated her. "You need to understand, my whole life is built around being a submissive." She shook her head. "No, that's not right, at least not totally. How I've played, before—the bratty sub, the girl who gets spanking and cuddles and wears cute lingerie... that defines me. And has since I was sixteen."

Xavier's gaze sharpened. "Sixteen?"

Mae leaned back against the wall. "I grew up in this nowhere town. My mom wasn't around, and my grandma raised me, but her health was bad, and she didn't really know what to do with me. When I was in high school, I started playing around online. I found these men who were willing to send me things in exchange for watching me play with myself on webcam."

"I'm sorry, Mae."

"It's not like that. I mean looking back I'm horrified, but I was lucky. Nothing really bad happened to me. Eventually there was this one guy. He told me that I was his baby girl, his sweet little girl, and that meant I had to do what he said. I got stuffed animals and cute toys in the mail."

"A Daddy Dom?"

"Exactly, though it took me a long time to learn the terms. He introduced me to D/s."

"You weren't even legal."

She shrugged one shoulder, not wanting to defend her past right now. "Without him and that relationship I wouldn't be who I am now. When we started you called me 'little girl.' For a long time that's who I was. That was my kind of submission."

Xavier shook his head. "A Daddy/little relationship is not the same as a Master sub relationship."

"I know. That's why I'm here. After a while it wasn't enough. I got older and the man who'd introduced me to all this wasn't as interested, especially because I wasn't happy playing with stuffed animals while I had a plug in my ass. I wanted something more. But that kind of submission is part of who I am."

"There's more to you."

"You've proved that." Her words were wry.

Xavier reached for her, but stopped just short of touching her. "Just because you're masochistic doesn't mean you have to have pain play. How you submit is your choice." He retreated to the far wall. "Because who you submit to is your choice. There are plenty of excellent Doms here who'd be careful with you."

"But not you?"

"I will not collar or be bound to a sub. That's a personal rule I've had for a long time."

It wasn't unexpected, but still hurt.

They were only a few feet apart, but it felt farther. They hadn't explicitly acknowledged that they wanted this relationship to continue. That was the issue they were skirting as they talked about all the reasons it couldn't work.

"Why?"

"I don't have to explain myself to you."

Mae's hand itched to slap him again. Each word was like the jab of a knife telling her that she wanted him more than he wanted her.

"No, you don't, Master Xavier." She made sure her tone was completely neutral, the words flat.

"Don't do that, Red. Don't hide from me." There was pain in his voice.

She wanted to comfort him, she wanted to scream at him for making her feel this way only to turn around and tell her that he wouldn't be her Master in the truest sense of the word.

"I can't be the only one who's vulnerable."

At that he looked up, eyes stark behind the mask. He held her gaze just long enough for her to detect a hint of resignation.

Pushing away from the wall, Xavier turned his back to her. In the candlelight he was all smooth gold muscles that she longed to touch, to mark with her nails the way he'd marked her with a whip.

He reached up, and Mae sucked in a breath as he began to undo the hidden zipper along the back of the mask. Inch by inch the leather parted, until he'd opened it all the way to the crown of his head. With his back still to her, Master Xavier pulled the mask off.

His hair was plastered to his head, but a few combs with his fingers loosened it. At first she thought it was blond, but he shifted slightly and she realized it was more silver than gold. For a moment she wondered if he was far older than she realized, and he'd gone gray.

Xavier turned to the left, just enough so she could see his profile and Mae sucked in a breath. He was gorgeous with a classically handsome profile—arched nose, high cheekbones, and strong jaw. There was a faint line along his cheek where the edge of the mask had pressed against him.

"You're the only one I would break that rule for." He didn't look at her as he spoke.

"Why do you wear the mask?" He was being so deliberate about not facing her, not letting her see him, that Mae began to wonder.

"I wear it because I prefer it. I am a better Master with it on."

She examined his handsome face. "Are you famous?"

He sputtered out a laugh, in his surprise almost turning toward her before he caught himself. "Why would you ask that?"

"You're ridiculously good looking. You hide your identity. That makes me think movie star. Or rock star."

He didn't smile or laugh. "You think I'm handsome?"

She examined his profile again, wondering why he was behaving so oddly. "Yes, I do."

Xavier turned to face her.

The first thing she noticed was that he looked like a Disney prince with his classic features. He was younger than his graying hair led her to believe. There were faint lines around his eyes and brackets around his mouth, and at a guess she'd say he was in his early forties.

In the second it took her brain to process that information, she also picked out what was wrong with the picture. Mae scrambled off the bed, her stomach in knots.

Jaw set, Xavier turned so that the right side of his face and head was clearly visible. A massive scar marred his face from his right temple all the way down the side of his cheek to his neck. His ear was mangled, the lobe missing. He pushed his hair up, showing that the scar tissue continued back from his temple and cheekbone, eating up a portion of his scalp.

"Xavier." She raised trembling fingers, but didn't touch. "Does it hurt?"

"Not anymore. It's been a long time."

She had questions, there were things she wanted to say, but they could wait. Mae gingerly placed a palm on each of his cheeks, pulling him down so she could kiss him.

He was stiff, almost awkward, but when she traced the seam of his lips with her tongue he came alive. Between one heartbeat and the next they went from standing to lying on the bed with Xavier's big body over hers. Mae spread her legs, cradling his hips. He covered her jaw and neck with hot open mouthed kisses as she reached between them to fumble with his pants. Together they got them off, shoving them down to his knees. His cock was long and hard, and when he slid into her, Mae clung to him. Xavier turned his head, presenting the unmarred side of his face. She kissed his jaw, wanting him to know that it didn't matter, she didn't care.

Then he was thrusting into her, and it was familiar. She looked into his eyes.

"I had a dream you fucked me," she whispered.

"It wasn't a dream."

"You, ah—" She had to stop as one particularly strong thrust hit her G spot, distracting her. "—fucked me while I was asleep?"

Xavier nipped her lower lip. "No one comes that hard while they're really asleep, but nice try."

Then there was no more time for words, no space to be Master and submissive. It was just two people, looking for something, someone, to help them make sense of the world.

For one shining moment they found that peace with one another.

CHAPTER 11

The sound of a spanking woke her.

Mae blinked, trying to orient herself. She was lying on a narrow bed in a small room with walls whose upper halves were vertical bars. In a second it all came rushing back—the branding, the talk, and most of all Xavier's face.

She checked all around the bed, but there was no note from him. No sign of him at all, except for one of her shoes from last night, sitting on the ledge of the stall door.

The sound of a beating—the distinct *thwack, thwack, thwack* of leather hitting flesh—echoed through the main part of the Conclave. Mae grabbed the sheet of the bed, folding and wrapping it around herself. Her body and emotions were both raw after the last few days, and if she was going to slink back to the Subs' Garden, she'd rather not do it naked. Her fellow members had seen more than enough of her yesterday.

She opened the stall door and peeked out. It was mid-morning judging by the light that spilled in through the windows in the end wall. To her left, a half-naked male sub was chained up, his arms stretched above his head, his lower body partially covered by silky boxers. Mistress Faith stood beside him, crop in hand. When she snapped the tool against the sub's ass, Mae winced. She did not want to interrupt one of the overseers at play.

"Aren't you going to thank me, boy?"

"Thank you, Mistress."

Mae gasped. That was *Xavier*.

Mistress Faith's attention whipped to her. "Good morning, Mae. Join me."

Feeling like Alice down the rabbit hole, Mae padded over to where Xavier was chained up, circling around so she could see him. He raised his head and a rueful smile twitched the corners of his mouth.

Mistress Faith struck his ass again and Xavier snarled, chain rattling. The change from hello smile to barely leashed fury was frightening.

The Mistress laughed. "Oh, you really have changed. A pity. You were a delightful sub."

Mae could not have been more shocked. Staggering over to a bench, she took a seat, gaze ping-ponging between them.

Mistress Faith touched Xavier's shoulder, her expression one of both affection and worry, and Mae felt the first stirrings of jealousy. "This boy used to be one of my favorite subs. He started out as a rich kid playing games, but he was born for this. After he was...hurt, he couldn't submit anymore. I taught him to top, taught him to be a Dom."

He turned his head, and Mae saw the full extent of the damage to his face in the daylight. Whatever had happened to him had burned most of the right side of his head. He'd been lucky that it missed his eye, but his ear was mangled as was the flesh all down the side of his face. In the morning light she could see the twisted ridges of the scar tissues, the skin both paler than the rest of his face and darker in places where it seemed a permanent red-wine color.

He cleared his throat. "After I was burned, I took some time away from this life. Years, actually." He shifted, the chains that bound him rattling musically. "Sessions with Mistress Faith were not only enjoyable, but how I dealt with stress, before. For a while I was too busy recovering, and making some other changes in my life, to miss this. But then I came back." He seemed at a loss for words, as if he didn't know how to tell the rest of the story.

Mistress Faith tucked the whip under her arm. "When he did come back he was a much darker person. Before, he was smart, sweet, and a bit sassy. Does that sound familiar?"

Mae nodded slowly.

Xavier looked surprised by the comparison, but that didn't stop him from continuing the tale. "I couldn't submit anymore. Any loss of control was horrifying, yet I wanted pain. I wanted to feel something besides anger.

"Mistress Faith taught me to be a Dom. She saved my sanity."

Mistress Faith smiled softly and touched his cheek. "You deserve to be happy, Xavier."

He nodded, but didn't smile.

"Is that why you won't collar someone?" Mae asked. "Because you might go back to being a sub?"

Xavier growled and tried to reach for her, but the chains brought him up short. "I'm not a switch," he snapped.

Mae raised one eyebrow. "Weren't you just getting spanked with a crop?"

Mistress Faith laughed while Xavier glowered. "Oh yes, I knew you two would be good for one another."

Mae tried to smile, but the need to understand was choking her. "Why?" she asked him.

Xavier's gaze locked with hers. "If I could do it for anyone, I'd do it for you."

Tears sprang to Mae's eyes. Rising to her feet, she dropped the blanket and ran to him, throwing herself against his body.

She wrapped her arms around his neck. With his hands bound, all he could do was bend his head to hers.

"You didn't have to do this," she said.

"I wanted you to understand that I know what it's like to change."

Before he could explain further, Mistress Faith cleared her throat, tapping Mae's ass with the crop. Mae jumped when the Domme touched her. She took a step back and bowed her head, nervous at being so close to someone powerful enough to have topped Xavier and yet angry that she was still here. Angry that this other woman had touched Xavier, and that she clearly felt affection for him, and he for her.

"I'll leave you two to talk." The Mistress used the butt end of her crop to lift Xavier's chin, and Mae realized where he'd gotten that particular habit. "Don't hurt each other."

"Yes, Mistress," Mae said politely.

"The controls for the chains are over there." The older woman laughed softly. "I suggest you make use of your time with him."

With that Mistress Faith left, her heels tapping against the floor.

Mae looked from the panel that controlled the chains to Xavier, her eyes widening.

"Don't even think about it, Red."

She could tell he was tense, that he didn't really like being chained up, or she suspected, not having his mask on.

"You want a sub who's obedient." Mae inched back toward the controls.

"Yes."

"And doesn't backtalk? Or speak unless spoken to?"

"Yes." Now he sounded wary.

"Then maybe this is the perfect time for me…" Mae tapped the buttons until she put a few feet of slack in each of the chains holding up his arms. When she had them where she wanted them, she locked the controls. Xavier growled and folded his still-chained arms. "To be the kind of sub you don't want."

"Right now you're not being submissive at all."

"Oh I am, because I know that when you do get free I'm going to be in trouble, but between now and then you're mine." She found a chair and dragged it over in front of him.

"You're mine," he countered.

"Then maybe we should belong to each other."

They stared at one another, tension taking the place of teasing. When he didn't say anything, Mae took a seat and forced herself to ignore the way her heart was breaking. She leaned back and braced her bare feet on his chest.

"You brought me my shoes."

"You keep leaving them. Like Cinderella." He grabbed her ankles, jerking her forward until her ass was on the edge of the chair.

"I don't mean to." Mae inched her feet apart and his gaze dropped to the apex of her thighs. She may have set up the positions, have made it clear what she wanted, but she wasn't brave enough to order him to pleasure her.

Luckily, she didn't have to.

Xavier knelt, the slack she'd put in the chain enough that he could do so, but now his arms were slightly raised, wrists by his ears, meaning he couldn't use his hands for much.

"Come closer, Cinderella," he whispered in that deep voice. For a moment Mae was frozen, unable to reconcile her mental picture of him, which included the mask, with the face looking back at her. Then their gazes met, and his green eyes were the same. Mae hooked one leg behind his neck, pulling toward her.

"Why don't you come here?"

Xavier lowered his face between her legs and Mae stopped thinking.

"UNDO THE CUFFS, RED."

In a post-orgasmic stupor, Mae reached out and undid the clip on one cuff, her body reacting to her Master's command. The sound of chain rattling as it swung free was enough to snap her back into focus.

"Uh oh."

Mae looked at Xavier's free hand and scrambled to get away, but it was too late. Her Master caught her, dragging her to the ground and pinning her down with a knee over her legs while he unfastened his other hand. He hauled her up, holding her tight around the waist with one arm as he freed his legs, then pulled her to her feet.

"How many times did you come, Mae?"

"I lost count, Master."

He jerked her head back by the hair. "You shouldn't have done that."

"Lost count?"

He growled, but there was a hint of amusement in it. "No, used me for oral sex."

"I'm...not even a little bit sorry, Master."

He dragged her back to their little room, and spent the next few hours reminding her who was in charge.

They didn't speak about the future, or about their relationship.

"I WANT YOU TO WAIT FOR ME." XAVIER STROKED Mae's thigh. She was cuddling on his lap, her worn-out body seemingly boneless against him. It was nearing dawn Monday morning.

"Did we finish all the items on our list?"

"No. Not yet." They could have. They'd spent all day together, but Xavier hadn't wanted to focus on anyone's agenda but his own.

"So next weekend?"

Xavier stroked her hair. "No. I might not be back for at least two weeks."

"Oh, that's not too bad."

"If not it will be nine months. Maybe a year."

"Oh." Mae sat up. "You mean you want me to wait for you... for months? I come here almost every weekend."

"Yes."

"You can't ask me not to play with anyone else when you've said that you won't commit to me."

"I don't want anyone else touching you."

She was tense for a moment, fighting his hold, but then she relented, resting against him once more. "I can't imagine being with anyone else. And I don't just mean for BDSM play." There was a hint of a question in her voice.

Hating himself, he said, "You'll have to remember this can't mean we have a formal relationship."

"You mean as a Dom and sub."

"I mean in any way."

"I still don't understand."

"To be bonded is an emotional commitment, not just a physical one. That I can't give."

She sighed. "You're married."

Married people were allowed to join Las Palmas, but their spouses, assuming they were not members, had to sign legal acknowledgements. The process was designed to ensure not only that members had clear understandings with their husbands and wives, but also kept Las Palmas's secrets from being dragged into the light as part of divorce proceedings.

"No, Red. I'm not married. I won't get married for the same reason I won't collar you."

He felt her surprise, but she didn't say anything. It would be better, for both of them, if he kept quiet, but he couldn't stop himself from adding, "There are reasons I've chosen to live my life this way, but if I could change for anyone it would be you."

They were quiet, but it was not the easy silence of a moment ago. After a few minutes the tension eased, the physical closeness helping to push away negative feelings.

"It's only been three days," she whispered. "How can everything have changed in three days?"

"I wish I knew." He took a breath, let it out. "Wait for me, Mae."

"Yes, Master."

Two hours later Xavier was gone from Las Palmas and Mae was getting dressed. He'd ordered her to wait for him.

So she would wait.

CHAPTER 12

It was cold in D.C. He missed California weather. He missed *her*.

The senator's son stepped off the train, laptop bag over his shoulder, tie in place. He expertly ignored the looks his ruined face got him—the long looks followed by a quick jerk of the head when they looked away. His appearance was just another tool in his arsenal. When he testified before government bodies, as he was here to do today, he carried not only the weight of his mother's name, but his own professional accomplishments and the very visible reminder of what he and others like him were fighting for.

"Dr. Xavier?" An anxious-looking aide with two cellphones and a clunky ID badge holder waved at him.

"That's me."

"Right this way. The chairperson wanted me to thank you for coming."

"Of course. Anything I can do to help maintain or increase funding for these programs."

Three hours later he read from his prepared statement, making sure to catch the eye of each congressperson on the panel. When the hearing was done he had lunch with his mother, one of the most powerful women in Washington even in her sixties, then headed for the offices of a national radio station to give an interview about the emerging health crises in Latin America.

THE AFTERNOON SUN POURED IN THE WINDOWS, making her office a well decorated sauna. She longed for the cool of the evening. She longed for *him*.

The owner of MissyMaven, a clothing and accessory brand that specialized in non-traditional sexy attire and lingerie, female-focused toys, and gothic and punk accessories with a sexy-cute spin, stood from her desk. The small offices were above the flagship brick and mortar store on a trendy street in Santa Monica. Below, her shoppers browsed the array of Rainbow Bright inspired thigh highs, princess dog collars, frilly panties, and white leather restraints embossed with black hearts. The rapidly growing empire drew a wide variety of buyers, from those steeped in the "Daddy/little" subculture where it had first started to tweens who had no idea why there were steel rings in the "chokers" they bought. They'd recently branched out into Goth attire, adding black to the color palette for the first time, but ensuring that all the Goth-style accessories featured plenty of bows and ribbons. In the spring they'd launch a line of steampunk wear and accessories, attracting an even broader client base.

Maven Block slipped out of her office and into the small kitchen area to grab a bottle of water. There were seven staff in this office, another ten in office space above the East L.A. factory where eighty skilled artisans made the bulk of their products, and two employees in a new satellite office in London, there to help the attempted expansion into an international market.

Forbes.com had carried an article on the company last year, extolling the virtues of identifying a niche market and providing high-quality specialized products. And somehow she was in charge of it all—over 100 people who depended on her and the decisions she made for their livelihood. The business had grown from her making ruffled underwear on her grandmother's old sewing machine and selling it to other "littles," into a recognized brand and soon to be international company.

"Is it hot in your office again?" Her assistant looked up, tapping a button on the keyboard to turn down the sound of the news radio show she was streaming. "I'll call about getting the AC repair person out here again."

"Don't bother. The air works fine, the sun is just at the wrong angle." Maven adjusted the neckline of her rockabilly style dress. "What are you listening to?" For one insane moment she thought she'd heard a voice she recognized.

"Just a news show."

"Turn it up."

The program went to commercial break and Maven told herself to just go back to her office, but instead she waited, carefully wiping the condensation from her water bottle with a napkin. Her assistant was giving her a funny look, but she didn't care.

"If you're just joining us now, we have Doctor Solomon Xavier with us on the program. Dr. Xavier is the son of Senator Jane Xavier and you may remember him as the surgeon who was injured while volunteering at a clinic in Bangladesh several years ago. Since then he's become an activist for world health and an ambassador for US-led international relief efforts. He has just returned from six months spent in South America. Dr. Xavier, thank you for being on the program."

"Thank you for having me."

Mae's heart clenched at the sound of that voice.

"Maven are you oaky?"

"I'm fine. Fine."

Locking herself in her office, she turned to her computer. A second later she was staring at the image of a blond doctor kneeling in the dirt, bent over a young woman, his hands pressed to her side. There was a stained rag tied over the side of his face. The scene around him was chaos, but the photographer had captured the shock and desperation of the moment.

Mae's heart broke as she looked at the image. "Oh my poor Xavier."

———

DR. SOLOMON XAVIER PICKED UP THE MAGAZINE someone had left on the seat. He'd forgotten to take his phone charger with him when he went to the hospital and the battery had died at some point while he was in surgery. A young woman he'd aided in getting asylum in the US had undergone reconstructive surgery on her hands, which had been smashed by her "husband"—a term he used loosely because she'd been thirteen when she was married.

He still had admitting rights at major hospitals in D.C., Atlanta, and L.A. but rarely had opportunities like this to actually be a part of the surgeries he helped arrange. There were days he missed the simplicity of surgery—taking a problem and fixing it. After Bangladesh, his life had changed in more ways than he could count. The most visible was the scar on his face, but the most meaningful was him walking away from a promising career as a transplant surgeon. He'd gone from having complete control over his professional environment to facing issues and situations that he was nearly powerless to fix.

He flipped through the glossy magazine out of boredom as the train took him to his hotel. He'd be in D.C. for another day, then he was off to U.N. headquarters in New York for a fundraiser and some meetings, before returning to the Philippines to do an assessment of the medical facilities and infrastructure that the U.N. had helped put in place after the floods.

Frowning, Solomon—Sol to his friends and family—flipped back a few pages to one of the ads.

A well-endowed blonde was posed with her ass to the camera as she twisted to look over her shoulder. She was naked except for a pair of pale green lace panties with a ridiculous bow on the butt and gold heels with bondage-style lacings up the back. The caption read "these are my big girl panties." There was a small logo in the bottom corner of the page—the stylized outline of a red-headed woman with the name "MissyMaven" under it.

Solomon laughed softly and traced his finger over the logo. "Hello, Red."

———

"DR. XAVIER, THERE'S SOMEONE I'D LIKE YOU TO meet."

Solomon picked his whiskey up off the table and followed the trim young staffer from the sponsoring organization. At the moment, he couldn't even recall what group was putting on the gala fundraiser, but the beneficiary of the proceeds was a health organization that set up vaccine clinics in rural areas around the world. He'd worked with them in the past, and agreed to attend the fundraiser. He was both cynical enough to know that his "tragic" past, coupled with his family connections, made him an excellent spokesperson for health issues, and pragmatic enough to not care that he was being used. As long as the money got where it needed to go he'd do whatever was needed.

"Who is it?" he asked, experience having taught him it was better to know who he was about to meet so he could tailor his response.

"A new donor. Her contribution was unsolicited, but big enough that we made sure to rush her an invitation to this event. She asked specifically to meet you. I think she heard that radio piece you did last week."

They approached an elegant woman in a floor-length white gown. Most of the women here tonight were in black, while the men wore tuxedos. She was a dove among ravens. There was almost no fabric along her back, the garment instead held together by dozens of small gold chains, a hint that there was more to her. Ruby-red hair lay loose over one shoulder.

Solomon's steps slowed. He set his glass down on a table they passed.

"Excuse me, Ms. Block?" The sponsor representative raised his voice to get her attention.

She turned, and Solomon found himself face to face with the woman he loved.

"Thank you for waiting." The slim young man was smiling in a way that meant the donation had been very large indeed.

"Oh, I've never been good at waiting." Her lips were glossy cherry, catching the light as she smiled. Solomon's mouth went dry.

Their gazes met, and nothing else signified. Every reservation he had—about committing to someone when his job was both dangerous and taxing, about mixing his life as a Dom with what he did outside a dungeon—melted away. How stupid of him not to realize until that moment that none of it meant more than her. She was the only thing that really mattered.

"Oh, well uh, Ms. Block, this is Dr. Solomon Xavier. Dr. Xavier, this is Ms. Maven Block."

She held out her hand—not to be shaken, but with her palm facing the floor. Xavier took it, bowing slightly. For the first time in a week he felt whole. For a moment her gaze dipped and her fingers trembled in his. He squeezed her hand and she looked at him through her lashes.

"Ms. Block."

"Dr. Xavier."

"It's a pleasure to meet you." He kept the words formal and polite while inside he ached to kiss her.

"And you."

"Would you care to dance?"

"I'd like that."

C IS FOR...

CHAPTER 1

J ames examined the single sheet of paper he'd pulled from the envelope labeled "C." When the overseers of Las Palmas Oscuras, LA's most exclusive BDSM club, called all members together, a club-wide sex game was the last thing he'd imagined they'd announce. Each Dom, Master, Owner, submissive, and slave was assigned a letter of the alphabet and everything that went with it. They had to work though each kink, toy, and fetish on the BDSM checklist, which all members filled out when they joined. It was a rather intriguing idea, made all the more interesting because the Doms didn't get to choose subs—the overseers had assigned everyone partners.

Over the past year, James had played with many of the uncollared subs in the club. He liked his BDSM play pleasure-focused and never engaged in scenes that lasted too long, or took either player too deep into that dark place of truth that was so dangerous.

Beside him, Xavier, a Master with a reputation for brutal play, opened his envelope. "Fuck."

James looked over. "Problem?"

Xavier held up a glossy photo of a woman James knew—in

the biblical sense. "Mae is a lovely sub," James told Xavier. "Don't let her looks fool you. She's also very smart and has a quick wit. She's a pleasure to talk to."

"I'm not looking for a fucking therapist."

James shrugged. "I didn't say she was one." He didn't add that a resident therapist wouldn't be a bad idea at Las Palmas, whose members were wealthy, powerful, and more often than not, wrestling with some demons.

And he was no exception.

"Isn't she the one who did that ribbon bondage presentation?" The other Dom's voice dripped with derision as he flicked through the stack of papers in his envelope—the submissive's BDSM checklist, and his own.

Frowning slightly, James folded his own nearly empty envelope in half. "Just...try not to break her." BDSM play was dangerous, and that danger wasn't just physical. The emotional and spiritual damage that could be inflicted inside the delicate world of the D/s relationship was far more lasting than bruises and welts.

The subs filed out of the large converted barn, one of many buildings on the expansive adobe-style estate and the only one big enough to hold all members at once. Shortly after, the Doms started filing out too.

Once outside, James circled the building until he was out of sight, staring out at the immaculate grounds, privacy fence, and beyond that, the gold and green hills of Malibu. Leaning against the wall, he once more opened his envelope. Xavier's had been thick, containing two checklists and a photo. He had only a single sheet of paper bearing a single typed sentence.

Return next week to meet your partners.

Partners?

The overseers had said that anyone who wasn't already bonded could be partnered with someone, or someones, new. It seemed that he was in for a ménage, which was never a bad idea. But the lack of a checklist meant he couldn't peruse the inventory of items and kinks that began with the letter C.

The only one he could think of was *collar*.

Closing his eyes, James leaned his head back against the smooth plaster of the barn wall.

Collars had a million uses in BDSM play—from simple non-weight bearing restraint to posture correction and animal play.

But the most dangerous, in James's opinion, was symbolic collaring—using a collar the same way you used a wedding ring. Collars showed more than just commitment, but ownership. At Las Palmas, members in Owner/slave or permanent Master/submissive relationships were recognized as being in an exclusive committed relationship by being "bound" together, rather than collaring. He, more than anyone, knew why Las Palmas used the distinction, though plenty of couples were both formally bound by the club's rules and used the elegant simplicity of a collar.

He tapped the envelope against his palm. He had a bad feeling about the letter "C."

BETH SHIFTED HER WEIGHT TO HER LEFT HAND, lifted her right off the wood floor and flexed her wrist. A crop struck her thigh.

"Be good, girlie."

Dropping her hand back to the floor, Beth resumed her position on hands and knees, serving as a footrest for her owner. Madame Cat lifted her legs a fraction of an inch off Beth's lower back, switching which ankle was crossed on top.

The floor of the library was one of the least comfortable places to be kneeling for long periods of time, but that was where Madame Cat had decided to have her dinner. Almost everyone else in the library was also eating, and Beth's stomach growled in reaction to the delicious food smells. People went quiet and Beth lifted her head just enough to look around. Master Xavier, recognizable from the mask he wore, was leading a lovely red-haired sub through the room.

They must have been paired up as part of the checklist game. Beth had played with Master Xavier once, over a year ago. He'd complimented her on her ability to obey and her responsiveness to pain, but Beth had been able to tell that he'd never ask for her again.

That was the story of her life. She was good, but forgettable…as forgettable as a piece of furniture, which she was now serving as.

Beth bit the inside of her lip, reminding herself that anything was better than nothing. Being collared by Madame Cat was an honor and a gift.

She watched out of the corner of her eye as the lovely redheaded sub was draped backward over a wine barrel and then pleasured by nearly everyone in the room. Beth was transfixed by the sight—though the sub had been ordered not to come, she'd clearly had orgasm after orgasm from mouths and hands dancing over her body.

Beth had been kneeling here, completely naked, for what felt like days, and the only physical contact she'd had were her owner's feet on her back and the occasional strike of the crop when she moved too much.

"I need her." Master Xavier's voice only a few feet away shocked Beth, but she held still.

"Of course." Madame Cat took her feet off Beth. "Go with Master Xavier."

Beth's heart was in her throat as she pushed herself up into a kneeling position. Keeping her head down, she waited for her orders, hoping, praying that it would be something dirty and sexy. Clearly Master Xavier remembered her from their one session. Maybe she wasn't as forgettable as she felt.

"Stand up. Come with me."

Ten minutes later Beth was positioned behind the barrel. Xavier had raised his sub's head and shoulders so they were no longer lower than her heart. Beth was serving as a support—the other woman's shoulders against her breasts, her bound arms looped around Beth's neck.

It seemed that her destiny was to be either furniture or a prop. Biting hard on the inside of her lip, she was able to hold in the murky feelings bubbling inside her. With nothing better to do, she analyzed, finally deciding that the predominant emotion she had at the moment was frustration, followed shortly by boredom.

Being part of the scene, even tangentially, was certainly better than being a footrest. She now had a perfect view of the woman's spread legs and the Dom who was currently licking her. Beth's own body throbbed in response. For one insane moment she considered running her hand over the smooth white skin bound and displayed before her.

But she knew better. That wasn't why Master Xavier had asked for her. Turning her gaze away to avoid temptation and stupid fantasies, her gaze landed on Master James.

Beth sucked in air. Master James looked like a movie star—not a grungy action star, but a classic clean-cut hero. Though he was wearing slacks and a simple button down shirt, he looked as elegant as other men looked in three-piece suits.

Master James was on the top of her wish list of play partners. She'd seen him sitting with subs on his lap, his style of domination a kind of casual yet intimate mastery—as if he had no doubt that he was in control and felt no need to make a show of it. She'd watched him kiss and pet his subs while in the common spaces, touches that seemed more like those of a lover than a Master.

And oh, she wanted that.

He smiled slightly and Beth blinked, then checked behind her, but there was no one there. Was he smiling at her?

His gaze dropped to her neck and the padlocked collar she wore. Golden-brown brows drew together and Master James looked away.

Beth lowered her gaze, her face warm—embarrassment the main cause, but there was another feeling in the mix, which she identified as shame. Luckily a moment later Master Xavier freed his sub's legs and helped her off the barrel. Beth waited to see if she was still needed. When everyone turned away, focusing on other things now that Master Xavier's scene was done, Beth dropped to her hands and knees and crawled back to her owner, wincing as Madame Cat plopped her feet into place.

Only five feet from where Beth knelt, a pretty blonde submissive was urged up onto a low ottoman. The girl had an open-style gag in her mouth, drool making her lower lip glisten. The Dom, who Beth recognized but whose name she couldn't remember, had her lie on her side. Smooth black rope was wound around the sub's limbs, creating wide cuffs that bound each wrist to the corresponding ankle, and knees to elbows. With her legs tucked up against her chest her ass and pussy were fully exposed. The Dom knelt beside the ottoman and ran his hands over the girl's back, adding the occasional spank as he whispered to her, the words low enough that Beth couldn't make them out, but she could guess that they were gentle from the tone of his voice.

The Dom pulled a small, jeweled plug from his pocket, slipping it into the sub's mouth through the open gag. When it was coated in saliva he spread the cheeks of the girl's ass with one hand then teased her anus with the blunt tip of the plug. Beth watched, unable to turn away—not that she wanted to—as little by little the Master coaxed, teased, and tormented the woman, using the plug to relax and loosen the muscles of her anus, until each time he pulled away the sub frantically twisted, trying to lift her hips, seemingly desperate for the penetration.

Beth understood the feeling. She'd been wet since watching

the scene with Master Xavier and his sub, and her current view wasn't doing anything to lessen the low burn of arousal. Her nipples were tight, making her aware of each breath she took.

When the plug was finally inserted, Beth had to bite back a moan that echoed the blonde's, her own anus clenching in reaction to what she was seeing. Next a large silver egg was forced into the sub's pussy. With the woman's squeals of pleasure ringing in Beth's ears, she shifted her weight, trying to relive the throb in her own pussy. Madame Cat rewarded her fidgeting with a sharp blow from the crop. Pleasure darted through Beth, and for one exciting moment she thought she might find release too, but then her Domme went back to her conversation.

The blonde's Master had risen and taken a seat, propping his ankles on the sub's hip. Another submissive footstool. He held a small control box, a wire leading from it to the egg buried deep in the sub's wet, pink pussy. He murmured something, then the girl started gasping and twitching, her toes curling, fingers grasping nothing but air.

Beth watched as the Dom leaned back in his seat, drink in hand, appearing relaxed and at ease, yet his eyes never left the sub, his fingers poised over the control box, adjusting it according to the sub's reactions.

It was painfully simple to make comparisons between the blonde's situation and her own. Beth wanted what the other girl had, but even as the sounds of female orgasm rose to impossible-to-ignore levels, Madame Cat was more focused on her conversation than on Beth. As Beth's Mistress, that was her right, to use Beth in whatever way pleased her.

Rather than continue to watch, Beth closed her eyes and tried to ignore the sounds, hoping her arousal would fade. Eventually, it did.

Maybe it was time to give up this life. She'd thought BDSM would help her, but instead it just reinforced the fact that Beth would never be like other women. No one wanted to play with her, no one cared about her pleasure. She was as alone here as she was in the outside world.

Madame Cat had dropped hints that she might be leaving the club, or possibly moving out of LA. When she did, Beth would resign her membership. Though it would effectively mean giving up most human contact, alone might be better than feeling like this.

Bottling up her feelings, Beth settled in to the boredom of serving as a footstool and started working through calculus problems in her head.

———

"MASTER MIKAEL." JAMES NODDED TO THE OLDER MAN as he closed his overnight bag into one of the lockers the Doms and Masters used.

"James." Mikael scrubbed a towel over his head, then unselfconsciously dropped the towel around his waist and started dressing. It was just after noon on Friday a week after the checklist game announcement, and still early as far as the club's patrons were concerned. Most people arrived between three and six pm on Friday nights and stayed until Sunday. Those with more flexible work schedules came on weekdays, though Las Palmas only had catered food in the dining room on the weekends.

James wondered idly what Mikael had been up to that he was showering at noon. Either it had been a long night or he'd gotten up early and already participated in a hot and sweaty scene. As one of three overseers of the club, Master Mikael was a force to be reckoned with. It was a testament to his personal authority that he was an undisputed leader among this group of powerful people.

When he'd finished pulling on pants, a shirt, and a vest, he turned to face James. "You're here for your checklist game?"

"I am. Though I don't know who I'm partnered with yet."

"Ah, yes. We have something special for you." Mikael smiled.

"Are you going to tell me?"

"Leo was going to do it, but since you're here now..."

Mikael unlocked one of the doors marked "private" and disappeared inside, only to return a moment later holding another large envelope with the letter "C" on the front, and James's name in the top corner.

"Join me?" Mikael gestured with the envelope and James followed him to the Doms' Lounge, usually just called the Den. There were areas of the estate that were reserved for Doms and Masters and this was one of them. There were matching places where the subs relaxed away from the presence of the Doms.

"A drink?"

James shook his head. Noon was a bit too early.

Mikael poured himself something. Together they selected armchairs near the empty fireplace and sat.

"Here." Mikael handed James the envelope.

Setting it on his knee, James didn't open it, sensing that it would be better to listen to the overseer than to do what he wanted, which was to rip open the flap.

"The game is an opportunity." Mikael relaxed back in his chair.

"For us, or for you?" James had no doubt that the overseers had ulterior motives embedded in the way they'd set up the game.

Mikael hid his smile behind his glass. "An opportunity for us to do what?"

"To experiment. To see what happens when you put people together who normally wouldn't play with each other."

Mikael dropped his hand, the smile now fully evident. "And what would you do, if you were us?"

"Maybe the same thing," James admitted.

"When we realized we needed to do something to break the

club out of the rut we'd fallen into, we realized that whatever we did would involve assigning partners."

"Because you think we aren't capable of picking our own?" James was trying not to be offended. He and the other members of Las Palmas were all powerful and in control of their lives. The overseer's insinuation—that they were incapable of making decisions for themselves—rankled.

Mikael shrugged slightly, his body language conveying a sense of "you said it, not me, but yes, that's what I think."

James was tempted to protest, tempted to say that they didn't need to be pushed. If members chose to come here and simply observe, or play with the same people over and over, repeating scenes that all parties enjoyed, then why should they step outside their comfort zone. But he couldn't say that. Las Palmas had many of the trappings of an expensive country club, from the elegant interior design to the five-star catered food and top shelf alcohol, but it wasn't a place to relax. It was a place to explore the darkness inside.

The ice in Mikael's glass clicked as he raised it and took a sip, the sound drawing James's attention back to the other man. "We know you're wary of the more serious play."

James stiffened. He didn't like being reminded that they knew what he'd done, and what he'd been through. And that without them he might not have survived.

Mikael waited for a comment that never came. After a moment of silence he continued. "Your checklist game partner is someone who knows nothing but serious play."

"Partner, not partners?"

"There's a third name in there, but that individual is not really participating."

"How is that?"

"You'll see. It's her information to tell. The reason that we held back your packet was so one of us could talk to you."

"You're talking, but I'm not sure I understand what you're trying to tell me."

"Have you ever been with subs who top from the bottom? And I don't mean purposefully manipulative." The overseer stressed that point.

James was slightly surprised by the question, but nodded. "I have. Though I don't let them do it for long."

"Why do they do it? Why do they try to control the play even as they give up control of their body?"

"They're not ready. They don't trust the Dom. They don't know how to let someone else be in command."

"Possibly, but it's also a way to make sure their needs are met. It's human instinct—they're making sure they get what they desire."

"That's fair, though a well negotiated scene should guarantee that everyone's needs are met."

"And what if the sub doesn't negotiate?"

"You mean what if they rely on their checklist alone?"

"No, I mean what if the submissive won't, or doesn't, tell the Master what they want?"

James sat back and considered. "Then it is up to the Dom to discover what they really desire and need."

"Exactly."

James shifted. "That kind of emotional interrogation is not what I come here to do."

"I know that. But you're good at it. I heard about what happened with Xavier and Mae. If you hadn't talked to Mae, helped her figure out her feelings, would she and Xavier have made it through their checklist last weekend?"

"They barely made it through as it was."

"But you could read Mae."

James took a breath and looked at the sideboard. Maybe it wasn't too early for a drink. "True."

"All I ask is that you do the same with this sub. Don't take her at face value. She's incredibly obedient, and completely closed."

James frowned. Who was Mikael talking about? He thought he knew most of the members of Las Palmas, if not by name then by sight.

"Open it."

James carefully peeled back the flap of the envelope.

CHAPTER 2

B eth wrapped her fingers around the metal bars of the cage. Tensing her arms, she lifted her body weight off her ass and right leg, which was curled under her. When she couldn't hold herself up any more, she relaxed, the crosshatched bars that made up the bottom of the cage settling painfully into her flesh.

Though she'd been careful, the slight movement was enough to set the cage rocking from side to side, the ground of the dimly lit playroom five feet below her shifting dizzyingly. Beth closed her eyes until the cage stilled again.

Madame Cat had said that today they were going to play the checklist game. Since she was collared, Beth had known who her partner would be, but she'd harbored a small hope that whatever her letter was would include things that might be more interesting and pleasurable than her normal play with Madame Cat.

Those hopes had been dashed when Madame Cat had put her into this uncomfortable contraption. Shaped like an old-fashioned domed birdcage, it was just tall enough that Beth was able to sit upright, but the diameter kept her legs bent at awkward angles. Currently she had her right leg half under her, foot sticking out between the bars, her left leg folded up so her thigh was against her bare breast.

Beth sighed and laid her cheek against her knee. The cage meant Madame Cat had drawn the letter C in the game. Beth had a very good memory and was fairly certain she knew exactly what lay in store. The rules of the game, and of the club, meant that Madame Cat couldn't do anything that Beth had indicated was a hard "no" on her checklist, but Madame Cat was creative —she could probably find a way to come close without crossing the line.

Whatever anticipation and hope Beth had when her Mistress had announced that this weekend was devoted to the game died as she sat curled in the cage repeating the "C" section of the BDSM Checklist in her head.

Cages
Caning
Cattle Prod
Cells
Chains
Chastity Belts
Choking
Chores
Clothespins
Clamps
Cock Rings
Cock Worship
Collar
Corset
Cuffs

"JAMES, DARLING, HOW ARE YOU?"

James stood as Madame Cat, a lovely African American woman, breezed into the Den. She wore slacks and a silk blouse, which was far from her normal leather and chains Domme wear. His confusion must have shown on his face, because she smiled as she leaned in to kiss his cheek in greeting.

"I know, not the ideal attire, but I can't stay long."

James frowned. He'd assumed that he and his partners would spend the weekend playing the game. It was slightly annoying to know he'd come all this way for essentially nothing.

Cat shook her wrist until the slim gold watch was perfectly positioned for her to check the time. "I want to be out of here by three. Hopefully I can beat the traffic headed south."

"I was unaware we were operating under a time limitation." James kept his voice as mild as he could. The weekend did not have to be a total loss—there would be plenty of people here to play with later, and he never had trouble picking up a willing sub for the weekend.

Madame Cat frowned. "Didn't Master Leo talk to you?"

"I spoke with Master Mikael earlier."

"And he didn't explain?" Now Madame Cat's voice held the same hint of irritation that his did.

"He gave me this." James held up the envelope. "All it has is your name and a checklist for your sub. He said the rest of it was up to you to explain."

"Ah, well." Cat settled back in her chair. "I'm afraid today is my last day at Las Palmas."

"Oh?"

"I'm moving to DC. Given my new position, it's best to cut ties with Las Palmas."

James nodded. He'd heard that Madame Cat did something involving politics, which had always seemed incredibly dangerous to him—a secret life as a Domme would be a wonderful political scandal.

"I'd thought to have more time," she continued, "but my flight leaves at 7. I'm only here to uncollar Beth."

James stiffened. "You're ending your relationship?"

"Yes, which is sad because Beth is so delicious. She's quiet and obedient. Everything I could want." True regret pinched the corners of Cat's eyes.

James tapped two fingers on the arm of the leather and wood chair. "And my role is to play therapist to your sub and distract her for the weekend?"

Cat's face showed her displeasure with his tone, but James didn't care. He had no desire to spend his time dealing with the emotional messes other Doms made of their subs.

"Hardly. Beth and I are not some great love story. We are more business associates than lovers. When I told the overseers I would be resigning my membership, they told me they were announcing a new game and suggested I uncollar Beth as part of it."

James sighed. Plucking the envelope off the side table he took out a glossy photo of the submissive in question. Beth was striking rather than pretty, with brown hair cut in a ruler straight line just above her shoulders. Her eyes were equally brown, and seemed large in her fox-like face.

He recognized her, though they'd never played. Beth was one of those subs who was always around, an excellent and obedient assistant in scenes focused on others. She was most often seen playing with Doms who preferred a stricter version of BDSM play than James used. If he was remembering correctly, Cat's favorite thing to do was to use her as a footstool, pushing Beth more into the realm of "slave" than "submissive."

"If you must know, you're not the Dom I would have picked for Beth." Though Cat's tone was neutral, James could detect the slight derision in her words, could tell that she thought his type of domination was too soft.

"And Beth is not the sub I would have picked for myself," he responded curtly. But when James looked at Beth's picture, all he could think about was what Master Mikael had said, his implication that while Beth was obedient, she was also "closed."

One thing James couldn't resist was a puzzle. It was why he was so good at figuring out people's emotional states, at "fixing" subs—he liked taking clues and piecing them together into a complete picture.

"I have her waiting. I'm afraid I didn't have time to tell her anything other than this weekend was for the checklist game." Madame Cat rose. "Shall we?"

Tucking the photo back into the envelope, James stood and motioned for the Domme to precede him. "After you."

BETH LIFTED HER HEAD FROM HER KNEE WHEN THE door opened, but kept her gaze down. There were two sets of footsteps, the click of heels which she recognized as Madame Cat's, and then another set she thought sounded like a man's. She closed her eyes when spotlights flicked on, the bright white beams focused on the cage.

Her eyes were still closed when the crop struck the bottom of her right foot. The blow was unexpected and painful. Beth sucked in a breath and jerked, then wiggled around until all her body parts were in the cage.

"You're such fun, girlie." Madame's words were soft and regretful, at odds with the harsh blow.

Beth opened her eyes, focusing on the ground. She could see her Mistress's feet. Madame Cat was wearing fashionable, shiny, cream colored stilettos and ankle length gray slacks, nothing like her normal wardrobe. Beth had noticed the clothes when her Mistress had locked her in her collar and placed her in the cage, but Beth had assumed that when she returned she'd have changed. The fact that she was still in street clothes had to mean something significant.

"You know how much I've enjoyed our time together."

What was going on? Beth didn't pause to try to figure it out, knowing waiting too long to reply was disrespectful. "Yes, Mistress."

"I will miss our time together. I doubt I'll have the opportunity to play with a sub again, let alone one as obedient as you."

Questions were poised on the tip of Beth's tongue, but she held them back.

"Lean forward so I can reach your collar."

This time Beth was so startled by the command that she didn't react in time.

"Beth." Madame's voice was sharp with warning.

Grabbing the bars, Beth struggled to shift her position to obey. She was finally able to get both legs under her so she was kneeling with her feet and ankles sticking out of the bars, her upper body bent forward slightly.

Madame Cat pulled a chain from around her neck, the small, shiny key to the padlock on Beth's collar glinting in the light.

"I'm leaving Las Palmas, and can no longer be your Mistress. As of this moment I am removing my collar from you."

Despite all her training she was so surprised she looked up, but the lights prevented her from seeing Madame Cat well. Now? It was all over now? She didn't realize her Mistress was planning to move so soon.

Beth dropped her gaze, hoping her breach hadn't been noticed. Plus it allowed her to hide her expression, which she feared would show something Beth herself didn't understand yet.

She was...upset.

It wasn't the loss of the collar, or of her Domme that upset her, but her Mistress's departure meant the end of her time as a submissive, the end of yet another failed attempt to interact with other people in a meaningful way.

Madame Cat stuck her hands through the bars, stroking Beth's cheek, then slapping it lightly. "I will miss you, girlie."

Intellectually Beth knew that Madame Cat wouldn't really miss her—she'd miss having a perfectly obedient sub, but still, those words, that hint of connection, were the one thing that had kept Beth coming back.

Madame Cat unlocked the collar, then gently pulled it off, slipping it out through the bars of the cage.

Beth curled her fingers into fists. Without the weight and symbolism of the collar around her neck, the cage suddenly felt foreign and intimidating, as if she really were some captured creature rather than a willing participant in a dangerous but controlled game.

"I didn't lie to you." Madame Cat toyed with the collar as she spoke, the metal clanking softly. "This weekend really is about playing the overseers' game, about exploring the letter C." Madame Cat laughed. "It almost sounds like a children's game if you say it like that.

"What you don't know is that you and I were not the only ones assigned to this letter. We have another player."

Though her gaze was focused on the floor, Beth saw Madame Cat check her watch. "I have to leave, so I'm going to turn it over to him."

"Him" must refer to the other set of footsteps Beth had heard.

"I got to play for two of the items. Collar and cage." Madame Cat gave the cage a gentle push. Beth quickly grabbed the bars and closed her eyes as she swung through the air. Her weight shifted along with the cage, alternately forcing her body weight painfully onto her knees and lower shins.

"The rest of the letter C I leave to him." Mistress Cat grabbed the cage, holding it still just long enough to reach in with the other hand and give Beth's left nipple a hard pinch. Still holding the tip of her breast, Mistress drew the cage forward and then let go. As it swung back, Beth's nipple stretched then pulled from her Mistress's grip. Beth let out a little hiss of pain, which seemed to be what her Mistress wanted. Madame Cat sighed regretfully, then stepped back and without another word walked out of the playroom. Leaving Beth with an ease that was anything but flattering.

Beth closed her eyes as the cage swung, quickly sorting through what had just happened, and trying to assign a feeling and conclusion to each thing, a technique she'd developed to help herself process events and conversations.

She was no longer collared. The timing was surprising, though the event was not. She felt...resigned, or was it relieved?

She was still a member of the club, and because of that was still subject to the rules of the game. This negated her plan to leave the club as soon as she was uncollared. She felt irritated at having her plan disrupted.

She was not alone in this room. The "him" Madame Cat had referred to had been assigned to the letter C by the checklist game. She felt excited.

Despite her resolution to end this part of her life, the idea of playing with a new Dom was thrilling. The unknown, the possibilities, the hope of experiencing the feelings and physical pleasures that other subs talked about, was enough to have Beth's heartbeat speeding up and her skin tingling.

Her eyes were still closed when she heard the man move closer. A moment later the cage stopped swinging, then warm hands covered hers where she clenched the bars.

Please, oh please, she thought. Let this time be different.

JAMES STILLED THE SWINGING CAGE, WHICH WAS suspended at shoulder level in one of the Iron Court playrooms. The sub kneeling awkwardly inside barely reacted, except for a slight relaxation of the tense muscles in her face.

He'd carefully watched her interaction with Madame Cat, warned by Master Mikael's words. Beth was either one of the quietest, most obedient subs he'd ever seen, was so deep in subspace that all her reactions were muted under a thick layer of knee-jerk obedience, or she was just going through the motions of submission with no real emotional connection to what was happening.

He hoped, almost desperately, that it was one of the first two.

James put his hand over hers, realizing that she was white-knuckling the bars, not merely holding on. He hadn't been able to tell exactly how tense she was in her body language.

She didn't look up, didn't open her eyes, leaving him staring at her glossy dark hair, which was parted in a perfectly straight line. She was naked, though in her contorted position he could see relatively little of her body. Tilting his head he caught sight of her reddened left nipple, the lingering mark of Madame Cat's fingers a testament to how tight the grip had been, and how much self control it had taken for Beth not to cry out at something that was surely painful.

James had never enjoyed subs who were either naturally secretive with their responses or who had been trained to stifle their reactions. Not that demanding quiet couldn't be a fun aspect of a scene, especially when it was a rule that couldn't possibly be followed, but he wanted to interact with a woman, to know what she was feeling. That was much harder to do if she just lay or sat there stiff and mute.

He wondered if Beth had been trained to be this way, or if it was part of her personality.

"Hello, Beth."

She shivered slightly when he spoke, and it was the first totally uncontrolled reaction he'd seen from her.

"Hello, Master James."

She knew his name. He was shocked, though perhaps he shouldn't be. There weren't so many members of Las Palmas that it would be extraordinary for someone to know everyone's name. But she'd identified him by voice alone.

"Let's get you out of that cage so we can talk."

"As it pleases you, Master James."

He was listening closely, watching her intently, so he caught the signs of relief—lowering of her shoulders, loosening of her grip on the bars.

It took him several minutes to find the control panel cleverly hidden in the stone wall. He turned off the spotlights, turned up the other room lights, and then lowered the cage, which was suspended from a mechanically controlled pulley.

Once it was down, he went back to the cage, unfastening the simple latches that held the door closed. Once it was open, Beth made no move to exit.

James stifled a sigh. "You can come out."

"Thank you, Master James."

She leaned her upper body out, planted her hands on the floor then slowly moved her legs. At first he thought she was scared to exit the cage, perhaps scared of a scene with him after having only a moment ago lost the security of a collar, but after a moment of watching her, he realized what he was seeing was not fear, but pain.

Crouching in a catcher's pose he held out his hands. "Give me your hands. I'll help you stand up."

Beth's head tipped up, and for a moment her eyes met his. What he saw in her gaze was a bright and powerful mixture of emotions—pain, anticipation, and lust. The force of her personality and desire was nearly enough to knock him back onto his ass.

Slowly she laid her fingers in his palms. Forcing himself to focus, James rose slowly, drawing her up until she was kneeling with her back straight. When the pressure of her fingers in his increased, James closed his hands around hers, giving her something to brace against as she rose to her feet.

Her lower legs from knee to ankle were marked with deeply embedded red lines, the crosshatch a perfect replica of the bottom of the cage.

James clenched his jaw as a wave of protectiveness washed over him. He held it back—subs were not princesses in need of rescuing. They were grown women who made informed decisions about their sexuality.

What she needed was to be cared for, not to be rescued.

James released her hands and knelt, rubbing her lower legs with firm, hard strokes. She made a small noise and swayed. For a moment her hands brushed his body as she instinctively reached out to steady herself. When she jerked back from the contact, she almost lost her balance. James grabbed her hip, fingertips against the flexed muscle of her ass.

"Don't fall; brace yourself while I rub the marks out of your legs."

He returned to working on her lower legs, but his attention was on her hands, on what she'd do. With rueful amusement he realized he was holding his breath waiting to see if she'd touch him. One hand settled on his shoulder. Her fingers were cold from clutching the metal bars.

The other hand brushed over his hair, the touch so light he almost didn't feel it, but then she did it again, skimming her fingers through his hair. James raised his face, and his gaze met hers.

Beth's breath caught, and her irises dilated with desire. Her hand clenched in his hair, not pulling, but possessive. A flush rose from her chest to her cheeks, darkening her skin to a dusky pink.

James rose to his feet, still holding her gaze as her hands slid down his body, the pressure of her fingers molding his shirt to his chest. Beth blinked, and with a jerk that shook her whole body, dropped her chin, eyelids now submissively lowered. She folded her arms behind her back, cupping the opposite elbow in each hand in a position that was physically demanding to maintain due to the pressure it put on the shoulders—it was a formal, stiff pose.

James just stared at her, utterly and completely fascinated. If anything, Master Mikael had undersold exactly what was going on with this incredible submissive.

For the first time since he'd gotten to Las Palmas this afternoon, James smiled. It was going to be a very good weekend.

CHAPTER 3

B eth kept her gaze down, emotions rolling through her. She tried to name them, but she was having trouble describing what had just happened well enough for her normal process to work. On the surface it was simple: he'd rubbed her legs, she'd touched his shoulder with one hand and with the other she'd petted his hair. That was inappropriate for a submissive, but surely one incorrect behavior was not enough to cause this chaotic mix of feelings.

Finally she pinpointed the moment they'd looked in one another's eyes as the real source of her turmoil, but in the next breath dismissed that thought as fanciful.

What she couldn't dismiss was the way her fingers still tingled from the contact with him—or the memory of how firm his chest was under the soft fabric of his dress shirt. She wanted to rip the shirt off him, wanted to feel those muscles against her own naked body.

James walked away, and Beth brought herself under control, taking measured breaths. What she knew about him didn't provide a clue as to how severe an infraction he would consider her behavior. Madame Cat would have reacted with immediate disappointment and correction. Remembering the items on the C list, Beth knew she was more than likely due for a caning, which she was not looking forward to.

Resignation made it easy to force out the last of those unidentified emotions Master James had raised in her.

The lights dimmed slightly, and there were more footsteps before Master James called out to her.

"Beth, come here."

Dropping to her knees she crawled towards his voice, keeping her gaze a discreet three feet in front of her. As soon as she saw his shiny black shoes she stopped, waiting for additional direction.

"Come all the way."

Beth continued until her head was only a foot from his knee —Master James was seated on a padded bench, his back against the wall. The muted light in the room gave it an almost cozy, twilight feeling.

"Stand up, please."

He said "please" the way all Doms did. It did not lessen the command, did not turn it into a request—merely added a note of formality.

Beth rolled gracefully to her feet, though she was still sore from the time in the cage. Her neck felt light and naked without the collar.

Once she was standing, Master James reached out and tugged her onto his knee. Beth froze.

Master James's warm hand settled on her back, the pressure firm but not intimidating.

"I understand you prefer a more formal style of D/s play. I merely want to talk, and this is normally how I talk to my subs, but if this position is uncomfortable, you can kneel."

Beth's mouth was so dry she couldn't speak. She was seated on Master James's right knee, her body angled slightly away from him by the position of her lower legs. He wanted to talk, not cane her. After a moment of silence, Master James nodded then started to push her off his lap and onto the floor.

Beth braced her feet against the floor and resisted, stuttering out an awkward, "N-no."

Master James stopped pushing, his hands resting on her back and thigh. "No?"

"No, Master James." What was wrong with her? Forgetting to use a proper title was the mark of a novice.

"I mean what are you saying 'no' to?"

"Oh. I meant no, I would not rather kneel." Beth frowned, her words not fully expressing what she wanted to say.

Master James seemed to sense that, because he said, "Beth, for the remainder of this conversation I want you to speak freely, as long as you tell me the truth."

"Yes, Master James."

"Let's start over." He tugged her towards him, then slipped her legs over his left knee so she was entirely on his lap. Beth put her hands on her legs, then dropped them to her sides, but that caused her to brush her fingers against his crotch. She jerked her hands up, folding them under her breasts, but that was a closed, defensive posture—inappropriate for a submissive.

Feeling frantic, she unfolded her arms, running out of ideas, when James caught her hands in his, forcing them against her legs.

"Beth, it's clear you're uncomfortable sitting on my lap. I don't want to make you uncomfortable."

"I don't know the position."

"What position?"

"The appropriate position for lap sitting."

"There's isn't one."

Beth frowned. She knew that wasn't right. "There's a rule for every situation, an appropriate pose, response, or action for every possibility."

"That is...the stupidest thing I've ever heard."

Beth jerked her head around to face Master James's bemused face.

"That's—but that's… BDSM is all about rules." Beth was practically stuttering.

"No, BDSM is about power, control, and kinky sex. The rules are part of the game, not the foundation of it."

Beth shook her head, so caught up in what he'd just said that she didn't consider how disrespectful it was. "Training and knowing the rules are what make a good submissive."

"The desire to submit and willingness to give up control make a good submissive."

"No. I don't like that." The words were out before she could stop them. Saying what she thought, and telling the truth, were her greatest weaknesses when it came to dealing with other people, and her greatest strengths when it came to her career.

"Why not?" Master James didn't seem angered by her response, which was unexpected, despite the fact that he'd invited her to speak freely. Usually "speak freely" was code for "I want to trap you so I can punish you."

"The rules are why I'm here."

He leaned his head back and the hand on her back started rubbing in small circles. "You want there to be rules—a set of rules that, as long as you follow, you know you're being a good sub?"

"Yes. BDSM is subculture that values hierarchy and defined roles, which presuppose a set of rules which all culture members have agreed to abide by."

His eyebrows rose and his lips twitched. "Well, that's one way of putting it."

Beth looked down, her stomach churning. She'd said the wrong thing, said something awkward, and now he was laughing at her. This was why she hated conversations.

Silence, which normally she was fine with, stretched between them, each second making her more aware of what a mess she'd made of the conversation the minute she forgot to behave like a sub. Embarrassment prickled along her skin like an itchy shirt. Yet his hand was still rubbing small circles on her back

"I should not have used the word stupid. That wasn't right. We don't know much about each other, though I've seen you participate in scenes. Clearly your training, and your preferred style of submitting, is more formal."

She relaxed a little, the tension that held her still easing with his words. "I need the rules," she said quietly.

"You need them?"

Beth nodded, gaze on her hands, which were held in place against her legs by his big hand. Though she was naked and he was fully clothed, she did not feel as if the nakedness was as important as it usually was. It was as if everything was secondary to their words, her nakedness a footnote to the conversation.

"To know what to do."

"But it's the Dom's job, and privilege, to guide a submissive, to make sure she knows what she needs to do or not do to bring them both the greatest pleasure."

"Pleasure..." Beth savored the word.

The hand on hers lifted, touching her chin. The pressure of his fingers guided her to look at him. She focused on his chest.

"Look at me, Beth."

"I am, Master James," she pointed out.

He huffed out a laugh. "Good point. I mean I want you to look me in the eye."

Sucking her lower lip into her mouth, Beth met his gaze. Master James's eyes were hazel—green and brown and gold, all mixed together. Between one breath and the next her nakedness became much more important. Her nipples tightened and she felt herself growing wet. Embarrassment almost made her look away, but she couldn't—she didn't know if it was the fact that he'd commanded her to look at him, or if deep down she simply didn't want to.

"Beth, would you be more comfortable kneeling?"

"No, Master James."

"You want to sit on my lap."

"Yes, Master James. I've watched you, with other subs. You touch them and kiss them."

"Are those things you want?"

"Yes."

"And you do them with other Doms?"

"No."

"Why not?"

"Because...I'm not that kind of submissive."

"You don't want to be."

Beth shook her head.

"You do want to be?"

Beth nodded. The tightness was back in her chest—she couldn't tell what Master James was thinking, what this conversation meant to him, and it made her nervous. Were her answers disobedient or rude? Was he going to throw her down and cane her any minute now?

"The last time I saw you, Madame Cat was using you as a footstool."

At that Beth dropped her eyes, blinking hard. "Yes, Master James.

"Do you find that kind of service particularly arousing?"

Beth had to take a second to compose herself before answering. "Being furniture is not meant to be directly arousing or pleasurable." She was proud that her tone was neutral, her answer both truthful and appropriate.

He was silent for a moment. "Were you being punished?"

"No, Master James."

"Is that kind of service the only way you can reach subspace?"

Beth didn't know how to answer that, didn't want to admit that she didn't really understand subspace, which seemed to be an emotional state that she had yet to figure out how to reach. She shrugged helplessly, knowing she needed to answer with words, but unable to do so. Bracing for correction at her failure to answer, she was taken by surprise with his next question.

"Then why were you there?"

"Because Madame Cat enjoys having a sub serve her in that way."

"All right. I think I understand."

Beth was glad someone did, because this whole conversation was confusing her.

"You said you've watched me with other subs."

"Yes, Master James."

"And you like the way you see me behave with them."

"Yes." The word came out as a sigh of longing.

"What if I told you that my subs don't follow rules, at least not many?"

"But how do they know what to do?"

"I tell them what I want, and—" he leaned forward to whisper in her ear, his breath against her neck making her shiver "—sometimes I change the rules, just because I want to, or because I think changing the rules will bring us more pleasure, make the submission sweeter."

"Pleasure..." Beth swayed towards Master James, raising her gaze to his.

His hand on her back curled around her waist in a possessive hold, while his other hand slid into her hair, holding her head still.

"Beth, when was the last time you had an orgasm?"

"Tuesday night."

"You were here Tuesday night?"

"No. I was at home."

"When was the last time you came for Madame Cat?"

"Never."

"You never had an orgasm for her?"

"I was supposed to come when I serviced her, but I never did. It was not technically disobedient because she never ordered me to come, only told me I could."

"You weren't able to come when you touched yourself?"

"No, I wasn't allowed to touch myself."

"Your last Domme assumed you were so deep in subspace that servicing her would be enough to allow you to orgasm with no physical stimulation?"

"I don't know, Master James. Madame Cat didn't talk to me much."

The fingers in her hair massaged her scalp and Beth's eyes closed in pleasure.

"Did it make you wet, watching me with other subs?"

"It made me jealous." The confession was quiet.

"Do you think that those other women were wet, when they sat on my lap while I played with them?"

Beth could only nod.

"And you, are you wet, Beth?"

"Yes, Master James."

Beth was in an almost dreamlike state—the warmth of his body was seeping into her bare skin, the pressure of his hands on her skin had a strangely calming effect and she was able to answer his questions with absolute truth without feeling awkward.

She was so lost in the feelings that she gasped when Master James grabbed her hips and spun her around so her back was against his chest. Firm hands grabbed her thighs and forced her legs along the outside of his, opening and exposing her sex.

"Raise your hands, put them on my head." His voice was rough.

Beth obeyed, but the peace of a moment ago was gone, every muscle tense with dread. She'd forgotten where she was, what she was, and now she'd be punished. Flogging and whipping of her pussy were on her list of hard limits, but experience had taught her that there were plenty of other ways her sex could bear the brunt of a punishment, and each was painful.

"I apologize for my disobedience, Master James." The words were the appropriate response to bad behavior. She waited for him to say something like "You won't make that mistake again" or "You need some correction."

Instead Master James brushed his lips against her ear and whispered, "I don't ever want to hear those words from you again."

One hand slid up to her breast, cupping the mound as he flicked the nipple with his thumb. The other settled between her legs, two fingers exploring her labia before slipping inside her pussy.

JAMES PRESSED HIS FINGERS ALONG EITHER SIDE OF her clit, rubbing gently. Beth's body arched, her fingers tightening in his hair as she gasped in startled pleasure.

He forced aside the rage that was churning in his gut, focusing on her. Rolling one nipple with his thumb, he pressed his lips to her neck, letting his breath stimulate the sensitive skin there.

Beth's hold on his hair became painful and the muscles in her thighs were vibrating. He'd been touching her for less than two minutes, but it seemed like she was going to come. Not surprising considering that she'd been denied pleasure for so long.

Ignoring that thought, he nipped her earlobe, pinched her nipple hard, and rubbed her clit with firm, quick pressure.

Beth's already taut body tensed like an archer's bow, the sleek lines of her gold-toned skin revealing lean, strong muscles.

She took a fractured breath and then started to shake, her limbs trying to curl in, as if to protect herself from the force of her orgasm—a force so strong he could see her thigh muscles quake.

He didn't try to force a second orgasm, but did press the heel of his hand against her clit, spreading the lips of her sex with all four fingers so he could feel the orgasm. He could have entered her, let her body clench around him, but he would save penetration for later.

Beth collapsed against him, breath shuddering in what was almost sobs. Part of him wanted to curl her up into a ball and hold her, but he kept her spread and open before him, hoping the physical openness would help trigger more emotional openness.

He ran his free hand over her torso, thighs, and arms, taking possession of her bare flesh with his touch. When her breath returned to normal, he took his hand from her pussy, wiping it against her belly so the smell of her orgasm would be more apparent.

He could tell the moment she shifted from a place of pleasure to awareness. She relaxed her hold on his hair, lifting her hands away from his scalp so her palms were only a light pressure on his head, still following his command but lightening the touch.

James eased her into a sitting positing, then helped her stand.

With her back to him, he took a moment to let his feelings show on his face. He could cheerfully horsewhip Cat—and every other Dom who'd ever used her.

True submission—stripping away a sub's walls to find the core of him or her—was the hardest thing a Dom had to do. It took time, planning and skill, because it went against most emotional and physical protective reflexes people, especially women, had developed by the time they were adults. Usually what happened was a submissive managed to keep some of those walls in place, resulting in a sort of half-submission that was usually fine, especially among casual partners. The trouble came when neither Doms, nor the submissive themselves, could tell that they weren't experiencing full emotional truth about what they wanted and needed.

That's what he'd helped Master Xavier and Mae overcome— Xavier had managed to bring out Mae's real submissive. She'd been begging Xavier for the kind of domination no one would have imagined she would want, but Xavier had his own demons to wrestle with and hadn't realized how deep Mae's need went. James had seen what neither of them could after watching the two of them together in a scene in the library. A scene Beth had been a part of, in so far as she'd been a prop.

In Beth it seemed there was the opposite problem—the perfect, obedient submissive who followed every rule, obeyed every command, and yet no one had touched the real core of her.

James doubted Mae would have submitted at that level to anyone but Xavier—chemistry between the Dom and sub played a huge role in how intense a scene or relationship could become. But it was much more common that good chemistry allowed for more intense play, rather than the apparent lack of chemistry in Beth's past relationships resulting in unfulfilling experiences for her.

There were people who found the greatest pleasure in kinks that dismissed their sexual needs while still making them sexual objects. Some "slaves" were used in that way, as were men who enjoyed long-term chastity or cuckolding. James was a firm believer in live and let live, though he had no interest in those styles of kink, nor it seemed did Beth, despite the way she'd been submitting.

Every knight in shining armor instinct he had was on alert after only a few minutes with her, which only made him angrier, because that was the last thing he wanted. Reminding himself once again that she didn't need to be rescued—she needed to be made to come until she couldn't remember the word "rules"—let alone what they might be. James promised himself that he wouldn't get emotionally involved beyond investing the time it would take to figure out how to make her let him in.

He was gathering pieces of the Beth puzzle, and though he still couldn't see how they fit together, he intended to figure it out before he let her go Sunday night. He intended to make her submit, truly submit.

Maybe for the first time.

A bubble of amusement at that thought helped him put aside his anger.

Beth's shoulders hunched slightly when he laughed. James squeezed her legs between his knees, reassuring her with physical contact. When she remained stiff he traced the line of her spine down to the crevice of her ass, spreading the cheeks with his fingers just enough to make her think about the possibility that he would fuck her there.

"Do you know why I'm amused, Beth?"

"No, Master James."

"It's because I just realized that I need to treat you like a virgin."

"Uh... I'm not a virgin." The tone of her voice suggested she didn't think he was particularly bright.

If there was one thing he didn't have to worry about with this sub, it was having her attempt to top from the bottom. That required manipulation, even if it was done subconsciously. Beth either didn't like to lie or didn't know how to. It was refreshing.

"I know you're not really a virgin, but you're a virgin to the type of submission I'm going to demand."

"I don't understand."

James rose, pressing his front against her back. She was half a head shorter than him and lean, but the kind of lean that came from muscles, not diet. He normally preferred curvier girls, but there was something deeply appealing about Beth's body.

"I know you don't," he whispered in her ear. "Raise your arms behind your head so I can look at you."

With quick, easy grace, Beth laced her fingers together at the back of her neck, thrust her chest out, and spread her legs. The arch of her back pressed her ass into his groin. It was suddenly easier to understand the appeal of such an obedient and well-trained sub. James put some space between them and stroked his hands from her elbows along her shoulder blades and down her back to her ass. Taking a seat, he kneaded the firm globes.

"Bend."

She didn't balk or hesitate. Keeping her hands behind her head, she bent to a perfect 90 degrees at the waist. Now he had a nice view of the rosette of her anus and her pussy. Both were waxed completely bare. Spreading her ass open with his thumbs, he blew against her rear entrance and was rewarded with a small shiver.

Her pussy lips were glossy from her orgasm, the scent of her pleasure heavy in the air. Palms on the back of her thighs, he now used his thumbs to spread her outer labia, examining the soft pink core of her sex. Her clit was large and partially erect from behind its protective hood.

Holding her open with index and middle fingers of one hand, he used the tip of his other thumb to press on the edge of her clit hood, trying to expose more of her clit.

Beth gasped and her posture wavered.

"Brace yourself."

She dropped both arms, bending further until she could brace both hands on the floor. It opened her up even more. James retuned his attention to her clit, using a precise, almost clinical touch. In a way it was showing off, making sure she knew that he knew exactly how to touch her.

Beth started to tremble. "Master..."

"Yes?"

She shook her head, hair brushing the floor.

Dipping his thumb into the cream that had pooled at her entrance, James coated her clit. The slick skin made his task more difficult but would keep her from getting uncomfortable. As he manipulated her clit hood—rubbing and pressing on it, occasionally giving it a light squeeze, Beth started to tremble.

He knew that rhythmic, steady touches to the clit were the gold standard for female orgasms. Multiple subs had told him that having their clit hood manipulated was sexy, and clearly the act of a Dom, but too strange to allow orgasm.

Acting on a hunch, James continued to toy with her clit hood, and when he finally had his thumb in the perfect position to hold it back, exposing the tiny core of her clit, he pressed hard, mashing her clit hood against her pelvic bone.

Beth screamed, her whole body shaking. He saw her knees start to give out and quickly grabbed her hips, easing them to the ground. Beth's body shook, and he could see through the hair that had fallen over her face that her eyes were squeezed closed, her lips clenched.

Pinching her labia closed he rubbed them in a circle, a muted caress of her clit. Her eyes popped open and her mouth opened too, though no sound emerged. Kneeling behind her, James slid one hand under her chest and forced her up, so that they were once more back to chest. He held her like that until her body stopped quaking. He'd never made a woman come like that. Her responsiveness was incredible.

"Master James?" She whispered his name, clearly hesitant to ask whatever question she was holding on to.

It was one of the habits he would break her of.

"Yes?"

"Are you going to…will we…is there going to be sex?"

She sounded so hopeful that his hold on her tightened. Denying or delaying orgasm was one of a Dom's best tools, but clearly that had been taken too far with Beth. Watching her orgasm was pure bliss, and he intended to become an avid Beth-orgasm viewer.

"Oh yes, if you're a very good girl there will be sex." He helped her to her feet then spun her around so she could see the promise of pleasure in his face, but she kept her eyes obediently lowered.

Tipping her chin up until she looked at him, he rubbed her lower lip with one finger, and she opened her mouth.

He wanted to see those pretty lips wrapped around his cock. He wanted to kiss her as he thrust into her, taste her pleasure.

"Yes. There will be sex." His voice was deeper than normal, his cock hard in his pants.

"If I'm a good girl." Her post-orgasm daze was fading from her eyes and she frowned. "Being good means following the rules, but you said there aren't rules."

"Yes…and no."

"That's confusing." She sounded disgruntled, which was strangely endearing.

"I'll make it simple." He grabbed her chin, putting enough pressure into the touch that it was not a caress but a command. "You'll obey my rules, you'll follow my commands, and you will submit."

Her pupils dilated and he could feel her relaxing into his control. Physically she was perfectly obedient and emotionally responsive. The challenge with her would be getting inside her head.

He released her, satisfied that her worry had been negated by her trust in his domination, but in the next breath she was frowning, the moment gone.

"Perhaps if you wrote down your rules, I'd be better able to follow them."

James smiled and started unbuttoning his shirt. "But if I do that I can't change the rules whenever I want."

She wasn't going to be an easy sub, but he had no doubt that when he finally put all the pieces of the Beth puzzle in place it would be something beautiful.

She was watching him undress with ego-stroking fascination. He was in good shape, but women rarely looked at him with such blatant admiration and desire, especially here where good-looking people weren't exactly scarce.

"Are we going to have sex now?" Beth licked her lower lip.

James was sorely tempted to say yes, though that was not part of the plan he'd come up with while she withered with pleasure in his arms.

He stripped the shirt off and held it up so she could slip into it. Beth looked at the shirt, then at him.

"You're giving me clothes." She eyed the shirt with trepidation.

Exasperated he said, "You're not a house elf. It's not going to free you."

Beth's face went completely blank and then she broke out in a huge grin. It transformed her face—she was suddenly so breathtakingly beautiful, and James blinked.

"Did you just make a Harry Potter reference?"

"I have nieces," he said, a bit defensively.

"Sure you do." Beth continued to grin. "I bet you have a Gryffindor tie."

He did. "What are you, psychic?"

"No, just good at guessing things about people. I'm a professional at that. It was logical that you'd have something like a tie."

James had no idea what that meant, and he was so thrown off by this weird conversational diversion that he blurted out the first thing that came into his head. "Don't play Vulcan mind-games with me."

Beth's grin widened.

James stifled a groan. What was wrong with him? Las Palmas was not the place where he let his geek flag fly.

Beth cleared her throat, then said somberly, "'The needs of the many outweigh the needs of the—'"

James threw the shirt over her head so he couldn't see that face. "Put it on."

Beth was still smiling as she slipped into the shirt, which had tails long enough to cover her ass and pussy. James ignored the voice in his head that asked why he wanted to cover her up before taking her out in public, or why the sight of her in his shirt was so pleasing. For both their sakes he needed to remain in control of the situation, though he was starting to suspect navigating between Beth's past as a submissive and her real personality which he'd just gotten a glimpse of would be more challenging than expected.

He reached out and undid the top two buttons of the shirt. Her breath caught when skin brushed skin, and the teasing of a moment ago was forgotten. He pulled the shirt to the side, exposing her breast.

"I want access to your body," he said by way of explanation.

"Yes, Master James." She shivered, but it wasn't from cold.

James pulled the shirt back into place, leaving the buttons undone so that a long V of skin was visible.

Placing a hand on her back, he guided her out of the playroom.

CHAPTER 4

B eth's body was still humming from the intense orgasms, there were butterflies of anticipation in her stomach, and she could feel the heat of a blush on her cheeks. Together those feelings helped her hush the internal monologue that was frantically pointing out everything she'd done wrong with Master James. From uninvited eye contact and not using his name and title when responding to direct questions to teasing him in a woefully disrespectful manner, she hadn't followed the rules.

Yet, he didn't seem to care, and the way he'd effortlessly taken command of her body, touching her both intimately and skillfully, made her feel far more submissive than the cage had. She was actually eager for him to command her, something she hadn't felt since her first few disappointing sessions.

Beth walked beside Master James, his hand on her back guiding her. It was a distinctly possessive posture, but nothing compared to being made to crawl, or being leashed.

He guided her to the lovely garden of the "Sub Rosa" court, so named because a massive pergola covered the courtyard in the center of the single-story adobe tile roofed buildings. Climbing roses in shades of white and pale yellow wove over and around the wood, shading the court from the late afternoon sun. There were four bedroom-like playrooms off this garden, and it was the "gentlest" of the play spaces. The sprawling complex that housed Las Palmas boasted a series of courtyards, each with its own themes that carried into the playrooms that opened off each outdoor space.

There was a small circular platform in the center of the court with two pretty wood lounge chairs positioned on it. Surrounding the stage were pieces of lushly padded outdoor furniture. Occasionally someone would take their play onto the small stage and put on a show, but most of the time this court-yard was used for lounging. Baskets set against the base of the pergola posts held flat pillows that could be thrown down over the tile to allow subs to kneel and woven blankets for use when the nights were chilly.

The sun was just starting to set, and rays of light cut through small breaks in the canopy of roses, angling golden sunbeams onto the smattering of people already there. At the sound of their approach, heads turned, and a few people called out a greeting to Master James, their curious gazes taking in his newest companion.

Beth's stomach knotted and her steps faltered when she caught sight of the other people. Their attention made her nervous—she wasn't the kind of sub who hung out and laughed and chatted in this casual space. Crumpling the cuffs of his shirt in nervous fingers, Beth wished desperately that he'd had her crawl here, or put her in some kind of bondage.

Last weekend she'd been disappointed to be part of the scenery—a piece of furniture or a human prop—but in that moment she would have cheerfully offered to serve as a foot-stool rather than have everyone looking at her with questions in their eyes.

She felt...vulnerable. It was insane, but she was more

exposed at this moment than she was when naked and chained to a wall in the dining room for display.

"Beth, look at me."

Turning her head, she kept her gaze on the ground.

"Beth." Now there was a warning in his voice, and that calmed her.

Raising her chin she met his gaze. His face was stern with command, but his gaze examined her, touching each feature.

"The only people who matter are you and me. The only person you should be worried about, or paying attention to, is me."

"Yes, Master James, I'm sorry—"

"No, don't apologize. If you feel unsure or scared, tell me. I don't want you to feel those things, so when you do it means there's something wrong."

"But that's topping from the bottom." Among subs, being accused of topping from the bottom was essentially being called a fraud or novice. There were a few subs at the club who cheerfully admitted that they liked or tried topping from the bottom, but their stories usually ended with sexy retellings of the "punishments" they earned for doing so.

The punishments those women described were not the kind Beth had gotten when she failed to follow the rules.

"No, it's not. Communication is the single most important part of a BDSM relationship." The corners of his mouth tightened, as if he were angry, but then his expression smoothed out. "I'm not always going to need you to talk to me. I'm going to be able to tell by the way your body responds, by how many times you orgasm..."

Beth lost the rest of what he was saying. Her whole body flushed with arousal as soon as he said the word orgasm.

"Beth?"

"Hmmm?" He had beautiful lips. Would he kiss her?

"How is it that no one has been treating you like the orgasm slut you clearly are?"

Beth was saved from responding—was orgasm slut a bad thing?—when Master James bent, put his shoulder against her midsection, and stood with her dangling over his back.

His hand across her calves held her in place as he carried her over to a large chair. The bottom and back cushions were heavy cream fabric, the frame and arms wide planks of dark wood varnished to a high gloss.

James set her on her feet only long enough for him to take a seat. A sunbeam touched his hair, making it glow the color of old gold.

He patted his thigh and raised one eyebrow. Beth took a half step, then froze, the voice in her head screaming at her that she should kneel, bow her head, put her arms behind her back. Years of training and practice were wrapped around her like chains, keeping her from moving forward.

"Beth, *I* want you on my lap, and *you* want to sit on my lap. That is what you need to focus on."

She blew out a breath, then repeated what he'd just said in her mind. He was her Master; he wanted her on his lap.

The fact that he cared if she wanted it also was just the cherry on top.

Beth slid onto his knee, ankles together, feet pressed against the tile.

Master James didn't say anything, but his hand slipped under the back of the shirt, fingers tracing patterns on her lower back. She slid back a few inches, wanting more. His hand flattened, now rubbing in large circles.

Another inch and his hand, still under the shirt, moved around to her belly, fingers coming oh-so-close to her breasts.

"Come closer..." His voice was both teasing and full of heat.

Beth slid all the way back, until her hip was pressed against his belly, her feet no longer on the floor.

Master James nudged her off his lap, wedging her between his body and the throw pillow positioned at the arm of the chair. Beth stiffened, sure she had done something wrong, but he positioned his arm along her shoulders, almost as if they were on a date at the movies. He tugged the shirt to the side, the collar falling off her shoulder and exposing her right breast.

"That's better." His fingers traced patterns on her breast, touching her everywhere but her nipple.

Beth closed her eyes, breathing deep, waiting, waiting for the moment when he finally touched her nipple. Her hands were on her thighs, palms up. When kneeling, palms up on the thighs was an appropriate "relaxed" posture. It made her feel better to adapt part of an approved posture for her current situation.

Soon the position of her hands was forgotten, all of her attention on her breast. She wanted, needed, him to touch her nipple, or maybe switch to her other breast. Better yet, for his fingers to slip between her legs and do those strange, wonderful things to her. She'd never had an orgasm like that before—nearly painful it was so intense.

"James, how are you doing?" The sound of an unfamiliar voice made Beth jerk, but Master James's fingers didn't stop.

"Good, how're you?"

Beth kept her eyes closed, trying to bring her body under control so she could pay attention in case Master James needed anything from her.

"Isn't that Cat's sub Beth?"

"Not anymore."

"Ah." There was a question in the sound, before the other Master said, "Oh, you got her for the checklist game."

"Yes."

Beth's breath caught in her chest as pain lanced through her. The emotion was so unexpected that for a half second she though it was an actual physical pain.

It shouldn't hurt her, the other Dom's tone or Master

James's response. She'd been the first to acknowledge that she wasn't the kind of sub Doms like Master James normally selected. Others were going to wonder why he was playing with her, and the game was the natural conclusion.

And the truth.

Though Master James was still toying with her breast Beth was no longer floating in a haze of aroused anticipation. She opened her eyes, though kept them submissively lowered.

Master James's fingers stopped moving, his hand flattening over her chest.

"Can you do me a favor?" Though she could tell Master James was looking at her, it was clear he was speaking to the other Dom.

"Of course."

"I need some things."

Beth remained still as Master James leaned away from her to whisper to the other man. When he'd left, Master James shifted slightly, adjusting pillows until he was in a more relaxed half-reclining position.

He tugged Beth's shoulders until she was reclining against his side, her head pillowed on his shoulder. "We haven't talked about our letter."

Beth found her tension slipping away as she lounged against him. "No, Master James, we haven't."

"I assume Madame Cat told you it's C."

"I figured it out."

"The cage and the collar, or lack thereof, were a rather large clue. How are you feeling about Madame Cat removing her collar?"

Beth shrugged.

"No, I want to hear how you're feeling. The truth." The command was clear in his voice.

"I knew Madame Cat was moving and leaving LA. I didn't know it was going to be today."

"That's what you know, not how you feel."

A valid point, and she should have known he'd ask what for her was a difficult question. "I didn't feel surprised when she removed her collar. I was…resigned. I'd planned to give up my own membership when Madame Cat left."

"Because you didn't want to submit to anyone but her?" He sounded both surprised and concerned.

"No, because being a sub is not what I thought it would be. I have not enjoyed it." She shook her head, because that wasn't quite right. "It has not been what I expected."

"You're disappointed."

"Yes. Disappointed." It felt good to say it, and it was true, but given her current position it was an odd statement. "In the Subs' Garden, when others talk about their sessions and scenes…" Beth didn't want to finish the sentence. Anything she said would sound pathetic, as if she were whining. She didn't want to do that.

"Your submission hasn't been fulfilling."

She was glad he understood. "Exactly."

"Have you considered topping?"

Beth sucked in air and almost choked. "No!"

"You don't find that idea appealing?"

"I could never do it. I could never be responsible for a sub."

"Why not? You said that you're good at reading people."

"Not their emotions, not in situations like this." She gestured to the courtyard, which was slowly filling with club members.

"Beth, sit up and look at me."

She rose and twisted, this time meeting his eyes without being prompted.

"Why did you join Las Palmas?"

Taking a deep breath, Beth finally said, "I won't answer that." The answer revealed too many things, asked her to expose too much of her own weaknesses.

Master James searched her face. "And you have the right not to. But I have to ask—are you sure you're submissive?"

Beth stiffened. "I'm a good submissive."

"You're a good rule follower. That's not the same thing. When you think about submitting, what do you imagine, what do you want? I don't mean physically. What do you want to feel?"

She almost left, almost stood up and walked away rather than answer. The last person to ask that was Master Leo at her interview for membership.

Master James cupped her neck, thumb pressed lightly to the underside of her jaw. The physical contact centered her.

"I want to not worry," she whispered.

"Worry about what?"

"About if I'm saying the right thing, doing the right thing. I want to be with another person, but know that I'm being with them the right way."

"And the rules of BDSM...that's how you'll know you're doing it the right way." He spoke slowly, as if he were processing what he was saying as he spoke.

"Yes."

"Beth, I have to ask, are you, uh..."

She knew what he was saying. Plenty of people had either assumed or accused her of being on the autism spectrum. "Does it matter?"

"No, and it was rude of me to say anything." His matter-of-fact tone lacked the pity she feared. "But I'm worried that this is some kind of coping mechanism, and not something you really enjoy."

"Oh, I hadn't considered that."

Master James ran a hand through his hair. "In light of what I'm planning to do to you, I'd feel a lot better if I knew you were actually going to enjoy it."

"You think I won't?" The question was serious, but held a

hint of teasing, something Beth wouldn't have dared with anyone else. It was him—he made her behave this way. The only reason she dared was because he'd pleased her far more than anyone else had, making the idea that he *wouldn't* please her laughable.

"Okay, now you're just insulting me." His lips twitched, the sparkle in his eyes inviting her to again tease him in turn.

"How am I insulting you?"

"You're implying I can't pleasure you."

"I didn't say that." She bit the inside of her cheek to keep from smiling.

Master James grinned. "What you're saying is that in all your years as a member here, no Dom has really pleasured you."

"Yes, so it's not just you."

Master James let out a bark of laughter and Beth lost control of her smile. This was fun.

Then Master James's laugh faded to a grin and he looked pointedly to the side.

Beth was suddenly aware that there was no chatter and almost every eye was on them. If it had been a movie, there would have been a screeching record to accompany the silence that fell after her words.

She sucked in a breath and stared wide-eyed at Master James. He continued smiling, as if this were still funny, but all Beth could think was that she'd just insulted nearly a dozen Doms, some of whom might have used her before and would take it personally.

Beth pushed herself to the edge of the chair, ready to drop to her knees. Master James grabbed her around the waist.

"Oh no, you don't."

"A sub should *never* speak disrespectfully about a Dom," she whispered frantically.

"A Dom should know how to pleasure a sub."

Beth shook her head. "You're confusing me. It's a sub's job

to pleasure the Dom, in whatever method or manner they find pleasing. A sub should get pleasure from that alone."

A strange laugh had Beth hunching her shoulders. The other Dom was back. He handed James a large bag. "Beth, my dear, if you really think that, then we've all failed you."

The statement elicited a smattering of laughter from those closest to them. Someone said, "Do you hear that, pet? You job is to please me in whatever manner I want, so come here and give me a kiss."

Beth was having trouble figuring out what was going on. "Are they laughing at me?"

"No. They're laughing because that's not the philosophy of most of the Doms here. Maybe if we were hanging out in the Iron Court it would be, but even then most Doms take pride in knowing they can make a sub come so hard she won't remember her own name. Or pleasure her so well that pain becomes pleasure."

"I still don't understand." She wanted to, but she didn't.

"I'm guessing that Madame Cat, and others, thought that you derived pleasure from serving and being treated like an object. There are people with that kink—you're just not one of them. You were sex misdiagnosed." Master James stroked her cheek until she looked at him. "As illuminating as this has been, we're done with this conversation. All you need to understand is that until Sunday evening you're mine."

"Yes, Master James." As the words left her mouth, a kind of peace settled over her.

He examined her before he nodded. "We were discussing our letter. Do you remember the checklist?"

"I do."

"And what do you think is on it, for the letter C?"

"Cages, caning, cattle prod, cells, chains, chastity belts, choking, chores, clothespins, clamps, cock rings, cock worship, collars, corsets, and cuffs."

Master James looked startled. "Er, yes, that's it exactly."

"Would you rather I not remember?"

"No, but I had planned to tease you with the possibilities. I'm guessing you've had time to think about them."

"I have. None of them are on my list of hard limits."

"Well, a few of them are hard limits for me."

"They are?"

"You're surprised."

Beth debated asking her question, finally giving in. "Why do Masters need hard limits? The sub can't make you do anything."

"True, but a sub might want or expect something I am not comfortable with, so a checklist helps make sure that no one is disappointed."

"I hadn't considered that. What are your—"

He pressed two fingers over her mouth. "I'm not going to tell you. You'll just have to figure it out. Now, come back here so I can play with you."

Beth shifted around until she was once more curled up against him. This time she didn't need any prompting to get comfortable. The shirt had fallen closed and she inched it off her shoulder, hoping his fingers might find their way back to her breast.

"Is that an invitation?" His whisper was warm against her ear.

"Yes," she answered truthfully, hoping that was acceptable.

"Well, it would be ungentlemanly of me to turn down such a pretty invitation."

CHAPTER 5

His fingers returned to her right breast, tracing patterns over her skin, but avoiding the aching peak. Her nipple budded tight, and Beth arched her back slightly, offering herself, begging him without words.

"Unbutton the shirt."

Beth's fingers trembled as she obeyed, eagerly peeling it open so her whole torso was bare. Reaching across his body, Master James began to tease her left breast with his free hand while cupping the outer curve of her right.

It was pleasurable, but not enough, not what she wanted.

Beth arched her back, her head pressed hard into his shoulder.

"What do you want, Beth?"

"I want..." She knew exactly what she wanted, but couldn't say it.

"Tell me."

The command made it easier to speak. "I want you to touch my nipples."

"Just touch?" His fingers feathered over the tips of her breasts in a barely there caress.

"More," she pleaded quietly.

Master James's hands stopped moving. "That didn't sound like begging."

"Should I beg?" Beth couldn't stop the note of desperation that tinged her words. The constant teasing touch was making her feel desperate, far more desperate than a complete absence of touch would have.

"That's up to you. I might give in, if you beg enough."

She didn't hesitate. "Please, please, please."

A silent laugh made his chest rumble. "Please what?"

"Please touch...uh, pinch my nipples."

"Hmm, a tempting idea."

Beth held her breath, but he didn't *do* anything. Her fingers curled into fists, nails pressed into her palms. She could feel him waiting, but she was waiting too, waiting for him.

He was the Dom, she was the sub.

It was her place to be quiet, obedient. If he wanted to do nothing more than hold her breasts, that was his right.

Master James bent his head over hers and kissed her shoulder, the crook of her neck, and then the soft spot just behind her ear. "The sooner you give in—the sooner you realize that your self-imposed control is the only thing standing between us—the sooner I can give you what you want. The sooner I can do the things your body is begging for."

"Please," she gasped, "please, Master James. Please play with my breasts. Touch, pinch, twist..." She stopped, unable to articulate anything more.

"Good girl."

He grabbed her nipples, pinching them firmly then tugging. Beth's teeth snapped together as bolts of pleasure shot from her breasts to her pussy, making muscles low in her belly clench.

"Arch your back more."

Beth obeyed, dropping her hands under herself to push her

butt up off the chair. He continued to tug and twist, but in her greed that wasn't enough.

"Master James, please, I need more."

"Good. What do you need?"

"I...I don't know. I don't know." She couldn't think. The burning pleasure within her made thought nearly impossible except for the single word that ran through her mind like a mantra.

More, more, more.

"Go get a pillow."

Beth didn't react until he released her nipples. Her butt fell back to the seat, the growing ball of heat and pleasure inside her deflating slightly.

With more reluctance than she'd ever shown as a submissive, she slid off the couch and padded over to the nearest basket, grabbing a large pillow.

Bringing it back, she set it down on the tiles in front of Master James's feet.

"Kneel on the pillow, with your back to me. Good. Now spread your legs so your feet are on either side of mine."

Beth situated herself, glad for the pillow that protected her knees from the tile. The fact that he cared enough to think of that caused a different kind of warmth to grow within her.

Master James kneaded the nape of her neck, then her shoulders, working his way to her upper arms, pushing the shirt as he went so it fell off, puddling around her wrists and draping over her ass.

"Lean back, rest on my knees. Keep your legs spread."

In this position Beth couldn't keep her chin down. Instead she let her head drop back, focusing on the canopy of roses between her and the twilight blue sky.

Master James cupped her jaw, forcing her to drop her head all the way back.

"You have a beautiful neck." Knuckles trailed down her

throat to her collarbones, which he explored thoroughly before moving south. Between one breath and the next Beth was once more flush with need. Her breasts were bare and vulnerable because of her position. As before, he spent time exploring her, this time moving his hands in tandem as he traced the soft crease at the bottom of her breasts, the outer edge of her dusky pink areolas.

When he finally grasped her nipples once more, twisting and tugging, Beth had to reach down and grab his ankles. She didn't think about it, didn't question it. She needed something to hold on to, needed the contact with her Master.

"You have incredibly responsive breasts. Have you ever pierced your nipples?"

"No, Master James." Her words were barely audible amid her deep, heavy breaths.

"They'd be lovely with bar piercings, far enough back not to interfere with these delicious tips." He flicked the puckered buds with his thumbs before pulling away.

This time she was content to wait, to trust Master James.

"Open your mouth, stick out your tongue."

The order was so unexpected that Beth shifted her gaze, in time to watch Master James pull a handful of clothespins from the bag the other Dom had brought him.

When he placed the wooden clothespin on Beth's extended tongue she winced slightly. The innocuous item seemed mundane, but the force of it was stronger than expected, especially on her sensitive tongue. She swallowed, the clothespin clicking against her teeth as she did so.

"You can't talk now, so you'll have to tell me with your body what you want."

Beth nodded once.

With a clothespin in each hand, Master James began to tease her, pinching her lower lip by placing the clothespin on it but not fully releasing it. With that same technique he moved down her upper body, pinching the skin of her shoulders, upper arms, and chest. The feelings were uncomfortable more than painful, and not at all sexy.

Except they were.

Except that as he repeated the path his fingers had taken not so long ago, Beth found herself whimpering helplessly. There was nothing obviously sexual about having a clothespin pinch the skin near her armpit, but each nip caused a corresponding throb in her pussy.

"There are two ways to use clothespins on nipples." Master James's words were almost conversational, but his tone was a bit deeper than it had been. "Placing them straight on so they stick out allows for more play—flicking and tugging. Perpendicular to the breast, especially when you first pull the nipple out a bit, leaves the very tip free to be played with."

The clothespins were set aside as his hands returned to her breasts, this time both hands on one breast, the left kneading the full weight while his right plucked and rolled the nipple.

"And then of course you have to decide if you're going for the exact tip, or if you're going back a bit, capturing some of the areola too. That allows for longer wear, but the first version is the stronger sensation."

Beth was shaking with need and anticipation. Hearing him talk about what he would do, how he would use and play with her, was enough to have her muscles tight with anticipation.

When he pulled his hands back, her left nipple was a hard pink bud, standing up bravely, if foolishly, from her breast.

Master James held the clothespin near her breast in a vertical position, the open mouth poised on either side of her nipple. Beth's breath shuttered with delicious dread at the pain that was to come.

He released the clothespin, letting it snap closed on the very tip of her breast. Beth yelped, nails digging into his legs through the fabric of his slacks.

Pain radiated from the tip of her breast, causing her to wince even as the feeling shot down to her pussy.

"Don't fight it. Give in. You can't stop it, you can't change it. All you can do is accept it. Know that I want it—I want to see your nipple pink and tight and pinched in the clothespin."

His words triggered something in her and Beth started to shake, her breath catching in her throat as her pussy spasmed. It was almost as if...

As if she were going to come.

Her eyes, which she'd squeezed shut, snapped open. Beth met Master James's gaze. Even if he hadn't silenced her with the clothespin on her tongue, she wouldn't have known what to say, how to explain that she might have been about to orgasm from a combination of the physical pleasure-pain of the clothespin and the emotional pleasure of his domination.

His eyes widened slightly, then narrowed.

With her eyes open she saw him pick up the other clothespin, watch him bring it to her unadorned breast. He plucked her nipple for a few seconds before quickly applying the clothespin.

Beth bit down, teeth making the clothespin dig into her tongue, the ache from that combining with the sharp pain at her breast.

Master James grabbed her, one hand around her neck, the other pressing against her trembling stomach. His touch grounded her, stopped her from shaking apart, at the same time it added another layer to the sensations that washed over her in wave after wave.

Beth was whimpering, a soft helpless sound she couldn't hide behind closed lips. Her whole body was moving from the force of her labored breaths. Each trembling breath made the clothespins on her breasts dance, and the faint breeze touched the drenched flesh between her legs, which so desperately needed his touch.

His hand at her neck tightened, not enough to cut off her air, but enough that she could not ignore that she was his—owned, possessed, controlled. She suffered because he wanted it. She ached with pleasure because he wanted it.

The hand on her stomach slid up to her breasts, sliding under the clothespins to knead each breast, increasing the circulation and preventing her tightly held nipples from going numb.

"You're going to come for me. You're going to come from having those pretty nipples tortured."

Beth shook her head, skull thumping his thighs. She wasn't able to come simply because a Dom demanded she do so. Even when it meant disobeying a direct command she hadn't been able to.

Don't make me disappoint you.

"You will come. Your body is telling me it's ready. The only thing standing in the way is your fear, your doubt."

Knuckles bumped over her nipples, catching the barely exposed tips in an exquisitely precise touch reminiscent of what he'd done to her clit.

"I will not let you fail. I will not let you disobey my command. You *will* come for me."

He will not let me disobey.

Though all her experience said otherwise, Beth believed him. Believed that he would make her come, believed that her body would obey him even when her head couldn't make sense of it.

She stopped worrying, stopped thinking about the rules.

Master James grabbed both clothespins, twisting her nipples a quarter turn. Beth screamed, hips lifting, offering her naked, wet pussy to him even as he caused her such exquisite pain.

When he released the pins, a fresh wave of feeling—no longer distinctly pleasure or pain, but something greater than both—zipped through her. He repeated the motion—twist, release, twist, release—until Beth's head was thrashing against his lap, pulling against his hold on her neck.

One final time he caught hold of both pins in one hand, grasping them firmly.

"Come for me."

He jerked both clothespins free. She had only enough time to inhale before shock waves of acute pain danced through her reddened nipples.

But it was sweet, sweet pain. She let out a small sob, her arms tensing with the need to rub the sensitive tips, before an entirely different feeling overcame her.

A dark, pain-fuelled orgasm sank its claws into her. What had been pain a moment ago became pleasure. Her skin was alive, the air brushing over her abused nipples a caress as powerful as if someone had been licking her. Beth's pussy spasmed, the need to have something filling her, for there to be something inside her for her body to clench around, the only sour note in the song of pleasure Master James had drawn from her body.

With no other physical stimulation, the orgasm faded more quickly than the previous ones, yet this was more intense, because it had come from someplace deep inside her, not just her body but her mind.

Master James pulled the clothespin from her tongue, then gently tilted her head up, massaging the tense muscles at the back of her neck as he did.

Beth curled her upper body forward, tears stinging her eyes, her hands slowly releasing their hold on his legs.

The instant she let go, a wave of fear washed over her, as if she were suddenly alone in rough seas. Turning on the pillow she wedged herself between his legs, wrapping both arms around his right leg and burying her head on his thigh.

His stroked her hair and back, whispering softly as she calmed.

"That was the most beautiful thing I've ever seen. I'm honored that you're submitting to me."

James looked up from Beth for a moment, taking in the stunned and admiring gazes of the small audience they'd accumulated. He could tell that at least some of those watching could tell exactly how amazing that had been—a true whole body orgasm from nothing more than nipple play, followed by the even more telling way she was clinging to him as she finished processing what had happened.

Beth was slowly relaxing against him, the tension melting from her as he stroked her. He wondered if she knew that much of that tension wasn't from the orgasm, but caused by her body reacting to the total lack of control she'd experienced. It was powerful and terrifying to have another person take control to such a degree.

When she'd relaxed enough that he wasn't worried about moving her, James reached down, scooped her up, and pulled her up onto his lap.

Beth curled against him, burying her face against his neck. He let her take the lead in this aftercare period, only making one small adjustment to her position. He forced her knees open, wanting to keep her aware of her pussy, which was no doubt desperate for attention. He wasn't going to give her the opportunity to use her closed legs to pleasure herself.

There was one thing he no longer doubted. Beth was submissive, and so submissive that James had to remind himself that she was only his for the weekend, so there was no point in fantasizing about all the ways he could train her to come from his voice alone.

CHAPTER 6

Master James kneaded the insides of her thighs, easing her legs further open. Beth lifted her head from where she'd tucked it against his bare chest, watching him touch her, his hand so tantalizingly close to her pussy. She was sitting sideways on his lap, heels planted on the seat next to him, one leg leaning against the back of the chair, the other fallen to the side, leaving her open and exposed.

"That was beautiful, Beth."

"Thank you, Master."

"How do your nipples feel?"

The tips of her breasts were still throbbing, and she doubted the sensation would fade any time soon. "Sore," she answered.

His palm covered her right breast, pressing it hard against her ribs. It both soothed and heightened the ache. When he'd repeated the caress with her left breast, his hand returned to her inner thighs, his other arm around her back, cradling her on his lap.

"How does your pussy feel?"

Needy. Beth wasn't prepared to say that aloud, so instead she said, "Empty."

Master James patted her pussy twice. "Then you're not going to like this. Stand up."

Beth rolled to her feet. His dress shirt was still dangling from one wrist and she shook it free, carefully folding the hopelessly wrinkled shirt and draping it over the arm of the chair. Master James watched her, and Beth got to take in the enticing tableau he presented. His upper body was well muscled, but his arms were particularly buff, which explained how easily he was able to handle her. His skin was a very pale gold, darker on his arms than chest, as if he spent some of his time outdoors in sleeveless shirts. His black slacks were tight over his thighs, which were spread in order to accommodate the obvious bulge of his erection.

Beth couldn't stop herself from staring at his crotch, wondering what his cock looked like, what it would taste like. His belt gleamed in that muted way that only nice leather did, and the buckle was a flat silver rectangle rather than a more pedestrian prong and frame.

"See something you like?" he asked, his heavy-lidded gaze examining her as she did the same to him.

"Yes, Master James."

"What do you want?"

"To see your cock."

"Just see it?"

"No, Master."

He waited, but Beth didn't speak. She didn't want to derail the scene by saying the wrong thing. The sooner they stopped talking the sooner he might do something to her, and despite the latest orgasm, she wanted more.

"Put the pillow away, then come back."

Naked, Beth took the floor pillow back to the basket. It was full dark now, though the landscape lighting kept everything well illuminated.

When she returned, sans pillow, there was a pile of metal

and black leather on Master James's lap. He motioned for her to stand in front of him. Beth positioned herself legs spread, arms raised, hands behind her neck.

Master James took a moment to look his fill, as if he hadn't already thoroughly inspected her. When he lifted the thing on his lap, chain rattled.

"Do you know what this is?"

"No, Master James."

"What if I hold it like this?"

He changed the positioning, until it was all too clear what he held—a chastity belt.

The waistband was a two-inch-wide piece of thin metal, backed by black leather with an adjustable closure on one side. Descending from the front was a second piece of metal that curved to the shape of a woman's body. The sides were straight except for a flared portion that would provide full coverage of the pussy. In the back, the strip of metal narrowed until it ended in two chains, which connected the crotch piece to the waist.

"It's a chastity belt, Master James."

He rose to his feet, the belt dangling casually from one hand. His big body crowded Beth, his bare chest brushing her nipples, his face so close to her that she could see the color variations in his irises.

"Do you want me to fuck you?"

"Yes, Master James."

He curled a hand in her hair, pulling her head back. "Do you want my cock in you?"

"Yes, Master." Her voice trembled. "Yes."

"Can you imagine it? My rock hard cock in you, my hands holding you down as I fuck you?"

Beth sucked in air, her nipples brushing against him as her whole body throbbed with need.

"Yes, Master James. I can imagine it. I want it." Her eyes fluttered closed.

"How much?"

"More than anything." The sounds of voices from others in the courtyard had died down, as if everyone was staying quiet in order to hear what she and Master James said.

"Well then." His lips feathered against her cheek. "Too bad you're not going to get it."

Beth's eyes snapped open and bright anger filled her. Her muscles tensed with the need to attack him, to push him down and rip open his pants and sink onto his cock.

The hand in her hair tightened, until her scalp tingled with pain. "Look at me."

Beth met his gaze, anger hot in her eyes, her hands, still behind her neck, curled into fists.

There was heat in his gaze, but it wasn't anger, it was arousal.

"Fuck me," she demanded. "Fuck me now." All thoughts of rules and submission were gone. She *needed* him and she would do whatever it took to get what her body craved.

"No."

James pulled her hard against his body, lips lowering to hers in a punishing kiss. Beth grabbed his upper arms, nails digging into him as they battled for control through the kiss. Metal clattered as the chastity belt fell to the tile, his free hand grabbing her naked ass, grinding her pelvis against his cock.

Teeth nipped, tongues dueled, and breath mingled as the kiss went on. Beth's hands slid up to his shoulders as she lifted onto her toes, pressing herself more fully against him. James continued to kiss her, pausing only long enough to change the angle of his mouth.

As the kiss went on, Beth's grip on his shoulders loosened, her hands no longer curled in anger and demand. Her head tipped back, yielding to the pressure of his kiss, and her lips parted, giving him unequivocal access to her mouth.

The urge to fight him, to take control and get what she

wanted at any cost faded, subsided under the need to yield, to give in and relinquish control, even at the expense of gratification.

They were both panting when Master James ended the kiss.

Beth's forehead dropped to rest on his collarbone. The fingers in her hair massaged her scalp, easing the residual sting.

When he stepped back, she kept her head submissively lowered—not out of fear, or for the sake of an arbitrary rule, but because he'd proven to her that he was in command.

Perched on the edge of the chair, he picked up the chastity belt, unfastening all the pieces before slipping the waistband around her middle. Once he sized it to her, he locked it in place, looping the chain dangling from the key over his neck so the small piece of cut metal glittered against his chest.

Reattaching the crotch piece to the front of the belt, he adjusted it until the widest part was pressed over her pussy, sealing it away from any hope of stimulation or penetration. At his command she turned, and he pulled the chains at the back snug. They were positioned to sit firmly in the crease of the buttocks, while also separating the cheeks slightly as the chains rose and attached to rings near the sides of the belt.

When the chastity belt was in place Beth shuddered, a final note of surrender.

Master James tugged at various places, making sure it was tight enough to make her aware of her bondage, but not so tight as to be painful.

"Go get the cushion." His voice was dark and rough. "I want you on your knees."

IF HE DIDN'T GET HIS COCK IN HER MOUTH WITHIN the next minute, James was going to lose his mind.

Beth's steps were tentative as she walked with the chastity

belt pressed tight against her pussy. Seeing the fire of her need, a fire that burned so hot it melted all thoughts of being a good rule-following sub, was incredibly sexy, but nothing compared to the way it felt to have her yield to him in a kiss.

That was true submission—to be driven to the point of near madness with desire and still yield control. It was easy to be submissive when the base need to fuck wasn't consuming. Only a true submissive would submit when every instinct screamed for her to take control and find satisfaction.

James scrubbed one hand over his face, taking a minute to pull himself together. Topping Beth was both challenging and easy—simply put, they had good chemistry.

When Beth returned, laying the cushion on the tile at his feet, he motioned for her to kneel, not trusting himself to speak. Part of him wanted to know what she felt, what she was thinking. A bigger part of him wanted her mouth on his cock, so the conversation would have to wait.

She must have sensed what he wanted, because she knelt facing him, her knees spread, hands palms up on her thighs.

When he unfastened his belt and unzipped his pants, he felt the weight of her gaze. Adjusting his slacks, he pulled his cock free, deciding it wasn't worth the trouble of standing up in order to get them all the way off.

He was rock hard and already wet from pre-come. Stroking himself a few times, he watched Beth lick her lower lip, which brought his attention to her pretty mouth.

James moved his hand, inviting her to pleasure him. She leaned forward only to stop, eyelashes flickering as she looked up. For half a second he was ready to punish her for teasing him, but reminded himself that it was more likely she was waiting for an order.

Clearing his throat, he forced himself to not make it simple for her. "I am going to come. Either from jerking myself off, and I'll come on your pretty face, or you can suck my cock."

Beth leaned forward, the tip of her tongue flicking the vein along the underside of his dick, before taking the head in her mouth.

James groaned, grabbing on to the cushion to keep himself from taking control—he wanted to know what she would do, how she would pleasure him without interference.

Inching her knees forward, Beth started to suck him in earnest, her head bobbing up and down, her tongue extended so that it was between her lower teeth and the sensitive underside of his cock. The head of his cock rubbed over the roof of her mouth and the inner edges of her back teeth, before bumping the back of her throat.

The angle meant she couldn't take him very deep, though he felt her try, listened for the change in her breathing as she timed it to coincide with her movements.

"Use your hands," he commanded, aware his voice was tight.

Slender fingers wrapped around the base of his cock, squeezing in time with her bobbing head.

As she drew back, he wrapped his hand around the back of her neck, controlling her by exerting gentle pressure just under her ears. She froze, lips still wrapped around the shaft just behind the head, her tongue stroking the slit in long, slow licks that were making him crazy.

"Look at me," he demanded.

Beth's gaze flicked up, brown eyes almost black in the shadows of the courtyard.

He urged her to move once more, this time while looking at him. James pushed her hair back from her cheek, tucking it behind her ear as she lowered her mouth towards his pelvis, moving with a kind of teasing slowness that he both hated and enjoyed.

"Faster," he demanded, knowing it wouldn't be long before he came.

Her movements became less controlled, less choreographed,

but it wasn't from a lack of care. He could see the desire in her eyes, the need that filled her and was being translated into pleasuring him, even as she was bereft of stimulation.

When he could no longer sit still, James pushed her away and rose to his feet. Beth's mouth was back on his cock in a matter of seconds, and now he could cradle her head in his hands, thrusting into her mouth even as she bobbed up and down on him. She released the base of his cock and clung to his thighs, not resisting his control of her head.

James pumped quick and hard as he felt the orgasm build in his shaft, then slowed for three final thrusts, bumping his cock against her throat with each deep penetration.

He came on her tongue, his fingers rhythmically massaging her scalp as he groaned in pleasure, the sight of her on her knees, lips wrapped around his cock, seared into his brain.

James collapsed back into the chair, his breathing heavy. Beth looked at him, her mouth half open, and he realized that she had yet to swallow.

A fierce wave of desire swept through him and he nodded, watching as she closed her mouth and swallowed.

He stroked her jaw, the curve of her throat, and the delicate line of her collarbone, before dropping his fingers to her nipples, tugging lightly.

She sucked in air and arched her back, the reaction too strong for the level of pressure in his touch, telling him that her nipples were still sensitive from the clothespin play.

It was still early in the evening, and the others in the courtyard were just getting into their play, the murmur of voices punctuated by the soft slap of a spanking. When a couple hopped up onto the stage, a coil of nylon rope held in the Dom's hand, James forgot his tentative plan of taking their play to the bedroom. It would be far more fun to spend time tormenting Beth and seeing exactly how responsive she could be.

WAS IT POSSIBLE TO GO COMPLETELY INSANE FROM sexual frustration?

When Master James had ordered her to kneel on the chair next to him, Beth's hopes had risen—maybe he'd take the chastity belt off and fuck her, if not with his cock then with his fingers. Instead, the devious man had decided to torture her, driving her to the point of almost assured madness.

Beth was kneeling beside Master James, her body at a right angle to his. Her feet were sticking out of the open space below the arm of the chair and he'd used his belt to strap one of her legs to the frame, keeping her thighs pressed firmly against the wood.

Tugging at the belt, Master James then tested the tension in the chains of the chastity belt. It was enough to add pressure against her pussy, the stimulation muted, but in her heightened state of arousal and awareness even that had her gasping.

Kneeling as she was, Beth was up against Master James, hands braced on the seat by his thigh, her shoulder against his chest and he felt her shudder.

"You have a very talented mouth." He massaged her back with one hand as he spoke, the other cradling a glass of scotch someone had brought him.

"Thank you, Master James."

"But..." He savored the word, and when Beth snuck an alarmed glance at his face she could see the hint of teasing in his eyes. "But, the checklist doesn't say blowjob. Or if it does, that falls under the letter B. It says cock worship."

"Yes, Master James." Beth wasn't sure where this was going, but she snuck a glance at his semi-flaccid cock, which he hadn't tucked back into his pants.

"So you're going to do precisely that, while we watch all these other people play, and you're going to do it all with that chastity belt on, knowing that the one thing you need you can't get."

Beth couldn't stop the small growl that escaped her.

"Is that a problem?"

"No, Master James." She bit off each word.

He tipped her chin up, and whatever he saw in her face made him grin. The jerk. Easy for him to smile when he'd gotten to come. Then again, she had come three times today.

"If you're a good girl I might be willing to give you some stimulation." His fingers kneaded her ass, then followed the path of the chains, stroking over her puckered anus, which Beth realized for the first time was protected only by the chain, not the metal plate.

"If I beg...you will fuck my ass?"

"Oh no, you haven't earned that. If you beg, I'll have someone else put a plug in that pretty bottom."

Beth shuddered as a wave of desire washed over her. She dropped her head, taking deep breaths as she tried to bring herself under control.

Master James gathered her hair in his hand, then urged her to lower her upper body. He shifted to a more reclined position so she could lay her cheek against his lower abdomen, allowing her to see what was going on in the courtyard.

Without any further prompting, Beth used one hand to flip his cock up, sucking the soft head into her mouth where she could "worship" it.

The Dom on the stage was in the middle of some complex rope bondage that included creating a cradle for the head of a large Hitachi Magic Wand vibrator, which he bound tightly to the sub's pussy. When the ropes were in place, the Dom flicked the vibrator on. The sub, helplessly suspended in rope, her legs bent, knees held open by a spreader bar, could only gasp and moan as the vibrator worked on her clit. The woman's thrashing made her sway slightly from side to side, and even from a distance Beth could see her muscles bunching under her skin as she strained against the ropes. When she screamed through the first orgasm, Beth sucked harder on Master James's rapidly stiffening cock. When she sobbed through a second orgasm, Beth sucked and nipped the length of his shaft.

When the sub begged to have the vibrator turned off and her master instead started gently spanking her, Master James was fully hard, and Beth bobbed her head up and down on his cock.

The act of servicing him this way, of being bound and controlled while pleasuring her Master, was arousing in a way Beth hadn't known, though on paper it was similar to many other situations she'd been in. She'd sucked and licked her share of cocks and pussies, but had never been so stimulated by the act—never seen it as a something that could or would stimulate *her*. She wanted his cock in her mouth, wanted to feel his hardness against her tongue, invading her throat.

When the well-pleasured sub was lowered to the stage and the ropes quickly cut away, Beth was not surprised that the woman crawled to her Master and ripped at his pants, devouring his cock.

Master James forced her mouth off, and Beth stared at the hard length of his dick, which was wet with her spit.

"Did you enjoy watching that?"

"Yes, oh yes." Beth started to lower her mouth once more, but Master James kept her head up with a firm hold on her chin.

"I think I'd like to see you like that, though I'm not a rope expert. Would you like to be bound and forced to orgasm?"

"Oh yes." Without the stimulation of his cock in her mouth Beth was itchy with need. She shifted as much as she could, trying to make the chastity belt press against her pussy.

"What do you want, Beth?"

"You, Master James."

There was a moment of stillness, as if she'd surprised him,

then he released her chin. "Remember what I offered you if you begged."

Beth paused, open mouth an inch away from his cock. Looking up she wondered if this was a test, if there was a wrong answer. What would a good sub do?

"No, Beth, don't think about it, trust me. I gave you a choice, an opportunity. I'm simply reminding you."

"I want to keep sucking your cock."

"Good, because I enjoy having your mouth on me."

"I would also like to have a plug."

"Why?"

Wasn't it enough that she wanted it? Did she have to explain everything?

"Why, Beth?"

"Because I want more. Serving a Master should be enough for a good sub, but it's not." Her stomach clenched with a feeling she could only describe as disloyalty, yet the honesty felt good. "Every time I come, I just want something else."

"Of course. Your sub isn't satisfied yet." His thumb stroked her lower lip. "Tell me exactly what you want."

"I want to kneel here and suck your cock with a plug in my ass. I want you to touch me and use me and abuse me until this need goes away."

Their gazes met, and something powerful passed between them.

Master James slid out from under her. Beth dropped her forehead to the seat cushion, looking up when she heard footsteps she knew were his.

Dangling from his right hand was a long silver plug with a flared base.

"I'm not willing to let anyone else play with your ass before I do."

He stepped up to the arm of the chair, and Beth twisted to

watch him. He coated the tip of the plug with lube, then turned his attention to her ass.

Pulling the globes of her ass apart he tugged the chains to the side. They were already tight and the added tension pressed the chastity belt hard against her pussy, hard enough that Beth felt her pussy lips throb against the unforgiving metal.

One slick finger rubbed against her anus.

"Relax," he demanded, burying the tip of his finger inside her. Beth moaned in pleasure at the penetration.

"Can you come from anal stimulation alone?"

"No, Master James." The answer was automatic, but then again, her body had responded to him in ways it had never responded to anyone before. "I don't know."

"Let's find out, shall we?"

Something cold pressed against her rear entrance, and for a second she tensed before reminding herself to relax. The tip of the plug slid in.

Master James applied steady pressure, forcing her body to open, forcing her to accept the penetration. As her sensitive anus was stimulated, Beth started to breathe hard, something coiling tight inside her.

"Are you going to come, Beth?"

She couldn't answer, only shake her head, not denying it, but telling him she didn't know.

The plug sank in, her body closing around the narrow neck.

Master James carefully moved the chains back into place so they were now holding the plug in place.

Beth turned to look at him, the small movement making the plug shift inside her. Master James returned to his seat, and without a word forced her head onto his rock-hard shaft. He was thicker than he had been a moment ago, a testament to the fact that plugging her ass had been stimulating for him too.

Beth devoured his cock, swallowing as she took him deeper

than she had before, the head of his cock filling her throat. She wanted it deep, needed to be overwhelmed by sensation.

Master James unfastened the belt from around her thigh. "Rock your hips back and forth while you suck me."

He had to help her find the rhythm, but soon Beth was rocking forward and back, as if meeting the thrusts of someone fucking her from behind, but there was no one there. Only the endless frustrating pressure of the chastity belt and the shifting of the plug within her. Her thighs smacking against the arm of the chair, her shoulder bumping against his chest. Beth moaned in frustration around his cock. Her nail dug into his leg, her brow furrowing.

She needed something more, just one more thing to push her over the edge, over an edge she didn't understand.

Master James's breathing was heavy, and one hand dropped to her head, taking control of the blowjob.

"I'm going to come," he panted. "I want you to come too."

It wasn't going to be enough. There was no direct stimulation, the plug held so tightly in place by the belt that its movement inside her was minimal.

The crack of leather striking skin took her by surprise, the sound registering before the flare of pain. Beth gasped and nearly choked as she realized he was spanking her with his belt. The second blow landed and distracted her, pushing her further from the precipice of orgasm, but the third blow brought all her arousal and need flaring back to life.

Master James's cock twitched in her mouth, his hand fisted her hair, and more punishing blows landed on her ass. His doubled-over belt smacked her ass in hard, sharp blows. It hurt. It made her pussy throb.

The orgasm ripped through her, a soul-shaking wave of pleasure without the sharp peaks of ecstasy she was used to. Master James forced her head down until her nose touched his pelvis. Come filled her throat as Master James came, the sensation causing a fresh wave of pleasure to rumble through her. She swallowed around the head of his cock.

Spots swam behind her closed eyelids, and Beth realized she needed to take a breath. His hand fell from her hair and she pulled back, sucking in air through her nose, the tip of his cock still in her mouth.

Her own labored breathing was mirrored by Master James's.

Exhausted, Beth's shaking elbows couldn't hold her up any longer. Letting his cock slip from her mouth, she collapsed on her side, knees curled up in a fetal position, her head on Master James's thigh. His hand stroked her hair back from her sweaty face.

Beth's body continued to hum and throb, but she finally felt content, despite, or maybe because of, the plug and chastity belt, which were still in place.

She closed her eyes, safe and satisfied, cradled against her Master.

CHAPTER 7

J ames woke first, the warmth of a woman beside him making him smile before he'd even opened his eyes. When he caught sight of Beth, who was sprawled on her stomach beside him, the smile widened. She'd fallen asleep on his lap in the courtyard, waking only when he carried her into the bedroom and had her bend over the bathroom counter so he could remove the plug and chastity belt.

Remembering how her ass had looked, red from the belt, spread wide as he removed the plug, he eased the covers down. There was one faint bruise on her left ass cheek—he must have hit that spot too many times in a row. The belt spanking had been impromptu and done with less finesse than was ideal. But there was something to be said for scenes driven by passion rather than planning, as long as he kept enough control to make sure he didn't really hurt her.

Beth had one leg bent to the side, seemingly begging him to touch her sweet pussy, which the position left exposed.

He wasn't the kind of man to ignore such an enticing invitation.

She stirred slightly when he laid his hand on her thigh,

stroking his way up to her pussy. Spreading her labia open with two fingers he used a third to tap her clit.

Beth came awake with a start, sucking in a surprised breath. She started to close her legs, but he tsked at her.

She froze, then turned her head on the pillow. Propped on one elbow he smiled at her, then pinched her labia together and tugged.

"Good morning, Beth."

"Good morning, Master James."

"How do you feel?"

"I'm not awake enough to answer that question."

He laughed, though he could tell she was serious. "Well, *I'm* awake."

He lay back and pushed the covers away, revealing his morning erection. Beth looked from his cock to his face, waiting for an order. He didn't want to give her an exact order, he wanted to see what she'd do. Rather than say anything, he pointed at his cock.

Beth got to her hands and knees, breasts dangling enticingly under her. James tugged on her nipples as she positioned herself against him. Her head lowered towards his crotch, but she stopped, looking at him out of the corner of her eye. He raised a brow.

Beth shot up and swung her leg over his hips, straddling his cock. Before he could stop her, or help her, she'd tilted her pelvis, his dick sliding through the folds of her pussy to her entrance. She wasn't that wet, but she lowered her hips, taking the tip of his cock into her body.

Her whole body shuddered, and the sight of her—head thrown back, nipples pink and soft, belly tight—was enough to have him ratcheting closer to an orgasm. Her sheath grew damp around his cock.

James grabbed her hips, pulling them down. Beth was tight —far tighter than he'd expected her to be. Her nails dug in to the skin of his lower belly, her breasts rose and fell with her breathing, and when her pussy clenched rhythmically around him, James realized she was coming.

Using his hold on her hips he urged her to move. She obeyed, riding him with slow, deep strokes.

"Faster," he commanded.

Her eyes snapped open. Bracing her hands on his chest she leaned forward a bit and sped up. As he raced towards his own orgasm, James found himself looking into her face, meeting her gaze. He could sense her desire, her need, and yet she was a mystery—there was something behind her eyes he couldn't name, more to her than he'd yet uncovered.

Needing more control, he rolled them over, tucking his forearms under her shoulder blades, hands curled over her shoulders from behind to hold her in place as he fucked her pussy hard and fast. When Beth tipped her head back and moaned, he bit her neck.

He came inside her, slowing but not entirely stopping his thrusts as his breathing calmed. Part of him was waiting for a signal from her—a restless squirm or frown that would signal she needed more, but her eyes were closed and whatever pleasure had overcome her when his cock first penetrated her seemed to have satisfied her.

At least for now.

James finally pulled out, lying back beside her. For a second he reached for her hand, prepared to lace his fingers with her, but then stopped. That was an odd gesture for a Master and sub —too friendly to be sexual, too romantic for a club setting.

"Master, may I leave the bed?"

He nodded, head still on the pillow, and watched her slip off the bed. He saw her hesitate, as if she weren't sure if she should walk or crawl to the en suite bathroom. She opted to walk.

Once she was out of sight, James rubbed his hands over his face. Mikael had been right—Beth had been ill-used, though the other Masters' mistake was understandable, if amateurish in his opinion. She was a fun sub when she stopped thinking so hard about what a sub should do. As she'd just demonstrated this morning, if she was given an opportunity to make choices, she opted for more overt sexual contact than her demeanor might otherwise indicate.

He opened his eyes when she approached the bed. Kneeling on the edge she lowered her head and cleaned his cock with her tongue. Fierce pleasure roared through him as he watched her service and care for him. By the time she was done he was semi-hard, and when she cleaned him a second time with a warm wet washcloth he was fighting the urged to bend her over the bed and fuck her.

After carefully cleaning his balls, Beth turned to take the washcloth back to the bathroom. He grabbed her arm.

"Usually I'm the one with the washcloth." Worry furrowed her brow and he stroked the pulse point in her wrist with his thumb. "That wasn't a criticism, Beth."

"Oh." She pursed her lips. "And you're not angry that I..."

"Rode me like a bronco?"

Now she smiled, and again it transformed her face. "You didn't expressly say you wanted my mouth on your cock."

"I didn't. I like that you wanted me in your pussy."

The blunt language had her licking her lips and swaying towards him.

"Do you know what I want now?" he asked in a low voice.

"No, Master. Tell me and I'll do it."

"I know you will." He grabbed her left nipple and tugged her down, until she was bent with her face only inches from his. "I want you to go to the dresser and open the top drawer. Bring me two sets of clamps."

Beth scampered away, detouring only far enough to toss the washcloth into the bathroom. James sat up, adding pillows behind his back and crossing his arms to avoid the temptation to stroke his cock.

She flicked through the selection in the drawer, which while far from comprehensive, he knew from experience had plenty of variety. Considering how much she'd enjoyed the clothespins he expected her to go for heavy clover clamps, but when she returned, she carried two pairs of delicate gold ones. One set were tweezer-style, which could be adjusted for tightness, and decorated with beaded gold tassels. The second were small screw clamps with black rubber tips, the screw part again allowing for adjustment of tightness. These were connected by three gold chains of differing lengths.

She poured them into his outstretched hands.

"Do you know where these are going?"

"I can guess, Master."

"And what's your guess?"

"My nipples and pussy."

"Pretty and smart." He pointed at her chest. "Play with your nipples."

There was a faint blush on her cheeks and James wondered if that was from arousal or if he'd embarrassed her. When her nipples were erect from tugs and flicks, he motioned her closer and applied the screw clamps, tightening them enough to keep them on, but not so much that they'd have to come off any time soon. The chains dangled between her breasts, the longest one falling nearly to her belly button.

"Spread your legs."

When he toyed with her pussy lips, he found that she was wet. Rewarding her for that with a few strokes to her clit, he then applied the tweezer clamps to her pussy lips, placing them toward the front of her pussy, where the inner pieces would bump her clit and the decorative tassels would be more obvious, drawing everyone's attention to her sex.

"Walk. I need to make sure they won't fall off."

Once he was satisfied they wouldn't slip off her pussy lips, he motioned towards the wardrobe. "See if there's a robe in there. I want you to put it on."

She frowned before obeying, flicking through the robes, bypassing terrycloth, kimono-style, and sheer black, selecting a long, white satin one. He was slightly surprised by her choice— it was a rather romantic, dramatic garment.

Beth slid it on, the white a lovely contrast to her tan skin, and he no longer doubted her selection.

He crooked his finger. When she stopped beside the bed, he pinched a fold of the smooth fabric and rubbed it against her clamped nipples. She jumped, then arched her back.

"Now I want you, my lovely Beth…"

He reached between her legs, flicking the tassels, then pinching the clamps together.

"…to go get us breakfast."

Her eyes popped open and her lips parted, as if she would protest. He waited, trying to hide his smile. She bared her teeth at him and he laughed.

"I'm hungry. We didn't eat dinner. Go get food."

"Yes, Master. What do you like to eat?"

"Meat."

"Turkey bacon?"

"What? No! Real bacon. Sausage."

Her eyebrows climbed as she looked at him, as if trying to figure out how he got away with eating that. The damned woman was making him feel defensive. "I run."

"Ah. That explains the tan."

"What?"

"Your arms are darker than your chest."

Was it that noticeable? "Er, yes."

Beth turned to leave, closing the robe and belting it in place.

"Beth."

She stopped and turned back.

"You can wear the robe closed on the way to the dining room, but when you get there, untie it. Make sure everyone can see your clamps."

Her eyes lowered and he could almost see her submission falling over her. There were some women who needed a constant level of domination and couldn't handle shifting dynamics. Clearly Beth could, which James was glad of. He didn't want to spend unnecessary energy making sure he was always in "Dom mode."

Beth returned ten minutes later, the robe open, exposing her naked body. Part of him wished he'd gone with her, wished he could have seen the admiring gazes she'd no doubt gotten. The tassels on her pussy clattered together cheerfully as she brought over a tray, placing it on the bed.

"Join me."

She sat cross-legged, the tray between them. Her plate held an egg white veggie omelet and fruit. His had a California omelet, three strips of bacon, sausage, and one strawberry.

"Is this your attempt to make sure I get some fruit?" He held up the berry.

"There's vegetables in the omelet, too."

"Ugh. Vegetables."

"I hope you're joking." She frowned at him.

"I am. I'll even eat this strawberry." He bit the tip off, then reached over and rubbed it against her nipples, smearing them and the clamps with the pink juice.

Beth's head dropped back. "If this is what it takes, I'm willing to sacrifice myself to make sure you eat healthily."

James roared with laughter. The rest of breakfast was punctuated by laughter as they teased each other about their eating habits, sexual play as he licked her nipples clean, then pretended to get his fork tangled in the nipple clamp chains, tugging them until she was panting.

When their plates were finally empty, James realized they'd

been sitting there enjoying one another's company for nearly two hours. With a start he realized this felt more like a lazy Sunday morning with a girlfriend than the precursor to a day of D/s play.

"Get rid of the tray." The command came out harsher than he'd meant it to and she recoiled slightly, eyes wide. James softened his tone, but turned away from her, getting off the bed. "If I'm not here when you get back, take off the clamps and clean them, then put them away."

"Yes, Master."

Without another word he left, ignoring the voice in his head that said he should just stay in bed with her, talking and fucking. They had a list, and it was time for the next item.

———

BETH HAD A FAIRLY GOOD IDEA WHAT WAS GOING TO happen next. She'd returned to the playroom to find Master James gone. Assuming a kneeling position near the cold fireplace, she looked up when the door opened, only to see a woman entering. The sub bustled over, holding out a cloth tape. Once she'd taken Beth's torso measurements, she left.

Another half hour passed before the door opened. This time it was Master James, and she was not surprised to see the corset he held under one arm, though the plastic bucket he carried was a bit more puzzling.

Once he spotted her, he detoured to the seating area by the fireplace, easing into one of the wide wingback leather chairs.

"Are you ready for our next scene?"

"Of course, Master."

"Stand up."

Beth rose, stepping up beside his chair. When he sat forward and shook out the corset, she raised her arms.

The corset was heavy reinforced satin, the black fabric seeming to glow with a muted shine. There were hook closures down the front and white satin ribbon lacing up the back. Smooth, cool fabric slid against her skin as Master James placed the corset around her back. Hook by hook he closed the corset down the front. The laces were loose enough that it wasn't difficult. Once it was in place Master James rose and moved behind her.

Beth gasped as he started to adjust the laces at the back, pulling the surprisingly stiff corset tight to her skin, then tighter still, constricting her waist and chest.

"Hold on to the chair."

Beth clung to the back of the chair as he tugged. She could no longer take a really deep breath, and the pressure against her nipples was sweet torment.

"There's something very satisfying about putting a woman into a corset." Master James's voice was a low grumble, deeper and with a note of menace that hadn't been there when they teased each other over breakfast.

"I've never worn one like this before."

"What kind have you worn?"

"A waist cincher."

"The ones that don't cover the breasts?"

"Yes, Master."

"For this particular scene I wanted to see you in a full corset." A final tug, and he stepped away. "There's a mirror over there."

Curious, Beth moved until she could see herself. Her breasts were two plump mounds above the sweetheart top, her waist almost impossibly tiny. Her sex seemed very naked compared to the stiff black fabric.

Master James stepped up behind her, seeming to loom over her, his hands settling on her cinched waist. Keeping his gaze locked on hers in the mirror, he dipped his head to nip her shoulder, then cupped one hand over her sex and lifted, forcing her onto her toes.

She was panting—the only kind of breathing she could really do—when he stepped back.

"You have your corset now, but we're going to kill two birds with one stone and take care of another checklist item at the same time."

He pulled something from the bucket and brought it over to her. The short black apron was trimmed with white lace. He settled it around her hips and tied it in place. It barely covered her sex, and from side to side was only wide enough to reach her hips, leaving her ass completely bare.

"You make a lovely maid."

"Maid?" Beth twisted, looking at her ass, which seemed rather large compared to her waist. The tails of the apron strings dangled along the crease of her buttocks.

"Chores are one of our checklist items." Master James brought her the bucket.

It was a simple blue plastic bucket. There were a few spray bottles, cleaning cloths, and a short feather duster inside.

"Chores," Beth repeated. She was turned on by the way he'd laced her in so tightly, but disappointed that now she was expected to clean. It was far better than being a footstool, and cleaning in a corset would at least be more interesting than the times she'd been ordered to help clean or set up playrooms while naked.

Master James returned to his chair, turning it so he could see the whole room. He placed one ankle on the opposite knee, resting his chin on his fist.

Beth placed the bucket on a side table and pulled out all the spray bottles, lining them up. Taking the first one, she started to read the directions for use on the back. When she was confident she understood that one, she set it down and picked up the second.

"Beth, what are you doing?"

"Reading the instructions."

"It's just cleaning."

"I'm not familiar with cleaning products." She kept her tone neutral.

"You don't know how to clean?"

"I pay someone to do this." This time her exasperation was clear. "I don't want to damage the finish on anything."

"Beth." His exasperation was a mate to hers. "I don't want you to actually clean anything."

"Then why did you give me a bucket of stuff?"

"I grabbed it out of some closet as a prop. Pretend to dust."

"Pretending to dust isn't 'chores'."

He thunked his head against the back of the chair. "No. But it means I get to watch you bend over in the corset and then punish you for being a naughty maid."

Beth's eyes widened in horror. "This is…this is role play?"

CHAPTER 8

"Why are you saying it the way people normally say 'dead baby seals'?"

"I *hate* role play. I'm *terrible* at role play." Beth's most traumatic high school experience had been when her best friend had cajoled her into being part of the school musical. She had a hard enough time figuring out what *she* was feeling, let alone pretending to be someone else and then trying to show others what the pretend person was feeling.

"Okay, Miss Literal. It's not role play." The corner of his lips twitched in a smile.

Beth had a white-knuckle grip on the bottle of glass cleaner. James frowned, realizing that she was not teasing, as funny as her fear might sound to others.

"Beth." Now his voice was sharp with command. "Put all the spray bottles in the bucket. Take out the feather duster."

Beth grabbed the feather duster, which was made of actual black and white feathers and had a short, thick wooden handle.

"Go dust the front of the wardrobe."

Feeling better at having simple, direct orders to follow, Beth went to the tall dark-wood piece and ran the duster over the doors.

"I don't think this is very effective." There wasn't any dust on the furniture—Las Palmas had a discreet cleaning service come in during the week, and two full-time people who lived on site and maintained the playrooms daily—but if there had been dust she was fairly certain the feathers would just move it around.

"Dust the top."

Beth rose on tiptoe, one hand on the doors, the other stretched up. For a large man, he was surprisingly silent as he came up behind her. When Master James grabbed her bare ass, Beth nearly lost her balance.

"I didn't say you could stop." He growled the words when she lowered her outstretched arm.

Beth went back up on her toes, struggling to maintain the position as he massaged her ass. When his lips brushed her ear, Beth shivered. The corset not only restricted her movement, but made her intensely aware of how naked her lower half was.

"The table over there needs to be cleaned."

He turned her by the hips, pointing her to the small side table positioned near the chair he'd been sitting in. The corset caused her hips to sway more than normal, but this time she played it up, sure from the weight of his gaze that he was watching her ass as she walked away.

It was an incredibly powerful feeling. She was the one in the binding corset, obeying his orders—yet she felt strong and in control.

She flicked the feather duster along the top of the perfectly clean table, heart thumping in her chest as she waited for him to make his next move. Master James resumed his seat.

"You missed a spot."

"I did?"

"Yes, stand right in front of me and you'll see it."

Beth's blood was humming with desire and anticipation as she positioned herself in front of him, her legs only a few inches from his knees. Again she flicked the duster, barely moving as she focused all her attention on the man at her back.

"There's dust on the shelf. Clean it."

There was a shelf near the bottom of the table, set with a lovely impressionist ceramic sculpture of a naked man and woman. Beth started to bend, then realized the corset made that problematic.

Bracing one hand on the tabletop she bent from the hips, not the waist, thrusting her ass back as she leaned forward.

A heavy hand on her back slammed her down the last few inches, so her chest was flat on the table. Master James grabbed the duster from her.

"I have a confession." He ran the soft feathers up her arm to her shoulder, then used them to push her hair off her face, the tickling feeling causing her to scrunch up her nose.

"This isn't really meant for dusting." He held it where she could see it. "Look at the handle."

The handle was about as long as her hand, from wrist to the tip of her fingers, and as wide around as a tube of toothpaste. Rather than straight it was curved, like the silhouette of a woman's body, with a rounded, tapered end.

"Can you guess where this is going?"

She could guess, but between the position, the corset, and the arousal that made it hard to think let alone talk, Beth didn't answer.

"I'm going to fuck your pussy with it, then going to shove it inside your tight ass."

With one hand on her upper back holding her down, he brushed her butt and legs with the feathers.

"Then I'm going to make you keep it in your ass, like a feather tail."

The smooth wood of the handle rubbed her inner thighs, then tapped against her mound.

"You're going to do some more chores, like get me lunch and a drink, all with a cute little feather tail."

Beth was panting with desire, the picture painted by his words driving her mad with desire.

The smooth, cool wood slid between the lips of her sex, the tip rubbing her clit.

"Then I'm going to take it out of your ass, so that I can fuck you. Or maybe you need to go over my knee for a spanking first."

The handle pressed into her, her desire-tightened body greedily clenching around the wood as it entered her inch by inch.

"I could say it's to punish you for this morning, but really it would just be because I want to spank you."

He started fucking her with the feather duster in earnest. Beth clung to the table, wanting to thrust back, but he was holding her in place, giving her no opportunity to move. She could only stand there and take it.

Leaving the handle buried in her, Master James rubbed two fingers between her pussy lips, gathering her body's own moisture and spreading it on her anus. He repeated the motion several times, pausing to fuck her on occasion, before pulling the duster handle out of her pussy and pressing it against her rear entrance.

The tip slid in smoothly, but the taper was not as gradual as last night's plug, and as he kept pushing, Beth squirmed.

"Tell me if I'm hurting you."

"You're not, Master," she whispered. There were twinges of pain but they were the good kind, the kind that let her know she was being used.

"Good."

When it was seated inside her to his satisfaction, Master James let her stand up.

"Time for the rest of your chores." He took a seat, the bulge of his erection apparent, his gaze hot with desire. "Get me a bottle of water and a glass of champagne."

"Yes, Master."

"Oh, and Beth..."

She paused.

"If you let it fall out, I won't fuck you for the rest of the weekend."

Now *that* was real punishment. Butt clenched, Beth slipped out of the playroom to complete her chores.

———

BETH SPRAWLED ON THE BED BESIDE MASTER JAMES, eyes closed. One of her arms was dangling off the edge in an awkward manner that was making it impossible to fall completely asleep, but she was dozing in a post-orgasm state of bliss.

"Beth, it's almost time to go."

"Hmm?"

Strong arms pulled her against a warm chest and Beth relaxed into the embrace.

"It's nearly six."

That woke her up. "PM? Sunday?"

"Yes."

Her stomach clenched. Their weekend was over. Yesterday had been a whirlwind of kinky sex, the feather duster giving way to a good long fuck with her bent over the table, followed by dinner in the dining room, while she wore cuffs and nipple clamps, a one-foot-long chain connecting each cuff to the corresponding clamp, which made eating an adventure and ensured that by the time they were done, her well-stimulated nipples had her so desperate for release that she'd literally jumped on James the instant they entered their room.

But it wasn't their room, it was a playroom—and one they'd be leaving shortly.

Today they'd taken it easy—the focus on getting Beth to express what she wanted in a way that fit with her rule-based view of BDSM. Master James had convinced her that she could still use the rules as a guide, but that wiggling her hips while standing in an appropriate posture was not "breaking the rules" but rather letting a Dom know that she was feeling sexy or playful.

Lunch had been memorable—she'd spent it cuffed wrist and ankle to a straight-backed chair on the stage in the courtyard. A straight-backed chair with the head of a wand vibrator mounted in the seat. James had used heavy chain in an X pattern to bind her upper body to the chair, the weight and pressure of the chains reminiscent of the feelings she'd gotten from the corset.

The restraints gave her enough space that she could move her hips, increasing and decreasing the vibration against her clit by sliding forward and back. After greedily coming three times in the first half hour, Beth had backed off, but found the audience that had gathered to watch her while they ate kept her aroused. Soon she was wiggling her hips forward, grinding her clit against the vibrator.

It was far from the first time she'd been put on display, but it was the first time she'd been putting on a *show*.

She'd spent nearly two hours strapped to the chair, and towards the end she begged Master James for more. He'd added heavy clover clamps on her nipples, then placed the short connecting chain in her mouth, allowing her to tilt her chin and increase the pinch on her sensitive buds.

Master James had finally called a halt, though Beth had been half-mad from all the orgasms by that point and protested. She'd sucked his cock before he finally tumbled her onto the bed for a long fuck that was both intimate and rough. Her pussy felt vaguely bruised from all the time she'd spent smashing it against a vibrator.

"How are you feeling?"

"Battered." It was the truth, but when he rolled her over and frowned down at her, Beth smiled. "It's a nice kind of battered."

He nodded once, but didn't smile back. "Good." He rolled off the bed and stretched. "Would you prefer to shower here or in the Subs' Garden?"

Beth sat up, struggling to figure out the sudden shift in his mood. Had she said something wrong? What was going on, and what did that nauseous sensation in her stomach signify?

"I don't have a preference."

"Then I'm going to jump under the shower here." He walked towards the bathroom door.

"James, wait."

He turned, both eyebrows raised in surprise. It was the first time she'd failed to address him as Master.

"Is this…are we done?"

His gaze searched her face. "What are you asking?"

The past forty-eight hours had been the most sexually satisfying of her life, and more than that, she was comfortable with him in a way she'd never been with anyone—in the scene or in vanilla life. The feeling that was making her stomach churn was fear. Fear of losing him.

"You said I was yours until Sunday."

"Yes."

Why was he being so distant, why was he making this hard on her?

Well, the one thing she wouldn't forget, wouldn't go back to, was staying quiet about what she wanted.

She pulled the sheet up over her chest, needing the courage that came with not being exposed. "We're not done with our checklist."

Finally, he smiled. "We're not?"

"No."

"And what do you think we missed?"

"Several things, actually, but there's one I want." It felt good to state her desires so simply.

"And what do you want?"

"A collar." Beth smiled. Collar was on their list, and if he collared her they would play together every time they were at the club. She'd hadn't been the kind of sub he favored on Friday afternoon, but he'd showed her that she actually enjoyed submitting to someone like him far more than she enjoyed submitting to a stricter Master. They made a good pair, and she was sure that he was as aware of it as she was.

James's smile disappeared.

Beth knew how inappropriate it was for a sub to ask to be collared, knew that even beyond that it was crazy of her to ask this after only a weekend together, but she knew what she wanted. She wasn't going to risk spending any more time dissatisfied because she didn't break this one rule and ask for what she wanted.

When James said nothing Beth tried to explain, to make him understand why she was asking this. "Submitting to you is unlike anything of my other experiences. I came to BDSM for the rules, but you showed me that they're not the important part. That I can be a good sub, that I can be comfortable and not worry if I'm acting the right way even without them. I trust you. I know it's only been one weekend, but I know what I want."

It was her first ever heartfelt speech, and Beth was rather proud of it. Maybe it wasn't the sort of thing that would ever end up in a Hollywood movie, but she'd been honest and said exactly what she wanted to say. The fear that had made her feel sick was gone, replaced by a lightness she identified as hope.

"No."

And just like that the sick feeling was back, but now it

wasn't fear. It was a slimy ball of emotions she couldn't fully name.

Beth looked down at the white sheet, tears making everything blurry. She touched her face. She never cried.

"You asked about my hard limits. Well, that's one of them."

Without another word he went into the bathroom and closed the door. Beth slipped from the bed, pulled on the long white robe, and left.

An hour later Beth stepped out of the showers in the Subs' Garden. The locker room was precisely that—with large wooden lockers the subs could store their things in, but the room was plush, with fresh flowers on the marble counters and delicate padded dressing chairs eliminating any possibility of a gym feel.

Dropping the towel in the bin by the door, she made her way through the smattering of other subs to her assigned locker. There was an envelope taped to the front.

Ripping it off, she pulled out the single sheet of paper. It was a copy of her checklist, the page that included the letter C items. Retreating to one of the chairs, Beth dropped down and looked at the list. Cages, chains, chastity belts, chores, clothespins, clamps, cock worship, corset, and cuffs all had checkmarks beside them. Lines were drawn through cattle prod, cells, collars, and cock rings—they must be James's hard limits. The only items that were neither crossed off nor checked were choking and caning.

Beth stared at the two unmarked items. This must have come from him, but there were no directions, no indication of what he was trying to say.

Folding the list, she got dressed, then tucked the paper into her purse. There was only one logical conclusion. James was telling her that they weren't done, that there were two items on their list they'd have to address.

Funny, but right now that didn't arouse her. It pissed her off.

CHAPTER 9

He should have hacked into the Las Palmas records, looked up her number, called, and apologized. James paced, hoping to hell Beth showed up this weekend, that she'd seen the list he'd impulsively left her and her rule-following tendencies would push her to come back so they could finish. He hadn't originally planned to deal with caning or choking. Though they weren't on his hard limits list, they weren't things that particularly interested him, and unlike Beth, he had no problem ignoring rules when it suited him.

He'd been a Grade A asshole the last time she'd seen him. How nice of him to spend all that time convincing her she should be more forthcoming with what she wanted only to shut her down when she asked for something. It was hardly her fault that she'd managed to hit on his one major trigger.

Not an hour had gone by this past week that he hadn't thought about her, and more than once his fingers had been poised over his keyboard, ready to break some rules, and laws, to get her personal phone number. Since his firm had been part of the team to develop Las Palmas's digital security, it wasn't really hacking in so much as using the back door he'd left for himself in case of emergencies.

It had felt like an emergency.

But then again, he'd already made one dick move and decided not to compound the problem with another equally dick move. An unholy amount of time playing *Grand Theft Auto* and some senseless murdering of digital characters had helped keep his mind off everything. Now that he was here, he had nothing *but* time to think about it as he waited to see if she'd show up.

There was an intercom system, and James had asked that an announcement be made every hour asking her to join him in the Orion Room, a well-outfitted playroom off the larger Constellation Court. Unlike their room from last weekend there was no bed—this room would never be mistaken for anything other than a BDSM playroom.

He'd been here since three o'clock, and it was now 6:45. So far, no Beth. But he wouldn't give up, not yet. There'd be another announcement in fifteen minutes.

James checked the setup, then went back to pacing.

SHE HADN'T BROUGHT ANY LINGERIE. IT WAS HARDLY a surprise—lingerie packing had never been part of her normal routine for coming here.

Arriving at 5:50, Beth had heard the six o'clock announcements, including a request for her to go to the Orion Room. Rather than rushing to obey, she took her time, even going so far as to ask the other ladies getting ready in the Subs' Garden if anyone had something she could borrow. It was the first time she'd ever really interacted with anyone in that space, and she was surprised by how readily people pulled out garments for her —and by the volume of brand-new lingerie everyone else owned and kept in their lockers. As someone said, "you never know what you'll need." She gravitated towards a frilly white corset, but after putting it on was gently told that it didn't really go with her "look."

Unaware she had a "look," Beth instead accepted the suggestion of a classic black bustier that stopped two inches above her belly button, boy-short style lace panties and thin satin slippers that were slightly too big. Then someone insisted on helping her with her makeup, the result heavy black cat-eye style liner, matte bronze eye shadow, and glossy lips.

When she stepped back to check her reflection, the blonde sub who'd helped her with her makeup smiled. "It's like Black Widow meets Playboy Bunny. Gorgeous."

Beth stared at her reflection. Her hair hung in a perfect straight line around her neck, the eye makeup drawing attention to her face. The lace panties kept the outfit from veering into leather-fetish costume territory. She looked strong and powerful.

"I don't look very submissive."

"So?" The blonde who'd done her makeup capped a small pot of liquid eyeliner and wiped the brush off on a tissue. "You want a Dom who's strong enough to handle you, in your complete bad-ass package."

Complete bad-ass package. She liked that. Beth smiled at her reflection.

With profuse thanks and promises to replace all the pieces, Beth left the Subs' Garden and headed for the Orion Room.

When she reached the door, she knocked once and opened it —she didn't hesitate or second-guess how he'd want her to show up. If he wanted her to crawl into the room then it was his job to tell her that. She had every right to expect a Dom to be clear with her...and for him to respect her desires, needs, and wishes.

The room was lit by cool blue recessed light, the high ceiling studded with small LEDs that mimicked the real night sky, the three stars of Orion's Belt slightly brighter than the others.

Master James stood in the center of the room, looking strong and dapper in black slacks and a gray dress shirt open at the collar.

"You got the list I left you."

"Yes...Master James." There was no denying the little blip of panic she felt because she'd purposefully paused before adding "Master James" to her sentence. Maybe this new bad-ass persona and worldview on how she was going to submit—and what it meant to be submissive—would take a bit longer to get used to than she thought, if such mild disobedience caused discomfort.

"There, under the chains."

Beth paused for a second to see if he'd include any orders on how he wanted her to get there, but he didn't, so she walked over to stand under the structure he'd indicated. The large metal frame looked like a piece of gym equipment—the kind used for pull-ups and cable exercises. One of the overhead cross pieces had chains dangling from it, giving the otherwise calm room a hint of dungeon atmosphere.

She took her position facing him, waiting with her hands relaxed at her sides. There were flutters of arousal dancing over her skin, but she wasn't lost in the feeling.

"Raise your arms." Master James stood in a shadowy area of the room, his face hidden from her.

Beth lifted her arms, helpfully positioning her wrists near the heavy padded cuffs attached to two lengths of chain.

The heels of his dress shoes clicked on the floor, and Beth dropped her gaze—not only out of submission, but because some stubborn part of her didn't want to look at him, afraid that if she did she'd lose the anger that was a cold ball of white light just behind her breastbone.

The cuff slid easily around her left wrist, buckling into place.

The fabric of his shirt brushed against her hip as he leaned across to cuff her right wrist.

Beth licked her lips, trying to hold on to the anger, to use it as a shield against the feelings his nearness caused. Her body didn't care that he'd shut her down when she'd asked for more. Her body remembered what it felt like to be touched, to be mastered by him.

When she was in place, her wrists at shoulder height, Master James walked away. Spotlights came on, bathing the area where she stood in bright light, and effectively blinding her to anything outside the circle of light.

"You look different." His voice and footsteps told her he was coming back, but she couldn't see him.

"Yes, Master James."

"It suits you."

"Thank you, Master James."

The tip of a bamboo cane appeared in the spotlight, inching towards her as if it were a sentient thing. The slim cane was long enough—nearly four feet—that by the time the pointed end came to rest on her breasts, only Master James's hand was visible.

"I wasn't sure you'd come today."

"We aren't done with our letter, Master." And I wouldn't turn down the chance to play with you again, even if you hurt me.

"Remind me, what do we have left?"

"Caning and choking."

"Have you been caned before?"

"Yes, Master James."

"Where?" He traced a pattern over the smooth fabric of the bustier with the tip of the cane.

Beth had to pause and think before replying. "My back and shoulders, thighs."

"And did you enjoy it?" The cane dropped to her panties, catching on the lace.

"No, Master James."

He stepped closer, his arm up to his shoulder now in the light. The cane slipped between her legs, pressing up on the sex.

"And do you think you'll enjoy it now?"

Beth closed her eyes. A caning was brutal by anyone's standards. She wasn't a pain bottom, so for her the pleasure from a caning would have to come from the submissive aspect of it. With anyone else she would have said no, would have accepted the caning because that's what a good submissive did.

Yet she knew, *she knew*, that with Master James even this otherwise terrifying implement of torture would lead to bone-melting pleasure.

"Beth, you didn't answer my question." There was a hint of chastisement in his voice. Instead of upsetting her, it pissed her off.

Her gaze snapped up, to the shadows where his face would be. "You know the answer to that."

"I want to hear you say it."

Beth jerked her chin to the side. "Why? You know how I react to you. You know I want..." *More. I want to wear your collar.*

The silence stretched, uncomfortable and tense.

"Take a small step backward, bend at the hips." The cane guided her, pushing against her pussy. "Back up more. Arms together, bend your elbows."

When he was done, Beth was bent at the waist, her torso not quite parallel with the floor, her arms together supporting her upper body weight, wrists higher than her head.

Master James laid his bare hand on the back of her thigh, and she felt the skin to skin contact along every nerve ending in her body. Unable to balance the physical demands of this position with the emotional work it took to hold on to her anger, Beth gave in, laying her cheek against her own arm.

"Beth..." His voice was soft, and lips brushed over the bare strip of skin between the top of her panties and the bottom of her bustier. Teeth nipped at the line of her spine.

"Master," Beth whispered, squeezing her eyes shut.

There was no room for the future or the past, there was only now, only this moment, this man.

He nipped her ass through the lace panties, then inched them down. She was wet despite her efforts to ignore him, and the lace clung to the slick folds of her pussy.

"I can smell you. I know how aroused you are. You should be terrified. A caning will hurt."

"I know, Master James."

"Are you scared?"

"*Yes, Master.*" *But not of physical pain.*

His hands, which had been roaming over her now-bare ass, paused, as if he heard the things she didn't say.

Finally he stepped back. "I'm going to cane your ass. Then I'm going to fuck you as I choke you."

The words were brutal, his plan containing none of the more obviously pleasurable elements of last weekend's scenes.

The first blow of the cane landed across the middle of both ass cheeks. The cane was quiet compared to the *crack* of a paddle, the whistle and small thump barely audible before Beth screeched.

It hurt—not more than was bearable, but enough that she couldn't stop herself from reacting.

Master James ran his fingers gently along the mark he'd just left. The skin was too hot for the touch to be pleasant, but when he wrapped one arm around her waist, holding her tight against his side as his fingers dipped into her pussy, Beth forgot about the pain.

"You're very wet, Beth."

"Yes, Master James." She moaned, arching her hips.

Two fingers stroked their way from her clit to the entrance of her pussy and back, moving with maddening slowness.

"I could train you to come from the caning alone." His voice was dark, the hand around her waist tightening. "I could bring you right to the edge of orgasm a thousand times, each time stopping to lay a nice welt on your ass. Eventually you'd be so desperate to come your body would use the pain as the final stimulus to push you over."

One finger entered her, curling to rub against her g-spot. Beth spread her legs more, rocking against his finger as much as she could.

"Eventually your body would associate the caning with orgasm."

Beth didn't understand why he was telling her this. That didn't seem like his brand of BDSM. Did he think that's what she wanted?

"We could get so lost, so wrapped up, that it would seem okay, seem normal."

The finger slipped from her pussy, and before she could brace herself the cane lashed against her naked skin. This one was lower, striking the soft skin where ass met thigh at her "sit-spot."

Again she screamed, this time dancing in place a little. Her underwear tangled around her ankles and she almost fell, but Master James again caught her, two fingers of his free hand sinking into her pussy. He fucked her gently until her panting breaths of pain changed into a different kind of pant.

"I once trained a submissive to come when I used the crop on her inner thighs."

"You did?" Beth couldn't hide her surprise.

"I wouldn't touch her except to tie her legs open and crop her. She'd come just from that. Then I'd put her on her knees, have her suck me off, and lock her in a cage. If she wanted to come again she had to beg me to beat her."

His grip on her waist had tightened and, ignoring all the rules, Beth broke out of his hold and straightened, turning to face him, one arm pulled awkwardly across her chest. In the harsh spotlights, the lines of pain on James's face were like gashes in his cheeks and forehead.

"James?" For the second time Beth failed to call him Master. This time it was out of concern. He didn't look like himself— she had no idea what that expression meant, but it couldn't be an indicator of happy feelings.

"The sub, the one I'm talking about, she wore my collar."

"Oh."

"And when we weren't at Las Palmas, she was my fiancée."

"Oh." Beth puzzled that over. "I don't understand."

James's gaze met hers, and slowly the lines in his face melted away, his lips curling up in a smile. "That makes two of us."

"Your fiancée was your collared sub, and you trained her to come only when being beaten..."

Repeating it out loud didn't make it any easier to reconcile the tale with the man she knew.

James sighed, nudging the cane, which he'd dropped to the ground, with the toe of one glossy shoe. "We got into the life-style together. She was the one who found out about Las Palmas, but joining—getting in—was a status symbol for her. We'd never been with anyone other than each other in BDSM play, and a year after we'd joined, and she'd put on the collar, things fell apart. We were pushing each other—using our sessions here to take out our aggression with the vanilla world. She started to fight me, push back, then accused me of being weak. So I'd take it up a level, try to be the Master she needed. Months would go by when we didn't even have sex, here or at home, yet we were always covered in bruises, especially her.

"Then she started asking to play with other Doms. So I'd give her to these other men, most of whom were way more gentle with her than I was, and she'd seem to enjoy it, but when the sessions were over, she'd break down and start sobbing, begging me to protect her. The next weekend she'd quietly ask if I was going to give her away, asking in a way that I knew meant that's what she wanted. And every time she'd come back acting like she'd been the victim of something. Once I even started a fight, accused another Master of abusing her. Right as I was about to throw myself at this guy I see her, out of the corner of my eye, sort of smiling, like she's enjoying this, enjoying watching me defend her.

"When it finally fell apart, she accused me of using the collar as a cover up for domestic violence. Our breakup was messy, and the cops were almost involved. The overseers stepped in—they didn't want anything about the club being mentioned in police reports. The last time I saw her, she threw the collar at me and called me a sick freak."

Beth took a step toward him, only to be pulled up short by the chains. She wanted to touch him, to reassure him.

"I'm sorry."

"Don't be. I haven't told anyone that story before, though plenty of people at Las Palmas know about what happened."

"That's why collar is on your hard limits list?"

"Yes. I'm one of the reasons Las Palmas has an alternative. There's too much potential emotional baggage with a collar."

Beth nodded. Partners or groups who wanted to be formally recognized as being in an exclusive relationship within the club had to be bonded. Often that meant collaring too, but bonding was actually a formal arrangement between the parties.

There were things she wanted to say, should say—that she was sorry for asking him to collar her, that if she'd known she wouldn't have asked, that she'd never been happier as a submissive than she was with him.

But the words wouldn't come, stuck behind a wall of awkwardness Beth would never lose, so instead she responded in a way she hoped he'd understand. Turning, she bent, resuming her position, waiting for him to continue caning her.

He didn't react, and Beth's stomach clenched with embarrassment and regret. Just as she was about to stand up, his hands cupped her hips. He stepped up behind her, and even through his pants she could feel the heat of his cock against her ass.

"Beth." Her name was a plea, a pledge, on his lips.

"Yes, Master?"

He moved away, and she wasn't surprised when she heard a faint whistle, followed by a line of fiery pain as he struck her for a third time.

This time she whimpered. "Thank you, Master."

"Don't. You don't have to say that."

"But I mean it."

"Why?"

"Because I know after this you're going to fuck me while you choke me and we're both going to come. Then we'll do something else, and we'll come some more and I won't have to worry about whether I'm pleasing you, or being a good submissive. That's all I want, and everything I need."

The cane struck again, this blow harder than all the others, and Beth screamed, throwing her head back, tears in her eyes, but the trembling that wracked her wasn't just from pain. Then he was there, his big body huddled around hers, his now-naked hips pressed against her abused ass, one hand on her back keeping her bent forward, while the other slid around her neck, pulling her head up.

Beth sucked in air, trying to process all the things she was feeling—pain from the caning, arousal because he'd caned her, anticipation from his naked skin against hers, delicious trepidation from his hand around her throat.

His hips shifted, his cock finding its way to the entrance to her sex. Fingers tightened around her throat as he thrust in. Beth sucked in air—she could still breathe, but she couldn't ignore or dismiss his hold on her, his control of her body.

Her pussy clenched in pleasure as his cock filled her. He was long and hard, just what she needed inside her.

"Beth." Still holding her by the neck, he used his other hand to jerk down the bustier until her breasts sprung free. Fingers closed over her aching nipples, plucking the tight buds.

"Master." It was nothing more than a whisper, but he growled in apparent pleasure and started fucking her in earnest.

Beth was buffeted by sensations—pain and pleasure chief among them. It took her a moment to realize she was fighting him, not physically, but emotionally, so focused on sorting out what she was feeling and what was happening that she hadn't given herself over.

All she had to do was trust him, give in and submit.

With a sigh she did exactly that—letting go of her anger at him, at herself. Releasing her worry and need to dissect what was happening.

"That's it," he whispered, as if he understood. Maybe he did. He knew her in a way no one else did, or ever had.

"I want to feel you come."

She couldn't respond, the pleasure and his hold on her robbing her of breath. Instead, Beth let her body tell him what he needed to know. When he pinched her right nipple hard, twisting the bud to the point of delicious pain, she tipped over that glittering edge, falling into the delicious darkness of pleasure.

Behind her, James groaned, jackhammering into her fluttering pussy as he too came.

"You didn't think we were done, did you?"

Beth opened one eye, looking up at Master James. He'd carried her to a mat in the corner, since this room didn't have a bed.

"We're done with our checklist." Beth responded.

"Do you want to leave?"

"No."

"Then spread your legs so I can put a clamp on your clit."

"Yes, Master."

"WHAT ARE YOU FEELING?"

James's voice and the fingers dancing along her naked back roused Beth from her semi-asleep state.

"My ass hurts."

He chuckled, the unrepentant sound unique to Doms. "Tomorrow I might give you a nice spanking, just to see what you look like with pink cheeks."

"A spanking on top of a caning?"

"Do you object?" There was a hint of steel in his voice.

A shiver of pure arousal shook Beth as she lay on James's lap, both of them seated on an elegant leather chaise lounge.

"No, Master."

"I didn't think so." He nudged her outside leg off the arm of the chair, her foot dropping to the floor. The new position spread her legs enough that her pussy, which had recently been free of a multitude of clamps, was open to him. "But you didn't answer my question. What I want to know is what you're feeling."

She sighed. "Don't ask hard questions."

He leaned down and kissed her forehead. "I'm not asking to make you uncomfortable." His voice was tender.

"Feelings are hard."

Master James stroked her inner thigh, saying nothing, but Beth could tell from the tension around his lips that he was holding back a comment or question. He'd trusted her with personal information, maybe it was time she do the same.

"I have low Emotional Quotient—low emotional IQ. I have trouble understanding my own feelings and figuring out other people's." James didn't reply, and when the silence continued

Beth kept talking, wanting him to know this about her. "I'm better than I was. I've studied emotionality and developed coping mechanisms."

"Coping mechanisms like becoming a submissive?"

"Yes."

"Numbers are what I'm good at." She wasn't even sure why she was telling him that. It veered dangerously close to talking about her job. "But I've never been diagnosed with anything other than low EQ. It was actually a roommate who first mentioned it. We spent all night downloading sample tests for me to take." Beth took a deep breath. "I like rules and labels because they provide structure, but I never got myself diagnosed beyond the low EQ."

"Beth." He cut her off before she could keep going.

"Yes?"

"It doesn't matter. The labels I mean. You are who you are. That should be good enough—for me and for everyone else."

"I...thank you."

"And who you are..." His voice trailed off and he her kissed long and deep, her nipples tightening in response. When he broke the kiss, his eyes sparkled with wicked humor, his half smile promising so many things. "Is an orgasm slut."

Two fingers found their way to her clit, which was swollen and sore, making his touch all the more exquisite.

"I meant to ask, is orgasm slut a bad thing?"

Master James chuckled as he tumbled her off the chair, then followed her down, his mouth going to her pussy. As his tongue brought her to another delicious orgasm, Beth decided being an orgasm slut submissive was a very good thing.

CHAPTER 10

"Beth, please come in."

James watched as Beth, in her street clothes, stepped in to the overseers' office. She was wearing jeans and a graphic T-shirt with a video game logo on the front. It was not the normal vanilla-world attire of a member of Las Palmas, but if there was one thing he'd learned about Beth, it was that she was different, in so many good ways. The setting sun, visible through the large picture window in the wall opposite the door, added red highlights to her hair.

Beth laid her purse and leather motorcycle jacket over the back of a chair positioned in front of the large desk Master Leo stood behind. James had been sitting in the other, but rose when Beth entered.

Her gaze flicked to him, and James couldn't help but smile.

"Why am I here?" she asked bluntly.

"Ah, Beth, never change." Master Leo laid out two sets of papers on the desk facing James and Beth. "Master James asked me to draw up—"

James cut him off, wanting to explain this part himself. "Beth, we're done with our checklist items."

"Yes. We finished on Friday."

"And did you enjoy the rest of this weekend?" It was sundown on Sunday night, and up until an hour ago Beth had been naked and bound, his to do with as he pleased.

She frowned. "I don't understand why you're asking that. You know I did."

James bit back an exasperated laugh. "Fair enough. We're done with our game, but I don't want us—" he gestured between them "—to be over."

Beth blinked, then a shy smile spread across her face. "You don't?"

"No." James took the papers from the desk and passed her a set. "You know that I won't use a collar, but at Las Palmas that doesn't matter. Beth, I want us to be bonded."

Beth looked down at the two-page contract, a simple statement of exclusivity used to formalize relationships between Masters and submissives.

He smiled, waiting for her to look up, waiting to see the happiness in her eyes when she realized that they wanted the same thing. Each other.

Beth set the papers down. "No."

James stared at her. "What do you mean 'no'?"

"I won't sign this. The best I could do is wear a collar."

"A collar is—"

"A stupid piece of jewelry. This is a contract. Admittedly probably not legally binding, but still, I won't sign anything giving anyone even pseudo control over my person."

James sat down, completely blindsided. "You're refusing?"

Master Leo started to laugh. "Sorry, sorry." He waved his hand in the air. "I've been waiting to see her reaction since you told me you wanted to be bonded."

"You knew she'd say no?" James glared at the other man, who looked wholly unrepentant. "Beth, is this because I said no to the collar? I told you, that's about me, my stuff. I'm trying to tell you that I want to be with you. Only you."

"I understand. But I won't sign this." She looked both worried and determined, the expression making her seem younger than she had a second ago.

"Beth has to protect herself. She's worth about twenty times what you are, and her major asset is herself." Master Leo's voice still held notes of amusement.

James looked between Beth and Master Leo.

"Let me rephrase." Master Leo held up a hand. "She's worth about twenty times what your whole company is worth."

"What?" James looked at Beth. "What do you do? I thought you said you were good with numbers." Right now she looked like a geek girl computer programmer.

"If I told you, I'd have to kill you." Her tone was flat but there was a tentative sparkle in her eyes.

"I can't even tell if you're joking."

Beth smiled, showing teeth.

"Seriously, is she joking?" James pointed at Beth while looking at Master Leo.

Master Leo shook his head. "I will tell you that some of our members who have ties to the DOD or any of its major contractors aren't allowed to go near her."

DOD—the Department of Defense. "Are you a spy?" James was trying, and failing, to make sense of this new version of Beth.

Her hair brushed her cheek as she shook her head and he had to fight back the urge to tuck it behind her ear and then kiss her neck. The unexpectedly tender urge was not appropriate in this context—they weren't in a playroom, weren't actively in their personas as Dom and sub. But he still wanted to touch her, sit with her, talk to her.

Dangerous territory. Especially if she's a spy.

"No, I'm not a spy. I'm good with numbers. I'm a mathematician."

"Uh huh." James didn't believe that for one minute.

"I'm a consultant—I write algorithms, do some coding." She shrugged lightly.

"For the DOD?"

"If they pay enough, and if I like the project. Sometimes other employers provide more *interesting* challenges."

"Holy shit."

"Why, what do you do?"

"I co-founded, and co-own, one of the West Coast's biggest digital security firms." James tried not to sound defensive.

"Military?"

"No."

"Oh, that's nice."

"*That's nice?*"

A little line appeared between her eyebrows. "I'm having trouble understanding your expression."

"This—" James pointed at himself "—is what it looks like when a man has been thoroughly emasculated."

She tipped her head to the side and studied him. "Emasculated?"

"Perhaps we could return to the issue at hand?" Master Leo rapped his knuckles on the desk to get their attention.

James opened his mouth, closed it, then ran his hand through his hair. With some effort he put aside what he'd just learned about her, which both made sense and horrified him—not the kind of work she did, but that someone with her credentials has been letting people use her as a footstool. "Let me get this straight—I won't use a collar, and you won't agree to be bonded."

"It seems so." Beth sat on the arm of his chair.

Ignoring all the rules of etiquette, he wrapped a hand around the back of her head and pulled her down for a kiss. "I'll fight for this. For us."

She blinked a few times, her eyes shiny with tears. The urge to protect her filled him, but this wasn't like with his ex—Beth wasn't trying to manipulate him by acting like she was in need of protection. She needed him, just as much as he needed her.

"What are we going to do?" she asked softly.

"You're going to do it the old fashioned way." Both Beth and James looked at Master Leo when he spoke.

Beth's brows drew together. "What's the old fashioned way?"

But James understood what the other man was saying. He touched Beth's cheek, urging her to look at him. "We're going to have to trust each other."

———

Thank you for reading the first three books of the Checklist series. Each book is a standalone story, meaning they do not need to be read in order. Turn the page for an exclusive excerpt from "*M is for...* " where the main checklist item is "medical."

———

RECOMMENDATIONS AND FREE BOOKS!

Love sexy stories set in BDSM clubs?
Check out the Orchid Club series, starting with
San Francisco Longing

Oh wait! How about a free copy ?
Sign up for Lila's Newsletter to get San Francisco Longing, as well as three other great stories, totally free.

Get four FREE ebooks when you join Lila's newsletter!
Go to
www.liladubois.net
and click on the "Free Books" link at the top of the page.

EXCERPT FROM "M IS FOR…"

Note: This excerpt depicts a scene already in progress. Cali and Zidan are roll playing as a slave and slave trainer. In the scene Cali's imaginary master has given her to Master Z to be trained and inspected.

In the center of the room, under a massive circular surgical light was a doctor's exam table. Instead of a bland tan or pale blue, the padded, sectioned top was covered in black vinyl. The base was a cream-colored plastic, with drawers in it, and there was a gray electric foot pedal sitting on the terra-cotta tile floor. There were also black leather straps dangling from the underside of the padded top.

It looked like someone had taken a real exam table and doctored it—har har—to make it appropriate for BDSM play. She knew she'd been in this room before but hadn't seen the medical exam table. She would have remembered. But then again, at any given time there were plenty of things subs didn't get to see. The corners of this room, and all the others she'd been in, were occupied by black-draped masses—unused equipment. When not in use, smaller things were stored in the person-sized cages that were a standard amenity in each Iron Court room.

"'Medical scenes' is a broad idea, with a variety of possible interpretations." Zidan brushed an unseen something off the corner of the exam table.

Medical play. When she guessed that M was their letter, posited what the other items might be, medical play hadn't been one she thought of. She'd come up with misbehaving, massage, and mummification.

Medical play...a medical exam?...that hadn't occurred to her.

"Since your checklist indicated only 'willing to try' for medical scenes, I decided to go with the most mundane." Zidan glanced her way, his gaze running up and down her body. "A complete physical exam."

He was going to strap her down to that table and look over every inch of her body. Her breath caught, even as her internal voice, in a calm, detached tone, pointed out that this wasn't all that different to what would happen at the start of most scenes. A visual "exam"—though it usually wasn't referred to as such—was often the first thing a good Dom did. To please themselves, perhaps because it helped the sub find the right headspace, but also to check for any bruises or tender spots they should avoid.

Zidan turned to fully face her. His head tipped to the side and down, so he was looking at her through thick lashes and lowered brows. It was a look she knew well. A look that was nearly a signature for him.

Reality wanted to intrude. If this was Cali scening with Zidan, there were things she'd say. Simple things, but also darker, angry things.

That's why he sent a gag.

But this wasn't Cali and Zidan. It was a master and an unnamed slave.

"Come here."

As she walked towards the exam table, Cali put up a thin emotional screen inside her mind. It wasn't Cali who would be strapped down on that table, but the slave she was playing. He'd given her several possible takes on this particular role, but as she walked up to him, she hadn't yet decided which she'd take.

"Up." He patted the table.

She could have resisted then, but she turned her back to the bench, her shoulder brushing his. Standing on her toes she wasn't quite tall enough to slide up, so she planted the palms of her hands beside her hips, the chain tight across her body, the cold of the heavy metal making her shiver even through the thin barrier of latex. Her nipples were visible under the latex of the tank top, and she felt his gaze drop to her breasts.

With a little hop she seated herself, then rested her wrists, bound in the heavy manacles, on her thighs.

"You were well trained," Zidan said. He grabbed the bit, tugging it out of her mouth—the straps digging in to her neck— and dropping it to dangle against her collarbone.

Cali inhaled, closed her eyes, then exhaled. She locked away the tangled ball of emotion that Zidan had knotted within her the instant he appeared.

When she opened her eyes, she kept her gaze submissively lowered and leaned in to the part she was playing. "Thank you, Master."

He made a pleased sound, then said. "You may call me Master Z. And for brevities' sake, you may also call me simply 'Sir' when needed."

"Thank you, Master Z."

He gripped her chin, underhanded, and lifted her face. She glanced once at him, then lowered her lashes, which meant practically closing her eyes since he had her chin raised.

"Time for your exam."

That was all the warning she got before he reached out and

grabbed her breast, squeezing just hard enough that her shoulders rounded and she leaned away from him.

"Chest out. Those breasts are mine to play with if I want to." His voice was hard, cracking with both command and disapproval.

"You're not my Master," Cali snapped back.

A sharp lance of pain pierced the wall she'd put up in her mind. Those words were too close to some truths that had no place here.

"You're right," Zidan—no, Master Z—said slowly. "But I am a Master. The Master who has custody of you, and whom you will obey."

She flinched at the last word, then slowly straightened her spine. Shoulders back, chest out, she waited for him to touch her.

Master Z pinched her nipple, giving it a warning tug, before he lost his grip on the slick latex. He slapped her other breast. She hissed out a breath, though it hadn't hurt, and managed to keep her posture.

"Obedient, but not totally so." Master Z grabbed her knees and forced her legs open, spreading her wide. Her heavy wrists stayed on her thighs, but the chain dropped down between her legs, poised on the edge of the table, then fell off the edge, clanking. The manacles pulled on her wrists, the weight uncomfortable and unfamiliar.

"Nothing you, or anyone, does, will make me totally obedient," she said in a quiet, grim voice.

"Total obedience isn't my goal."

"And what is your goal...Sir?"

"For you to know your place."

Cali swallowed, nerves making her stomach tight, even as her sex pulsed. "My place?"

"To know that you exist to be used." Master Z slid his fingers along the inside of her thigh, swirling little patterns until he reached the edge of the latex shorts, which had ridden up towards her crotch when he spread her legs. "To please your master, and yes, occasionally, to be pleasured."

"To be used." She hadn't meant for the words to be bitter, but they were.

Master Z turned away for a moment. She regretted the words. She was also harshly satisfied to see they affected him.

"Never forget you chose." His words were barely above a whisper.

Was he talking to Cali, or the slave? The statement worked both ways, though the choice Cali had made had been an impossible one.

The words she wanted to say would have nothing to do with this scene, or the role she was playing, and everything to do with her past.

Their past.

And so Cali made another choice. Or rather, she chose to believe he'd been speaking as the Master to the slave. Chose to participate despite the danger. It was the choice she'd made outside when she'd walked towards him. She'd chosen to accept what was, and to live in the moment.

"I agreed to come to you for training because I knew it would please my Master," Cali said, building her character's backstory with each word.

In her mind's eye she pictured the fictional master—tall, blond, deadly. Maybe his name was Ian...

"I can see why he cherishes you." Master Z turned to face her. "You're lovely, clearly submissive, but not without spirit. However, you will benefit from being humbled by this assessment." He cupped her chin once again, raising her face to his. "Look at me," he commanded.

She raised her gaze to his, but could only meet his eyes—brown, nearly black—for a moment before she had to look away or risk falling out of character.

"This will not be easy for you. I will expect total obedience, and you will be punished for failure."

"I will…do my best, Sir."

"Some of what I order you to do, and what I will do to you, you might find humiliating."

A little moan of fear and need escaped her.

"Including this medical exam." He slightly stressed the "m" sound at the beginning of medical.

Master Z's hand dropped to the curved neckline of her latex tank. Two fingers slid into her cleavage, and then he pressed out on the material from the inside. She loved latex clothes because of the smooth, high-gloss look. Latex was a second skin, thin and delicate, unlike rubber or leather which could both be tight and glossy, but were thick. She even liked the ritual of putting latex items on— coating her naked, clean body in powder or a dressing aid lubricant. Carefully sliding the clothing on, using a flat hand so she wouldn't risk tearing it. Then, once it was on, using a soft cloth and a bit of Pjur latex shine to polish the clothing until light reflected off it.

There was a reason latex had a general "no fingers" rule for getting it on. Master Z's fingers stretched the fabric past its breaking point, and a small hole appeared. He pushed his fingers through the hole and spread them, ripping the fabric along a vertical line. The upper edge parted, her breasts, which had been lightly compressed, swelling lewdly.

Master Z grabbed the edges and yanked, splitting the tank top down the center front. The latex squeaked as it curled up along her sides.

"Lovely breasts." He grabbed one of her tits casually, lifting and looking at the underside before dropping it.

Her cheeks felt hot, and Cali started to raise her hands, planning to cover her tits with her palms. The heaviness of the manacles and the clank of the chain stopped her from making a mistake.

"All the way up." He patted the bench beside her hip. "Then lie down."

Master Z stepped out of the way so she could swing her legs onto the exam table and then slowly lie back. Her shorts squeaked against the vinyl, and if she hadn't been fairly certain he was going to rip them off, she would have been worried about tearing them. She was too far down—her legs were hanging off the end—but before she could adjust and scoot up, Master Z grabbed her ankles.

"Bend your knees."

He guided her feet until her heels were nearly touching her ass, soles flat on the padded table.

"Do you think I want your knees together?" Master Z asked sharply.

"Would you like me to spread them, Sir?" She couldn't see him; he was at the foot of the table and her own legs blocked her view.

"We will not be playing that game."

"What game, Sir?"

"You are smarter than that, Princess."

"I'm not a princess. We've both acknowledged what I am."

Master Z's hands slid from her ankles up to her knees. She was ready for it when he shoved her legs apart. Her knees butterflied out to the sides. If she hadn't been in good shape, and limber, it would have pulled on her groin and thigh muscles to be manipulated like this.

"I want to hear it," Master Z commanded in a hard voice.

"I'm a sexual submissive..." She stopped when he ran his hands from her knees down her bare inner thighs towards her pussy, which was protected from him by a thin layer of delicate latex.

"You're more than that." He raised a finger, waiting for her to focus on it, on him, and then lowered the digit to the apex of her thighs. He placed the tip of his finger low over her pussy, closer to her entrance than her clit.

"What are you, Princess?" He dug his finger in, and the latex made contact with her labia. Her stomach muscles twitched, causing her to jerk as a flash of arousal, of need, ripped through her.

"I'm a sex slave," she whispered. "I belong to my master. I'm his to use, abuse, pleasure, punish, fuck…" Her words ran out, and her next inhale was choppy.

He was pressing harder, enough that the tip of his finger was between her outer labia—which were slightly spread thanks to her position—and touching the inner lips of her pussy. Cali had particularly sensitive pussy lips, and liked having them tugged on. When she was really aroused her labia minora would swell up, visible even when she had her legs closed.

And Master Z was applying pressure directly on those sensitive folds of flesh.

Master Z wiggled his finger, adding a bit more pressure, and the latex ripped. Cali shrieked in shock and pleasure as his fingertip poked the sensitive valley of her sex for a second before sliding down and into her vagina. As she was wet and swollen with need, the sudden penetration of his finger was both shocking and sweet. Her pussy clenched down on his finger, the presence inside her wonderful, but also not enough.

She wanted more.

Master Z removed his finger from inside her and ripped the latex. It split side to side, opening up along her thighs where a seam would have been on a normal garment. She felt the cold air on her lewdly gaping sex. He grabbed and ripped. What had been latex shorts was now a tattered skirt that left her pussy and ass exposed.

Master Z walked away, and Cali carefully adjusted the remnants of her clothing so it wasn't pulling and pinching at her armpits and around her waist.

She shouldn't have bothered because when he came back, he held a stiff black bag with a handle. An old-fashioned doctor's bag. He opened it and took out a pair of orange-handled medical shears. A few snips at her shoulders and stomach and the last of the latex fell away.

"Lift up, raise your hips."

She did a bridge, and he pulled the ruined latex out from under her.

"Arms above your head."

Master Z circled around as she raised her arms, letting the manacles weigh her wrists down in place above her head. He grabbed the chain, pulling it off the top edge of the bed. She felt tugs, and heard a click as the chain was connected to something.

Master Z came to stand at her right hip, looking down at her with one hand casually resting on her bare stomach.

She was naked, her legs lewdly spread. The bit-style gag was still around her neck, the bar resting on her throat, not painful or restrictive, but also not easy to ignore.

The way he was looking at her was so intense, so…intimate, that she couldn't handle the silence.

"Is it time to play doctor, Sir?"

Master Z casually pinched the underside of her left breast. A bite of pain enough to make her twitch, but not flinch away.

"No, we won't be playing doctor. We won't be playing at all." Master Z went to the foot of the exam table, bending to look at something she couldn't see.

"Your master didn't send you to me so we could play a game." His accent deepened, the words even more delicious and terrible because of it. "What I am about to do to you…how I examine and use you, will require utter submission."

Cali's pussy clenched in reaction to his words, and she could feel how wet she was. He'd be able to see, smell, her arousal.

Master Z pulled two stirrup arms out from the end of the bed, lifting and latching them in place. Gynecological stirrups.

Shock and embarrassment slapped her. She'd known he would examine her pussy, but she'd thought he'd keep her legs like this. Gyno stirrups...no. Just no.

Cali slammed her legs together and rolled off the side of the exam table. Landing on her feet, bent at the waist so she didn't yank on her wrists, Cali managed two quick steps towards the head of the table—she had a vague plan of unlatching the chain so she could get as far from the exam table as possible—before he grabbed her.

Zidan jerked her against his body, her back to his front. She tried to grab his forearm, but the manacles and chain arrested her arms just short of touching him.

"Safe words," Zidan whispered in her ear. "Milk to pause the role play. Macbeth and three fingers for a full safe word stop."

She didn't want the reminder that this was a scene, because that meant thinking about the real word.

Thinking of him as Zidan instead of Master Z.

Cali flipped her wrists, grabbing ahold of the chain, and jerked herself away from him.

She gained a few seconds of freedom, but then he was on her again, this time slamming her facedown over the exam table. She grunted as her cheek made contact with the vinyl, one arm half under her, the manacle digging into her ribs. His body-weight on her back increased the pressure and made her wince.

"Very well, if you will not submit to your examination with the obedience and grace expected of a slave, we'll begin with a punishment."

READY TO KEEP READING?

M is for...

M is for medical, but an intense medical scene is only first of the things Master Zidan had planned for Cali.

Their past is complicated, but what they once had is long

dead. To survive the game, Zidan decides they should role play…as the most extreme versions of dominant and submissive possible. The role play, plus the letter M, means they'll both be pushed to their limits. Physical…and emotional.

When their past refused to stay dead, the checklist game becomes a catalyst for a fight that's been years in the making. They're about to find out that the checklist game is not for the faint of heart, or those whose hearts could still be broken.

And don't forget, you get
four FREE ebooks when you join Lila's newsletter!

Go to
www.liladubois.net
And click on the "Free Books" link at the top of the page.

ABOUT THE AUTHOR

Lila Dubois is an award winning, multi-published, bestselling author of erotic, paranormal and fantasy romance.

Her book "J is for...", the tenth book in the bestselling checklist series, won the 2019 National Readers' Choice Award. Additionally, she's been nominated for the RT Book Reviews Erotic Novella of the Year for "Undone Rebel" and the Golden Flogger.

Having spent extensive time in France, Egypt, Turkey, Ireland, and England Lila speaks five languages, none of them (including English) fluently. Lila lives in California with her own Irish Farm Boy and loves receiving email from readers.

Visit Lila online:
www.liladubois.net
author@liladubois.net

Made in the USA
Monee, IL
09 July 2021

72649138R00216